TWO
MOTHERS

BOOKS BY KATHRYN CROFT

TWO MOTHERS

Kathryn Croft

bookouture

Published by Bookouture in 2024

An imprint of Storyfire Ltd.
Carmelite House
50 Victoria Embankment
London EC4Y 0DZ

www.bookouture.com

ISBN: 978-1-83525-646-6
eBook ISBN: 978-1-83525-645-9

For Paul G

PROLOGUE

Rachel

She stares at Luna, asleep in her pink and white toddler bed, and for a fleeting moment the little girl could be her daughter. They have the same light brown, almost blonde hair – which Evie must have got from Damien's side; Rachel's is far darker, almost black.

'I promise I'll keep you safe,' Rachel whispers. 'Always.' Tears blur her vision, making the little girl look even more like Evie.

But Evie is gone. All it took was a second. One devastating moment. A single drop in a vast ocean that changed all of their lives.

Rachel looks away, blinking to stem the flow of her salty tears. This isn't Evie's room. It's too messy, too crammed full of things. Cuddly toys spill over the top of a large pale pink basket with Luna's name on it. Shelves filled with board books and more cuddly toys. Things everywhere. Chaos. The opposite of Evie's minimalist room with cream-coloured walls and a light grey carpet. Toys neatly put away. Everything in its place.

Now Evie's door remains firmly shut, and their house is mostly silent. Rachel's son Logan rarely speaks. He's a year away from being a teenager so surely this reticence shouldn't be happening already. But events change people. Rachel knows this more than most. And now she has a silent son she can't reach. And a daughter whose voice she'll never hear again.

Logan always has his head buried in a book, or he's engrossed in that computer game. *Fortnite.* The one all the kids seem to be obsessed with. Rachel had resisted allowing it at first – she's a teacher and needs to set an example – but in the end she could see it was doing him more harm to be the only kid in his friendship group who wasn't playing it. And hasn't it actually been good for him? A distraction from his sister's absence.

And as for Damien... He might be there in physical form, but he's a stranger to her, and was long before Evie.

Damien is not a good man. But she doesn't tell anyone that. He's Logan's father, and she'll do what she has to in order to protect her son and shield him from the truth.

She and Damien don't argue; what exists between them is worse than that. And what's there to fight about when nothing matters any more? Evie is gone. And a thick black line has been drawn under their lives in permanent ink. An ending of some sort. And the beginning of something Rachel didn't sign up for.

Leaning down, she strokes Luna's soft cheek. Evie's cheek. *Holly's* daughter. The little girl squirms, her mouth forming a tiny circle as she settles back down. Peaceful once more.

She doesn't have long. Holly will be back soon, and then Rachel will be making the short walk back to her soulless house, where grief sucks her breath the second she steps through the door. It doesn't have to be like this. Rachel could have her life back. There is a way, and it starts right here in this room. Tonight.

She reaches down with both arms to lift Luna from her bed. Is she a light sleeper? Rachel can't remember. And Holly doesn't talk to Rachel about her any more – not about toilet training, or any of those milestones Luna will be reaching. Rachel's aware that it's out of concern for her feelings, but it only serves to sever the smooth edges of their friendship.

Her hands slide behind Luna's arms – and then Rachel hears the door.

And a voice calling to her.

ONE

NOW

Holly

To begin with, it's like any other morning – Holly surveying the mess her two-year-old has made within the space of ten minutes, Elijah distractedly eating his breakfast while tapping out an email on his phone. And Alexa blasting out Heart FM from the corner of the kitchen.

Holly opens her mouth to ask Luna to tidy up, but thinks of Rachel and reconsiders. Her friend would do anything to swap places with her – to be living in this chaos once again. Toys everywhere. Crayon on the walls. Signs of life. Holly silently begins gathering Peppa Pig figures and colouring pens, while Luna grabs handfuls of Cheerios and shovels them into her mouth, laughing as most of them spill onto the floor.

Elijah finally finishes his email and glances up. 'Won't Luna be late for nursery?'

'I thought you were taking her today.' Holly rolls her eyes. 'Remember? I've got an editorial meeting in half an hour. I'll never make it if I don't leave in a few. They're doing those infuriating roadworks on Parkway, aren't they?'

He grimaces and scratches his head. 'Oh, yeah. Sorry. Um. I have a meeting too.' He checks his Apple Watch. 'And if I don't leave now, I won't make it. Traffic's terrible on the A3 at this time. And as for trying to get to Fulham in rush hour—'

'Okay, I get it.' Holly sighs. 'Maybe I can ask Rachel to drop her off on her way to school.'

Elijah's mouth twists. 'No, don't do that. She's probably busy. I'll take Luna.' He jumps up. 'Come on, little miss. Time to go.'

Holly watches him scoop up their toddler, and in less than a minute they're out of the door.

And all it took was the mention of Rachel.

'I think there's a story here,' Ross, Holly's editor at the online newspaper says, a few hours later. He closes the door and walks back to his desk, gesturing for her to sit. 'But we need to push. And you're perfect for it. You know how to get people talking when they might be reluctant.'

Holly stares at Ross. He looks tired today, and it's the first time she's noticed dark shadows under his eyes, a contrast against his golden skin. 'Ross, I'm not sure if I'm comfortable with this one. It's—'

'All the charges were dropped against the Hobbs boy.'

'I know. But I'm keeping an open mind. He might still have done it. It could just mean she was too scared to pursue it. He could have put pressure on her to drop the charges. Or her family did. Either way, I'm not sure I want this story.'

Ross frowns. 'Holly, don't you want to get closer to the truth? That's why you do this job, isn't it?'

He's right; even as a child, she'd harboured dreams of being a journalist. Someone who would hunt out the truth, no matter the cost or the effort. Put the world to rights. Perhaps working for *Surrey Live* didn't always utilise the full spectrum of her investigative skills – most of the time she was reporting on car crashes or library closures. Even potholes. Nothing that needed digging into beyond the surface layer. Of course, technology has changed the landscape dramatically since she was a child, for the better, as far as Holly is concerned. They can reach more people online, and update stories as they're happening. It excites her. She's happy here. Content. She respects Ross; he's good at what he does, and she's still learning from him.

Besides, Luna needs her right now. There'll be time to think about moving on when her daughter's a little older.

'So this kid,' Holly says. 'Oscar Hobbs. Are any of his family willing to talk?'

Ross grimaces and flicks off the lid of his pen, jotting something down on a Post-it note and sticking it to his computer screen. 'Not exactly. But they might be if *you* approached them. You have a knack for getting people to open up – I've seen you do it many times. The mum's called Shania. It's just her and Oscar at home, but I think the dad's in the picture still. Might be good to get a perspective on what it's like being on the other side of such a... dreadful thing.'

Holly's noticed that Ross can never bring himself to say *rape*. She understands. It's a horrible word for a heinous act. But he's right: although it's rare, sometimes people do make false allegations.

Holly stands. She can never resist a challenge. 'Okay. I'll do it. Better than the review of parent and baby groups I'm about to start working on.'

'Give that to Paul,' Ross says, smiling. 'Might do him some good.'

Holly pulls into the only available space near Shania and Oscar's house. The Hobbs's home is in a new development of flats and townhouses, all of them crammed so closely together it makes her feel claustrophobic. Even though the developers maxed out every inch of viable space here, it's pleasant, and the small grassy play area in the centre gives it a wholesome family feel.

But Holly's learnt from seven years of working for *Surrey Live* that anyone can lurk behind the doors of a seemingly picturesque place.

As if to prove this, the woman who answers the door is not who Holly has imagined. *Never make assumptions*, she reminds herself. In the emails they'd sent back and forth, this woman had seemed confident and assertive, yet the person standing in front of her cowers behind the door, shrinking back as if she wants to disappear. She's thin, and shorter than Holly, and her long denim maxi skirt touches the floor. Her narrow shoulders give her a childlike quality.

Holly holds out her hand. 'Hi, I'm Holly Fisher from *Surrey Live*. We messaged earlier. Is it still okay for us to have a chat?' She moves forward.

Half-hidden by her long dark fringe, Shania's eyes narrow, and she seems to wither away even more. 'I suppose. But—'

'I can assure you, I'll run the article by you before anything gets published. And you can veto anything at all you're not happy with. Also, we won't mention your son's name. We want to protect all the children involved.'

This seems to work, and slowly Shania's shoulders drop, her face visibly relaxing. 'I suppose you can come in. Just for a bit.'

From the narrow hallway, a living room leads into a small adjoining kitchen with a table in the centre. Beyond that, two French doors open onto a tiny lawn with no patio. Although it's tiny, it's clean and bright. Shania has made the best of the limited space, and it's clear that she takes pride in her home.

'Oscar must be at school?' Holly asks.

Shania nods. 'He likes school. He's got a lot of friends. Or at least, he did. Do you want tea? I don't have coffee. I never drink it.' She leads Holly through to the kitchen.

'Tea's great.'

Holly prefers coffee, but she'll drink whatever will help her bond with this woman. She sits at the small table in the middle of the kitchen and watches Shania. She must be at least mid forties, but it's hard to be sure.

With slow, deliberate movements, Shania sets about making the tea, and Holly wonders if she's stalling. Giving herself time to prepare. Why would she need to, though? The truth doesn't need any rehearsal.

She finally places one steaming mug on the table.

'Aren't you having one?' Holly asks.

'No. Gone off tea. I was living off it when all of this first happened, and now I can't seem to stomach it. Is that weird? I dunno. Maybe it reminds me of what happened. Triggers me. God, I hate that word. The way it's bandied about. There has to be a better one.'

Holly's learnt that very little in life is actually unusual. If you're doing something, or feeling something, then it's likely there are many others going through the same thing. 'It must have been very difficult,' she says. 'I can't imagine how awful it was.'

Shania tilts her head and studies Holly. 'Still is. And are you trained to say that? To get people to speak? You must be. It's your job.'

'We do have training, yes. But I mean what I say to people. I honestly can't imagine what you went through. How painful it must have been.' Briefly, she thinks of Rachel, and the immense suffering her friend endures every day.

'Do you have children?' Shania enquires.

'Yes, a daughter. She's two.'

Shania nods. 'Ah, well fast-forward a few years and I hope you never have to go through what I have with Oscar.' She leans forward. 'They change, you know. Right in front of you. Every second. You might not notice it too much at first, and then suddenly they're this sixteen-year-old and it's like... they've built a brick wall around them and you just can't get to them.' She stares down at her hands. Her fingernails are already short, bitten to the skin.

Holly sighs. Luna is already strong-willed, but she loves that about her daughter, and she doesn't ever want to dampen her spirit. 'I'm sure it's hard raising a teenager.'

'Yes, it is. Did you know our brains aren't fully developed until around twenty-five? That's insane, isn't it? It means they have no fear of consequences. I've read up about it.'

'I've actually heard that,' Holly says. But caught up as she is in the toddler stage, Holly can't yet see beyond toilet training and tantrums. 'What was Oscar like as a young child?'

Shania pulls out a chair and slides into it. 'He was a gentle boy. People used to say that to me. "Oh, Oscar's so soft and gentle. What a lovely boy." He would never tear around the house, wild and crazy. He'd prefer to sit and draw. But I had nothing to compare it to because he was my first. And last.' She looks down again, and Holly senses sadness behind her words.

'We'll probably stick with one,' Holly says. Ross always taught her the importance of making connections with people if you want them to talk.

Shania raises her eyebrows. 'Well, it's an individual choice. I split up with Oscar's dad when Oscar was around eight, and I've never met anyone else to settle down with. It's fine, though. People need to learn to be happy with what they have instead of focusing on having more of everything.'

Holly nods. 'I think you're right. So, can you tell me what happened leading up to the... accusation.'

'*False* accusation.'

'Sorry, yes – false accusation.' Even as Holly says this,

though, a flicker of doubt ignites in her mind. *How can anyone ever know what really happens when two people are alone?*

'He was seeing that girl. *Megan.*' Shania says the name as if it leaves a horrible taste on her tongue. 'I know he was. They'd be up in his room all the time. Door shut. For hours on end. It doesn't take a genius to guess what they were doing.'

Holly wants to ask her if she condoned this happening under her roof, but she stops herself. 'Did Oscar tell you they were together?'

'Oh, no. But he doesn't tell me anything that's going on in his life. He insists they were just good friends. Still, I told him to be careful. Megan's only fifteen. But he'd just get angry and tell me it wasn't like that. And then the next thing I know, the police are knocking on the door accusing him of... of *forcing* her.'

'That must have been a shock. And frightening. For both of you.'

Shania nods. 'Our lives have been destroyed because of *her* lies. Oscar hasn't been the same since it happened. Oh, he puts on a brave face, but I see beyond that. It's messed him up.'

'How long was it before Megan dropped the charges?'

'Eight weeks. Almost two months of hell. We had all kinds of abuse from people. Even people I know. People I thought were my friends. And Oscar just shut himself away and became a hermit. He's only just starting to rebuild his life now. He'll never be the boy he was. It's been so hard for him. He wants a weekend job so that he can start saving for a car, but no one will give him a chance. And I can't afford to give him much.'

'It's unimaginable,' Holly says. 'Just awful to have to go through something like that.'

'Well, I hope you never have to know pain like it,' Shania says. 'Because it rips a part of you out and you never fully heal.'

A deep chill runs through Holly at Shania's words. She needs to wrap this interview up as quickly as possible.

. . .

With Elijah out with work friends this evening, Holly's on her own getting Luna ready for bed. After giving Luna a bath and brushing her teeth, Holly switches off all other thoughts and focuses on colouring with her daughter. Her mind's been scrambled since her chat with Shania Hobbs. Something about what Shania said doesn't feel right. Holly has no evidence to support this, but her instinct warns her that she's missing something.

Luna rubs her eyes, but carries on scribbling all over her colouring book. 'Look, Mummy!' she says, smiling. 'I colour!'

'A pink elephant – lovely! Okay, little miss, I think some-one's tired. It's time for bed.'

'No, finish,' her daughter says, jabbing the paper with her pencil.

Glancing at all the white space left on Luna's colouring page, Holly tells her they'll finish it tomorrow.

Too tired for her usual grumbling, Luna complies and climbs into her bed, pulling the duvet up to her chin. 'Mummy read to me?' she asks, pointing to her Peppa Pig book on the bookshelf.

Before Holly's reached the last page, Luna is asleep. With her thoughts returning to Oscar Hobbs, Holly kisses her daughter goodnight and leaves her to sleep.

She makes herself a strong coffee and sits at the kitchen table with her laptop. The heat is stifling after the recent burst of unseasonable late-spring warmth, so she opens the bifold doors, but the early evening air does little to cool her skin.

She taps on her keyboard, shaping the story she wants to write. The devastation caused to an innocent boy and his family. A warning not to jump to conclusions about a person's guilt or condemn them before they've had a trial.

After a couple of hours, her eyes feel heavy – a sign that her brain is close to powering off. She closes her laptop, ignoring the niggling sense that something feels off.

While she's brushing her teeth, a WhatsApp message from Rachel comes through. A year ago, she would have been delighted to see her friend's name on her screen, and they would have spent at least an hour messaging back and forth, filling each other in on every part of their days. On everything Luna and Evie got up to. Now, though, her heart sinks a little. Even before she's read the message, she worries about what reply she can offer.

Holly climbs into bed and messages Elijah to say she hopes he's enjoying his evening. She deletes the last word, and writes *childfree evening* instead, with an army of exclamation marks to follow.

Then, she takes a deep breath and reads Rachel's message.

> *I miss our chats. I miss US. I'm still me, you know. Anyway, if you need a break, how about I take Luna to the park tomorrow after I finish at school? There's something I need to talk to you about.*

The guilt Holly always feels spreads over her like a thick, heavy blanket. She's said no to Rachel the last few times she's asked to see them, making feeble excuses that Rachel is bound to see through. It's not that she doesn't trust her – of course she does – but she worries it's doing her more harm than good to be so involved in Luna's life.

Luna isn't Evie.

Holly taps a reply. *That would be great.* But as soon as she reads the words back, she deletes them. A bit of distance will probably do them all some good. And save her from having to listen to Elijah complaining that Rachel's trying to take over with Luna.

So sorry, but Elijah and I are taking Luna out tomorrow after nursery. We've hardly spent time with her all week. But I'll let you know when I'm free and we can have a chat.

She's not lying to her friend – she'll make sure they do take Luna out. Holly presses send, and her message vanishes into the ether, finding its way to Rachel, where she can only imagine it will be met with disappointment and sadness.

Putting her phone on mute, she turns over and closes her eyes, but it's a while before the overwhelming guilt allows her to sleep.

Just after three a.m., Holly wakes, her eyes springing open. Beside her, Elijah softly snores. He's home safe. Everything is fine. Evie's death has taught her never to take anything for granted.

The house is silent, so she has no idea what woke her. It's the Oscar Hobbs story. She's missing something, and it's bugging her. Why would he and Megan pretend they weren't together? There was no apparent reason to hide their relationship. They spent plenty of time together, so clearly their parents weren't against it.

Holly climbs out of bed – walking helps her when there's something her brain needs to probe more deeply, even if it's just a stroll around the kitchen island.

On her way, she stops outside Luna's room, peering in. Luna's night light is on – a pink cloud that infuses pale light into the room – but her daughter isn't in bed.

'Luna?' she calls, stepping into the room and turning on the light. 'Are you hiding?' But why would she do that at this time of night? Luna rarely wakes up, and usually Holly or Elijah has to prise her from her bed in the morning.

Then Holly notices the slight chill in the air. She rushes to the window and pulls up the blackout blind. The window is wide open, letting in a draught of cool night air.

'Luna!' She panics now, checking the room, just in case Luna *is* playing a trick on her. But she's not under the bed, or in the wardrobe, and there's nowhere else in here she could be.

Outside in the hall, she calls her daughter's name, throwing open doors and checking each room for her daughter.

'What's going on?' Elijah calls from the bedroom, sleep weighing down his voice.

'I can't find Luna!'

Holly hears him scramble out of bed but she doesn't wait, she's already downstairs, turning on lights and calling for her daughter.

But there's no sign of her. And when she sees the security chain isn't on the front door, she knows that Luna has gone.

TWO

NOW

Rachel

There are so many things grief tears from you, and sleep is one of them. That's why Rachel is never surprised to find herself awake at night, while the rest of the town sleeps. She sits in her living room with the blinds open, staring out at the deserted street. It's like looking at a picture; nothing moving, everything calm and still. In a small way, it reassures her.

Marriage is another thing grief pilfers. But she and Damien were disintegrating long before what happened to Evie.

They hadn't planned to have another child. Logan was enough for them, and they were settled into life as a family of three. She didn't have that feeling of not being complete that many women talk about. But then she found herself unexpectedly pregnant again. She was a teacher with a nine-year-old son, and on the path to a senior management position at her school.

Sometimes she wonders if it's her fault that Evie is dead. Because – and she never tells people this, not even Holly – she almost didn't have her. Rachel had been in turmoil when she found out she was pregnant. How could she bring another child into this sham of a marriage? So she'd booked an appointment at a clinic. But ultimately, she couldn't go through with it. The seed of life was growing within her again and she would get on board with it. Love the baby, and put her life on hold.

And now she doesn't have to, and she'd give up anything to have her little girl back. The little girl whose face brightened any room. Who, at one and a half, could charm people with only her smile, just like her father.

Reaching for her phone, she reads Holly's text again, while a blanket of guilt wraps itself around her. She analyses each carefully constructed sentence, trying to see through the words. Grief changes the structure of friendships because, sooner or later, even the people you're closest to will no longer know how to be around you.

This is the fourth time Holly's made an excuse for Rachel not to see Luna, and it's beginning to make her paranoid. But it's not paranoia if it's real – and Holly is definitely avoiding her. Their friendship is playing out its last days, and the pain of it makes Rachel's bones ache. Sucking her strength.

And when she thinks of Luna now, Rachel's stomach clenches with that familiar hollow feeling of being a mother without her daughter. Luna is the only one who can bring her any peace.

She hears Damien's harsh words. *You still have Logan. Your son. He needs you, so start being a better mother to him.* He looks at her with disgust now, barking at her as if he's talking to one of his employees. No, that's wrong. He treats the people who work for him with more respect. He has to – otherwise he'd have no workforce.

Of course, Rachel's there for Logan; she can't let Damien cast doubt on herself as a mother. But her son does put up walls. Shuts himself in his room and won't open up to her, despite her attempts to coax him out. She's aware that it's his way of dealing with his sister's death, but she doesn't know how to reach him. And it hurts to try.

Not for the first time, Rachel wonders if she's losing her mind. Just another thing grief has robbed her of.

The neat pile of red exercise books on the coffee table catches her attention. She leans forward and picks up the top one. It's dog-eared and full of illegible graffiti, but she doesn't have the energy to care. Marking these Year 10 essays is the only thing that will get her through this night. She's nearly there. Everything is coming together. She just has to be ready to face tomorrow, and whatever that will bring.

'Not again.'

Her eyes snap open and Damien is standing over her, his arms folded, that contemptuous look she despises plastered across his face. She wonders what other people see when they look at him. A handsome man with light brown hair and hazel eyes that fix on you and appraise you, making you feel like you're the only person in the world? Or can they see what she does? What she knows. That he is nothing his outward appearance suggests.

If Rachel closes her eyes, maybe he'll have disappeared when she opens them again.

'How much longer d'you think you can stay up all night without coming to bed? How will you be fit to teach today?'

Rachel ignores him, letting his words bounce off her. Sometimes she's grateful for the numbness that grief has left her with. She glances at the clock on the wall. Five past six. She has plenty of time. 'I'll be fine. I'm okay.' She pulls herself up to prove it. 'I just need a shower.'

Damien shakes his head. 'You need to sort yourself out, Rachel. This can't go on. It's...' He falls silent. 'And the front door was unlocked. But I know I locked it before I went to bed. Did you go outside?'

She frowns. 'No. Why would I go out in the middle of the night?'

'Who knows with you?'

'Maybe it was Logan?'

'No. He was fast asleep. And we normally have to drag him out of bed. I've just checked on him.'

Which means Damien is mistaken and he didn't lock the door after all. He'll never admit that, of course. 'If we're all here, then there's no point worrying about it, is there?' She moves her legs over the side of the sofa. It's time to face the day.

Refreshed from her shower and on her way downstairs, she stops outside Logan's room, listening. Damien has woken him now, and she can hear him rooting through his wardrobe and drawers, pulling out his school uniform. She hovers by the door, wanting to knock and poke her head in, to say good morning, smile and tell him she loves him. But she's frozen, so instead she heads downstairs.

Mechanically, she makes coffee and gets the breakfast things out. She never knows what cereal Logan will want, so she pulls out everything they have in the cupboard: Weetabix, Corn Flakes, Cheerios. The same cereals he's been having since he was a toddler. Everything the same, even though nothing is any more. The absence of Evie is like a gaping wound that can't heal.

The muffled sound of a ringing phone catches her attention. It's her ringtone – Damien's is some rock song she's never heard of – so she rushes to the living room, where the sound grows louder.

She finds her phone on the windowsill and answers without checking who it is first. It must be urgent for anyone to be calling this early in the morning. 'Hello?'

'Rachel... I...' Her friend erupts into tears.

'Holly, what is it? What's happened?'

'I've been texting and calling you for ages.' Again, the tears drown out her words.

'I'm so sorry, I haven't checked my phone. Are you okay?'

'Luna's gone!'

'What do you mean, *gone*? What's happened?'

'The police are here. I... I went to check on Luna in the night and she wasn't in her room. She wasn't in the house. She's gone!'

'I'm coming. Right now.' Rachel ends the call before her friend can object.

Instead of shouting up to Damien and Logan, Rachel scrawls a note for them and leaves it by the cereal. *An emergency. Gone to Holly's.*

It's only when she's in the car, driving away from her house, that the enormity of this hits her. *Everything will be fine. Everything will be fine. Everything will be fine.* Rachel repeats this mantra aloud the whole way to Holly's, until her words mingle together and no longer make sense.

The road she knows so well is unrecognisable. Police cars blocking the drive. People scattered around, fear and anxiety on every face. She doesn't recognise a single person. Are these all friends of Holly and Elijah? Work colleagues? Everyone has rallied around so quickly, yet she's only just heard what's happened.

Rachel parks her Peugeot behind one of the police cars and makes her way through the crowd, straight to Holly's door.

A woman she's never seen before answers, staring at her, appraising her. She looks younger than Rachel, and even though she's fairly short, she has a presence that can't be ignored. 'Can I help?' Her voice is deep and direct, but somehow still kind.

'I'm Rachel, a friend of Holly's. Her closest friend. She just called and told me what happened so I came straight here.'

The woman ushers Rachel in. 'I'm DC Michelle Evans,

from the child safeguarding team. I'm the family liaison officer.'
She doesn't smile, but scrutinises Rachel. 'We'll need to speak to
you,' she continues. 'Is now a good time?'

For a brief moment, Rachel wonders what would happen if
she said no, that it isn't a good time at all. 'Can I just see Holly
first?'

'They're in the kitchen,' Michelle says. 'But don't forget to
find me for that chat.'

Before she can move, Holly appears, rushing towards
Rachel and flinging her arms around her. Her hazel eyes are
swollen, and even her dark blonde hair seems damp.

'Where is she?' Holly cries. 'Where's my little girl?' She
pulls back. 'You haven't seen her, have you?' She looks desperate, and Rachel longs to tell her that everything will be okay.

'No. I wish I could say I have.'

Holly takes her hand. 'She couldn't have got out of the front
door by herself. She can't reach the handle. We always lock up.
Every night without fail. Elijah double-checks before bed. But
the chain wasn't on the front door.' She breaks down, tears
erupting from her eyes like a burst hosepipe.

By the front door, Michelle Evans watches them both.

'They want to speak to me,' Rachel says, and a rush of
anxiety flushes through her.

Holly nods. 'Not just you. They're talking to everyone in
Luna's life. Just to find out everything they can.'

Silently, Rachel is pleased. She's part of Luna's life. That's
all she's wanted since losing Evie. 'What time was it, when you
noticed she wasn't in bed?'

They go through to the living room.

'It was around three a.m. I've been working on a story,' Holly
says, dabbing her eyes. 'I woke up and thought of something I
need to probe more deeply. I got up to write some notes – in case
I forgot them by morning. And when I checked on her... Luna

was gone!' Tears glisten in her eyes, making them darker. 'Someone's taken her! And it's my fault – I left the window open. I never do that! Wide open! I only had it open that wide because it was so hot. And the window's too high for Luna to reach.'

Rachel hugs her friend. 'It's not your fault – please don't blame yourself. They'll find Luna. It *was* hot yesterday. And Luna's room always feels like a sauna. I would have done the same.'

Holly shakes her head, but doesn't speak. She's not wearing any make-up and she looks younger, her skin a few shades paler. Rachel's heart aches for her. And Luna. *But Luna will be okay. Nothing will happen to her.* She wishes she could say this to her friend, but being in the midst of despair, Holly wouldn't hear it, wouldn't thank her for her optimism.

'Elijah was out with work friends but he checked on her before he came to bed around midnight, and she was fine. So it happened between twelve and three.'

The despair on her friend's face is familiar. Rachel's seen it before on her own face, staring at herself in the hospital mirror when they rushed Evie to hospital, hooked her up to all sorts of machines.

'I'm going out to search. Before school starts.' Rachel reconsiders. 'Actually, I'll tell the school I can't come in. Then I can spend all—'

'No... don't do that,' Holly interrupts. 'Thanks, but you need to go to school. You never take time off...'

They both fall silent, because this isn't exactly true. Unable to face leaving the house after Evie's accident, Rachel had seven months off work. The thought of standing in front of classes full of children, all watching her expectantly, waiting for her to perform, was too much for her. It was her counsellor who encouraged her to go back. To grab her life and rediscover her purpose. It *has* helped – the kids are a distraction, and for most of each day she's too busy to think about anything outside of the school walls.

'Okay. Well, I'll spend as long as I can before I go in,' Rachel says. 'I've got a free period first thing so no one will miss me.'

Holly nods. 'Thanks. Someone from the police is organising the search so you'd need to speak to them. They want to make sure they're covering all areas and people aren't just going over the same spots. Wasting time.' She takes a deep breath. 'My poor Luna.'

Rachel hugs her friend, wishing she could siphon out all of her pain and take it on herself. What difference would more suffering make to her anyway, when she's already overloaded?

They're interrupted when the door opens and Elijah peers in. 'I'm going out to join the search,' he says. He glances at Rachel. 'I didn't realise you were here.'

'Of course. I had to come,' she says, fully aware that her tone is defensive. Elijah's contempt for her seeps from his pores, but Rachel is mindful that he's in pain, so she needs to give him a break. 'I just want to help in any way I can,' she continues. 'I'm joining the search in a minute, at least until I have to leave for school.'

Elijah stares at her, and she immediately realises that his despair is the only thing holding him back from making some contemptuous comment. 'Michelle will want to talk to you,' he says. Rachel should have known he'd find a way to antagonise her.

As if she's been summoned, Michelle Evans appears, holding a laptop. 'Ready for that chat?' she asks Rachel.

Elijah takes Holly's hand and leads her out. 'We'll find her,' he whispers into his wife's hair.

. . .

After talking to the FLO, Rachel steps outside and takes a deep breath. As numb as she is to this trauma, she needs to join the hunt for Luna. *Their* little girl. That's what she feels like, what she's always felt like since she met Holly. That Luna and Evie belong to both Rachel and Holly. Luna and Evie. Evie and Luna. It's remarkable how similar the two girls are. *Were.*

There's a large green in front of the house, with the neighbouring houses forming a crescent around it. At the edge of it, close to the main road, are two enormous oak trees. If they had eyes, they would know what happened to Luna. But the trees will keep their secret for longer than Rachel, or any of them, will be around.

She shivers, despite the muggy warmth of the morning. She's been told to join the group searching the woods behind Holly and Elijah's house, so she makes her way there, shielding her eyes from the harsh sun. As she follows the path that leads around the back of the houses, she scans the trees. *As if there's any chance Luna could have climbed up there.* Rachel's never been out here before, and has only ever seen it from Luna's bedroom window.

Her phone rings and she pulls it from her pocket. Damien. No doubt calling to tell her she's done something wrong by rushing off. Stuffing it back in her pocket, she ignores the incessant ringing and focuses on the woodland in front of her.

It's creepy, even under the bright glare of the sun. The chorus of voices calling Luna's name echoes through the trees – chilling and mournful.

'Luna!' she shouts. 'It's Rachel. Are you here?'

Two women turn to her, acknowledging her presence with small nods. It's funny how it takes something like this to bring a community together.

For nearly an hour Rachel tramples through dry mud, calling for Luna. She would do this all day if she thought it would help, but she knows it's futile. Luna is far away from here by now.

'Terrible, isn't it?'

A man appears next to her. She recognises his face but can't place him. He's in his late fifties with a grey-speckled beard.

'Yes.'

'They say that if a child isn't found within three days, then there's pretty much no chance,' he says.

This thought makes Rachel nauseous. 'We'll find her,' she says.

The man nods. 'You're right. Got to be positive.' He studies her. 'Know the family, do you?'

'Luna's mum is my closest friend. Luna's like a daughter to me.'

His eyes widen. 'Oh. I'm sorry. This must be hard for you too.'

Rachel nods, feeling the prick of tears sting the corner of her eyes. 'Do you know the Fishers?'

He shakes his head. 'No. But I live round the corner. Glendale Drive. My wife's here too. We've got grown-up kids. I can only imagine how the parents must be feeling. It's a different world now. Kids just aren't safe anywhere. When mine were—'

'Luna will be fine,' Rachel says. 'She'll be somewhere. We'll find her.' Even to her own ears, her voice sounds robotic, devoid of emotion.

The man shrugs. 'I hope you're right,' he says, placing his hand on her shoulder.

Rachel resists the urge to squirm, and is relieved when he tells her he'd better join his wife. She watches him walk off, heading towards a woman in a dark denim jacket and hiking boots.

A police drone flies above, able to cover areas faster than any of the team on the ground can.

The alarm on Rachel's phone blares from her pocket. It's time she made her way to school.

If she's honest with herself, Rachel doesn't much like this Year 11 class. Not the kids individually, oh no – she cares about every one of them, and she's taught them for two years now. But as a whole, the twenty-four students make up a mass of... what? She's not sure. Something unpleasant, distinct from them all as individuals. From the second they enter the classroom and sit, there's a tense atmosphere, and they stare at her, unsmiling, their minds a flurry of negative thoughts, she's sure. She just hasn't been able to gel with them as a group.

Oscar Hobbs strolls in late, while the others are reading silently. 'Sorry, Miss. My mum's alarm didn't go off so she forgot to wake me.'

Normally, Rachel would respond to this with a comment about how perhaps he's old enough to set his own alarm, but she doesn't have the energy this morning. The search through the woods still haunts her.

Instead, she raises her eyebrows, folding her arms as she sits on the edge of her desk. 'Okay. Silent reading,' she reminds him. Many of the Year 11s are taller than her, so it gives her confidence to be physically higher than them, even when she's sitting.

Rachel walks round to the computer to mark Oscar present on the register. Last year, he tried to test her, push her boundaries to see what he could get away with. But Rachel stood firm. Wouldn't be intimidated. And out of that grew a mutual respect. And she has to admit, Oscar seems to have calmed down since he turned sixteen. And gradually, she's grown quite fond of him. She knows about all the trouble he got in with Megan Hart, and she's sure that has something to do with his metamorphosis. Oscar's not a bad kid. Others might not get him, but she sees through the bravado. His desperation to be liked. That's what it is, she's sure.

Rachel glances up and sees that he's pulled out his reading book, and she lets out the breath she hasn't realised she's been holding in. For Luna.

She works the class hard today. Exam practice questions, one after the other. Dull but necessary, especially when the exams are only weeks away. She's pleased to see Oscar fully engaging, instead of staring into space. And while they're working, she thinks about Luna, how frightened and alone she must feel. Unless... Rachel's chest constricts and her body becomes a furnace.

With two minutes to go before the bell, she tells her class to pack away and stand behind their chairs. A little bit of order in the chaos of what's happening outside these walls. She couldn't control what happened to Evie, but she can determine much of what happens in her classroom.

Lyra Hunt stops by her desk as the kids shuffle out. Her eyes are glassy, as if she's been holding back tears but can't quite stop them.

'Are you okay, Lyra?' Rachel asks.

She shakes her head. 'Did you hear about that toddler? Luna someone? She's been snatched.'

'We don't know that for sure.'

'But what else could have happened?'

'She might have wandered off and got lost.' *Impossible. She can't reach the door handle.* 'They'll find her.'

'But it was the middle of the night. She was sleeping.'

As much as Rachel wants to support Lyra, this conversation sends sharp shooting pains across her body. Luna. Evie. Both little girls intermingle and become one being. 'I know her mum. She's my closest friend.' Rachel's not sure why she's saying this. She never talks about her personal life to her students. Giving things away makes her feel vulnerable.

Lyra's mouth hangs open. 'Sorry, Miss.'

'Let's try to be positive. I think that's always better, don't you?'

Lyra nods, but she's not convinced. 'I've got a bad feeling. Something feels all wrong, Miss. And I've got a little sister not much older.'

Rachel glances towards the corridor, where students criss-cross in all directions. 'Try not to think like that. Nothing will happen to your sister. You'd better get to your next lesson before the second bell goes.'

Lyra turns to leave. 'Bye, Miss. Thanks.'

Once she's alone, Rachel shuts the classroom door and sits at her desk. She has another free period now, and she still has a few books left to mark before her next class. She opens the first one, and then her bag under the desk catches her eye. With a glance at the door, she places it on her lap.

And then she reaches in and runs her hand over the soft grey fur of Luna's cuddly lamb.

THREE

NOW

Holly

'I wasn't there for her,' Holly says when Elijah joins her at the living room window. Outside, reporters have gathered on the other side of the street, huddled together chatting and holding cups of coffee. Even though she's a reporter too, Holly feels an intense rush of anger that to them this is just another job. Something exciting that will attract eyeballs to their stories.

She turns to Elijah. Just like her, dark grey shadows hang under his grey-green eyes. His dark hair has grown quite long, falling across his forehead. 'For Luna?' he asks. 'Of course you're there for her. Always. She couldn't wish for a better mother.' He wraps his arms around her. She's always felt secure when he holds her; at almost six foot, he towers above her. But today, his embrace does nothing to comfort her.

Holly pulls away, unable to bear being touched when her daughter is... gone. 'I don't mean Luna. I mean Rachel.'

'Why are you thinking about *her* now?' Elijah huffs. 'Our daughter's missing and—'

'Rachel lost her daughter too.'

'Luna's not dead,' he says, his words echoing across the room, rebounding off the walls.

All day their house has been full of people, most of them strangers, and she just wanted them out. But now she and Elijah are alone, and the house only feels hollow, stark in Luna's absence.

'This is completely different to what happened to Evie,' Elijah continues.

Holly ignores his comment. 'I didn't know what to say to Rachel when it happened. I turned away from her because I couldn't bear her grief. What kind of friend does that make me? I just couldn't find any words to say to her. My closest friend.'

Elijah puts his arms around her again. 'You've got lots of friends,' he points out. 'Who you've known a lot longer.'

Again, she doesn't address what he's just said. It's as if they're having separate conversations. 'Now look at me. Now I know, don't I? I finally understand what it must feel like for Rachel.'

'Our daughter is not dead,' Elijah insists, his voice commanding, his words fervent.

It's so out of character that Holly stares at him, wondering how much of a stranger he'll become to her before they find their daughter. Will this tear them apart? She's known of the healthiest marriages being irrevocably broken by grief. 'I should have supported Rachel more,' she says. 'I should have known what to say.'

'You *did* support her. You were in contact with her every day for months. Dropping everything if she needed you. And let's face it, she's—'

Holly glares at him. 'Please don't.' Besides, it's not true. Maybe for a few weeks she was in daily contact, but it soon petered out a bit, especially when Rachel didn't reply to half her messages. 'She's always there for me. She spent her lunchtime yesterday putting up posters in the school. Every spare second she's been searching. It's more than I did for her.' Holly had felt helpless when Evie died, out of her depth because what words can comfort a mother who's lost their child?

'Stop it, Holly. Don't do this.' Elijah's voice snaps her back to the present. 'We need to focus on Luna.'

'I know! That's what I'm doing! I've been out all day. Putting up posters. Talking to anyone who will listen, to see if they've seen her.'

Elijah pulls her towards him, and she feels herself flopping in his arms like a ragdoll. None of what she's been doing is enough to bring Luna back.

'I need a shower,' she says, pulling away. She's not sure she'll make it through even a quick wash, but she just needs to be alone for a moment, to work out how she'll find their daughter.

Upstairs, she stands outside Luna's room, and her breath catches in her throat. It's now a crime scene – blue and white tape across the doorway. A warning not to enter. She knows this is to avoid contamination, but still it feels like a violation. This is Luna's room. That's all it should ever be. Swiping away tears, she heads to her and Elijah's bedroom and sits on the bed, pulling her phone out to note down everything she can remember about who they've come into contact with in the last few days.

It's an hour later when she goes back downstairs. She didn't make it into the shower, but she's dressed and ready to face what the rest of this day will bring.

Elijah appears from the kitchen and hands her a mug of coffee. Holly doesn't want anything, but she thanks him and takes it, placing it on the bookcase in the hall. She's about to tell him that she's going out to search again, but the doorbell rings before she can speak.

'I'll get it,' Elijah says.

But Holly's already rushing to the door, her chest constricting as she flings it open, desperate for it to be someone bringing Luna back to them.

It's Ross on her doorstep. 'I'm sorry I didn't come yesterday,' he explains. 'I was out looking, though, in the evening. As soon as I could.'

'You don't have to apologise,' Holly says. Ross had called several times throughout the day and that had been enough. She holds the door open for him.

'Hi,' Elijah says, appearing behind her. 'Thanks for coming.'

'I wasn't sure if you'd want any visitors,' Ross says, stepping inside. 'Thought the house would be full of people.'

'It has been,' Holly says. 'But no one's here now. Michelle, the FLO, will be back soon, though. She doesn't leave us alone for long.'

'That's good,' Ross says. He looks unsure of himself, and shoves his hands in his pockets. Holly can't remember a time when she's seen him like this. He's a father – he understands, maybe even feels a tiny part of her pain to imagine it could be Harry missing instead of Luna.

'*Is* it good?' Holly asks. 'I feel like Michelle doesn't trust us. Like she thinks we've got something to do with Luna disappearing.' Tears roll down her cheeks, stinging her skin. 'Is that what people are thinking? *As if we could hurt our baby.*'

'No one thinks that,' Elijah assures her, leading her and Ross into the living room.

'Of course they do,' she says quietly. 'They always look at the parents first. Michelle's not just here to help us, she's also here to investigate.'

'There's truth in that,' Ross agrees. 'But the police just want to find Luna. Try to keep that in mind.'

In the living room, Elijah offers to make Ross coffee. 'Thanks, but I won't stay long. I'm getting back to the search in a minute. I just wanted to run something by you both.'

Silently, Holly and Elijah sit down, and Ross does the same.

'You'll know that we covered what happened yesterday. Anything to raise awareness and get people looking. But I wondered what you thought about getting your side out? It might get more people paying attention. And you never know if someone's reading the story who might know something. Or has heard something.'

Holly had wondered about this. Normally she would have been the person begging Ross to give her this story, and now the thought of that makes her shudder. Her little girl *is* the story. She looks at Elijah. 'We're doing an appeal this morning at the police station. Could it just tie in to that? I can't think about anything else yet.'

'Of course. This is national already. Everyone pulls together for children.'

Holly knows that Ross is just trying to reassure them that people are on their side, all united in the hunt for Luna, but this isn't exactly true. Most news stories exist only for entertainment.

'You'll be at the press conference, then?' Holly asks.

'I'll be covering this myself. Sensitively and respectfully. And I'll be out looking for Luna every moment I can.'

A few seconds of silence pass. 'I don't want you worrying about work,' Ross continues. 'Take as much time as you need. I can give the Oscar Hobbs story to Paul.'

Normally Holly would fight to keep any story she's invested in, but right now she doesn't care about anything other than finding Luna. 'Yeah,' she says. 'I... I can't even think about that right now.'

'Like I said – take all the time you need.'

Holly stands up. 'Thanks. I, um, I need to go. I need to look for Luna.'

'Michelle wants us to stay here,' Elijah says, standing up. 'We should do what she recommends.'

'I'm not going to sit around here when Luna is out there somewhere, scared and crying for us.'

She leaves the two men and rushes from the house, taking in a huge lungful of air when she gets outside.

Rachel

She gets home just before four p.m. and heads straight upstairs. She hesitates for a moment before knocking on Logan's bedroom door; trying to talk to her twelve-year-old son since Evie died hasn't been easy. But she won't give up, no matter how hollow she feels inside. Gutted and hollowed out. And now it's more important than ever that he knows she's here for him, and always will be, no matter what happens.

'Yeah?' he calls after a moment.

'It's Mum. Can I come in?'

'Yeah.'

This is the best Rachel will get from her son, so she opens the door and steps inside. Although Logan is rarely talkative, his room isn't typical for a boy about to enter his teenage years. It's clean and tidy, almost compulsively so this last year.

'What are you up to?' she asks, hovering by the door.

Her son is sitting on his bed, clutching his phone. He shrugs and looks up at her from under his flop of dark wavy hair. 'Nothing. Did you need me for something?'

Rachel crosses to him and sits on the edge of his bed. 'I just wanted to see how you are.' She pauses. 'I didn't see you at school today. You'll have heard about Luna?' She couldn't bring herself to talk to him about it yesterday, but she's assuming Damien must have.

Logan nods. 'Everyone's heard. It's all anyone's talking about at school.'

Rachel nods. 'We have to be positive and believe that they'll find her.'

His face pales. 'What if they don't? Look what happened to Evie!' His words remind Rachel how young he is, how maturity has been thrust upon him too quickly, because of his sister's death.

Gently, she takes his arm. 'This is different. Evie was hit by a car. A horrible accident. There's every chance they'll find Luna. This is nothing like that.'

'Yeah, I hope,' he says, doubt lacing his words.

'I love you,' Rachel whispers. Perhaps lately she hasn't said these words enough, or maybe she's said them too much. She no longer knows what she's doing right any more. Everything is charred, like burnt edges of paper. It's important to tell people how you feel about them when they're still here – that's all she knows for sure.

Logan's head jolts up. 'Is something wrong?'

'No, no. I'm fine. Everything's fine. I just want you to know how much I love you.' She has to assure him she's okay; everyone around her believes she isn't, and it's a battle she's fighting so hard to win. 'Are you hungry? I can make you something to eat before I join the search again.'

'No, thanks.' He looks up at her. 'But can I go out searching too?'

Rachel raises her eyebrows. She'd never imagined that her son would want to come with her. He's such a home body. 'Um, of course. I'd love it if you came with me.'

He bites his bottom lip. 'Um, I meant with some friends at school. It's already been arranged. Dad said it was okay.'

Panic engulfs her. Logan rarely leaves the house, and if she's honest with herself, she prefers it that way. Where she knows he's safe. When Logan goes out, how can she control what might happen to him? *He could end up like Evie, and I can't lose him too.*

'I don't know,' she says. 'I'd prefer if you came with me. Or even Dad.'

'Dad said he's got some work to do tonight. He can't go out searching.'

She's not surprised that he knows more about Damien's movements than she does. 'Logan, I—'

'Course you can.' Damien's voice booms from the hall, and then he appears in the doorway. 'I'll drop you off.'

Rachel turns to face him. 'It's getting late.' She tries to keep her voice measured. She doesn't want to be accused of overreacting. Being irrational.

Damien rolls his eyes. 'He'll be back before dark, won't you, son?'

Logan promises he will, and the matter is settled without Rachel having any say in it.

Downstairs, she confronts Damien once they're alone in the kitchen. 'I don't want Logan wandering the streets at night. How can you think that's a good idea?'

'Rachel, you can't keep him trapped in the house just because you're scared something might happen. That's not living, is it? We need to give him some freedom. Besides, everyone's out looking for Luna. Nothing's going to happen to him.'

'He's twelve. And it'll be dark soon.'

'In a few weeks he'll be a teenager, and what do you think will happen if you try to stop him going out? It's hardly late, Rachel. And it doesn't even get dark until after eight. You've got to stop this.'

She'd ask Damien what he means, but she already knows. Her anxiety, that borders on psychosis. Her overprotectiveness, even though he always tells her she no longer engages with their son. *But I'm doing everything I can to keep Logan safe.*

In the pocket of her jeans, her phone vibrates. She pulls it out and glances at the screen, quickly shutting it down when she sees who it is.

Damien watches her, his eyes narrowing before he turns

away to start the coffee machine. 'You've changed,' he says. 'And it's not good, is it?'

Rachel considers what he's said. She's noticed that since Evie died, it takes a while for her brain to formulate responses. To get things straight in her head before she speaks. People wouldn't want to hear to hear the first thoughts that come to her mind. 'How can you expect me to be the same?' she asks Damien, trying to keep her voice measured. She doesn't have the energy for another argument.

The truth is, he wants her to get over it. He thinks a year is long enough for her to have wallowed, and somehow she should miraculously snap out of her grief, shed it like a second skin she doesn't need. 'I can't do what you do,' she says. 'I won't just act as if we never had a daughter.'

'That's not what I'm doing!' Damien shouts, his anger erupting with no warning.

She keeps her eyes fixed on him. If she looks away, he'll take it as a sign of weakness. And despite what he thinks, she is anything but that.

'What's going on?' Logan says from the kitchen door.

Before she can move, Damien rushes over to him, placing his hands on Logan's shoulders. 'Nothing to worry about. All this stuff with Luna's just been getting to us.'

Logan stares at the floor. 'I hope she's okay. What if she's not? What if something's happened to her?'

Again, Damien steps in before Rachel has a chance to comfort her son. 'This isn't Evie, son. Luna must have just got lost somewhere. They'll find her.'

How can she have got lost in the middle of the night? Rachel loathes the way he's sugar-coating it, as if Logan's a toddler who needs to be shielded from the harsh reality.

When Logan doesn't respond, Damien attempts a different approach. 'How about we go and grab something to eat before you meet your friends? Nando's?'

Rachel has to hand it to him – he's always there to support their son. He wouldn't win any awards for husband of the year, but his parenting skills can't be faulted. And that's where the problem lies. Her heart aches at the thought of how much she's failing Logan. How much Evie's death has stolen from them.

Logan's face brightens. 'Yeah. Thanks, Dad.'

Damien looks at Rachel. 'Shall we go then?'

His invitation is so unexpected, it catches her off guard. 'I can't. I've got to re-join the search.'

He sighs, but doesn't say anything. He won't in front of Logan.

When they're ready to leave, she gives Logan a hug by the door.

'Are you sure you're okay, Mum?' he asks.

'She's just worried about her friend,' Damien says. 'Come on, let's get going.'

Rachel watches them leave. She waits a few minutes before grabbing her handbag from the side table by the front door and pulling out the soft grey lamb. She considers washing it – she has no idea when it last had a clean, but she doesn't want it to lose its smell. She heads through the kitchen and out into the garden, clutching it to her chest.

The shed at the bottom of the garden seems further away tonight than it ever has. She makes her way there, pulling out the padlock key to unlock the door.

FOUR

BEFORE

Rachel

She can sense Damien's eyes on her as she sits on the living room floor playing with Evie. It makes her uncomfortable, and she shouldn't have to feel like that in her own home. This should be a safe space, where she can be herself, and not have to walk on eggshells. Tiptoe around a man she's come to despise. There. She's thought it now. She doesn't like her own husband. Does that make her a terrible person? *It's not your fault. It's not your fault.*

Rachel shifts her focus onto Evie, who picks that precise moment to turn to her mother and smile, filling Rachel's body with warmth. Damien might have pushed her to have this little girl, but the love she feels for her daughter explodes from every pore in her body. Logan, too, of course. But right now Evie needs more of her time.

'You've made her clingy,' Damien says. 'It's not healthy, is it? You'll be back at school soon and she'll have to go to nursery. How will she settle if she won't go to anyone else?'

As he says this, Evie crawls across to her, nestling onto her lap.

'See what I mean.' He stands up and reaches for their daughter. 'Come to Daddy, Evie.'

Evie's smile vanishes and her eyes start to glisten. She holds out her tiny arms to Rachel as she attempts to wriggle out of Damien's grasp. But he won't let go. And then the wailing starts, as loud as an air-raid siren.

Rachel takes her from Damien and immediately Evie stops crying, beaming at her mum and nestling into the crook of her arm.

'This is exactly what I'm talking about,' Damien says. The contemptuous look he throws Rachel only serves to put another nail in the coffin of their marriage. 'Don't you see what you're doing? You're making her want only you. This is *your* fault, Rachel. If you'd just let other people hold her when she was a newborn, this wouldn't be happening. And...'

Rachel tunes out. She's become good at this over the last few years. She's not being passive – she'll never be that – all she wants is to keep the environment calm and peaceful for the children. She won't have them growing up in a verbally aggressive house, like she did. Memories of being plonked in front of the TV and left to fester all day still haunt her. No, she just wants them to have a healthy and functional family life. *Then why, Rachel, did you choose this man?*

'I don't understand you sometimes,' Damien is saying, when she allows herself to tune back in. 'You didn't even want another baby and now look at you. I don't know what you've become.'

Perhaps she is as much a stranger to him as he is to her.

'My own daughter won't let me hold her,' he continues. 'And it's all because of you.'

Rachel's often wondered if Evie can sense what kind of person he is, and that's why she rarely goes to him. She looks down at her. 'Can Daddy have a cuddle?' she asks. 'Cuddle for Daddy?' Of course Evie's too young to understand exactly what Rachel's saying, and she just smiles and coos, tightening her grip on Rachel.

'I offered to do night feeds with a bottle,' Damien continues. 'But no, it had to be you, didn't it? That's all bullshit about breastfeeding. It doesn't matter. As long as the baby's fed. You do know that, don't you?'

Rachel doesn't care either way. Breastfeeding Evie was one thing Damien couldn't take from her. Those nights she'd spent sitting on the rocking chair Damien's mother had bought them were special. Just the two of them. And sometimes she'd go into Logan's room and feed Evie in there, just so it could be the three of them with no Damien around. She smiles now to think of this.

'What the hell are you smiling at?' Damien says. 'I think you're disturbed, Rachel. You need to see a doctor. Maybe you're depressed. Remember how you got after Logan? I think it's happening again. We need to get you help.'

We. As if they are a team, the two of them united against the rest of the world. Rachel feels her shoulders sag. That's how marriage is supposed to be. Not *this.* 'I'm not depressed. I've got two amazing kids and a job I love. What more could I want?'

Damien shakes his head. 'I'm going to work,' he says. 'Somewhere I'll be appreciated.'

Rachel waits until she hears the front door click closed then rushes with Evie to the window. 'There goes Daddy,' she says. 'Wave bye-bye!'

And within seconds, the heavy fog that drowns her every time Damien is here begins to lift. She kisses Evie's forehead. 'Whatever happens, my sweetheart, you'll always have me. Me, you and Logan. The three of us. That's all we need.'

FIVE

NOW

Holly

She's too exhausted for all the questions Michelle is asking. One minute Holly feels as though she's being interrogated, the next it's as if she's talking to a close friend. It unsettles her, but she'll deal with whatever she has to. She just wants her daughter to be found. Safe. Unharmed.

But with every ticking second it feels as though the chances of that are dwindling.

'I need you to think really hard,' Michelle is saying. 'Are you sure there's no one you can think of who might want to harm Luna? Or get to you or Elijah in some way?'

Holly glances at Elijah, whose face crumples. He's as distraught as she is at this thought. They've been out searching all day, and now night-time has fallen and the search parties have dwindled, she can't bear to be sitting at home, doing nothing while Luna is still out there somewhere. 'No,' she says. 'I can't imagine why anyone would want to hurt Luna.'

'Anyone who's been paying an unusual amount of attention to her lately?' Michelle continues. 'Even if you didn't notice it at the time, have a think now. Something that seemed insignificant could be really important now.' She looks at them both with her large brown eyes and carefully applied black mascara. Michelle is on their side, Holly reminds herself. She's here to help find their daughter.

Elijah clears his throat. 'Holly has a friend,' he begins, shooting his wife a glance.

'Go on,' Michelle urges.

Holly shakes her head. She knows exactly who Elijah's talking about and she needs to stop him, but would that make things worse? 'I don't think—'

Elijah grimaces; perhaps it's a silent apology. 'She's a good friend of Holly's. You've already spoken to her. Rachel James. She's a teacher at the secondary school around the corner. She was here yesterday.'

Michelle's eyebrows rise. 'Yes, I remember. Okay. Go on.'

Elijah looks at Holly, shrugging. 'Sorry, but it has to be said.' He turns back to Michelle. 'Rachel had a daughter around the same age as Luna. They went to nursery together. But around a year ago Evie got hit by a car... and died.'

'I remember that,' Michelle says. 'Devastating for her family.'

Elijah glances at Holly again before continuing. 'Well, since then Rachel's been... she always wants to... to be around Luna. You know, offering to babysit all the time, taking her out on her own when Holl needs to work. That kind of thing. It's... Oh, God, I sound like a monster, but it's a bit... well, it makes me uncomfortable.'

Michelle nods. 'I see.' She turns to Holly. 'And how do *you* feel about it?'

'Rachel's my closest friend.' There's no hesitation in her answer. She can't believe Elijah would even entertain the possibility that Rachel could be involved in this. 'And yes, it's been hard for her. But I think being around Luna helps her. That's all it is. She misses her daughter and it comforts her to be involved in Luna's life.' *Enough to take her?* Holly forces the thought from her mind. 'And she has a son. She's still a mum.'

'Course,' Michelle says. She pauses for a moment. 'Has Rachel done anything lately that's caused you any concern? Anything out of character?'

'No. Nothing.' She glares at Elijah, a wave of guilt rushing over her. They've always been able to communicate well, and iron out their differences. Is this going to rip them apart?

'I'll speak to her again,' Michelle says, almost to herself.

Holly stands, unable to face the stifling atmosphere in here. *Luna, where are you? Mummy just wants you back safely.*

She leaves the room and hears Elijah and Michelle speaking in hushed voices the moment she's out of sight.

In the kitchen, she fills a glass with cold water, drinking it so fast that it feels like glass slicing into her throat. Her phone beeps and she quickly grabs it from the worktop. It's Ross, checking how they're holding up. There are other messages too, none of which Holly has replied to, or even read. There's one from Rachel, sent this morning, telling Holly that she's praying for Luna. Her friend would be devastated if she had any notion of what Elijah's entertaining in his grief-stricken mind. It's desperation, that's all it is. Holly's sure he'll come to his senses and realise this is *Rachel* they're talking about.

Holly replies immediately, thanking her for keeping them in her thoughts. It's a bit formal, but she can't worry about that. She just wants her daughter back.

Elijah nudges her awake, and it takes Holly a moment to realise she must have fallen asleep on the sofa. 'What time is it?' she asks, pulling herself up.

He gently strokes her arm. 'I left you to sleep but thought you'd be more comfortable in bed. It's nearly eleven.'

She doesn't recall falling asleep, or even sitting down on the sofa. 'I'm shattered,' she says.

Elijah sits beside her, rubbing her arm. 'I know.'

'Any news?' she asks. But of course there isn't – he would have told her by now.

He shakes his head. 'You need to eat, Holly. Let me get you something. You didn't have anything for dinner again.'

She jumps up. 'No, I can't.'

'You need the energy for searching, don't you?'

Elijah's right. What good will she be to Luna if she can't drag herself off the sofa? 'Okay, I'll have some toast.'

They've just finished eating when her phone rings. Holly freezes. It's nearly midnight – this has to be something to do with Luna. She doesn't recognise the number, and her breathless voice is barely able to greet the caller.

'It's DC Clarke.'

His voice is deeper than it sounds in person, and Holly holds her breath, waiting for him to continue. 'Someone's found a young child fitting Luna's description.'

Holly's heart races. 'Where? Where is she? Is she okay? Is it Luna?'

'We can't say for sure, but we think so. She was found wandering alone in the park but doesn't appear to be hurt. She's being taken to A & E to be checked over. You can meet us there.'

Holly can barely speak to thank him. She hangs up and throws her arms around Elijah, who is hovering by her side. 'They think they've found her!' Tears flood from her eyes like a waterfall, even as she's grabbing her phone and car keys.

'I'll drive,' Elijah says, taking them from her.

The doctor who examines Luna is a friendly woman who looks

to be in her mid forties. Her voice is smooth and melodic as she tries to reassure Holly and Elijah.

Only minutes ago, Holly held her daughter for the first time in two days, and she was overcome with sadness and grief, but also joy. Luna is safe. She's back with them and never again will they allow anything to happen to her.

Her daughter, who clings to Holly with all her strength, still wears the pyjamas she wore to bed two nights ago, but they're grubby and stained with what looks like mud. And even though she's been doing so well with her toilet training, there's a large wet patch at the back of the trousers. Holly fights back tears.

'Physically, Luna looks fine,' the doctor says.

Holly looks up from Luna and nods. It's of little comfort, given that they don't know where she's been since Monday night.

Michelle sits beside them, her eyes scanning them all, silently taking everything in.

'So she hasn't been physically hurt?' Elijah asks, his voice rising with hope and desperation. He grips Holly's hand. 'That's good, then.'

'It doesn't appear that way,' the doctor assures them. 'There are no physical signs at least.'

'But she's not talking,' Holly says. 'She hasn't said a word since we got here. She hasn't even said *mummy*.'

'Whatever's happened over the last couple of days, I think it will just take time for Luna to adjust to being back at home.' She rearranges the stethoscope draped around her neck. 'Let's give it a few days, and if she's still not talking, we can think about referring her to a child psychologist. But Luna's very young – her grasp of language will limit what she can express. Please try and remember that.'

As the doctor says this, she glances at Michelle, and Holly wonders if this doctor is in over her head with this. How many child abduction incidents would she have dealt with?

Luna grows heavy in her arms, her eyes slowly closing. A tear she can't stop falls onto Luna's head, and Holly clutches her even tighter.

'Please bring her straight back if you have any concerns,' she says. 'Anything at all. Or you can take her to your GP.' She turns to Michelle. 'We've cleared a room down the corridor for you to use for as long as you need.'

Michelle nods. 'Thanks.' She turns to Holly and Elijah. 'With your permission, of course, we'd like to take some swabs of Luna's hands and face. It won't hurt her at all, we'll just use a cotton swab.'

Holly can guess why they need this, but she asks for clarification.

'There might be DNA evidence from the person who took Luna,' Michelle explains. 'We'd also like to take her clothing to examine. You'd be surprised what DNA can be left, even with a minimal amount of contact. We'll get some clean clothes she can wear.'

'Okay,' Holly says, despite it feeling like a violation of their daughter. If it brings them some answers, then of course she won't object.

Michelle nods. 'Normally we'd take you and Luna to a different location, but given that she's been through so much already, we'll get everything done here.'

'Then we can take her home?'

'Yes, we see no reason why you can't. It just might take a while.'

It's over an hour before they're allowed to leave. Michelle explains that they had to hold an emergency safeguarding meeting before they could let Luna go home. 'But everyone's satisfied that Luna will be safe at home with her parents.'

'Of course she is!' Holly almost shouts.

'Please understand, we just have to be sure,' Michelle says. 'I'll come and see you tomorrow.'

But Holly barely hears her; she's already gathering their things and lifting up their sleeping toddler.

'I'm worried about her,' Holly says.

She and Elijah watch their sleeping daughter, whose eyes closed the moment her head touched Holly's pillow. Elijah didn't object when Holly insisted Luna had to sleep in their room with them.

'Something terrible must have happened to her. Otherwise she'd say something. You know what she's like. She talks non-stop, saying every little thing that goes through her mind.'

Elijah squeezes her hand. 'Like Dr Humphries says, we have to give it time. Luna's traumatised. Didn't Michelle say something about her possibly retreating into herself? Like some kind of protective mechanism. We just have to keep showing her all our love and support. That's all she'll need. Then... she'll start talking again. Course she will.' He turns back to Luna. 'We have to just be grateful she wasn't physically hurt.'

Usually Holly shares Elijah's optimism, but it tears her to shreds to think of what her daughter could have experienced over the last two days, even if there are no marks on her little body. All she can think about is who she was with. Why they took her. Whether they hurt her without leaving any marks. A tidal wave of nausea spreads through her body when she thinks of this, and she sinks to the floor. 'What if... what if whoever took her didn't let her go? What if she somehow got away from them? What if they try to come back for her?'

Elijah joins her on the floor, taking her hand again. 'We can't think like that.'

Holly shakes her head. 'Don't you see? It's the only way to think. It will keep us on high alert. We can't let anyone take her again. I won't let that happen.'

Somewhere in the house, Holly's phone rings, forcing away

these crushing thoughts. She can't remember where she's left it
– it could be the police with further news, so she rushes out of
their room, following the sound of her ringtone.

It's still ringing by the time she locates it on the kitchen
island. The screen shows a number she doesn't recognise and
she answers quickly, trying to catch her breath.

'Holly, it's Damien.'

It takes her a moment to register this – his voice is so out of
place on her phone.

'I'm sorry to call at this late hour. But I wondered if you've
seen Rachel. Has she been out searching?'

'No, I haven't seen her today. And we've found Luna! She
was left in the park a couple of hours ago.' It's only now Holly
realises she's completely forgotten to let Rachel know.

'Oh, that's... that's great.' Damien falls silent for a few
seconds. 'Rachel didn't come home from school this evening
and no one's seen her. She didn't say she was going anywhere. I
just assumed she'd go to yours and then be out searching again.
Her car's still in the drive so she must have walked.'

'She definitely didn't come here, and she didn't say she was
joining the search again. I just thought she must have something
on at school. Are you sure she wasn't going somewhere? Maybe
she was meeting someone and she forgot to mention it? With
Luna missing, it could have slipped her mind to tell you.'

'No. Rachel doesn't forget things. You must know that.'
Damien sighs. 'And she doesn't go out in the evenings.'

This is true. Even before Evie died, Rachel preferred to be
at home. 'I can try calling her.'

'Don't you think I've done that? She's not answering or
replying to messages. And when Logan saw her at lunchtime
she said she'd see him at home after school.'

'Oh.' Now it's Holly's turn to fall silent.

'I've called everyone I can think of,' Damien continues. 'It's not a long list. Rachel keeps to herself, doesn't she? You're the only friend she sees.'

Holly doesn't know what to say. She's been so distracted with Luna being taken that she has no idea what's been going on with Rachel the last few days. Or weeks, if she's honest. Then she remembers. Right before Luna was taken, Rachel had messaged her saying she wanted to talk about something. What was it she had wanted to say? She's about to tell Damien but stops herself. It could have been something she didn't want him to know. 'She'll come home,' Holly says.

But when they end the call, with promises to keep in touch, Holly replays the conversation in her head. Rachel wouldn't just disappear. She'd never leave Logan.

That's when Holly knows with certainty that something is wrong.

SIX

BEFORE

Rachel

Sometimes she tries to tell herself that Damien changed overnight. That suddenly, with no warning, he was no longer the charming, attentive man who somehow silently convinced her to let down her guard and allow another person into her life. For years Rachel had been fiercely independent, owning her own home in her early twenties, living alone and not depending on anyone for anything. Until she met Damien.

But the truth is, there were signs, even before Logan came along. She just didn't want to believe that she might have made a dreadful mistake.

She told Damien things she'd never before spoken of. Things she'd kept locked away in a box, never to be opened. How her parents, both university lecturers, left her unsupervised for most of her childhood, not caring or worrying about what she was up to. Too consumed with their jobs, their own lives, themselves, to let having a child change anything. She even admitted to him something she'd never even wanted to acknowledge herself: that when they both died in a car crash when Rachel was in her early twenties, the first thing she felt was relief, before the excruciating pain kicked in. She would never have closure. Never get to confront them about the childhood they'd given her. To ask them why they'd bothered to have a child when they didn't want to look after her.

And when she told this to Damien, lying in bed together the first time she'd let herself sleep with him, he'd listened silently, a tear forming in his eye. That must have been the moment she let her defences down.

'They didn't deserve to be parents,' he'd said, taking her hand and pressing it to his cheek, slowly kissing away her pain. 'I'll look after you now.'

Rachel had laughed, despite the tears forming in her eyes. 'I don't need looking after,' she told him.

With a smile, he'd said, 'That's what people like to think. But deep down we all do.'

Now she knows that when it came to Damien this was certainly true. Since she'd had the children, and less of herself to give him, his resentment had grown and become something far more sinister. If only she'd read more into the words he'd said to her in those early days. The clues were there if she'd paid attention. But then what? She wouldn't have Logan and Evie, and no matter what, she'd never be without them.

'Is the baby still sleeping?'

Rachel looks up from her book and sees Samantha, Damien's mum, standing in the doorway of the guest room where she and Damien have been sleeping. Evie too, of course, in her travel cot. They've come up to York to visit his parents, and Rachel has taken the opportunity while Evie naps to hide away in the bedroom and read. She hadn't wanted to come here, protesting that she'd rather not drag Evie around when she'd only just had her vaccinations the day before. 'She'll be cranky. Or ill,' Rachel had warned. But of course Damien had insisted, and Rachel didn't want to stop his parents seeing the kids. She'd never fit in with Damien's family, but she had to make an effort, for the kids' sake.

Samantha strides into the room, making no attempt to keep the noise down. 'She's been sleeping a long time, hasn't she? Do you think you should wake her so she'll sleep properly tonight? She should be over all that night waking by now.'

'I have done this before, Samantha,' Rachel says, forcing her voice to be soft and calm. Quiet so Evie doesn't wake.

'Oh, I know. But none of us are above taking advice from those who came before us, are we?' She places her hands on her hips and peers into the cot. Samantha is a female version of her son, in so many ways. They both have the same light brown hair and hazel eyes, skin that tans so easily and effortlessly. And they're both tall, holding themselves with confidence and fierce self-belief. She used to find this attractive in Damien; now she sees it's never been a good thing.

Rachel needs to appease this woman. She can make life difficult for Rachel, just like her son does. 'You've done a great job raising Damien and Joseph. But I'm just doing what I feel is right.' The smile she forces makes every inch of her face feel tight.

Ignoring her, Samantha leans over and gently nudges Evie. 'Come on, little one, it's time to wake up. Your brother wants to go for a bike ride and you could do with some fresh air. Mummy doesn't always know best, does she?' Samantha flashes her a smile. One that seems to say *don't even try to defy me*.

Rachel's cheeks burn, and she puts her book down on the bed and jumps up. 'Please stop. I want Evie to wake naturally. Her body knows exactly how much sleep she needs. I'm sure it won't be long now.'

'Then no harm if I wake her early, is there? There is such a thing as too much napping, you really—'

'What's going on?'

Damien appears, and Rachel sighs. He'll back her up. He's

always talking about how important it is for Evie to sleep as much as she needs. 'Your mum was trying to wake Evie up. I tried to explain that we let her sleep until she wakes naturally, but Samantha—'

'I'm so sorry, Mum,' Damien says. 'You'll have to forgive Rachel's rudeness. Remember what I told you? She's been really struggling with postnatal depression, and it's affecting everything. I can barely even cuddle my own daughter.'

Rachel stares at him, unable to form a response.

Samantha nods. 'I knew something was wrong.' She pats Rachel on the arm. 'Well, you need to get straight to the doctor as soon as you get home. You don't want to leave it and let it get any worse. I mean, hiding up here all day. We've hardly seen you all weekend.' She tuts. 'There's nothing to be ashamed of, you know. Lots of women struggle. I didn't, of course. I don't let things get to me.'

'I'm not—'

Evie begins to stir, letting out a soft moan.

Before Rachel can get to her, Samantha has scooped her out of her cot. 'Come on, let's get you changed and wrapped up warm, then we can all go out for that walk.' She takes Evie to the bathroom.

Rachel's about to object when she catches sight of Damien glaring at her. 'Let Mum do it,' he says. His voice is harsh and cold now that Samantha's out of earshot. 'I've promised Logan he can ride the new bike Mum and Dad have got him. It's our thing, isn't it? Father–son bonding.' He starts to walk out but turns back to her, lowering his voice. 'Oh, and please don't be rude to my mum. Whatever issues you've conjured up in your mind, it's not fair for you to take it out on my family.'

'I wasn't. I just wanted Evie to have a full nap. You know what happens if she's woken up. You always say it yourself.'

He walks over to her, leaning so close that she can smell mint on his breath. 'I don't care, Rachel,' he hisses into her ear.

'We're in my parents' house and you need to show them some respect. What's wrong with you?' He pulls away and starts delving into Evie's nappy bag. 'And what are all these?' he says, pulling out the new clothes Rachel bought Evie the other day and throwing them onto the bed.

'What does it look like?'

'She doesn't need any more. She'll have grown out of them in days. Why are you wasting money? Just because I'm doing all right doesn't mean you can splash out and waste it.'

'It's my money,' Rachel says. 'What I do with it is up to me.'

Damien edges towards her, his fingers curling into a fist, but then stops. 'We'll be leaving in five minutes. See you downstairs.'

Once he's gone, Rachel flops down on the bed and forces deep breaths. If she was a different person, then right now she might be wondering if Damien is right. That this is all *her* fault.

But Rachel knows the truth.

While she sits on the bed, gradually calming down, she considers telling Damien and his parents that she's getting the train home with Evie. Logan loves it here so she would let him stay if he wanted. Besides, she knows he adores Damien, and despite everything, the man is a good father to their son.

But then she thinks of her childhood. How she'd sometimes hide in the downstairs cupboard to escape the verbal battle-ground her parents would create whenever they were around each other for longer than a few minutes.

That will not be her children's life. She will die before she lets that happen.

So for now she will continue watching Damien, and waiting. Because his time will come.

SEVEN

NOW

Holly

Luna is safely sleeping in their bed, yet Holly has barely closed her eyes all night. She's lost count of the number of times she's gone downstairs to check the doors are locked, and that every window is shut tightly, trapping stifling air inside the walls.

Just after four a.m., Damien had sent her a message saying that Rachel still wasn't home, and Holly's tried calling her phone several times since, only for it to go straight to Rachel's voicemail message. She never turns her phone off, and never lets the battery run low, let alone completely down. This isn't like Rachel. Even in the depths of her grief and despair, she was present for Logan and Damien. What would keep her from them now?

While Elijah and Luna sleep, Holly makes herself coffee to set herself up for the day, whatever it might bring. It's still dark outside, but through the window a hint of an orange glow is emerging. Holly tries calling Rachel again. Straight to voice-mail. It's only five a.m., though – it's possible she came home late and went straight to bed, avoiding Damien for some reason.

Her phone rings, blaring into the silence, and she rushes to answer it before it wakes Luna. It's Damien. His number is now stored in her phone. 'Any news?' she asks, without a greeting.

'No, nothing. She still hasn't come home.' His voice sounds strange, almost detached. 'I don't know what to do.'

'Have you called the police?'

There's a pause, and Holly can hear his breaths. One, two, three. 'Isn't it too early for that?' he asks. 'She's not a child.'

'No, but has she ever done this before? It's out of character.' And as she says this, that sensation of dread Holly felt earlier chills her bones. 'Is Logan okay?'

'He's not saying much, but I can tell he's upset. He thinks...'

'What?'

Silence.

'Say it, Damien.'

'He thinks she's left us. Oh, God – is that true? Did she say anything to you?'

'Of course not. We've hardly... with Luna being taken there hasn't been a chance to talk about anything else.'

Damien falls silent again, and it's impossible for Holly to read into what that might mean. She feels sorry for him. Even though he's always seemed a bit cold whenever she's crossed paths with him, she can imagine how he's feeling right now.

'I'll come over,' she offers. 'See if we can work out where she might be. But I'm bringing Luna with me. I'm not letting her out of my sight.' She pauses. 'Is that okay? I know it might be—'

'I have no problem with that,' Damien says, ending the call.

Upstairs, both Luna and Elijah are still asleep. Normally by this time their daughter is running around the house demanding breakfast. Everything has changed.

She gently nudges Elijah, and waits for him to open his eyes. He's never been a morning person and takes a while to rouse himself. 'What's going on? Is Luna okay?' He rubs his eyes and turns to Luna, who is still sleeping soundly.

'I've just heard from Damien again,' Holly whispers. 'Rachel still isn't home. Come in the bathroom – I don't want to wake Luna.'

Elijah's eyes widen and he stares at her, slowly pulling himself up. 'Where is she?' He follows Holly to the en suite.

'I have no idea. Nobody's seen her. It's not like her, though. First Luna, now Rachel. This is weird.'

Elijah falls silent. 'I don't understand. Where could she be?'

'I wish I knew,' Holly says. 'But I'm going over there now. I don't think Damien has any idea what to do.'

'Does Rachel know we found Luna?'

'After Damien called to say she hadn't come home, I messaged her. Told her that Luna had been found safe. But she didn't reply. Her phone seems to be switched off. I just—'

'She's... troubled,' Elijah interrupts. 'Maybe—'

'She lost her daughter. She's grieving, not troubled.'

He doesn't say anything, but glances back into the room. 'This can't be a coincidence,' he says, echoing Holly's thoughts. 'First Luna. Now her. And Rachel always wants to be around her.'

'Spending time with Luna helps her. It's nothing more than that,' Holly says, trying to keeping her voice low.

Elijah sits on the edge of the bath. 'I know you don't want to hear this,' he says, 'but I've been thinking about this. What if it was Rachel who took Luna? And then she changed her mind and left her in the park. It might explain why she wasn't hurt.'

Holly shakes her head. 'No. Don't do this. Don't say things you won't be able to take back.'

'I'm just—'

'Rachel would never do anything like that,' Holly says, though a flicker of doubt laces her words. She can't entertain that notion. Not now. Not ever. It's the worst betrayal of her friend.

Elijah sighs. 'Anyway, I'm sure she'll turn up for work this morning. Maybe they had a row? How do we know what's going on their house?'

Holly picks up her toothbrush. 'I need to take Luna with me. To Rachel's.'

'What? No, you can't wake her. She needs to rest.'

Holly peers into the bedroom where Luna still sleeps, her face angelic and at peace. Elijah's right. 'Will you promise me you won't let her out of your sight while I'm gone?'

'Of course I won't. That's why I've taken the week off work, isn't it? So we can both be here for her.'

Holly nods. 'I'll be as quick as I can.'

Damien is dressed in jeans and a sweatshirt when she gets there. His steel-toed boots sit neatly on the door mat, and his high-vis jacket hangs on the coat hook. 'Thanks for coming,' he says, letting her in. 'Logan's still asleep.'

It occurs to her that she doesn't know much about her friend's husband. All she knows is that he's a property developer with a huge portfolio. A workaholic like so many people these days.

They stand in the hall, and Damien folds his arms. Holly wonders if he feels as uncomfortable as she does. They've never been alone – they've had no reason to. And over the years, Holly gave up trying to get the four of them together. Either Damien or Elijah always had something on, and then she and Rachel just stopped asking. They settled into a friendship that only involved the two of them, and the kids.

'I've called the police,' he says. 'After I spoke to you. They're sending someone over. Do you want coffee or something? I'm not sure what you like.'

She doesn't point out this is because he never shows an interest in Rachel's friends, and every time she comes over he vanishes upstairs or out somewhere. 'I'm fine,' she says, gesturing to the kitchen. 'Shall we go in there?'

Damien shrugs. 'Yeah, okay.' He leads the way, and it strikes her how different the house feels without Rachel in it. How devoid of warmth. Even in the months following Evie's death, there was something alive in Rachel that grief couldn't extinguish.

Without being invited, Holly pulls out a chair and sits at the table. 'When did you last hear from her?'

Damien hovers by the door, as if he'd rather be anywhere else but talking to Holly. 'Yesterday morning. I was rushing to work and she was getting ready for school. It was... everything was normal. *She* was normal.'

Holly's used to asking questions – digging for information that will shine some light on things. 'Did you message each other during the day?'

'No.'

'Is it normal that you don't talk to each other through the day?' She and Elijah always message about something or other most days, and she'd worry if she didn't hear from him at all.

'How can we?' Damien says. 'I'm always on site. Or in meetings. I rarely have a chance to check my phone. And Rachel's teaching. She can't exactly message me in the middle of a lesson.'

Holly bristles at how rude he is, but chooses to ignore it. 'Was there anything she said in the morning that seemed unusual?'

'No. I've already said that. There was nothing. It was a normal morning. And then she told Logan that she'd see him after school.'

There's anger in his voice – he doesn't like Holly questioning him. 'How was she with Logan in the morning?'

He glares at her. 'Same as always. She'll do everything for him but she's... distant. Going through the motions with him. You know, getting his breakfast, checking he's got everything for school. But it's like she's a robot or something. It feels like she's emotionless.'

For the second time this morning, Holly jumps to Rachel's defence. 'She's doing the best she can. She loves him.'

'But would it hurt her to tell *him* that?' He raises his voice. 'Show it to him?' He stares at the floor. 'Sorry, I'm just worried. Where the hell is she? Logan's distraught. I've played it down, of course. Tried to tell him she just needs some space or something, but he's not stupid.'

'The police will ask you if you argued,' Holly says. She studies Damien's face, hoping to find clues about what he's thinking. But how can she read him when she barely knows him?

'Well, we didn't.' Damien's tone is defensive. He must hate not being in control. 'You have to have passion and feelings to argue. I don't think Rachel... Never mind.'

'Have you checked her things? Is anything missing?'

'You mean, did she pack a case because she's left us?'

'That's not—'

'Do you think I haven't thought about this? It's kept me awake all night. And the truth is... I don't know what was going on in her mind. She didn't pack anything. There's nothing missing that I can see.' He pauses, and stares at Holly. 'I don't know her any more.'

'She lost her daughter. It's bound to—'

'I know, but it's been over a year. And we *both* lost Evie. But we have to be here for Logan, don't we? He's still here. Life has to carry on. I've tried to tell her that. But she doesn't hear it.'

'Rachel *is* there for him. He means everything to her.'

'Then where is she?'

Damien's words sit uncomfortably between them.

'What about Rachel's other friends? Anyone she'd feel able to stay with if she just needed to get away for a bit.'

'Only you.' Damien sighs. 'She doesn't seem to have any other friends. Not ones she bothers with. And then after Evie died, the few she did have dropped away. Apart from you. Have you ever known Rachel to take a single day off work?' Damien asks. 'I don't mean after Evie, but before that. And since she went back to work after bereavement leave?'

Holly had joked about this once to Rachel – how she soldiers on no matter what illness might afflict her. She shudders to think of this now, but she told Rachel she'd be teaching lessons on her deathbed. *I can't let the kids down*, Rachel had insisted.

'No, she never has,' Holly says. 'So maybe she'll turn up this morning.'

'Do you really believe that? No matter how I try and frame this, it doesn't look good.'

Holly needs to get out of here. Damien doesn't need or want her help – not really. She doesn't really understand what he wants. 'Let's see what happens today,' she says. 'I'll keep trying to call her and I'll let you know the second I hear anything.'

Damien nods. Would it hurt this man to utter the words *thank you?*

'You shouldn't be here.'

Holly looks up to see Ross standing in her office doorway, his arms folded.

'I needed to come in.' She doesn't add that she'd have gone insane if she hadn't. She and Elijah have taken it in turns to watch Luna like hawks since Holly got back from seeing Damien, and their little girl still hasn't spoken. Or smiled. She didn't touch her breakfast either, even though she'd pointed to the Weetabix box. But at least she'd started playing with her Peppa Pig house, prising herself away from Holly's arms for a few moments before running straight back to her. It's progress.

And now Luna's here with Holly, napping in her buggy. Holly had ignored the inquisitive stares from her colleagues as she pushed Luna along the corridor.

Ross walks in, lowering his voice when he spots Luna's buggy. 'Oh. Um...'

'It's fine. I just came in for a couple of hours while she's napping. I didn't want to leave and risk her waking up to find me gone. Not after...'

'Course. It's no problem. I just meant... you can take some time off. As much as you need. You've been through an ordeal. I can't imagine what it would be like if Harry had been taken.'

'This Oscar Hobbs story needs to be finished, and—'

'Paul can do it. I really think you should take some time—'

'It's my story,' Holly insists. 'And I need to finish it. I'm interviewing Oscar after school today. Elijah and I are taking it in turns to be with Luna, so she's never without one of us.'

Ross nods. 'Oscar's mother's agreed to it?'

Holly won't explain that it's taken a multitude of emails back and forth to convince her, and that even when she had, Shania had wavered. 'She's on board. But I need to go and talk to her before she changes her mind.'

'Oh. Good going. Don't know how you did it. Shania was adamant she didn't want her son speaking to the media.'

Holly shrugs. 'What can I say? We just... clicked. As mums. You know?'

Ross frowns, but he nods his agreement. 'Well, if you're sure you don't need a break, go for it.'

Holly doesn't mention that from now on, wherever possible, she'll be taking Luna with her. Until they know what happened, how can she be sure her daughter is safe?

The second Ross has left her office, and with Luna still sleeping, her thoughts turn to Rachel. Holly messaged Damien this morning to see if she'd turned up for work, but he hasn't replied, though he's read her message. She tries again now, holding her phone for a moment to see if he reads it. But after a few seconds, it remains unread, so she places it on the desk. She tries to reassure herself that Rachel is right now sitting in her classroom, teaching her lessons, and that maybe she just wanted some space from Damien. It's not hard to see why. She would have told Holly all about it if Luna hadn't been taken.

Holly glances at Luna. 'What happened to you, my sweetheart?' she whispers. 'Where were you?'

Turning back to her laptop, she tries to focus on work.

Someone coughs, and Holly spins around to find Paul striding into her office, dressed as he always is in smart trousers and a shirt and tie. At around five foot eight, what he lacks in stature, he makes up for with confidence. And arrogance. He's a few years older than Holly, and she's acutely aware that he feels threatened by how quickly she's progressed in her career, while he seems to have plateaued. It's no surprise, given he does the bare minimum he can get away with. In every interaction he has with her, his words are laced with resentment.

'Glad she's been found,' Paul says, pointing to Luna. 'Must have been tough.'

'Yeah, it was.' And it's far from over. They still don't know why she was taken or by who. And until they do, it will hover over them, a dark threat overshadowing everything they do.

'Why are you here?' Paul says, walking in and perching on her desk. He always does this; it's as if he needs to be physically higher than her to feel good about their working relationship.

'Because I work here,' Holly says. 'And d'you mind not sitting on my desk?'

He glares at her but slowly rises, walking across to the chair in the corner of her office. 'Excuse me for being concerned.' He looks at Luna again. 'Probably not a good idea to bring your young child into the office. There are all kinds of hazards here, aren't there? And toddlers get into everything, don't they?'

'Thanks for your concern, but I'm keeping a close eye on

her. She's asleep and I've only come in for a bit to grab some things I need.'

Paul surveys her desk.

'I've just spoken to Ross and he has no problem with it,' Holly continues.

'Course he wouldn't.'

'What's that supposed to mean?'

Paul stands up, shrugging. 'Nothing. I'll leave you to it.' At the door, he turns back. 'By the way, I'd started working on the Oscar Hobbs story before Ross took it away. I had a great idea for it. Let's see what you come up with.'

Holly's cheeks burn and she's about to shout after him when Luna stirs. 'Oh, sweetheart, I'm sorry for waking you.'

Luna opens her eyes, and her mouth forms a circle as if she wants to say something, but instead she reaches out her arms. Holly unstraps her from the buggy and lifts her out. Luna's getting heavy, but Holly will never stop picking her up if that's what she needs. 'Are you okay?' she asks, holding her breath while she waits for a reply she's sure won't come. Luna just stares at her. 'How about some lunch? Mummy's hungry. Are you?'

Luna buries her head into Holly's arm. She's aware that she needs to give it time, but if nothing changes in the next couple of weeks, then Holly will go back to the doctor.

'And where's Rachel?' Holly says, her voice almost a whisper. Luna tightens her arms around Holly. 'Where could she possibly be?'

Carrying Luna in one arm and pushing the buggy with her other hand, Holly speeds up as she passes Paul's office.

'Holly? One second.'

Too late. Clearly he's ready for round two. 'What is it?' she asks. 'I need to get Luna home for some lunch.'

He clasps his hands together, leaning back in his chair. 'Just wondering if you'll reconsider the Oscar Hobbs story. There's a new angle I want to explore. It's important.'

'What is it?'

'Oh, no. I'm not giving you my story ideas. Surely you've been here long enough to know that's not how it works.'

Holly should just ignore him and keep on walking; she's risen to his bait before and it never ends well. But she won't be silenced or kept in a box. Her outspokenness is what Ross said he admired about her. Her need to speak the truth, no matter the cost. 'I'm working on this story,' she says. 'But thanks for offering to help.' She turns to leave.

'You're only here because he's interested in you. You know that, don't you?'

Again, she stifles the urge to offload onto him. She wouldn't do that in front of Luna. 'Why don't you tell Ross that? See what happens.' She flashes the largest smile she can muster before heading off.

But Paul hasn't finished with her. 'Watch your back,' he calls.

EIGHT

BEFORE

Rachel

Rachel stands by the kitchen window, watching Damien and Logan playing basketball in the garden. Damien has just bought a new hoop for their son, all to foster that bonding he's always talking about. Rachel knows he's overcompensating, showering affection onto Logan because he's worried he has no bond with Evie, but she keeps this to herself. If Rachel took a photo now, and captured this moment in time, nobody would ever believe that Damien was anything other than a doting father. The joy on their faces is as real as the ball Logan's dribbling. It's everything else that's a lie.

This is what she struggles to comprehend. How Damien can be such a loving father to Logan, yet still be capable of such hatred towards his own wife. Nobody would believe her if she told them. They'd say she was delusional. Fabricating things. Because how could such a perfect father be so dark and twisted?

She checks the time. Twelve forty-five. One hour until Damien drags her to the GP. He might be forcing her to go, but he can't control what she says when she's alone with the doctor. She's banking on the fact that what happens in that room is confidential. A few minutes that Damien will have no part of, and no control over.

Footsteps on the stairs interrupt her thoughts. Samantha or Tobias. Damien insisted that his parents come and stay for Christmas, even though after a day he'll be moaning about them. He and his mother are too similar; eventually they end up driving each other mad.

'Are you ready for your appointment?' Samantha asks as she joins Rachel in the kitchen.

'There's really nothing to get ready,' Rachel says, smiling. 'It's just a GP appointment.'

Samantha tuts. 'Yes, to help you. You can't go on like this. It's not good for you or the children. And it's definitely not good for Damien. Your mood affects him terribly. And even babies pick up on things. Everything you're doing now will affect Evie in the future.'

Rachel ignores this, lets it wash over her like a tide across sand. There's nothing wrong with her. It's Damien and his family who are the problem. Always making her feel that she's doing something wrong. Evie crawls over to her and Rachel scoops her up, breathing in her freshly washed hair. 'Not you, though,' she whispers. Her shining light. Logan too. Without them she'd be empty.

'What was that?' Samantha glares at her.

'Nothing. Just talking to Evie.'

Tobias walks in, wincing with every step. His leg must be playing up today. He has days like that, where he can hardly walk. An accident a few years ago that he doesn't talk about. And Damien has never told her what happened to his dad – he seems to enjoy keeping her in the dark, on the periphery of his family.

'Are you okay?' Rachel asks, because despite how they treat

her, she feels sorry for Tobias. And he's not as bad as Samantha. Mostly he just ignores what goes on.

'He's fine, stop fussing,' Samantha says, shaking her head and holding out her arms. 'I'll take Evie. You need to get ready.'

Sitting in the doctor's office – away from Damien – Rachel feels like she can breathe again. She's never seen Dr Nicopoullos before, but she seems patient and friendly as she waits for Rachel to explain why she's here.

'I'm... my husband thinks I might need help.'

Dr Nicopoullos frowns, leaning forward so that Rachel catches the scent of her perfume. Flowery. One she's not familiar with. 'Well, I'm more interested to know what *you* think. How *you* feel.'

'I've just had a baby. Well, not just. Evie's eleven months old now.'

The doctor smiles. 'The time just goes so fast, doesn't it? And are you coping okay? Babies and toddlers can be challenging.'

'Evie's not my first. I have a son. Logan. He's ten. I love the baby part of it all. I didn't think I would, but I'm really enjoying it. Evie and I have a really strong bond.'

'Then is there anything else worrying you?'

Where to start. Damien. That she's chosen the wrong man to be the father of her children. That she worries every day what to do about it. 'No,' Rachel says. 'I'm doing okay.' She looks down at her trainers. They need cleaning.

Dr Nicopoullos's neatly plucked eyebrows knit together. 'I want you to know that this is a safe space for you to talk. Everything you say is confidential. If you're worried about anyone in your family knowing what we discuss, then please be assured that it's completely private.'

Rachel doesn't say anything, but briefly glances up from her trainers into kind, warm eyes. She's never seen eyes that bright shade of blue before. *Now is the time. Tell this woman everything. She can help. This is my chance.*

Seconds tick by and her brain becomes frazzled, foggy. What she really wants to say to this woman wouldn't make sense. She remembers Damien's words to her last night. A vice grip around her throat. *You'll lose Logan. I'll make sure of that. You don't want that to happen, do you?*

And then she looks the doctor directly in the eyes. Right eye to left eye. She's heard on a podcast that this is how you bond with people. 'I'm really having trouble sleeping,' she recites. 'And then I feel tired all day. My husband is worried that I'm so exhausted. Is there something you could give me for that? And also, I think I might need anti-depressants.'

NINE

NOW

Holly

Elijah's sitting at the kitchen table, his laptop in front of him, when Holly gets home. 'Just catching up on some stuff while you and Luna were out,' he explains. 'This is the trouble with being the only IT manager at the company. There's no one else who can step in when I'm not there. At least not anyone with the security access I have.'

'It's okay. I get it. I've been at work too.'

Elijah stops typing and looks up. 'What? You said you were taking Luna out for a walk.'

Luna clings to Holly's jeans, looking around as if she doesn't know what to do with herself. 'Let's get you some lunch,' Holly says, taking her hand and walking her to the table, where she scoops her up and places her in Elijah's arms. 'I did take her for a walk. Then she fell asleep so I thought I'd pop to the office. I needed to check some things.' This is all true, but what Holly had needed most was some normality. Something to distract her brain from the trauma of this past week. Throwing herself into work might be the only way she'll get through this.

'Any news on Rachel?' Elijah asks.

'She didn't turn up for work,' she tells Elijah. On the way home, she had finally received a reply from Damien.

Elijah looks down at their daughter and strokes her cheek. 'Probably gone off to start a new life somewhere. It's not surprising. When people go through something so traumatic, they—'

'Run off and leave their son?'

'I'm just saying that maybe she was... I don't know. Not thinking straight. Troubled.'

But would it take a whole year, when she's just started healing, to then decide to discard her life? 'That's the second time you've called Rachel that. And I keep telling you it's grief.' She pulls out bread from the bread bin, checking the date. She can't remember the last time either of them went shopping. 'It doesn't feel right. I know she wouldn't run away. She loves Logan and she loves her job.'

Elijah pauses for a moment. 'And her husband? What about him?'

'I'm not in their marriage so I have no idea.' Holly rummages around in the fridge. 'Oh, we're out of peanut butter. Is cheese okay, Luna?'

Luna looks up at her but doesn't respond.

'Yeah, yummy cheese,' Elijah says.

'We just don't know what goes on in other people's relationships. Just like nobody knows what happens in ours.'

Elijah frowns. 'But we're okay, aren't we? We've been through—'

'I didn't mean it like that,' Holly assures him. 'I just meant how things look on the outside aren't always how they really are.' *But if this is the case, why didn't Rachel confide in me?*

Holly needs to end this conversation. They'll never see eye to eye about Rachel, and she can't listen to his criticism. It always comes back to one thing: how obsessed Elijah believes her friend is with Luna.

'I've got to interview someone for this story I've been working on,' Holly says. 'At their house. I'm taking Luna with me.' She cuts Luna's sandwich into quarters and slices some cucumber and carrot. 'I'll take some toys with me – she'll be fine.'

Elijah shakes his head. 'You can't take her with you. I'm here – she'll be fine with me.'

'I just don't want—'

'I know you're worried, but Luna is back with us. Whoever took her changed their mind. They let her go.'

'But someone took her for a reason. Maybe they didn't mean to let her go. We don't know anything. And until we do—'

'I'm perfectly capable of keeping Luna safe,' Elijah says.

Holly sighs, knowing it won't do Luna any good to drag her to Shania's house, especially with what she and Oscar will be discussing. 'Okay,' she says, taking Luna's plate to the table and pulling her onto her lap. 'Mummy will be home as quickly as she can.'

Shania Hobbs paces the kitchen while they wait for Oscar to come downstairs. 'I don't know why he's taking so long to get changed,' she explains to Holly. 'But I can't blame him for having second thoughts. What's he going to gain from this story of yours?'

'I understand your concerns. But Oscar hasn't been able to put his side of it forward. Isn't it important he gets the chance to do that?'

Shania stares at her. 'I don't think I know what's important any more. Maybe we just need to forget the whole thing ever happened.' She sighs. 'And I'm sorry about what happened to your little girl. It must have been—'

'It was awful. But I'm just grateful she was found.'

'I have to admit, I nearly called you to cancel this. I've been away for a few days and it gave me time to really think about whether Oscar should do this. But then I thought of what you've been through, and I guess that made me change my mind. Anyway, I hope they find who took her,' Shania says. 'The right person. Not just someone who can be a scapegoat. Case closed. That kind of thing.'

Before Holly can answer, someone coughs and they both turn to see Oscar standing in the doorway. He's taller than she expected him to be, and she's surprised by how grown-up he looks. A child in a body that's morphing into adulthood. She's seen photos of him while she was doing her research, but he doesn't look like the young boy in those photos. He goes to Woodbridge School, where Rachel teaches, and where Logan is in Year 8, and she'd asked Rachel about the allegation when it first happened. But Rachel had said she couldn't discuss any of her students, even with Holly.

He walks into the kitchen, scrutinising Holly. 'So, you're here for me to get my story out? The truth? There's no, like, hidden agenda?'

'No, I promise. All I ever want is the truth,' Holly says.

Shania walks over to him. 'We can trust Holly. And I'll be right here while she's asking her questions.'

'No, Mum – I don't want you to. It's... you won't like hearing all of it.'

'You're still a child,' she replies. 'I need to be in the room.'

'I'm sixteen. Stop treating me like a baby. I can handle this.'

Shania hangs her head and walks to the sink, filling a glass with water.

'Your mum should stay,' Holly says. 'Until a person is eighteen, I'd need their parent to be present.'

Oscar shakes his head. 'I guess I don't have a choice, then. Come on, can we please get this done?'

While Oscar and Holly get settled at the table, Shania sits on a chair in the corner of the small kitchen, watching them.

Holly tries to push Luna and Rachel from her mind, and forces herself to focus on this story. Everything depends on her telling this the right way. Now Luna is safe, there is no way she's letting Paul have it.

Holly places her phone on the table. 'Did your mum explain to you that it would help me if I can record this? It will be quicker than me having to jot notes down. Is that okay? I'll just be using this.'

Oscar stares at it. 'I guess.'

'Okay, let's start at the beginning. How do you know Megan?'

He takes a deep breath. 'She's in the year below me at school. I never talked to her there, though. We met properly when I was hanging out with some friends in town. She walked past with a couple of her friends.'

Holly nods. 'So you knew Megan was younger than you?'

He looks down. 'Yeah, but not much. She's sixteen in September. She's one of the oldest in Year 10.'

'And he's only just sixteen,' Shania chimes in.

'Megan's fifteen.' Holly has to point this out, even though she's not entirely sure the few months between them makes that much difference. They're both children.

'Nothing happened with us,' Oscar says, clenching his fists. 'I didn't like her like that. I mean, she's pretty, yeah, but I didn't want to do anything with her.'

Holly glances at Shania and she looks away. It must be uncomfortable for her to hear this.

'So you were just friends? Never anything more?' Holly kicks herself for putting words in his mouth – it goes against everything she believes in. The story has to come from him. Too late to retract her question now.

'Yep. That's exactly it. We were *friends*.' He stretches the word out, and Holly wonders if he's being sarcastic. But underneath the bravado she senses fear. If he's innocent, then what's he afraid of?

'Did you spend much time together?'

He shrugs. 'Yeah. She always wanted to come round here. Hounding me. You know.'

'It sounds like that's not what you wanted.'

'No... I'm not saying that. I mean, maybe I didn't want her here *all* the time. But it was cool spending time with her. Made a change. She was different to my other friends.'

'And what would you do when you hung out together?' Holly needs to hide her frustration. Getting anything out of this boy is proving difficult. And her mind keeps wandering. She wonders what Luna's doing right now. She resists the temptation to ask Oscar to wait a moment while she texts Elijah to see how Luna is.

'We'd just watch stuff in my room. YouTube, mostly. TikTok.' Oscar fires a glance at Shania, and again she looks away.

'I've told him I don't like social media,' Shania says. 'But you try getting any kid off it once they've had a taste.'

'Mum!' Oscar says, shaking his head.

'What? It's true.'

Holly's grateful that she's got years before she has to deal with that issue. And she's hoping the whole landscape will have significantly changed for the better by then. 'And what happened that day in February?' she asks, getting the interview back on track.

'Nothing. That's just it. Megan came over and we were in my room.' He rolls his eyes. 'She was in a weird mood that day. Hardly said anything. Left early.'

'I remember that,' Shania says. 'She'd only been here around an hour and I remember thinking it was strange that she was leaving so soon. Normally she'd be here for hours and I'd have to go up and encourage her to go home.'

Oscar rolls his eyes. 'I asked her what was up and she said "nothing".'

Holly's phone vibrates on the table. 'Sorry,' she says, grabbing it. 'I need to get this. Won't be a sec.'

She makes her way into the hall as she answers. 'Damien, any news?'

'No. What the hell am I supposed to tell Logan? He'll be back any minute. He said he was sure she'd be at school and was planning to look for her. I can't go on pretending she's just having some space.' His voice is fraught, almost unrecognisable. A side of him Holly's never witnessed.

'Um, Damien, listen, I'm just doing an interview, but I can stop by when I've finished. In around an hour. Are you at home?'

'Yeah. I came back early to be here when Logan gets home.'

'I'll be there as soon as I can.'

Oscar and Shania are staring at her when she returns to the kitchen. 'Everything okay?' Shania asks.

'Sorry, yeah. Shall we carry on?' She sits back down, but now she can't focus. 'Was there anything else unusual about that day? Anything Megan said or did.'

'Nope.' Oscar looks down, staring at her phone. 'But maybe we did kind of have a bit of an argument. Well, kind of. Not really an argument.'

That grabs Holly's attention. This is something nobody's mentioned before. 'Oh?'

'Yeah, it was nothing. She just kept going on about one of our teachers. Miss James.'

Rachel. 'You mean *Mrs* James?'

Oscar shrugs. 'We all just call her Miss James. She doesn't mind.'

Holly stares at Oscar. Her head feels heavy; she doesn't want to ask this question but knows she has to. 'Um, what was she saying?'

'How Miss James is... crazy. After, you know, her daughter was killed.'

'Of course that would be hard for anyone. That doesn't mean—'

'I know,' Oscar says. 'That's what I told her. Miss James is nice. She's one of the only teachers I like. I kept telling Megan not to say those things, but she wouldn't listen.'

'Is that why she didn't stay here with you, like she normally would?'

Oscar shrugs. 'I guess. I dunno. She seemed to want to argue about it. I didn't. I defended Miss James.'

'And what else did Megan say about your teacher?'

Oscar glances at his mum. 'Is this important? What she did to me hasn't got anything to do with our teacher.'

'Everything's important, Oscar,' Holly insists. 'Every tiny detail you can remember about what Megan said that evening. Because it was straight after that she made her accusation, wasn't it?'

'False accusation,' Shania says.

Oscar chews his lips. 'Oh yeah, that was it. She said she could prove Miss James was a nutjob. Megan told me that earlier, Miss James told her she had to leave early that day to pick up her daughter from nursery. But why would she say that, when her daughter died ages ago?'

TEN

BEFORE

Rachel

Sometimes the weeks pass calmly, as if she's floating on gentle waves, lulling her into a false sense of security. She's barely seen Damien this Easter. He's been working late every night and she's always asleep before he gets home. It's a new development he's thrown himself into, and it's taking up even more of his time than usual. And then he's up and gone before Rachel stirs. She likes it like this. If it was always this way, then perhaps she could put up with everything else. Their marriage would be like a business transaction, mutually convenient, nothing to do with love.

Rachel smiles as she pushes Evie's buggy, with Logan riding his bike in front of them. Every few metres he stops to let them catch up. He's a kind, sensible boy. She's lucky to have them. This is all that matters.

They stop at the park, and Evie screams to be let out. She hates being confined. Buggies. Car seats. High chairs. They all strip her of the freedom she desperately craves. Logan was never a runner, but her daughter would be out of sight within seconds if Rachel ever took her eyes off her. They're lucky to have this beautiful park on their doorstep, where she can let both the kids roam free while she safely monitors their every move.

Inside the park gates, Logan balances his bike against a bench and rushes off to the climbing frame. He's one of the oldest children here, and towers over the younger ones, making it to the top with such speed that the other kids look on in awe.

Evie toddles after him, and Rachel has to run to catch her before she gets hurt. 'How about we go on that?' she suggests, pointing to the baby swing with a safety chair.

Evie beams and runs towards it, almost getting bowled over by a boy who doesn't even notice she's right in front of him.

Despite knowing she'll have to spend the next hour chasing after Evie, Rachel smiles. To her, this is bliss. Just the three of them.

Rachel manages to get Evie into the swing, and she pushes her daughter back and forth, revelling in Evie's excited squeals. She wishes she could capture this moment, freeze it so that she could thaw it out whenever she needs to relive it. To cling on to a moment that could be permanent if she could sort out a way to make it happen.

When Logan says he's hungry, the three of them sit on the grass on their picnic rug, and Rachel spreads out all the food she's brought. Sandwiches, cakes, crisps, yoghurts and vegetable sticks. It's far too much for just the three of them, but Rachel doesn't care. The kids are happy. She's happy. And Damien will be working late again tonight.

Evie starts to grizzle when they've finished eating and Rachel tells them it's time to head home. 'You need a nap, sweetie,' she says, just as Evie starts rubbing her eyes.

'No! Stay!'

Logan puts his arm around his sister. 'We can come back tomorrow, Evie. Can't we, Mum?'

'Yes, we can,' Rachel says. 'Anytime. But right now, we need to get you home for a sleep, little miss.' But their attempts to pacify Evie don't work, and she wails even louder.

'How about I let you walk?' Rachel says, desperate. 'No buggy home.'

Evie stops crying and smiles. 'Evie walk!'

'Yes. Come on, then.'

Evie helps them clear up, throwing things into the picnic bag and smiling as she misses and everything lands on the grass.

'Thanks, Evie, that's really helpful,' Rachel says, laughing.

She sings to Evie as they walk home, clutching her tiny hand in one of hers, and pushing the buggy with the other.

Up ahead, Logan cycles, carefully stopping and waiting whenever they get to a road. Rachel tells herself it's not so bad letting Evie walk a bit. It will be good for strengthening her legs, and no doubt she'll be exhausted soon and demand to get back in the buggy.

It all happens so quickly. Up ahead, Logan wobbles on his bike, then tumbles off, smashing to the pavement with a thud. Rachel's heart races as she scoops Evie up, leaving the buggy and rushing towards him, taking in the blood gushing from a gouge in his leg. 'Jesus! Um, don't panic. Um, let's get this covered up.' She places Evie down beside her and pulls off her cardigan, tying it around Logan's leg to stem the flow.

There are tears in his eyes but he doesn't cry. He's being so brave. A wound that deep has got to sting. 'Come on, let's get you home and cleaned up. We might need to get you to hospital.' She's not sure whether this constitutes a trip to A & E, but the sooner they get home the better.

She helps Logan up and is about to grab Evie and put her into her buggy when she hears the screech of brakes. She looks up, and the scene before her plays out in slow motion: the grey car swerving and mounting the pavement, the thunderous smash as it slams into her daughter.

'Evie!' she screams.

More shouts. Screams. Car doors opening and slamming. Noises she will never forget.

Her daughter's tiny body lies on the pavement, metres from where she was standing. Silent and still.

ELEVEN

NOW

Holly

Driving to Rachel's house – she refuses to call it Damien's –
Oscar's words crash around her head. *She had to leave early
that day to pick up her daughter from nursery.* It doesn't make
sense when Evie died over a year ago. Why would Rachel
have said this so many months after Evie's death? It must
have been Luna she was referring to – there's no other
explanation.

But Rachel hasn't picked Luna up from nursery since Evie
died. She's asked many times, but Holly has always avoided
letting this happen.

When he answers the door, Damien's dressed in jeans and a
khaki green T-shirt. He stares at Luna. 'I didn't realise you were
bringing her,' he says, shutting the door behind them.

'Is that okay? I've been away from her all day and she needs
me more than ever right now.'

'Course it's okay,' he says. 'Why wouldn't it be? It's
just... last time you warned me and then you ended up not
bringing her. Never mind. It's just taken me by surprise.' He

ruffles Luna's hair. 'Well, you haven't been here for a while, have you? Come in.'

Holly steps inside and puts Luna down, hoping she'll wander off and explore as she always used to when she was here. But instead, Luna clings to her leg, gripping tightly.

'You haven't heard from Rachel, then?' Damien asks.

'Nope. Not a thing. I keep trying to call her but her phone's still off.' Holly takes Luna's hand as they follow Damien into the kitchen.

'I'm afraid there's nothing for Luna to play with,' Damien says. 'Rachel wanted to keep all Evie's toys, but I didn't think it was healthy. It's not, is it? I put them in the loft. It was a compromise. They're still in the house, just not where we can see them every day. That's not good for anyone.' He glances at Luna. 'Anyway, she's probably outgrown all those toys now. It's been a while.' Damien's eyes become blank as he stares into space, only shaking his head and snapping out of his trance when Holly speaks.

'It's fine. Luna hasn't been playing much since she was... taken. She just wants to be with me all the time.'

Damien nods, his eyes once again shifting to Luna. 'Have you tried asking her anything? She might be able to tell you something.'

'She's stopped talking. Unless it's to call us if she wants something. Otherwise it's just nods or head shakes.'

'Can't say I'm an expert, but the whole thing must have traumatised her. She's probably hidden it away in some deep part of her, and it might do more harm than good to try and retrieve it.'

Holly's no expert in psychology, but she doesn't agree with this. Burying things just keeps them inside, where they fester until they explode. She wants Luna to be able to talk about what happened. To heal.

And this is none of Damien's business. He's never before

shown any interest in Luna so Holly's not about to start sharing things with him now. 'We need to find Rachel,' she says. *She had to leave early that day to pick up her daughter from nursery.* 'Do you know if Rachel had to leave school early for an appointment or anything since she went back? Did she mention anything like that to you?'

Damien narrows his eyes. 'No. Why? There's nothing I can think of. She always makes doctor's appointments and things like that for after school or the holidays.'

'That's what I thought.' She should have known Damien wouldn't know anything. There are clearly things Rachel's been keeping from him. Holly glances at the calendar hanging on the wall. 'Does Rachel write everything in that?'

'Yeah. I keep telling her to use her phone calendar but she says she prefers to see it written by hand.'

'D'you mind if I have a look?'

Damien sighs, but reaches for the calendar and hands it to Holly. 'There's nothing useful in there.'

Holly pores over the last few months, carefully checking each neatly written entry. There's a dentist appointment for Logan, his after-school clubs, swimming lessons at the weekend and not much else. Nothing for Damien. And nothing that would mean Rachel had to leave school early.

There's every chance that Megan was lying – it wouldn't be the first time if the allegation she made against Oscar truly is false. She hands the calendar back to Damien. 'Thanks.'

'First Luna goes missing,' he says, hanging it back on the wall, 'and now Rachel's gone.'

'What are you saying?'

He sinks into a chair. 'I don't know. I don't know what to think. Why would she just leave without a word?'

This has been playing on Holly's mind all day. 'Rachel wouldn't. I'm worried something's happened to her. She'd never leave Logan. Or the kids at school. That can only mean one thing.'

Damien leans forward, burying his head in his hands. 'But you think she'd leave me?'

'I didn't say that.'

'Has Rachel said something to you?' Damien raises his voice. 'Do you know where she is?'

'No! I—'

'Hi, Holly.' Logan wanders into the kitchen, forcing Holly to hold back her words. 'Are you talking about Mum?'

'Yes, we were,' Damien says. 'We're just trying to work out where she could be.'

Logan pulls off his glasses and wipes them with his sleeve. 'She wasn't in school. I looked for her. And people were saying there were supply teachers taking her lessons.' He glances at Luna, but doesn't say anything to her, like he always used to. It must be difficult for him to see her; a constant reminder of Evie.

'You must be worried,' Holly says. 'But she'll come home.'

'I'm glad Luna's okay,' Logan says, gesturing to where Luna sits on the floor with her cuddly bunny. With his dark hair and eyes, Logan looks so much like Rachel.

Damien stands and walks over to his son, placing his hand on his shoulder. 'Did your mum say anything at all to you? Anything to suggest she might not be happy or might want to leave?'

'Course not. You've already asked me that. I'd tell you if she did. Mum never says anything about what's going on with her, does she? But I know she hasn't been happy since Evie died. How could she be?'

'That's true,' Damien concedes. 'But did anything happen in the last few weeks to show she might be deteriorating?'

Logan shrugs. 'I don't know.' He opens the fridge and pulls out a bottle of Prime, pouring it into a glass that's been left on the worktop. 'I posted on Facebook. In the community group.'

Damien frowns. 'What? What exactly did you post?'

'I just said Mum is missing and posted a photo of her. So people can contact us if they see her. Online is the quickest way to find people, Dad.'

'You should have run it by me first,' Damien says. 'I don't know if I approve of this. I don't want our business plastered all over social media. We're a private family. Please take it down, Logan. I need to think about this first.'

'Dad, there's no time,' Logan protests. 'We need to find her.'

Damien shakes his head. 'The police are looking.'

'Are they? It's not like when Luna was taken.' Logan glances at Holly. 'Sorry, but Mum's not vulnerable. They won't be looking for her.'

'I agree with Logan,' Holly says. 'The more people who know Rachel's missing, the quicker we'll find her. It can only be a good thing.'

Damien shakes his head, turning to Logan. 'They are taking this seriously, I promise you. They know your mum's history.'

Logan stares at him. 'What history?'

'I just meant with Evie and how your mum's grieving.' He flashes a look at Holly. 'Look, I understand why you did it. But from now on can you just run things like that by me first? We don't want to do anything that interferes with the police search, do we?'

'Okay.' Logan finishes his drink and takes his glass to the dishwasher.

Damien watches him. 'I just need to talk through some things with Holly. Do you mind giving us a few minutes?'

Logan looks as if he wants to object, but he nods and leaves the kitchen.

'He shouldn't have done that,' Damien says, once Logan's upstairs and they hear his bedroom door shut. He pulls out his phone. 'But there's something I didn't want to say in front of him.' He pulls a small bottle from his pocket. 'I checked

Rachel's pills this morning, and she hasn't been taking them. This is full. I found it hidden at the back of her wardrobe.'

'What pills?' This is news to Holly – her friend has never mentioned being on any medication.

'Anti-depressants. And if I think about it, I don't think she's been taking them for months. Maybe longer. She hasn't... seemed right. She must have told you she was on them?'

Holly thinks quickly. 'Yeah... of course. Since Evie died. Well, it's been tough—'

'No, long before that. When Evie was less than a year old, in fact. She's been on them ever since. Or was supposed to be, at least. It scares me to think what she might do without them.'

Holly's stomach drops, but she's not about to admit to Damien she had no idea. 'Oh, yeah. Of course.'

'You didn't know, did you?' He studies her face. 'I can tell. You had no idea.' He sighs. 'She's not who you think she is, Holly. Rachel's good at putting on an act. She's a teacher – they have to perform to their classes every day, don't they? Hide what's really going on with them. My wife is good at that. And clearly you're not the only one who didn't know her.' He shakes the pill bottle.

'Maybe she didn't need them any more.'

He shakes his head and starts scrolling through his phone. 'Here's Logan's post.' His eyes dart back and forth as he reads, and when it becomes apparent he's not going to show Holly his screen, she reaches for her own phone and hunts for the post.

Before she finds it, Damien grabs her arm. 'Someone's just posted a minute ago, saying she saw Rachel at the nature reserve yesterday evening.'

Holly finds the post and reads it for herself. The woman's called Gabriella Ortiz. Holly doesn't recognise her name.

She taught my kids a few years ago, so I recognised her and stopped to chat. She didn't look right.

'Do you know this woman?' she asks Damien.

'Never heard of her,' he says. 'But what was Rachel doing there after school?'

Holly keeps reading. 'I don't know, but apparently this Gabriella has already told the police that she saw Rachel.'

Damien paces the floor. 'I need to call them. They need to be at the nature reserve looking for her. Now.'

'It was yesterday, though. She won't still be there.'

'But it's the only thing we have,' Damien says, stalking out of the kitchen.

Holly can only assume he's gone to make his call in private. She calls goodbye to Logan and then leaves them to it.

She needs to find Gabriella Ortiz.

TWELVE
BEFORE

Rachel

She stopped living the moment Evie died. There was a flicker of hope, tangible yet brief, when the paramedics informed them her heart was still beating, but less than two hours later it was extinguished when Evie's little body gave up trying as she lay in her hospital bed.

Now, six months later, Rachel's just existing, and she supposes this is how life will be from now on. If she tries really hard, with all the energy she can muster, she can force a smile that will never reach her heart. And as for laughing – muscle memory has failed her and she no longer remembers how to do this.

Damien has changed too. He's backed off, just a tiny bit, and is less likely to snap at her or complain about everything she does. But she knows that what lies deep inside him is just biding its time. Rachel has to hand it to him, though – he's really been there for Logan when she is barely able to drag herself out of bed.

She turns to face the alarm clock. Nine fifteen. Damien left for work hours ago, and Logan will be at school – where *she* should be. Her son amazes her. He hasn't taken a single day off and is powering through his grief, throwing himself into his schoolwork. Logan doesn't know this, but she's spoken to his teachers, sent them confidential emails asking how he's doing. The replies from each one of them are identical. *He's excelling.*

Robotically, Rachel turns on the shower and steps inside, wincing as the hot water burns her skin. She clasps the knob to turn it down, but changes her mind. The physical pain is preferable to the emotional pain.

By the time she's finished, her skin is red, but she ignores it and gets dressed. Jeans and a thin jumper. No need to dress smartly when she won't be setting foot outside.

Downstairs, she boils the kettle, grateful for the rumble it makes in this ghostly silence.

When the doorbell rings, she's tempted to leave it. But there's a chance it's Damien, and he's forgotten his key. If she doesn't answer, then what? Or maybe it's a test. He's already disgusted with her wallowing in grief. As if it has an expiration date and by now she should be over Evie's senseless death.

It was like dominoes: Rachel agreeing to let Evie walk, just to get her out of the park without too much fuss. Leaving when they did. Logan falling off his bike. The car turning the corner at that precise moment, swerving to avoid that damn cat who rushed out in front of it. And her poor Evie, excitedly chasing after it, while she was busy sorting out Logan.

Rachel stands behind the door as she opens it, as if it's a shield that can defend her from whoever is out there. Perhaps, ironically, she really is losing her mind this time. It's what Damien has always hinted at. Not even hinted. Told her blatantly, leaving no shadow of doubt, no room for misinterpretation. Now, she wonders if he's been right all along. Even before Evie's death.

Holly is standing on her doorstep, her arms folded against

the cold. She's wearing a bobble hat and scarf, her thick winter duvet coat.

'Rachel. I know you don't want to see anyone. But I had to come. What kind of friend would I be if I didn't? I'm on my own.'

Rachel knows immediately why she's said this. Holly thinks it would hurt her too much to see Luna. Evie's best friend. The same age. One of them living, the other dead.

'Can I come in?'

No. Go away. I don't want to see anyone. 'Yes,' Rachel says. 'I was just...' She wasn't doing anything. Not working. Not life admin. Nothing. Barely even thinking. 'I've just boiled the kettle.'

'Let me make it. Tea?'

Rachel nods. 'I can do it, Holly. I'm not sick.' She looks at her friend as she takes off her coat and hangs it on Rachel's coat hook – freshly washed hair, clean smart clothes, a life as smooth as silk – and suddenly resentment swells inside her. She's never been the jealous type, but for a fleeting moment she wishes this had happened to Holly instead of her. 'I'm not good company,' Rachel says, re-boiling the kettle.

'You don't have to be. We can just sit in silence if that's what you need. Anything. I just had to come and see you.'

Rachel takes a deep breath and closes her eyes. Perhaps once she reopens them, Holly will be gone. Poof. Evaporated. Perhaps she's not even here at all.

'Let me do that,' Holly says, prising the kettle from Rachel's hand.

Rachel doesn't have the energy to argue, so she lets her friend take over, look after her as if she's a child. Holly's been here enough times to know where everything is in this kitchen, so all Rachel has to do is sit at the table and wait.

'How's Logan doing?' Holly asks, placing their mugs on the table. No coasters, but Rachel's too numb to care.

She shrugs. 'Not good. He blames himself.' Rachel constantly tries to reassure him that it's not his fault he fell off his bike. Still, they will both carry their guilt around like luggage they can't put down. 'How is little Luna?' Rachel asks.

Holly's eyes widen. 'Um, she's okay. Getting bigger every day.'

'She must have grown loads since I last saw her,' Rachel says. 'Nearly two. Time flies, doesn't it?' The words shrivel and die in her dry throat. Evie will never see her second birthday. She takes a sip of tea. Far too strong and not enough milk, but she wouldn't tell that to Holly. Before, perhaps, she'd have made a joke about it, but not now. 'How's work?'

'Oh, you know. Not bad. Super busy. Can't complain, though – I love what I do.'

The perfect family. Perfect life. Rachel stifles her anger. 'I'm sure it helps that you work for Ross.' She stares into her cup, avoiding her friend's inquisitive gaze.

'Yeah, he's a good friend as well as my boss. I know how lucky I am.'

'Some people say we make our own luck,' Rachel says. 'Do you believe that?'

'No. I think we make our own choices, but luck just happens alongside it all.'

'I'm going back to work,' Rachel says, taking herself by surprise as much as Holly. She hasn't set foot in a classroom for six months, and doesn't even know if she can do it again, but she's got to start rebuilding her life.

'That's... great. Are you sure it's not too soon?' Holly puts down her mug and studies Rachel closely.

'I'm not sure of anything. I just know it's time. The kids need me, not a different supply teacher every week. That doesn't help them. They need consistency.'

Holly shifts in her seat. 'I know. But you need to take care of yourself. You're always worrying about everyone else. It's about time you cared for yourself first.'

Wouldn't that make her selfish? Rachel wonders if people care too much about themselves these days. What she needs to do is *not* think about herself – it's the only way she'll make it through a life without her beautiful Evie.

'Damien says I need to get back to work. He reckons it will be good for me. That it's just what I need.'

'Do this because *you* want to.'

Rachel stares at her friend. Holly is kind. A good friend. She could tell her everything now, and be free of the dread that weighs her down every day. Then she pictures Damien's face, how it can change from affable to irate within seconds, with no warning. 'I *am* doing it for me.'

'How is Damien doing, anyway?'

Better than me. He seems to have put Evie out of his mind far too easily. 'He's thrown himself into work. That's his way of dealing with things.'

Holly opens her mouth but doesn't say anything, picking up her mug and sipping her tea instead. 'We all deal with things differently,' she says. 'There's no right or wrong way to handle grief.'

Rachel considers telling Holly how Damien's dealing with it okay because he never bonded with Evie. Their daughter never wanted him to hold her so he gave up on her, instead of putting his own feelings aside and realising she was just a baby. With Logan, though, it's another story. 'You could have brought Luna,' Rachel says, her voice hoarse. Perhaps she's coming down with something and she should go straight back to her bed when Holly leaves.

Holly looks flustered. 'Oh, I... I didn't think it... I wasn't sure it was a good idea. I would have definitely brought her if I'd thought...'

'I love Luna – you know that. She's like a daughter to me.'

'I know. Sorry. Shall I bring her next time?'

Rachel smiles, without even realising what she's doing. 'I'd love to see how she's grown.'

'She's hard work,' Holly says, a faint laugh escaping from her lips.

Rachel nods. Evie would have been too, she's sure. But it would have served her well as she grew older. Tears form in Rachel's eyes. 'I think it would be good for me to see Luna,' she says.

'If that will help you, then for sure I'll bring her,' Holly says. She takes Rachel's hand and gives it a gentle squeeze. 'I'm sorry. Shall we talk about something else?'

Silence falls around them and Rachel wonders if their friendship has permanently changed, just like everything else. Cracked wide open beyond repair. She doesn't want that – she needs something in her life to stay the same. Someone.

Rachel longs to say something to break the silence, to prove that their friendship is still solid. She should tell Holly about the messages she's been getting for a couple of months now. At least once a week. And she's started to wish it was more.

But no, she can't tell anyone about that.

THIRTEEN

NOW

Holly

Holly's not surprised to find Ross still at the office this late, so engrossed in whatever he's doing on his computer that she has to clear her throat to get his attention.

He jolts up. 'God, you scared me! What are you doing back? Is everything okay?'

She steps inside, hovering by the door. 'Can we talk?'

'Course.' He gestures to the chair in front of his desk and waits for her to sit. 'Talk to me. As long as it's not to hand in your resignation.' He smiles.

Holly takes a deep breath. 'After what happened with Luna, this is all a bit... difficult to comprehend. But my close friend has gone missing. You've met her before. Rachel. Do you remember her?'

Ross frowns. 'The teacher? The one who lost her—'

'Yeah, that's her. She didn't turn up for work today. Her husband and son haven't seen or heard from her since she left school yesterday afternoon. Her phone is going straight to voicemail.'

Ross places his elbows on his desk, resting his head on his hands. 'That's not good.'

'Rachel wouldn't just leave. There's no way. Oh, I know people always say that, and I get that sometimes people do want to disappear. But not Rachel. I know her. She wouldn't do that.'

'She has been through a lot, Holl. I mean, can you imagine losing a child? If anything ever happened to Harry, I don't know what I'd do. I know he's only five, but it feels like he's always been in my life. I just can't imagine...' He pauses. 'I take it the police know?'

'Yep. And her son posted on Facebook and got a reply from some woman. She said she'd seen Rachel at the nature reserve and she was acting strangely. I think the police are sending a team out there to search the area.'

'What can I do to help?'

Holly is touched by Ross's kindness, but that's not why she's come here tonight. 'I need you to let me cover the story.'

Ross's eyes widen, and he frowns. 'I'm not sure that's a good idea. You're too close to it. It could get—'

'I know all that, but I need to do this. For Rachel. I'm the only person who can write this story. It has to be me, Ross.'

He studies Holly for a moment, his face gradually softening. 'Paul won't like it. He's already mad that he didn't get to work on the Oscar Hobbs story after I'd said he could.'

'I don't care what Paul thinks.' She remembers Paul's words and her cheeks burn. *You're only here because he's interested in you.* 'Let me do this, Ross. Have I ever let you down before?'

'No.' He sighs. 'Okay. But if it gets too much at any point, you'll tell me, won't you?'

She nods. 'It won't get too much, because by tomorrow I'll be writing about how she's been found and reunited with her family.' Holly hopes saying these words will inject her with belief.

'So, what's your plan?' Ross asks, picking up a pen and scribbling something on a green Post-it note.

'I've already messaged the woman who said she'd seen Rachel to see if she'll meet me. Her name's Gabriella Ortiz.' Holly had wasted no time sending her a private message on Facebook the second she got in her car outside Rachel's house. 'I know she's already spoken to the police, but hopefully she won't mind going over it all again.' Holly pulls out her phone. Gabriella still hasn't read her message, and she sent it twenty-two minutes ago. But there is a message from Elijah – a selfie of him with Luna, their daughter sleeping next to him while he works on his laptop.

Holly stands up, a heavy ache in her stomach. She needs to get home to Luna as soon as she can, even if she's asleep.

'I hope Rachel comes home soon,' Ross says. He glances at his watch. 'Jeez, I'd better get going. I'm supposed to be meeting someone.' He glances at her. 'It's kind of a date, and it won't look good if I'm late.'

Normally Holly would ask Ross all about it, but tonight she can't find the energy. 'No, you don't want to be late,' she says instead.

'Especially when I've got my ex-wife's words ringing in my ears. What was it she said? I have no work-life balance. What even is that? Shouldn't our careers be our passion? Why is that so bad?'

'It's not,' Holly says. 'But it's also important to give your time to someone you care about, isn't it? But if you do ever meet anyone who's got that balance right, then point me in their direction.'

He smiles. 'I know. You're right. As usual.' He laughs. 'What would I do without your advice?'

'I need to go,' Holly says. Usually she has all the time in the world for Ross, and she senses he needs to talk to someone, but right now she's got some digging to do. 'Let's talk soon,' she says.

Screw what Paul thinks. She and Ross are good friends –
nothing more. They have a close bond, and she will never apologise to anyone for that.

Her phone pings when she's driving home, and she turns
into the next road and parks up to read it. Her heart races when
she sees it's a reply from Gabriella Ortiz.

> *Yes, I can meet you. But I've already told the police everything
> so not sure what help I'll be. I'm off work tomorrow morning if
> that's any good?*

But tomorrow is too long for Holly to wait – she needs to see
this woman now. She replies to Gabriella's message, asking if
they can meet now, telling her that it's important they get this
story out quickly.

The message-read tick appears, and seconds tick by, turning
to minutes, before Gabriella finally replies.

> *I'm about to finish a shift at the Surrey Park Clinic. Meet me
> there in half an hour.*

With no time to go home, Holly calls Elijah. 'Is Luna okay?'

'Hello to you too.'

'Sorry. Where is she?'

'Right here next to me. Didn't you get my photo?'

'Yeah, I did. But that was a while ago.'

'Holly, it was a few minutes! Where are you, anyway?'

'I popped into work after seeing Damien. Rachel was seen
by the nature reserve. Acting strangely, according to the woman
who saw her. I'm covering the story. Had to check it was okay
with Ross.'

Elijah is silent for a moment. 'Is that a good idea?'

'I'm her closest friend. I owe this to her.'

'You don't owe her anything. It's not your fault—'

'If Luna wakes up, tell her Mummy will be home very soon.'

'Aren't you coming back now?'

Holly explains that she's meeting the witness who saw Rachel, and waits for him to try and talk her out of it.

'I get it,' Elijah says, to her surprise. 'If it was one of my friends, then I'd be out there all night if I had to be.'

'Thanks.'

'But that doesn't mean I like this. It's all too much of a coincidence. First Luna and now Rachel. I don't know what's going on, but it feels as if this won't end well.'

There are only two other cars in the large car park outside the women's health clinic when Holly pulls up. She'd quickly checked Gabriella's Facebook page, trying to get a sense of who she is, but it had no details about her job. All Holly's learnt is that it looks like she has two older children, possibly college age.

Holly presses the buzzer at the main door and within seconds she's let in. It feels odd being here so late, as if she's doing something criminal. There's a dental clinic in here too, and she finds the door for the Surrey Park Clinic to the right of the reception area. Inside, a woman is sitting behind a large reception desk. Gabriella Ortiz – Holly recognises her from her Facebook profile, although in person she looks older, and her hair is shorter.

'Hi. You must be Holly. Either that or I've let some random stranger into the building.' Her voice is friendly and soft, and Holly detects a faint Spanish accent.

'Is it okay for me to be in here?' Holly asks as she approaches the desk.

'Yes. No one's here. I'm locking up tonight. Just need to add something to the patient database.'

'Are you a doctor?' Holly asks.

Gabriella smiles. 'No, clinic administrator. Part of the furniture. Been here since my kids were little.' She turns to her computer screen and taps on her keyboard.

Minutes tick by slowly while Holly waits, resisting the urge to message Elijah again. Finally, Gabriella shuts down her computer. 'All done. Sorry. I'm ready now. So, you're from *Surrey Live*? Um, I don't actually read it. Sorry. There's just no time, is there? I work long hours here and then I have two dogs who need walks and attention. So even with the kids being older, I'm still very busy. Wouldn't have it any other way, though.'

Holly smiles. As desperate as she is to get straight to the point, she needs to indulge Gabriella to get her onside. That way, she's more likely to spill every detail. 'I have a toddler at home so I get it.' Holly pauses. 'As I said in my message, I'm covering the Rachel James story so it would be really helpful if you could talk me through what happened when you saw her.'

'Well, I put it all in my post, but I was walking the dogs at the nature reserve. I always go there. They love it. I'm not usually there at that time, though, so it was just chance that I was. I had a half-day here as I'd accrued some extra leave. Anyway, I always walk along the river path. You know it?'

Holly nods. 'But I don't get to go there much.'

'Beautiful place. In spring and summer when it's not too muddy. I was walking Milly and Rolo when I saw her. She was just standing by the river, staring at nothing. I didn't recognise her at first. I thought maybe she was a dog walker who'd let her dog off the lead and she was waiting for it to come back. But as I got closer, I recognised her.'

'So you know her, then?' Holly already knows this from the Facebook comments, but she's starting from scratch here, just to make sure she doesn't miss anything.

'Yes. She taught both my son and daughter when they were at school. I think they liked her. They never complained about her so they must have. I feel sorry for teachers—'

'Then what happened?'

Gabriella frowns. 'I went up to her and said hello. Told her she used to teach Sam and Penny. She stared at me for ages before she answered. It was like I was speaking a different language. I know I have an accent, but my English is good. I've been here years.'

'Your English is perfect,' Holly agrees. 'And what did she say?'

'After she snapped out of her weird trance thing, she told me that of course she remembered them. Then she looked past me, kind of just staring blankly. I thought maybe she was ill or something so I asked if she was okay and she just said she was fine. It was like she wasn't really listening to me. I can take a hint. She didn't want to be bothered. She kept looking around. She seemed... maybe nervous. Almost... like spaced out. Very strange. I also thought it was weird that she looked quite dressed up. She had on jeans and a pretty white top with a huge pussycat bow on it. I remember thinking her clothes were too nice for a walk through the nature reserve. I told the police all this.'

'I know,' Holly says. 'Sorry you're having to repeat yourself.'

'If it helps to find her, then I don't mind.'

'What happened after that?'

'I take the hint, of course, and say goodbye. She just lifted her hand and kind of waved. I thought it was a bit rude. But we all have bad days, don't we? When we can't be bothered to talk to anyone. And you never know what's going on with someone. It's like an iceberg, isn't it? You can only see the tip, but underneath, out of view, there's so much more to it.'

Holly nods. 'That's very true. So after you said goodbye, was that it?'

'No. When I walked off with the dogs, I turned around and she was still standing there, staring at the ground. For ages. I kept turning back expecting her to be gone each time, but she was still there.' She frowns. 'I should have gone back, shouldn't I? Made sure she was okay.'

Sharp spasms shoot through Holly's body. *What was Rachel doing?* This doesn't sound like her at all. But it does sound like a woman in need of help, and Holly was nowhere around. *But Luna needed me.* 'It wasn't your fault,' she tells Gabriella. 'It sounds like she didn't want to talk to anyone.' Standing up, she pulls her phone from her pocket. 'Thanks for talking to me. I really appreciate your time.'

Gabriella stands too. 'I hope it helps. That poor woman. She's already lost a child, and now this.'

Holly can't get to her car fast enough. She wasn't expecting to hear that Rachel had been hanging around the nature reserve like that, anxious and distracted. The two of them had been there for a walk last summer, but other than that, she can't remember Rachel ever mentioning the place.

Her phone rings, piercing the silence. Damien. She takes a deep breath and answers.

There's a long pause before he speaks. 'The police have found Rachel's bag with her phone in it. Jesus, Holly! What's happened to my wife?'

FOURTEEN

BEFORE

Rachel

Coming back to school should have made her feel more like herself. When she's in the classroom she's not Rachel the mother, or wife. She's Rachel the teacher. As if nothing else exists outside these walls. But now, standing here waiting for her Year 10 class to filter in, she feels as though she's a stranger, and she's not sure she'll find the words to begin her lesson. Her throat feels like sandpaper, and there's a tight knot in her stomach.

Tommy Harris comes in first, early as usual. He smiles at her briefly then stares at the floor while he makes his way to his desk. Normally he's full of chatter, telling her all about whatever he's been up to with his family at the weekend. But that was before grief tainted her, and made her unapproachable.

They're almost fifteen minutes into the lesson when Megan Hart strolls in. Without a word, she heads to her desk at the back and dumps her bag on the table. The thud it makes echoes through the room. As she wrestles her books from it, everyone turns to Rachel, eagerly awaiting her response.

'You're late, Megan. Where have you been?'

Megan eyes her defiantly. 'I didn't know. Sorry.'

Rachel could do without this. Most of the kids have been making a huge effort to be on their best behaviour, but not Megan. 'That's fine. Luckily it's lunchtime after this so you can make up the fifteen minutes then.'

'What? No!' Megan scowls. 'That's so not fair.' She throws her bag on the floor, mumbling something Rachel can't make out, and is not sure she wants to.

Ignoring Megan's outburst, Rachel instructs the class to carry on with their writing. In her pocket, her phone silently vibrates. She sits at her desk and pulls it out, keeping it hidden. It's the same number again. No name attached to it because he's not part of her life. Rachel does a quick calculation: eight days since she's heard from him. And today, for the first time, she admits to herself that the silence has tormented her. She needs to reply otherwise the messages will stop, and now, after all this time, she's sure she doesn't want them to, despite the times she's prayed for her phone to stop buzzing.

She slips her phone into her bag and pushes it under the desk. Now is not the time.

'How did today go?' Holly asks when Rachel answers her call. It's strange to hear her voice here in the staffroom – Holly is a separate part of her life, a part that has never intermingled with her work life until now.

Rachel stops typing the worksheet she's been creating for her Year 10 class tomorrow. It's challenging, but they need to be stretched. 'It was... um... I got through it.'

'Course you did. I really admire your strength. Not just now. I have done since we met.'

Although Rachel's grateful for these kind words, Holly can't possibly mean them. What's strong about taking almost seven months to go back to work? And is it showing strength to be convinced she won't get through the next hour, let alone day? Week? Term?

'Actually, I'm still at work,' Rachel says, hoping her friend will take the hint. Words don't seem to come easily to Rachel now, with anyone.

'Yeah, sorry. I just wanted to quickly ask you something, and please don't feel you have to say yes.' There's a brief pause. 'Um, our babysitter's just called to say she's sick, and Elijah and I are both supposed to be going out tonight. Elijah says he's happy to cancel his plans, and to be honest, I could too, but I was just wondering—'

'Of course I'll look after Luna,' Rachel says, feeling a smile form on her face. 'Neither of you have to miss anything.'

'Are you sure? That would be great. Thank you so much. This really helps us out.'

But the truth is, it's Rachel who should be thanking Holly; for the first time in months, Rachel feels the heavy fog lifting. Only slightly, but there is hope. *With Luna, there is hope.*

A shot of anxiety hits Rachel as she stands at Holly's door. Imagining something never feels the same as actually doing it. She's got the whole evening to look after Luna, to once again be the mum to a little girl that she was meant to be. So why does it terrify and fill her with joy in equal measure?

Her thoughts drift to Logan. When she'd left the house, he'd been playing *Fortnite* with Damien. Father–son bonding time. He will be fine this evening without her, because one thing she can trust is that Damien will never show his true colours to his son. It's his mission to remain unseen to everyone but Rachel. That's how he convinces the world that everything is in her head.

She takes a deep breath and presses her fingertip to the bell, getting ready to plaster a smile on her face to hide how nervous she is.

Holly looks beautiful when she answers the door. Her hair hangs in loose waves around her shoulders and she's wearing a black wide-leg jumpsuit with a diamanté belt. 'Thanks so much for this,' she says, her voice breathless. 'I've really been looking forward to it.'

'Where is it you're going? You look lovely.'

Holly waves off her compliment. 'Our work Christmas meal. At The Ivy.'

'Oh. I didn't realise that's what it was.' A shadowy thought flickers through her mind like static. *Ross will be there. Is that why Holly's made so much effort?* But Rachel knows Holly loves Elijah, and would never hurt him, or anyone else, so she dismisses this notion.

'I'm so sorry but Luna's already asleep. I tried to keep her up until you got here, but she was ready to crash. She had nursery today and started yawning straight after dinner. I'm hoping she'll still sleep through.'

Briefly, Rachel wonders if this is true. Or if Holly wanted to keep Luna out of the way. But no one can force a toddler to sleep. 'It doesn't matter if she wakes up,' Rachel replies, already harbouring ideas about reading her stories.

Holly nods, ushering her in. 'Are you sure this is okay? It must be diff—'

'It's fine. I'm fine,' Rachel assures her. She stands straighter, as if to prove this, and holds her head up. She read somewhere that it's important to always stand tall and keep your head up, so as not to diminish yourself. She can't remember the exact details but it was something like that.

Inside, the house is still and quiet. 'Has Elijah already gone?'

'Yeah, he just left. He's got dinner with a client. He'll probably be back before me.'

'It's fine. I don't have to rush back. Both of you can take your time. Enjoy yourselves. It's hard to do that with a toddler.' A sharp pain shoots through her abdomen.

Holly smiles. 'I'll just finish getting ready, then. Forgot my perfume. Make yourself at home.'

Rachel holds up the book she's brought with her. *Doctor Faustus*. She's teaching it to her Year 12s next week and needs to re-read it.

'Some light reading, then.' Holly laughs.

In the living room, Rachel sinks into the cream sofa, curling her legs underneath her. She stares around the room. There's too much in here for her liking. Ornaments and photos taking up every space. It's homely, no doubt, but it's too cluttered. Another fleeting thought assaults her. What would it be like to be Holly? To have this life instead of her own. With a living, breathing daughter who she'll get to see grow up. A husband who's kind, who loves her.

She blinks away tears. She loves Holly like a sister. Why is she having these thoughts?

'How do I look?'

Holly's voice shatters through Rachel's subconscious. She turns to look at her friend, who has now completed her make-up and looks even more stunning.

'Too good for a work Christmas do,' Rachel says, forcing herself to laugh.

'Well, when I get my next invite to the Oscars, I'll be sure to replicate this look.'

'And I can be your guest and wear these,' Rachel says, tugging at her Adidas joggers. She laughs, and it feels strange. Wrong somehow.

Holly's effort is all for Ross, it has to be. 'Have fun,' Rachel says, getting up from the sofa to see Holly out.

As soon as she's alone, Rachel heads upstairs to check on Luna. The stairs creak with every step she makes, but she keeps going. If Luna wakes, then she'll cuddle her until she falls asleep again. Sing to her. It's been a long time since she's been able to do that. Her heart races. *Evie. It will be like holding Evie again.* And if she were to close her eyes, it would be her daughter in her arms.

But when she reaches Luna's room, the little girl is sleeping soundly, soft snores emitting from her like purrs as she clutches her grey lamb.

Rachel leans down and strokes her cheek. 'Sleep tight, little one,' she whispers.

Downstairs, she reads for a while, annotating the book with key points she wants the kids to know. When her eyes begin to ache, she turns on Netflix, scrolling until something catches her attention: *The Big Bang Theory.* She's never seen it before, but it makes her chuckle, as if she's carefree, the grief that she wears each day like a winter coat almost forgotten. Perhaps it's being here alone, having sole care of Luna, if only for a few hours. This is what she needs. And it feels good to be helping Holly too.

She's upstairs checking on Luna again when she hears a key in the door. Ten o'clock. Far too early. Rachel was hoping Luna would wake up and call out for her, but she hasn't even stirred. She's sure Holly would have told her she'd be babysitting tonight.

'Hi. All okay?' Elijah calls quietly.

Rachel makes her way downstairs. 'Yeah, fine. Luna hasn't woken at all. She must have been tired.'

'I think nursery was a bit full-on today,' Elijah says, peeling off his coat.

In the living room, Rachel picks up her book and pencil, putting them in her bag. 'I'll get going, then.'

'You don't have to rush back. It's not that late, is it? And it's Friday. Why don't you stay and have a drink?'

For a moment she doesn't believe she's heard him right.

Elijah's always been pleasant to her, but they're hardly drinking buddies. And she hasn't set eyes on him since Evie died. He signed his own name in the card, of course, but that's about the only thing she's heard from him. She's about to decline his offer when she thinks of Luna upstairs. There's still a chance she might wake, and if she does, Rachel will ask – no, tell – Elijah that she will go to her. 'Okay,' she says. 'I'll stay for a quick one.'

'Good,' he says. 'I don't drink that much, but you know when you do, you just don't want the buzz to wear off so you keep topping up? Ha, I'm probably at that stage right now.'

So he's drunk. That's why he's being friendly. Not a good idea to leave him alone with Luna, then. Perhaps she should stay until Holly gets home.

Rachel follows Elijah into the kitchen, noticing how he stumbles as he walks. 'Are you sure you want another one? Would coffee be better?'

'I'm not drunk,' he insists. 'I've only had...' He begins counting on his fingers. 'Three. Four.' He laughs.

And the rest. Still, he's a grown man. Who is she to suggest he doesn't need any more?

Elijah pours them each a glass of red wine and hands one to Rachel. She's not sure she wants it; she hasn't touched a drop of alcohol since before the accident. Not that she was a big drinker, but she'd at least have a glass occasionally to celebrate whatever occasion Damien thought demanded it.

'Please sit,' Elijah says, gesturing to the table.

Rachel would rather not – she's been sitting all evening and needs to stretch her muscles, but she does as he suggests, noticing that when he checks his watch, his smile vanishes.

'Something wrong?' she ventures.

'Nope.' He picks up his glass and takes a long gulp before placing it down again. 'I just thought Holly might be home by now. She's not one for late nights. Unless she's working.'

'You shouldn't worry about her, you know,' Rachel says. 'She can take care of herself.'

'Don't I know it. It's not that. It's... never mind.'

'It's because she's out with Ross, isn't it?' Rachel says, emboldened by the wine she's sipping. And the fact that Elijah probably won't remember this conversation in the morning. 'That's what's bothering you.'

Elijah stares at her for a moment before looking away, absently picking up his wine again, smoothing the glass with his free hand. 'What makes you say that?'

Rachel shrugs. 'Call it a gut feeling. Instinct. I don't know.'

'Has Holly said something to you?'

Lines crease Elijah's forehead as she studies him, trying to see through his words. His actions. 'No, she hasn't. There's nothing to say. Nothing is going on with her and Ross.'

Elijah finishes what's left in his glass. 'I didn't say there was.'

'But you're thinking it. You're worried. You must know that Holly would never do that to you, even if—'

'Even if what? She likes him?' Elijah slurs his words, almost spits them at Rachel. She'd expect this from Damien, but not this man. *Alcohol does strange things to people. Or brings out their true selves.*

Rachel's about to respond but he doesn't give her a chance. 'I've suspected it for years – that there's something between them – even if it's not physical.' He gets up to pour another glass, placing it down with such force that wine sloshes over the rim. 'Somehow, that makes it worse. I could deal with it if she just cheated on me—'

'Holly would never—'

'I'm just saying, *this* is even worse. That they could both be hiding feelings for each other because of me and... maybe this is why Ross got divorced?'

'Elijah, it's the alcohol making you feel like this. You've had the merry part where everything's wonderful, and now comes the melancholy. It's a depressive.' Even as she says this, she takes another sip of her own wine. It's numbing her, smoothing her jagged edges. This is why alcohol exists: to erase our pain. She laughs, despite everything.

'Are you okay?' Elijah asks, staring at her.

His gaze on her makes her feel vulnerable, as if he can see through to her core. Nobody should witness what's inside her. Rachel wishes she didn't know herself. 'No,' she says quietly. 'But I'm okay with not being okay – does that make sense?' She drinks more wine, as if she's racing against time to empty her glass.

'I'm sorry,' Elijah says. 'I can't even imagine...'

'You'll never have to. Luna will always be fine.'

He continues to stare at Rachel, lifting his glass. 'You're remarkable. How you carry on each day. And I'm a jerk for moaning that someone has a crush on my wife. That's nothing compared to—'

'We all have our stuff to deal with,' Rachel says. Then she silently berates herself for reducing her daughter's death to *stuff*. 'I mean... you know.'

'I do,' Elijah says. 'No need to explain it to me.' He sighs. 'Listen to us! I don't think we've ever had a conversation this long, and we're talking about the most personal stuff.' His lips form a thin smile. 'Life can take us by surprise, can't it?'

When he offers her another drink she says no, but all it takes is him to start pouring and she's laughing instead, reaching for the glass he's filled. 'I see why you and Holly are such good friends,' he says. 'You complement each other. You're so different but somehow in sync.' He shakes his head. 'Is that how she is with Ross?' He hisses the name, as if it tastes vulgar on his tongue. *Ross*.

'You've got to stop this,' Rachel warns. 'You have an amazing wife. A beautiful daughter. A great life. Don't let this... this jealousy tear everything apart. Because it will, you know. It's toxic.'

'I know, you're right,' he slurs. 'I'm a lucky, lucky man.'

The night begins to blur, Rachel's head becoming fuzzy. She doesn't feel like herself – this kind of thing definitely isn't her – drowning her pain in drink, alone with her best friend's husband. A good man. Not Damien.

Elijah pours more drinks. They laugh. At what, she's not sure. Everything seems funny, she is a million miles from her grief. She can't even see it in the distance, even though she's aware it must still be there somewhere. Hiding. Waiting for her. 'I've parked it!' she declares. 'Maybe I'll be able to leave it where it is. Wouldn't that be something?'

'Eh?' Elijah says. 'What are you talking about?'

'My grief. That's what I'm talking about.' She giggles and it hurts. The emotional pain, because even in the clutches of alcohol, she knows Evie is still there.

'Come here,' Elijah says. 'I think you need a hug. And in the absence of Holly, you'll have to make do with me.'

Rachel laughs again. It's ludicrous that she's here now, drinking with Elijah. All she wanted was to be with Luna, to feel like a mother again. To *be* a mother again, because somehow, even though she still has Logan, sometimes she feels like that part of her died with Evie. A gush of sadness explodes inside her. She just wants her Evie back. Nothing else. That's all she wants.

'I don't want a hug,' she says.

But Elijah pulls her up from the kitchen chair and leads her into the living room. 'Much more comfortable in here,' he says.

And as they sit on the sofa, Elijah lets her sob into his shoulder, dampening the smart navy blue shirt he's wearing. And then he's holding her tighter, as if he's trying to draw out her pain and free her of it. Kindness, that's what it is. He's a good man. What would it be like to be married to one of those?

She closes her eyes and feels as if she's floating. Away from here. From everything.

And then she feels his lips kiss the top of her head. Her cheek. Then his mouth finds hers and his lips feel so different to Damien's. Soft. Passionate. This doesn't feel like it's really happening. Perhaps she's only imagining it.

But then her body starts to respond, waking up from the coma it's been in since Evie died, or perhaps even long before that.

And then she doesn't want it to stop. Because for the first time in months she isn't thinking about anything else.

FIFTEEN

NOW

Holly

'She's dead.'

Holly feels as if her heart has stopped. 'No... no, she isn't.'

Damien shakes his head. 'They've found her bag... her phone. That can only mean one thing. What else could it be?'

Holly steps inside. 'No, it doesn't. Nothing's happened to her.' She wonders who she's trying to convince more – Damien or herself? 'I'm sorry I couldn't come until now. Luna needed me. And I've been...' She stops herself. Damien doesn't need to know that she barely slept last night, trying to piece together everything she knows about Rachel's disappearance. All the things leading up to it that didn't strike her as unusual at the time. Things that involve him. 'Do you want something to drink?'

'No, I don't want anything. Just my wife back.'

Holly should feel sorry for him, but he's an unpleasant man. It simmers beneath the surface, rendering anything nice he says null and void. Meaningless. 'What exactly have the police said?'

she asks, following him into the living room, where Rachel's aura is absent.

'I had to go and identify her bag and phone. A jogger found it underneath a bench near the lake. Not the river – the lake that you first come to after walking from the car park. The bag's definitely hers. That blue one. And everything was in it. Her purse. Her make-up. Keys.'

The crossbody bag Rachel loves and always uses for school. Holly can picture it now.

'And her phone with that battered sparkling case she never changes,' Damien continues.

'Because Evie liked it so much.'

'Didn't help her with her grief, though.'

Didn't. Damien is already giving up on her, assuming she's dead.

'She's in the lake. I know it,' he says, confirming this. 'Why else would her things be left there?' He paces the room. 'I think she's done this... to herself.'

'No. She wouldn't do that to Logan.'

'But without those pills – who knows what state her mind was in?'

Damien still hasn't answered Holly's question. 'But what did the police say? What are they doing?'

'They've cordoned off the area to search it properly. And they've sent an officer here. An FLO. She left just before you came but said she'll be back to meet Logan after school. You must have had one when Luna was taken?' He stops pacing and waits for Holly to answer.

'Yeah. Michelle. She was nice. Helpful.'

'Well, this one isn't. DC Kendra Marks. Every time she looks at me, I feel like she's judging me. Asking questions to try to catch me out.'

'That's not—'

'That *is* what they do. It's their job. You must know that?

They want to work out if family members are guilty of anything, and they dress it up as being there to support you.' He resumes pacing. 'As if I'd ever hurt my wife.'

But there's been something going on. Something isn't right in your marriage. 'I need to tell you something,' Holly says. 'But just hear me out until I've explained it all.'

Damien perches on the arm of the sofa, folding his arms. 'What's that?'

'This is going to have a lot of media coverage. And I'm covering it for *Surrey Live*. I just wanted to let you know. I'm writing Rachel's story. I couldn't let anyone else do it.'

He stares at her, and she refuses to look away. Holly knows how he will react to what she's just said and she's ready to fight. 'But you're her friend. Surely that's not ethical? You can't do it. It's too... too personal.'

'That's exactly *why* I'm the person who needs to report on this. I *know* her. Every word I write will be personal, and it has to be. We need everyone out there looking for her. Isn't that what you want?'

'Someone else can do it,' he says, ignoring her question.

'I'm afraid not.'

'Then I'll—'

'Just hear me out, Damien. It will either be me, or my colleague who doesn't give a fuck about anyone other than himself and will turn this into... I don't know what. All I do know is you won't like it. This isn't about gossip. This is a loving mother we're talking about. Wife. Friend. And I'm determined to find Rachel. That's my only agenda.'

Damien doesn't respond, which she takes as a good sign.

'Also, I'd like to interview you. Let people see the woman behind the story. Set the record straight about Rachel, because the trolls are already all over this on social media.'

Seconds tick by before he responds, and his words take her

by surprise. 'Of course I will. Anything to help find my wife. I just want Rachel home, where she belongs.'

Holly nods. 'Great. I've got a bit of time now if that works for you?'

'Sadly not. There's a meeting at work I can't miss. I can't just sit around at home, letting this eat away at me. I need to keep busy. Logan's already seen his mum fall apart, he doesn't need to witness his father doing the same. Come back tonight. In fact, no. Not here. I don't want Logan hearing anything. I need to shield him as much as I can. I'll come to your office. Eight o'clock.'

Holly's about to object but she reconsiders. She'll put up with Damien's demand if it gets him talking.

But he's not behaving like a man desperate to find his wife.

At home, Holly sits on the floor with Luna, making animals out of Play-Doh, in the hopes that Luna will join in. There's been a little progress this morning. Luna is smiling. And she's been playing more independently. But still with Holly or Elijah right beside her. Holly shudders to think once more of what her daughter went through, and it still concerns her how easily Luna was returned. Have they given her back for some other reason?

'Mama,' Luna says, turning to her and holding out her arms.

'I'm never letting you get hurt again,' Holly whispers, hugging her. 'It's my job to keep you safe, and I didn't do it well enough. But never again will I let that happen.' She smooths Luna's hair from her eyes, then takes another piece of Play-Doh and begins rolling it into a ball. Luna just stares at it. 'And now I've got to try and find Rachel,' Holly adds.

Luna's eyes widen. 'Ray-Ray,' she says.

Holly's so shocked that for a moment she thinks she's imagined Luna's voice. 'Yes, Ray-Ray.'

'Luna and Ray-Ray.'

Holly frowns. Her heart races as her mind scrambles to work out what Luna means. 'Have you seen her? Ray-Ray? Has Luna been with her?'

Luna blinks and grabs the Play-Doh bunny that Holly's just made, her small hand repeatedly smashing down on it. 'Ouchy,' she says, continuing to slam her hand into the Play-Doh until it's flattened.

Holly jumps up the second she hears Elijah's car in the drive, rushing to the door. 'I need to talk to you,' she says, pulling him inside.

'What's happened? Is Luna okay? Where is she?'

'She's watching TV. She's fine.'

He pulls off his jacket and throws his keys in the bowl on the cabinet, peeking into the living room before they go through to the kitchen. 'Any more news on Rachel?' he asks. 'Did they find anything in her things that might help find her?'

'I don't know yet.' She sighs. 'I'm still trying to get my head around what it means. But that's not what I need to talk to you about. Something happened earlier with Luna. I don't know what to make of it.'

'What is it? You're worrying me – just tell me.'

Holly recounts the incident with Luna, every detail readily available to her because she's spent the last hour picking it apart, analysing the words she spoke, every facial gesture, every movement. The sound of her pummelling the Play-Doh. All of it Holly describes to Elijah, hoping together they can come to understand it.

'That's weird,' Elijah says. 'I've never seen Luna do anything like that to her Play-Doh before.'

'No, she hasn't. She's never been aggressive with anything. That's not in her nature, is it?'

'No. So what does it mean, then?'

'I was hoping you'd help me figure that out. I just don't know.'

'So she said "Luna and Ray-Ray"? Then "ouchy"? Like we say when she's hurt herself.'

'I know.'

'Holl, you won't want to hear this but I told you something was weird about Rachel. How she wants to be with Luna all the time. What if Luna meant that's who'd taken her? Otherwise why would she mention Rachel now? She hasn't seen her for weeks.'

'I've been thinking about this, and the thing is – we've been talking about Rachel a lot the last couple of days. She's probably taken it all in and that's why she mentioned her.'

'I don't know, Holl. That doesn't sound right. It's more likely that she's seen her.'

'Rachel would never—'

'You can't say that. About anyone. Don't you think we're all capable of anything if we're pushed to our limits? We're human. Flawed. What if Rachel took her but then changed her mind? It would explain why she was given back. And then maybe she couldn't bear the guilt so she disappeared?'

Holly's been trained to think through every possible scenario, and to reserve judgement until she has evidence. But no part of her can entertain the notion that Rachel had anything to do with Luna's abduction. That would shake the foundations of everything she thought she knew. She shakes her head. 'No. She wouldn't do that to Luna. To us.'

'Maybe not ordinarily, but think about it – Rachel's been grieving. She lost her daughter, and Luna was Evie's best friend. They were the same age. Went to the same nursery. Is it beyond possibility that she did it out of grief? That she wasn't in her right mind?'

Holly has to admit he has a point. 'Then there'll be evidence, won't there? Sooner or later, the truth will come out.'

She turns to go back to the living room to check on Luna. 'But in the meantime, we don't know what happened so we need to keep our little girl safe. My instinct tells me this isn't over, Elijah.'

The office building is eerily quiet and she lets herself in, grateful when the motion-sensor lights finally kick in, brightening the space. She's never been here alone before – usually there's at least someone around, even on one of the other floors. But not tonight. She wishes Ross was here; she'd get him to sit in on the interview, because something about Damien's words doesn't match his behaviour. She knows grief. Even if it was brief, she was profoundly immersed in it while Luna was missing, as was Elijah. And what projects from Damien is nothing like grief.

It's a quarter to eight – she's got fifteen minutes to prepare for this interview. The worried husband. Does he know something? What had Rachel wanted to talk to her about before she went missing? She'd been so distracted with Luna being taken, everything else had seemed unimportant. But now she knows it wasn't.

She switches on her computer, and her notes flash up on her screen. Oscar Hobbs. She needs to write up the story. And she needs to speak to Megan, the girl who accused him. This girl might be able to shed some light on the argument she had with Oscar over Rachel. Everything feels so intertwined.

It's ten past eight before Damien calls to tell her he's outside. Holly takes a deep breath and goes to let him in.

'Is it just us here?' Damien asks when she lets him in. He glances around. 'Feels odd.'

'What did you expect at this time of night?'

'It's not that late. Many of my employees are still at work.'

She wants to tell him that this says a lot about his management style, but she swallows her words. 'Have a seat,' she says, gesturing to the chair in front of her desk.

Damien doesn't move. 'Bit like a job interview,' he says. 'Not sure I'm up for that.' He points to the sofa in the corner of the office. 'How about there? Then I won't feel like I'm being interrogated.'

'Fine.' She picks up her phone and a pen and paper. 'I'll need to record this. That okay?'

'Yes. If this is what it takes to find out what's happened to my wife, then of course. Anything.'

Anything except sit at her desk. Still, he's here and this is Holly's opportunity to analyse every word he says. 'I want this to feel like it's just a conversation between friends. In some ways it is. Casual. Honest. Let's see what we can work out about Rachel disappearing.'

Damien studies her for a moment, eventually nodding his agreement as he sits on the sofa.

'Can we go back to two days ago, when Rachel went missing? Wednesday.'

'Yep. The same day Luna was returned.'

Holly's well aware of this – she doesn't need him bringing it up. 'Let's just focus on Rachel.'

'Sure. Whatever you want. I woke up around six, and Rachel wasn't in bed. That's not unusual. She often falls asleep on the sofa. She has terrible insomnia – I'm sure you know that. Actually, it was the second night in a row I'd found her downstairs with a pile of exercise books on the coffee table.'

This is interesting. Would Rachel bother marking her students' books if she was planning on running away the next day? It's possible. She hated loose ends. If anything, she'd have done it for the kids she teaches. But her bag and phone? She'd need them, wherever she was going. Holly's stomach cramps. 'What did you talk about that morning?'

'Can't remember. Mundane stuff. What we were having for dinner. She said she'd make a roast. I thought that was weird for the middle of the week, but I wasn't about to turn it down. I told her I'd make sure I was home early so we could all eat together.'

'And how did she seem?'

Damien falls silent, and Holly wishes she could hear his thoughts. He's holding back, she can feel it. There are things he isn't saying. His words seem too carefully constructed.

'Can you stop recording?'

'Why?'

'Please just stop.'

Reluctantly, she does as he asks. 'What's going on, Damien?'

He leans forward, resting his elbows on his knees. 'The truth is... I didn't tell you this before. You're her friend and I wanted to protect her privacy. But the police know, so it will come out sooner or later.'

Holly holds her breath. 'What is it?'

'Rachel was begging me to have another baby.'

Holly stares at him, shock rendering her speechless.

'I told her it wasn't a good idea,' Damien continues. 'I said we couldn't just replace Evie. It was far too soon to even think about her getting pregnant again.' He shakes his head. 'It's made things... really tense at home. She's been holding it against me. Resenting me. A few weeks ago we had a huge argument about it. She said she wasn't going to let anything stop her being a mum again. That she'd do whatever it took.'

Holly takes a moment to let this sink in. It's thrown her off course.

'Did you know?' Damien asks. 'Did she ever talk to you about it?'

'No.' But then Rachel hasn't talked to her much about

anything lately. Only wanting to see Luna. Even though this has thrown Holly, the urge to defend Rachel kicks in. 'It doesn't make sense. Before Luna, Rachel told me she was happy with just having Logan. She'd never planned to have more.' As she says this, Holly wonders if this is what Rachel wanted to talk to her about.

'You're right. But then she had Evie. And Evie dying changed everything for her. You must know that? But this is what I was saying – it was a really bad idea for Rachel to try and get pregnant again so soon. She wasn't doing it for the right reasons.'

Guilt forms a heavy lump in her throat. 'I... was distracted. I wasn't there for her. Maybe she thought she couldn't talk to me about any of this.'

'That sounds like Rachel,' Damien says. 'She's a very private person. She doesn't share much with people.'

'I should have let her know I was there for her. That she could tell me anything.'

'Your daughter had been taken. Of course you weren't thinking of what Rachel might be going through. Besides, people are good at covering things up when they want to. Or need to.'

'Why are you only telling me this now?'

Damien sighs. 'Because I thought she'd be back by now. And I was protecting her privacy. But things are different now.'

'What d'you mean?' The fact that this is supposed to be an interview for her story fades into the background, and right now her sole role is as Rachel's friend. Holly hasn't expected Damien to come out with all of this.

'The police are looking for her,' he explains. 'Spending time and resources. When I think I know what's happened to her.' He pauses. 'I was worried at first, but now I see clearly what she's done. Vanished. She's deliberately left us and made it look like something happened to her.'

Holly lets his words settle in the air, fragments that she can't digest. Doesn't want to. She can't talk about this in the story. She won't sully her friend's name. 'I don't believe that.'

'It's too convenient, isn't it?' Damien continues. 'That her bag and phone happen to be found. I think she wants people to believe she's dead.'

'No. Rachel wouldn't—'

'How do you know that? I'm beginning to realise neither of us really knows her.'

Holly stares at him. 'This is why you wanted to do the story here instead of at your house, isn't it? You didn't want Logan to hear the awful things you're saying about his mother!'

Damien holds up his hand. 'I'm just trying to protect my son. I need you on side with this, Holly. I need you to believe me. Because the story you put out there needs to be the truth.'

'No. I don't know any of this is true.'

'What if I have evidence?'

For the second time tonight, Holly is stunned into silence. 'What evidence? You can't have.'

Damien shakes his head, reaching into the inside pocket of his jacket. 'Do you recognise this?' He pulls out his hand and thrusts something towards Holly, forcing her to reel backwards. She stares at the object he holds in his hands. She knows exactly what it is, but her brain can't make sense of what it's doing here. How Damien has it in his hands.

Luna's grey cuddly lamb.

The one she's sure she hasn't seen since the night Luna went missing.

SIXTEEN

BEFORE

Rachel

She saw a TV show once where the characters took pills that could erase their short-term memory. Something to make mistakes go away rather than having to live with the consequences. She's not sure whether these actually exist, but even if they did, Rachel would steer clear. No amount of medication or alcohol or anything else will change the fact that last night she slept with Elijah. Her closest friend's husband. She shudders to think of how intimate they were – how she'd let it happen. For the life of her, she can't understand why. She's never cheated on anyone before, not even when she was a teenager.

There is no excuse for what she's done. Not grief. Not alcohol. Not Damien. All she knows is that she has to put things right somehow. Because Holly means a lot to her.

'What's up with you?' Damien says, sitting across from her at the table. Logan hasn't come down yet and his cereal bowl sits empty, waiting to be filled.

'I'm fine,' she says, taking her mug and getting up from the table. Sitting with Damien this morning is making her more uncomfortable than usual, and Rachel feels as if there's barely any breath left in her. Perhaps Damien will notice, and see through her. See exactly what she's done. What would he do? It doesn't bear thinking about. Even though it pales in comparison to what he's done.

At the sink, she pours her lukewarm coffee away and tries to drown out Damien, but his words are too loud, too demanding.

'Logan's suffering because of you,' he says. 'It's bad enough he's lost his sister, and now you want him to lose his mother as well? Can't you just get a grip? Are you even taking your pills?'

Rachel takes a deep breath and counts to three. She knows what he's doing, and this time she won't rise to his bait. 'Yes,' she says calmly. 'Of course I am.'

On the worktop, her phone pings. Luckily Damien doesn't notice and continues his tirade. She tunes it out this time – her thoughts dominated by the need to read her message in privacy. She glances at the screen and it's not who she's expected – or hoped – it would be. It's Elijah. She doesn't open the message but can imagine what it says. There are things they either need to talk about or ignore completely, as if nothing happened. But Elijah messaging her suggests he's not going to forget anything.

She tunes in to Damien again when he comes closer, staring down at her with that darkness in his eyes. 'It makes me sad to say this, Rachel, but if it wasn't for Logan, I would have left a long time ago.'

He's never said this before, but nothing that comes out of his mouth surprises Rachel. She's learnt to expect anything, to always be ready. 'Why don't you, then?' she hisses, conscious that Logan might wake up any moment, even if this doesn't seem to concern Damien.

'Because I won't let you have Logan. I can't trust you to look after him. Look what happened to Evie when she was under your care.'

Rachel feels as if she's been struck by a hammer. Even for

Damien, these vitriolic words are far worse than anything he's said to her before. Until now, he's never used the children as a weapon against her. 'It was an accident. You know that.'

'You should have been watching her more closely. Then you would have seen the car veering towards her. Even if you were helping Logan, you should have known exactly where Evie was. If you'd kept her in her buggy, she'd still be here.'

'You don't even care, anyway!' Rachel shrieks, unable to control the volume of her voice now. 'You never loved her. You couldn't stand that she just wanted to be with me. Never you.'

The pain as his fist smashes into her jaw is like nothing she's felt before, and she topples backwards, only just managing to grab the worktop to stop herself falling. She catches sight of the knife by the sink. She could thrust it into his arm or leg, it would be nothing less than he deserves. But then she thinks of Logan, and she knows she could never do it, no matter what Damien has done to her.

He stares at her, his eyes wide with shock. For a moment he opens his mouth and she senses he's about to apologise. To make excuses like many abusers do, but instead he shoves her aside and walks out, leaving her to clean up the pool of blood dripping onto the floor.

Rachel sits on a park bench, trying to let the warmth of the winter sun comfort her. It's not the same park that she took the kids to on Evie's last day of her life. No, Rachel hasn't been able to set foot in there since. So instead she drives to Woking Park. She'd never got round to taking her daughter, but she used to bring Logan here all the time when he was younger.

Her face still stings, but at least the bleeding has stopped. The fight with Damien hadn't woken Logan, but by now he must be up and asking questions about where she is.

Today has been a first for several things. The first time

Damien has told her he wanted to leave her. And there she was thinking she was the one desperate to break away. The first time she's truly realised that this man will never let her be free of him. It's also the first time he's hit her. He's acted aggressively on other occasions, but never crossed the line he stepped over today. Rachel knows it won't be the last time; it's a door Damien will never be able to close now that it's been opened.

A young couple in their twenties passes by her, laughing with their heads huddled together, lost in their own world. Rachel has never romanticised love, or believed there's a soul-mate for everyone. No, you meet someone and try to make it work. Only, she hadn't counted on meeting someone like Damien. A skilled charmer who stops at nothing to get what he wants, even if it means playing the role of a decent man. And that can't be easy for him.

She pulls out her phone and scrolls WhatsApp for Holly's last message. It had been light-hearted and simple. Thanking her for babysitting. It came this morning, right around the time Damien was pummelling his fist into her face. Rachel hadn't replied. Through guilt, shame, and the pure absence of words. But now she's desperate to speak to her friend. To offload and finally tell her friend about Damien and what he's been doing. Not just the violence – that's a new level of threat – but the way he's been manipulating her, twisting her world to make it fit his agenda. Making her... appear insane. She knows she isn't. But then, isn't that what someone who was actually of unsound mind would think?

And then there is the other thing that he's done.

Ignoring Holly's message, she deletes Elijah's without reading it, before finding the one she does want to reply to. She's ready to see him now. After all this time. Everything has led to this.

Rachel re-reads his last message, sent only yesterday.

I know you won't reply to this, but I'm messaging anyway. I won't give up hope. I went for a long walk today. Never been a walker but a friend recommended I reconnect with nature. Something like that. Anyway, not sure it helped but it felt good. Knowing I'm just a tiny insignificant dot in this vast world. Hope you're doing okay. I know you won't be, but maybe just a tiny bit. That's what I hope.

Reading his words again, Rachel's head feels lighter, just a fraction. She takes a deep breath and begins typing.

I'm sitting on a park bench feeling exactly the same. Please stop messaging me.

The moment she sends it she hopes she hasn't made a mistake. What if he actually listens this time and she never hears from him again? She doesn't want that. She can't explain why, all she knows is that she feels connected to him.

Empty seconds tick by, and when they turn to minutes, Rachel wonders if all he needed was one response from her. And now he can put her behind him. Move on with his life. Nausea swirls around her stomach.

She's about to get up to walk back to her car, back to a life that lies in pieces, when her phone pings.

Tell me where you are and I'll be there.

Rachel's only seen him in the flesh once, but his face is as familiar to her as her husband's. She's scrutinised everything she could find about him online, sucking up all his information as if it's medicine that will cure her. Nobody knows what she does in these private moments, or that they've been communicating – or at least he has with her. And now, as he walks towards her, she scans the park to make sure there's no one around she recognises. This park is ten miles from her house, but there could be someone here she knows.

Jack Parsons is a couple of years younger than her, and she knows he's a data analyst. She has no idea what that involves on a daily basis, and wonders if he even still works. He slows down when he sees her. Probably nervous. More so than her.

He's taller than she remembers, and his light brown hair looks freshly cut. His face is kind. Friendly. And he's a man whose messages over these months have brought some lightness to her days.

He's also the man who killed her daughter.

SEVENTEEN

NOW

Holly

Holly stares at Luna's soft toy, and a thousand questions fire around her head. 'Where did you get that?' she asks. It's unmistakably Luna's – it has the small red pen mark on its back leg. The one Luna had made when she'd found Holly's Sharpie pen.

Damien takes his time to answer. 'I found it in our shed. It was padlocked and I haven't been able to find the key for months. Haven't had time to even look. But then I found it in Rachel's bedside drawer. It was weird. She's always so organised, so it wouldn't have got in there by mistake.'

Holly thinks of Rachel's colour-coordinated filing system. How everything in her home has a place. She urges Damien to continue.

'I haven't been in the shed for so long,' he says. 'I was curious. So I went and opened it. And inside I found this lamb, wrapped in one of Evie's baby blankets.'

Holly struggles to get her head around this. 'It doesn't make sense,' she says. 'Maybe Evie had one?' But she knows it's

Luna's. Too much of a coincidence that Evie would have had
the same lamb, with the same red pen mark.

'No. Evie never had a toy like that. I'd remember if she did.'
He hands the lamb to Holly. 'Despite what you might think of
me, I pay attention to my kids.'

Holly brings it to her face and sniffs the fur, but it doesn't
smell of anything much. 'I'm sure Luna had this in her bed the
night she was taken. And I haven't seen it since.'

'Course you haven't. Because Rachel had it locked in our
shed.'

'But—'

'Come on, Holly – you're an intelligent woman. You know
exactly what this means. Rachel had it. There's only one
conclusion we can reach from that.'

Despite the overwhelming evidence, Rachel isn't here to
speak for herself so Holly needs to be her voice. 'Rachel
wouldn't take Luna.' But her words aren't as forceful as she
wants them to be, and doubt seeps in.

'The police haven't found anyone, have they? There's no
evidence to point them in any direction. Nothing. Child
abduction is a serious crime – just because they've found Luna
it doesn't mean they've stopped trying to work out who took
her.'

'Have you told them you found this?'

'No.'

'Why?'

'Because it was found in *my* shed. And with Rachel not
here, I don't want them looking at me. As if I'd take Luna. My
baby days are long gone, and I certainly wouldn't want them
back.' He points to the lamb. 'Do what you want with that, but
please leave me out of it. And if you tell anyone where you
found it, I'll just deny it. But I'm giving it to you because I need
you to believe me. Rachel took Luna. She's guilty and that's
why she's run.'

His words echo Elijah's, but this time there is evidence to support it.

Holly gets up and puts the lamb in her desk drawer.

'Now, do you want to turn that back on?' He gestures to her phone.

Blindsided, Holly stares at him. 'No... I... I think I've got all I need.'

Damien stands and picks up his jacket. 'Fair enough. I trust you'll be honest in this story.'

Holly watches him head to the door. 'Wait.'

He turns around. 'What is it?'

'What do you want to come out of this? You don't seem upset at all. Your wife's missing. Anything could have happened to her, and you don't seem to care.'

'Not that it's any of your business how I handle things that happen to me, but I'll tell you why I don't seem *upset*. It's because Rachel died a long time ago. The woman I've been married to for years is a stranger to me now. Satisfied? Is that a good enough answer?'

Holly doesn't reply – he doesn't deserve a response – and she walks him out in silence.

'All of this is on purpose, Holly, can't you see that? She planned the whole thing. And we're all pawns in her game. She doesn't care who she's left behind. Logan. Me. You. None of us mean anything to her, because she's made this choice to run instead of facing the consequences of her actions. I don't know why she changed her mind and gave Luna back – only she knows that. But I know she's sick and needs help.'

'You're not going to tell Logan all this, are you?'

'Of course not. I'm all he's got now, and I'll protect him as much as I can. I just hope you come to your senses and don't try to sugar-coat the story. You need to tell it how it really is.'

He stalks off, and Holly quickly closes the door. A cold chill runs through her as she turns around, even before she sees who's standing by the reception desk, watching her, his arms folded across his chest.

'What are you doing here?' she asks, as he emerges from the darkness.

Paul smirks. 'I could ask you the same thing,' he says. 'But I don't need to. I just heard the whole of your conversation with that man. Your missing friend's husband.'

'It's none of your business,' Holly says, marching back to her office, her face burning.

He follows her, grabbing her arm. 'I hope you're planning to write the truth. Like he says.'

'Hey! Get the hell off me.'

He lets go. 'Your friend's husband thinks she had something to do with your daughter's abduction. No point denying it – I heard every word.'

There's no point denying it, or trying to put any kind of spin on it.

'And I know he has evidence,' Paul continues. 'Some toy of Luna's. What is it?'

At least he didn't see, then. 'Nothing to do with you. And Rachel had nothing to do with—'

'Of course you're defending her. She's your friend. I can't believe Ross let you have this story.'

'That's exactly *why* he let me have it.'

'Not any more,' Paul says, smiling. 'You're going to tell our boss that you want me to do it. You've had a change of heart and think it would be too difficult for you to cover it. Not when it's all so... raw.'

'There's no way I'm—'

'You don't have a choice. I'm about two seconds away from calling the police – telling them about the conversation I've just overheard.' He pauses, letting his demand sit with Holly for a moment. 'So, what's it to be? I'll need that decision now.'

She doesn't like being blackmailed or coerced into anything.

Holly's never in her life let that happen. But if she doesn't go along with his demand, she knows Paul won't stop at just going to the police. He'll make sure Rachel's name is smeared, that she'll never be able to come home. Holly can't let that happen.

'What about if you take the Oscar Hobbs story instead?' Behind her back she crosses her fingers.

'Nah, I'm afraid not. That ship has sailed. This story has much more spark in it. Who knows what the outcome will be? And something like this has got to be good for my career.'

'You're a despicable human being,' Holly spits, grabbing her bag and pushing past him.

'I'll take that as a yes, then,' Paul shouts after her.

The first thing she does when she gets home is check on Luna. She's in her bed, lying on her stomach, facing the wall. Holly kneels by her bed and strokes her forehead. 'Who took you, sweetheart?' she whispers. *It wasn't Rachel. I won't believe that.*

Her phone pings – a message from Ross.

Paul's claiming you've given him Rachel's story. Is this true?? What's going on?

She doesn't want to deal with these questions right now, so she types back *Yes* and leaves it at that.

Downstairs, Elijah's sitting at the kitchen table with his laptop. 'Told you she was fine,' he says, without looking up. 'I've been checking on her loads. And before you ask – the window is locked. Nobody's getting in there. And I've ordered a Ring doorbell.'

'Thanks,' Holly says, filling a glass with water. 'Has Luna said anything else?'

'No, not much. I let her watch TV for a bit and she was engrossed in that. You know I wouldn't normally let her watch that much, but, well, after everything she's been through, I just thought...'

'It's fine. TV isn't what we need to be worrying about right now.'

'You've got to stop thinking like that, Holly. Whoever took Luna gave her back. I'm sure they wouldn't try and take her again. Everyone will know we're on high alert.'

Holly wonders how Elijah can be so relaxed about it. *Because he thinks Rachel had something to do with it, and now she's gone. The danger is out of the way.*

'How was your chat with Damien?' he asks, turning back to his laptop.

Driving home, Holly had debated whether or not to tell Elijah about what Damien found. Even though it feels like a betrayal of her friend, he's her husband and this concerns Luna, so he has a right to the truth. 'He found something in his shed. Luna's cuddly lamb.'

Elijah's head jolts up. 'What?'

'He said the shed had been padlocked and the key went missing ages ago, but he found it in Rachel's bedside cabinet. And when he went to look in the shed, there was the lamb. At first I thought it couldn't be Luna's... but it's got the pen mark she made on its leg. Maybe we left it there and Rachel found it and it ended up in the shed.' She's misleading Elijah, but she needs more time to work all this out, and she knows he will jump on this, use it as definitive proof of Rachel's guilt.

Elijah shakes his head. 'I thought you said the lamb was only missing since Luna was taken, that she had it that night when you put her to bed.' He frowns. 'So that can only mean one thing.'

'I could be wrong. Luna has so many cuddly toys. I can't be sure it was Baa Baa.'

'You were sure when you gave your statement to the police, though,' Elijah reminds her.

Holly knows this, but somehow she can't bring herself to admit it to him. 'I could have been wrong. I can't be certain now. I just don't know! I'm not going to condemn my friend when I can't be sure.'

'You've got to face facts here, Holl. Surely now you must see Rachel's involved?'

In the furthest edges of her mind, perhaps Holly can, but sometimes things aren't as straightforward as they seem. 'I don't make judgements until I have all the evidence,' she insists.

Elijah shakes his head, exasperated. 'Don't we owe it to Luna to find out what happened to her?'

'Yeah, of course.'

'Anyway, it's up to the police to find out now,' he says. 'Then hopefully we can draw a line under this and move forward. This evidence will help them.'

'Um, Damien isn't going to the police.'

'What? Why?'

'Because he doesn't want to, and neither do I. At least not yet.'

'But that doesn't make any sense. They need to know. Someone needs to tell them about this.'

'We can't,' Holly says. 'Damien won't say anything, and I can't prove he gave it to me. He says he'll just deny it.'

Elijah shakes his head. 'This is messed up.'

'All I know is that I need to keep Luna safe and find Rachel. That's all that matters.'

'I'm sorry, Holl, but I don't think you're thinking clearly. If Rachel's somehow...' He stops, and stares at her with an expression she can't read. Seconds tick by. He closes his eyes for a moment. 'Okay,' he says. 'Have it your way. I have to trust that you know what you're doing.'

Holly's confused. She's never known Elijah to backtrack on anything – he can be even more stubborn than she is. She's about to question him when Luna cries out.

'I'll go,' Elijah says.

But Holly is already racing upstairs to their daughter.

For over an hour, she sits on Luna's bed, singing to her. 'Frère Jacques', 'Twinkle, Twinkle'. Anything to soothe her.

'Can you tell me what's wrong?' Holly asks, when Luna can't settle, clinging to Holly with her strong grip.

Luna doesn't speak, but stares at her with wide eyes.

'I wish Mummy could understand how to help you,' Holly says, blinking back tears. 'Can you tell me what happened? Who was Luna with? Were they kind to you?'

Blank eyes continue to stare, so Holly sings again. 'Rock-a-Bye Baby', even though Luna's no longer a baby. This time, it seems to comfort her, and soon she's drifting off in Holly's arms.

For almost half an hour, Holly doesn't move, cherishing every moment of this time. Her daughter is safe. And she's going to find Rachel. She can't let people think her friend would take her daughter. And though tiny doubts niggle away at her, Holly buries them.

Elijah's still downstairs when she climbs into bed. She considers calling for him, asking if he's coming up soon. But instead, she pulls out her phone and starts scrolling, searching for everything she can find on Rachel's disappearance.

And then she sees it. The rumour she's been trying to prevent right there for everyone to see.

That woman took her friend's little girl. That's why she's disappeared. She should be in prison.

And underneath it, hundreds of comments – all of them agreeing what a heinous person Rachel James is.

EIGHTEEN

BEFORE

Rachel

'Thanks for agreeing to meet me,' Jack Parsons says, hovering in front of her, but keeping a bit of distance. She can understand why he's nervous – being face to face with her can't be easy. 'I understand why you haven't replied until now,' he says, shifting from one leg to the other.

'Are you going to sit, then?' Rachel says, shifting to the edge of the bench so that they won't be sitting too closely together.

Jack sits, with a sharp intake of breath. 'I'm so grateful,' he says. 'This can't be easy for you.'

Rachel doesn't respond. Surely he doesn't expect her to be happy that he's grateful? Or to feel anything. Hatred. That's the emotion she *should* be feeling. That's what anyone else would be consumed with, so why isn't she?

'I think about her every day,' he says, looking up at the sky. There are faint wisps of white cloud in the bright blue sky. 'Still. It doesn't get any less as time goes on. Every time I see a child around her age, it's like a knife slicing into me. And I

deserve it, I know that.' He looks at Rachel again, and she can
see the glimmer of tears in his eyes.

Rachel's had months to think about this, to pull it apart and
analyse every aspect of what happened. That black and white
cat hurtled across the road, out of nowhere. Jack panicked and
swerved to avoid it. Most people would have done the same –
she definitely would have. There's no way she'd want to be
responsible for an innocent animal's death. And now she's sure
Jack would pick this over her daughter's death if he could go
back and change things. It's not his fault that Evie happened to
be right there at the exact moment, dashing towards the cat. She
doesn't know who's ultimately responsible. It's too easy to say
Jack. But she was the one who let Evie out of her buggy.

'What do you want from me?' she asks him. 'Why did you
contact me on Facebook?' It's a reasonable question; Rachel has
the right to know why he won't leave her alone. Why he
messages her more than she and Holly used to, even before Evie
died.

'I don't know. I just... I wanted to apologise face to face. Oh,
God. Apologising seems so... inadequate. It's not enough.
Nothing ever will be. I'm so sorry.' He shakes his head and
stares at the ground, sighing.

'We're all looking for redemption,' Rachel says. 'But another
person can't give it to us. We have to give it to ourselves.'
Rachel's not entirely sure where her words come from. It must
be because of what she's done. She's also responsible for
wrecking a life. Her friend's. And Luna's too. Where does
it end?

'I can't forgive myself,' he says. 'And I don't want to. I want
to pay this price.'

She turns to him, taking in his appearance. He's an attractive man, underneath his pain. She imagines that before this, he
had his life together. Probably a girlfriend. Lots of friends. A

social life. She'd bet money on the fact that everything's changed for him now. What she hasn't expected is to feel sorry for him.

'I'm quite sure you're already paying in so many ways,' she says. 'Has your life changed?'

He nods. 'Yeah. I still go to work. I have to. Bills to pay. But I don't see anyone. I can't socialise. How can I sit there laughing and having a drink when I know what I did? I don't drive any more. Can't seem to get behind a wheel. The thought of it terrifies me. I rode my bike here today. It's locked up at the leisure centre.'

'You'll find a way to live with it,' Rachel says. 'So will I. Because what choice do we have?'

Silence sits between them, but surprisingly it's not uncomfortable. It feels familiar, the silence that might exist between friends. After all the messages he's sent her, she does feel as if she knows him a bit. So much of what he writes is him talking about his day, or what he's been doing. To begin with she found it disconcerting, but it grew into something reassuring.

'Can I ask what happened to your face?' he says. 'That looks painful.'

Rachel brings her hand to her mouth. She'd forgotten how she must look. 'I tripped,' she says. Jack's caught her off guard and it's the first excuse she can think of.

His eyes narrow, but he doesn't question her further. It's none of his business, anyway, and she'd have no problem telling him that. 'This park's nice,' he says. 'I've never been here.'

'I can't go to my local one now. Not after...'

'I know.' He sighs again. 'How's your son doing?'

Rachel's not sure how to answer that question, or even if she wants to. It was one thing receiving Jack's messages, but she never replied and shared anything about herself. She's not sure she's prepared for whatever this is to be more balanced. 'He's as

okay as he can be,' she says. The truth is, like her, Logan will
never be okay. She just has to help him live with it.

'Jesus,' Jack says. 'This is... I'd do anything to change it all.'
He stops to wait for an elderly couple to pass. 'I was even
hoping I'd go to prison. Penance, you know.'

'It doesn't do any good thinking like that,' Rachel says. 'Like
I said, you're already paying a heavy price.'

Again, silence engulfs them, as warm as the sun on their
skin, until Jack breaks it. 'Do you think maybe... is there
anything I could help you with? Anything.'

'Like what? Doing my garden? Fixing things that break in
my house?' It's almost laughable that he thinks this might
help her.

'No, I don't mean that.' He turns away. 'I don't know what I
mean exactly. But not that. If you needed to talk to someone,
though. About anything. I've been told I'm a pretty good
listener. Maybe it's from having three sisters.' His mouth forms
a thin smile. 'Anyway, I'm no good at gardening. Or fixing
things.'

Despite herself, Rachel laughs. 'Then you're no good to me.'

Across from them, a woman arrives with two children, one
of whom looks around the same age as Evie. Rachel watches
them, and her body feels heavy, as if she'll never be able to lift
herself from this bench.

Jack follows her gaze and his eyes fall on the little girl.
Without a word, he takes her hand, and they sit in silence.

She flinches at the contact, but doesn't let go of his hand.
His skin is warm and smooth, and feels so different to Damien's
rough, dry touch. She should pull away but she doesn't want to.
They are united in their different forms of grief for the same
little girl.

She's not sure how long they stay like that, but eventually
Rachel snatches her hand away. 'I have to go now.'

'Wait, can we get a coffee or something?'

'I have to go,' she repeats.

Without giving him another chance to persuade her otherwise, she rushes off, hearing him call after her.

'Can I see you again?'

But Rachel can't entertain that notion. It will only lead to trouble.

NINETEEN

NOW

Holly

Morning hasn't come quickly enough for Holly. Once again, she's barely slept, and as much as she knew scrolling through all the comments from online trolls would do her no good, and serve no purpose, she soaked it all up, needing to read every word. And it's clear what people think.

Rachel took Luna.

Now, she sits in her car outside Megan Hart's house, waiting until nine o'clock to knock on the door. She'd never normally turn up at someone's house without an invitation, but there was no time to call ahead. And she's sure Megan's parents wouldn't have agreed to a meeting if she had. Besides, this isn't about Megan and Oscar Hobbs – it's about Rachel.

The blinds in the downstairs windows are open, so she assumes at least someone in the family is up. Two more minutes, and then she'll rock up to the house as if she has every right to be there. In her head, she does; this is for Rachel.

While she waits, she runs through everything she knows about Megan. She turns sixteen at the beginning of September.

Parents still together, and she has eight-year-old twin brothers. Never been in any trouble at school, or outside of it, as far as Holly can tell. *Why, then, would this girl tell such an awful lie about Oscar Hobbs?* Even though Holly's here for Rachel, the journalist in her is hoping to shed some light on what happened there too.

At one minute past nine, Holly gets out of the car and makes her way up the short path to the front door. The second she rings the bell, a dog barks, loud angry yaps that make Holly feel uneasy. Then footsteps, and a voice commanding the dog to be quiet.

The man who opens the door doesn't say anything, but waits for her to speak. Megan's father, she assumes. He's tall, with curly dark hair and wiry limbs.

Holly holds out her hand. 'Hi, I'm Isobelle Simons from *Surrey Live*.' She's picked her middle name and her mum's maiden name – so she doesn't forget.

Tentatively, Megan's father shakes her hand. 'Oh, right. I don't read papers. Who does these days?'

'It's an online news site.'

He shrugs. 'Still don't have time. How can I help?'

'I'm covering the disappearance of Rachel James, the teacher from Woodbridge School.' Holly's not used to lying, and has spent her life trying not to, so she hopes guilt doesn't show on her face like a beacon.

'Yeah, I did hear about that. She's my daughter's English teacher.'

'That's why I'm here, actually. I've been talking to anyone who might have seen her in the last couple of weeks. Staff. Students. Anyone who might be able to help me build a picture of Rachel James. We all just want to find her, don't we?' She doesn't give him a chance to answer. 'Also, it must be quite disruptive for your daughter with Mrs James away, and she must have mock exams coming up?'

He nods, but his eyes have narrowed. Mistrust is creeping in. Holly needs him to let her in fast if she's to stand any chance of talking to Megan. 'I'm sure you and your family will want to do everything you can to help find Rachel. Can I ask your name?'

'Aaron Hart. And what exactly are you asking for?' he asks. 'I can't agree to something until I know what I'm expected to do.'

Holly nods. 'With your permission, I'd like to talk to Megan about Rachel James. In your presence of course.'

'I don't know. I'd have to speak to my wife. She's having a lie-in this morning. Can you come back later? Or tomorrow.'

'I totally understand, Aaron. But it would really help me if I could just do it quickly now. As I'm here. I promise it won't take long, then I'll leave you to get on with your day.'

Megan appears behind her dad, eyeing Holly quizzically. Holly recognises her from her social media trawl when she was researching Oscar Hobbs. She's a pretty girl, with curly brown hair that sits on her shoulders. She's wearing navy velour joggers and a white crop top. Behind her, a golden retriever wags his tail.

Stepping forward, Holly holds out her hand. 'Hi, Megan. I'm Isobelle from *Surrey Live*. I'm covering the disappearance of Rachel James. I believe she's your teacher?'

Megan frowns. 'Yeah. But there are, like, fifty thousand of us she teaches. Not just me. I don't know anything about her.'

'I know. But I just had to pick a few people.'

'How exactly did you find us?' Aaron asks.

She needs to think fast. She can't mention Oscar, as that's likely to evoke hostility. She takes a gamble. 'I know your neighbour – in that house across the road.' Holly points to a random house.

'The Hurleys. Yeah, they're good people.'

'They certainly are. So can I have a few minutes, then?'

Megan's dad frowns, but holds the door open wider. 'I suppose so.'

The first thing Holly notices when she steps inside is the damp smell of dog. The place looks clean and tidy, though, and they're clearly a family who take pride in their home. The hallway wall is filled with family photos, including some of the dog, and there's a blush pink rug running all the way to the door at the end of it.

'I don't know what help you think I'll be,' Megan says, traipsing into the living room. 'I don't know what happened to her. What am I supposed to say?'

Holly sits on the sofa. 'What I'd like to do is build a picture of Rachel in the weeks leading up to Wednesday afternoon, when she disappeared. I need to get this story right, and show people who the person behind the headlines is. Does that make sense?'

Megan shrugs, folding her arms. 'Yeah, I guess. People are saying she took that little kid.'

'I try not to listen to speculation. I'm a journalist and try to work with evidence.' She needs to veer this girl in a different direction. 'Megan, all I need from you is honesty. Don't just tell me what you think sounds good. The truth is all that matters.'

Megan's eyes roll. 'I'm not a liar,' she insists. 'Just because of—'

'You don't need to talk about that boy,' Aaron insists. He's been so quiet up until now that Holly's almost forgotten he's sitting on an armchair by the window. 'That's got nothing to do with anything,' he adds.

Thankfully, Megan ignores him. 'Yeah, but now because of him, people think I'm a liar, and I'm not.' She looks at Holly. 'I withdrew my statement because—'

'Megan, I'm warning you.'

'Shall we just focus on Rachel James?' Holly says, even though she'd love to know what Megan was about to say. Right now, she just needs to defuse the tension between Megan and her father. Maybe he'll start to trust her and might leave the room for a moment.

'Good idea,' Aaron says, settling into an armchair.

'Dad, you don't need to be here,' Megan says.

'Oh yes I do. You're fifteen. Still a child.'

Rolling her eyes, Megan turns to Holly. 'So what do you want to ask me?'

'What is Rachel James like as a teacher?'

Megan rolls her eyes again. 'What's that got to do with anything?'

'Just trying to build a picture. Anything you can tell me will help.'

'And you want the truth, right?' Her mouth twists. 'No matter what it is?'

Holly nods, unsure she's prepared for what she's about to hear.

'Everyone thinks she's such a good teacher. And they feel sorry for her after her kid died. But nobody could see what she's really like. Until now. It's all coming out, isn't it?'

'And what's that?'

'She took her friend's baby. I knew there was something weird going on with her.'

Holly should put her straight, but she needs to know what Megan's trying to say. 'What d'you mean by that, Megan?'

'Well, she was going around school acting as if she still had a daughter. And we know she's only got her son in Year 8.'

Even though Holly has already heard it from Oscar Hobbs, she asks Megan to give her a specific example.

'Like one time, she said she had to leave school early to pick her daughter up from nursery. Other people must have heard – it couldn't have been just me. But no one said anything.'

'Are you sure she said that?'

'Yeah. I was standing right there. Walking into the lesson. She was smiling. She seemed kind of... happy.'

'Can you remember when this was?'

Megan shrugs. 'Not sure. Hang on. Maybe in Feb. But her daughter died a year ago. When I was in Year 9.'

Although Holly has already heard this from Oscar, she's not sure how to respond. She'd hoped Oscar Hobbs had been lying, and that Megan would set the record straight about Rachel. But all she's done is corroborate what Oscar claimed they'd argued about.

Megan could be lying, though. Just because she said this to Oscar, and is repeating it now, doesn't necessarily make it the truth. 'Is there anyone else in your class who might remember hearing Rachel say this? You said others heard.'

'It's weird you calling her Rachel. She's Miss James. When you say Rachel, I just think you're talking about someone else.'

'Okay, then. Miss James. Who else might remember?'

Megan shrugs. 'She said it at the beginning of the lesson when people were still wandering in, so I don't know who heard. And then halfway through class the cover teacher came and Miss James left without a word. Also weird, by the way.' Megan crosses her legs and waits for Holly's next question.

'This is all very helpful,' Holly says, smiling. Even though it's not true. She'd have known if Rachel had been acting strangely. *But I've been so busy with work the last few weeks. And so conscious of the amount of time Rachel wanted to spend with Luna. I've let her down.* 'Is there anything else you can remember?'

'Everything she did was weird,' Megan replies, pulling lip balm from her pocket and dabbing it across her mouth. 'Where do you want me to start?'

Holly ignores the gibe. 'Just tell me anything you can think of.'

'Um, I dunno.' She picks at a loose thread on her joggers.

'Actually, there was one thing. I'd forgotten about it. She's got this sparkly phone case. It's all battered but she never gets a new one. Then, one lunchtime I saw her out by the art block talking to someone on her phone. But it wasn't her usual phone, it was a weird old phone like they had in the old days. You know, those ones that don't even connect online.'

Holly scrambles to think of a reason for this. 'Are you sure?'

Megan rolls her eyes. 'I know what I saw. I know about phones.'

'Maybe she lost her phone, and it was a temporary replacement?' Yet Holly doesn't remember Rachel mentioning this, or having a new number.

'No,' Megan says. 'That's the weird bit. When I saw her at the end of school that same day, she had her old sparkly phone again. I told my friends and we all made a joke that Miss James must be a drug dealer or something and needed a burner phone.' She laughs.

But to Holly, this is far from funny.

Why would Rachel need two phones?

TWENTY

BEFORE

Rachel

They've met up a few times now, and the more she sees him, the more she relaxes in his company. He does too, it seems, and the man standing outside South Kensington Tube station stands taller than he did in the park three months ago on that first meeting. He smiles as she approaches, and instinctively she smiles back, before reining it back in, letting it fade.

It was Jack's idea to visit the Natural History Museum. Rachel loves it here, and had told him about when she'd brought Logan as a toddler. It had seemed a good idea at the time, but after five minutes he'd grown tired and bored, and begged her to go home, so Rachel had hardly seen anything. She'd meant to come back – on her own – but had never found time, until now.

And in London, they can move freely, without fear of being recognised. She can breathe. Her steps are lighter.

'I have to confess,' Jack says, 'I thought you'd bail. I thought – there's no way Rachel's coming up to London to meet me here.'

'I'm not missing the chance to see this place,' she says.

'Wandering around with no toddler begging me to go home.' As soon as she says this she thinks of Evie, and immediately regrets her words. She'd give anything to have her little girl drag her back home.

Picking up on her silent anguish, Jack tells her he gets what she means. 'Let's go,' he says. 'There's a lot to see.'

For a couple of hours, Rachel loses herself in history that has nothing to do with her pain. While they're wandering around the human evolution section, Jack takes her arm. 'What makes us human?' he asks. 'I mean, the fundamental thing. I know there are lots of components.'

Rachel considers his question. 'I want to say our ability to love. But animals can love, I think. So maybe it's more to do with our ability to hate. Animals might feel something like hate as it relates to fear. They don't want to get attacked or eaten. But us? We're awful. Our capacity for hatred has little to do with survival – it comes from jealousy, resentment...'

Jack smiles. 'I think you're right. I want to believe there's goodness at the core of all of us, though. Somewhere. Maybe in some people it's just unreachable.'

Rachel thinks of Damien. How, no matter how much she's tried, she can never extract anything decent from him. Except his love for Logan. That's it. Did he even love Evie? She doesn't want to think about that. 'What are we doing?' she asks.

'We're discovering the origins of humanity. Seven million years' worth.'

'I don't mean here. I mean what's going on with *us*. Why are we doing this? Talking. Meeting up all the time.'

'Let's sit for a minute.' He leads her over to a bench in the corner of the room. 'Because I think we can help each other. I need it, and I know you do too.'

She turns away, swiping away the tear that rolls down her cheek, stinging her skin.

'It's not right,' she says. 'You...'

He hangs his head. 'I know. But don't you see – exactly why we need each other. To heal, even in a small way.'

In some way, Jack is right. Spending time with him does help her. She'd never have imagined it could. The man who caused Evie's death. It's insane. But at the same time, he's the antidote to Damien, and she needs that, now more than ever.

'Has he hurt you again?' Jack asks.

It had taken her a while, but after a few weeks, Rachel had confessed to the real reason her face was a mess that day in the park. And Jack had listened to her, holding her hand and letting her cry silent, painful tears. Then he simply told her he was there for her. No matter what.

'I don't need anyone,' she'd said. 'Just my children. And my job. I don't need any man to make me whole.'

'Oh, I know you don't. And that's not what I'm offering,' Jack had replied. 'I just want you to know that I'm here. That's all.'

'No, he hasn't touched me since that day,' Rachel says now. 'But... everything else has got worse. I can't trust him. I don't feel safe.' This is what's been simmering in her subconscious, but she's never dared articulate it. Until now.

'You need to leave. You and your son. Both of you need to get away from him. I know he hasn't hurt Logan, but look what he's done to you. Who knows what he's capable of?'

Rachel doesn't think he'd hurt Logan, but how can she be totally sure? What about when Logan's a teenager and challenges them? 'He'll never let me take Logan,' she tells Jack. 'Never. He's got too much pride. And also... he does love him. I'm the one he has the problem with.'

'Because he knows you're too good for him.'

Rachel's shocked to hear these words. She's not used to being complimented. But Jack's words aren't true. Elijah flashes into her head. It's been a couple of months, but their betrayal hovers over everything she does. She opens her mouth to tell

Jack what she did. That she is an adulterer, and even worse, it
was with her friend's husband. But Rachel likes the lens Jack
sees her through and doesn't want to taint it, so she stays silent.
She wants this man in her life, even in this small way. 'Shall we
get some lunch?' she says.

On the train home, while dusk settles outside, Rachel leans back
and closes her eyes.

'You've got nothing to feel guilty about,' Jack says, taking her
hand.

Her eyes open. 'Where did that come from?'

'Going up to London. Meeting me in obscure places. At
weird times. We're not doing anything wrong. It's not as if we're
having an affair.'

'I know we're not. But no one would understand what we're
doing,' she says. She doesn't even fully understand it herself.
'Especially Damien.' He'd use it against her, a way for him to
take Logan from her. Something to suggest she's an unfit
mother. *You see, she's having some kind of emotional affair with
the man who killed our daughter.* She can almost hear Damien's
words, if he were to find out. 'And it's no one's business,' Rachel
continues.

'True. I just don't like secrecy. Deceit.'

'I'm not lying to him. Damien was already out when I got
up this morning, and Logan's with Damien's parents for a few
days over half-term. So... no lies.' And if he'd actually asked her
where she was going – what would she have said? Anything but
the truth.

'Semantics,' Jack says.

'Well, if you're so worried about it, why don't you knock on
our door and introduce yourself?' Now that she's got to know
Jack, she's sure he wouldn't be afraid to do this. He would stand

up to Damien. But that's because he doesn't know the full extent of the monster she married.

'I'd never do that,' he says. 'Not without your go-ahead. And I'm not concerned about Damien. It's *you* I have to think of.'

Rachel's not sure why, but she feels belligerent this evening. Maybe it's the thought that in less than an hour she'll be at home again, alone with Damien. It's always harder when Logan isn't there.

'You're welcome to come back to mine for a bit if you like?' Jack says. 'If you're worried at all. It might have to be a takeaway for dinner – I haven't had a chance to do any shopping this week.'

Rachel laughs. 'Sounds like you're asking me on a date.'

'No, definitely not.' His cheeks redden. 'Really? Is that what you think of me?'

'Well, you have been stalking me for months.'

He smiles – a rare sight, Rachel realises. 'Guilty as charged.'

'Maybe another time,' she says. 'If you're paying.' She nudges his arm.

The rest of the short journey passes in that comfortable, familiar silence, but when they arrive at their station, anxiety once again consumes her, suffocating her. *Maybe Damien will be out. He's been working such long hours lately. The new development he's working on.* Or at least that's what he claims he's doing. She only half believes it; while he's clearly a workaholic, there are other things he does outside the house. And one day it will all catch up with him.

'Bye,' Jack says, briefly putting his hand on her shoulder. 'I'll be in touch soon.'

What would he do if she said no? That what they're doing – this unlabelled thing they're partaking in – has to stop now. The words sit at the edge of her mouth, all she has to do is push them forward. She folds her arms across her chest. 'Bye, Jack.'

.   .   .

The house is dark and silent when she lets herself in – too quiet without Logan, even if he barely makes a sound when he's in his room. No Damien, that's the main thing. A sense of relief spreads over her, slowly filling her as if she's had an infusion of a calming drug.

She makes herself a cup of ginger and manuka honey tea and takes it to the living room, flicking on the light.

'Where have you been?'

Rachel jumps, her cup slipping from her trembling hands. It crashes to the carpet, a pool of tea spreading across it.

'That was clumsy,' Damien says. 'Answer my question. I asked where you've been.'

'Just... out.'

'Out where?'

Her brain scrambles to build something credible. 'With Holly. We took Luna to a soft play.' That's feasible. Damien isn't in contact with her friend.

'Is that right? Which one?'

Heat floods to Rachel's cheeks. 'Woking. The leisure centre one in the basement. She loves it there.'

Damien checks his watch. 'Bit late for it to be open, isn't it?'

'We went back to Holly's. I helped her get Luna ready for bed. Elijah isn't home.' She should keep the details sparse to avoid catching herself out, but she wants to make her lie believable.

'Stop!' Damien shouts. He stands and strides towards her. 'I know you're lying. I saw Holly and Elijah about an hour ago at the petrol station. They'd been out together. Her mum's watching Luna. Now do you want to explain why the fuck you're lying to me?'

But there's nothing Rachel can – or wants to – explain to this man who masquerades as a husband. 'I need to clean this up.' She turns away, heading towards the kitchen to get a cloth.

Damien grabs her neck, forcing her backwards. She doesn't

even scream. After last time, she's half expected this. But she's not going to give him the satisfaction of knowing how terrified she is.

And even when he throws her to the floor, picking up the mug, ready to smash into her face, she stays calm and rams her knee into his groin. But he's too quick, and manages to dodge sideways. 'I knew you'd fight back,' he says, and there's a smile on his face. He's enjoying this. And all the time she'd assumed he wanted her to be passive. No, in his twisted way he's trying to draw something out of her.

She waits for the assault, but it doesn't come. Instead, he laughs, dragging her up. 'The thing is, if I lay a hand on you, then you've won,' he says. 'And there's no way I'm letting that happen. Not after everything we've been through.'

Rachel's confused. There are many things he could be referring to. But with his next words, she knows exactly what he means.

'Death follows you everywhere, doesn't it, Rachel? Evie. Will. Your parents. You wouldn't know, would you? Have you ever stopped to wonder who's next?' He moves closer to her. So close that she can smell his Aramis aftershave. She'd liked it once. It had made her want him.

'I'll tell you this much, Rachel. It's not going to be me.'

TWENTY-ONE

NOW

Holly

The outpouring of rage against Rachel continues online. The police will be looking into this angle too; there's no way it's something they'll put down to gossip. Holly has to scroll through a plethora of comments expressing this opinion before she finds one dissenting voice. Someone who will defend a stranger.

'Luna, can you get me your Peppa Pig bag? We're going out for bit.' Holly grabs some snacks from the cupboard.

'Where, Mama?'

Holly's so happy to hear her daughter speaking that for just a second, she almost forgets everything else. 'Come here, sweetheart,' she says, holding out her arms. 'Do you know how great it feels to hear your little voice?'

'Mama,' Luna repeats. But then, as soon as she's spoken, blankness falls across her face again. They've got an appointment with a child psychologist this afternoon, though Holly and Elijah know that Luna might be too young for it to yield any results. Anything is worth a try, though. She just wants her daughter to be okay.

This means Holly has a brief window of time to find Damien and question him about the second phone Megan Hart claimed to have seen Rachel with. Elijah is out visiting his grandmother this morning. He said he'd take Luna – that it would do her and Jean some good, but Luna had burst into tears and clung to Holly, so that was that.

It takes longer than she'd anticipated, and hoped, to get Luna ready, and it's nearly noon by the time she's found Luna's bag and filled it with everything they'll need. 'Okay,' Holly says, strapping Luna into her car set. 'Mummy just has to do a few things, and then maybe we can go to the playground?'

Luna stares at her, silently.

Holly pats her arm. 'Well, let's see later, then. But for now, Mummy's got to find someone.'

Logan answers the door, squinting at her as if she's an apparition. Her heart breaks for him; she can imagine the devastation he's feeling, not knowing where his mum is. Or if she's okay. And having to read those poisonous comments from strangers. 'Hi, how are you bearing up?'

He shrugs. 'I dunno. It's weird. Sometimes I forget she's gone and I come down to ask her something but it's just... silent.' He reaches out to touch Luna's arm. 'Hello, Luna.'

'Sorry, I was just looking for your dad.'

'He's gone to work.'

'Oh, course, yeah. Saturdays are just another work day, aren't they? To me too.'

'Yeah.'

'We'll find your mum, Logan. The police are doing everything they can. I am too. I hope you're not reading all that stuff online. It's not true.'

'I know. Mum would never take Luna. Never.'

'You and I both know it, don't we? Even if it feels like we're swimming against the tide.' Luna's words ring in her ears. *Luna and Ray-Ray*. What did her daughter mean? And Luna's grey lamb. The one she was so sure Luna had that night when she put her to bed. 'Logan, can I ask you something? Do you know if your mum ever had to use a different phone?'

Logan frowns. 'No, why? She hasn't updated her phone for years. I keep telling her she needs an upgrade, but she just says one iPhone is the same as any other so there's no point.'

'And you definitely never saw her using a different phone? Not an iPhone. Like an old-style one?'

'No. Why?'

'Never mind.'

'I miss her,' Logan says. 'I never tell her how much I... you know, how much I love her. And now she's probably—'

'Hey, your mum will be fine. She'll be coming back to us. She needs us to believe in her.' Holly glances back at the car. 'Is your dad due home soon? Maybe Luna and I could come in and wait for him?'

Logan shakes his head. 'He's on site. Said he won't be back until dinnertime. He said we could order pizza.'

'Do you know where exactly he'll be?'

'That new housing development, I guess.' Logan shrugs.

'The Hilltop Park one? By the motorway?'

'Think so. We don't really talk much about his work, so I'm not totally sure.'

'I'll give it a try. Thanks, Logan.'

Once more, he glances at Luna. 'Can I... um, give her a cuddle?'

'Oh. Um... are you sure it's not too upsetting? I've tried to keep her away from you as much as I can. Who knows if that's the right thing.'

'No, it'll be good for me. She was Evie's bestie. Is she... okay now?'

Holly's mouth twists. 'She's not talking much. But we're

seeing a doctor later, so maybe they'll be able to help her. The thing is, Logan – she's being a bit clingy and won't really go to anyone else. She just wants me all the time. Or Elijah a bit.'

Logan's shoulders sag. 'That's okay. Maybe next time then. Mum was devastated when she was taken. That's why I know it wasn't her.'

'You don't have to convince me,' Holly says.

But as she straps Luna into her car seat, waves of doubt engulf her.

The Hilltop Park development is well underway. The structure of the houses has been erected, and she's in awe of the mind Damien must have to be able to design these plans, and see them through to completion. She might not particularly like the man, but he works hard, she'll give him that.

There's space to park on site, and she pulls out her phone and calls Damien. She can't see him, and there's no way she's taking Luna onto this hazardous building site, or leaving her in the car.

He picks up on the second ring. 'Holly,' he says. 'What can I do for you? I'm a bit busy.'

'I need to talk to you. I'm at Hilltop Park. In the car with Luna. Can you come to me? I can't leave her here or bring her to you.'

A few seconds pass. 'I'm at work, Holly. Now's really not a good time. Unless you know where Rachel is, then—'

'This *is* to do with Rachel. You need to come and see me now. I'm not leaving Luna in the car.'

He hesitates for a moment. 'Give me five minutes.'

It's nearer to fifteen by the time Damien strides over to her, wearing a blue shirt and smart trousers that contrast with his heavy steel-toed boots and white hard hat.

Holly gets out of the car. 'Mummy will just be a second,'

she tells Luna. 'I'll be right by the car window. You'll be able to see me.'

But when Luna looks like she's about to erupt into tears, Holly pulls out her phone and finds Peppa Pig on YouTube. 'Here, sweetheart. Watch Peppa for a minute.'

That seems to appease her, and Holly gets out of the car.

'I hope this is important,' Damien says. 'You shouldn't be here. It's not safe.'

Holly wastes no time. 'Did Rachel have two phones?'

He frowns. 'No. Why would she?'

'Someone saw her with a different phone. An old one, not a smartphone. Can you think of any reason she'd have it?'

'No, it's ridiculous. Like I said, why would she need another phone? That doesn't make any sense. And who told you this?'

'I can't name sources, Damien. Sorry.' She's about to explain to him that it proves there was something else going on with Rachel. But looking at Damien now, she knows he's not the person to talk to about this. Especially when he thinks Rachel's guilty of child abduction. 'You're right,' she says. 'It doesn't make sense. I have to go.'

He watches as she gets in the car, then leans through the open window. 'The police are searching the lake right now. Then the river next. Such a terrible waste of resources, when she'll be miles away by now.'

Holly rolls up the window and drives away, watching Damien grow smaller in her rear-view mirror.

Luna has fallen asleep by the time they get to her office. It worries Holly that she's sleeping so much. She mentally adds it to the long list of things she needs to speak to the doctor about.

Somehow Luna stays asleep while Holly eases her out of her car seat and into her buggy, reclining it so that Luna's more comfortable. Ross's black Tesla is in the car park, and thankfully there's no sign of Paul's Audi.

Inside, she heads straight for Ross's office, further along the hallway from hers. He's sitting at his desk and looks up from his laptop, smiling, as she approaches. 'Just the person.'

'Oh?'

'Nothing bad.' He closes his laptop. 'I hope Luna's doing okay?'

'No change, really. But we've got an appointment later to see a child psychologist.'

'That's good. I hope it helps. Um, I just wondered what's going on with Rachel's story? It doesn't make sense that you'd give it to Paul.'

Holly pushes the buggy near the far wall and sits at Ross's desk. 'I think it's better if he does it.'

'Hmm. Not sure I can agree with that, but if you say so. You were adamant that you should be the one to write it. Has something happened?'

'I've had time to think since then.' *And be blackmailed.* 'I actually want Paul to do it. It's too much for me.'

Ross scrutinises her. 'I didn't think anything could ever be too much for you. But fine. Your choice. Okay, next thing – I know you've had a lot on your plate, so do you want me to take over the Oscar Hobbs story? It's not a problem. You've got enough to deal with right now. And I really need it in the next couple of days.'

'No,' Holly says. 'I'm doing it. I spoke to Megan, his accuser, although not about him. But I think she grew to trust me in that short time. I'm planning to speak to Oscar's dad to get his take on it. I know he doesn't live with them any more, but it would be good to get his point of view.'

'I don't want you burning out,' Ross says. 'And I'm saying that as a friend, as well as your boss.' He smiles. 'Mostly your friend, though.'

'And I appreciate it. Look, I need to talk to you, but I don't want Paul to know any of this.' She stands and goes to the door, checking there's no one in the corridor before shutting the door, something she wishes she'd done when she was interviewing Damien.

'Go on,' Ross says.

Holly glances at Luna before sitting again. 'When I spoke to Megan Hart, it was about Rachel. I... I told the family I was working on the story. I gave them a different name.' She holds up her hand. 'I know what you're going to say, but I had to. Anyway, she told me that at school once she saw Rachel with another phone. Not her usual iPhone. It was an older phone. Megan called it a burner phone. And when I said Rachel had perhaps lost hers, Megan said that later that same day she had her normal phone again.'

'So she has two phones. Not that unusual.'

'I know. But I've never seen her with a different phone. And neither has her husband or son. Rachel's never mentioned having another one. So seems like it was something she was hiding.'

Ross taps his pen on his desk. 'Why, though?'

'That's just it. I have no idea. I can't think of any reason she'd need one. And if she did, why wouldn't she tell me about it? We've always shared things.' Holly's chest tightens. Because it's not true. There are things she's never shared with Rachel. Forcing this aside, she turns her attention back to Ross. 'I need to find my friend. I don't know what was happening in her life. What would make her disappear. Or if it was even her choice.'

Ross sighs. 'Do the police know about this phone?'

'No. And I'm not telling them. Not until I know for sure it exists. I'm planning to find out if it does.'

'What if she's got it with her?' Ross says.

Holly's considered this. Rachel's normal phone was found by the lake, but if anything Damien says is true, she might have left that on purpose. But Damien is wrong about something. 'What if...' Holly can't believe she's even entertaining this idea, but being here with Ross feels like a safe space. The only one she has. 'What if she did disappear on purpose? If she had no choice?'

Ross frowns. 'You said she'd never leave her son.'

'No. But what if something forced her to. What if she felt it was safer for him than if she stayed.'

'Like what?'

'That's just it. I have no idea.'

'Then we need to find out.'

'We?'

'I'm here for whatever help you need. But just be careful. There are people out there who don't know Rachel and will get a kick out of assuming the worst. It's entertainment for them. We've always said that, haven't we? The trolls have nothing else in their lives but to tear other people down for their own sense of worth.'

'It's bad already. Have you read the stuff they're saying about her?'

He nods. 'A little. But without proof it's all hearsay. Gossip.'

Holly looks at Ross and makes a split-second decision. There has to be at least one person she can trust, someone else who will fight for Rachel. But it's a gamble telling him. She takes a deep breath and tells Ross about Luna's cuddly lamb. How it went missing when Luna did, and Damien found it in their shed.

Ross raises his eyebrows.

'I know it doesn't look good. But I can't just assume the worst. Damien could be lying. I thought Luna had it that night when I put her to bed, but now I can't be sure. And I'm not going to convict my friend when I'm not certain. Luna has so many cuddly toys, and she seems to pick a different favourite every day. It's hard to keep track.'

'Okay,' Ross says. 'Then you need to find another plausible explanation. Did someone put it there? Did she find it and was keeping it to give back to you but forgot? Either of these could be likely.'

And both of which point the finger away from Rachel. 'I need to get proof,' Holly says. *Either way.*

'Remember what I said,' Ross says. 'Whatever you need, I'm here.'

Instinctively, Holly gives him a hug, pulling away when she feels something she's unable to describe pass between them. *It's friendship, that's all.*

Outside in the car park, as she's getting Luna into the car – this time fully awake – Holly glances across the road and sees a man watching her. He's standing by a red car, leaning against it, his arms folded. He's too far away for her to make out any of his features, and his head is covered with the hood of a red sweat-shirt with a large white logo on it.

When he notices she's seen him, he gets in his car, driving off before she can register what's happening.

Uneasiness spreads through her. 'Come on,' she says to Luna. 'Let's get you home.'

On the drive back, Holly wonders if she's being paranoid to think that man was watching her. Now that she's away from him, and Luna is safely in the car, it's easy to tell herself she overreacted.

But that feeling doesn't last; Holly trusts her instinct. And she knows that man was watching her and Luna.

TWENTY-TWO

BEFORE

Rachel

'Death doesn't follow people around,' Jack says. 'Damien's trying to mess with your head.'

They're in Richmond Park, on a bench by the lake, the picnic Jack's brought spread in front of them. Sandwiches, crisps, cupcakes, a platter of fruit and vegetables. He's thought of everything. It's warm for April, more like a summer's day.

Rachel wishes Logan could be here. He'd like Jack, she's sure of it. But introducing them would be like setting off a time bomb.

'What Damien says is true in a way,' she says to Jack. 'There's been a lot of death for me. More than most people. And I'm the common denominator.' She wonders how much she should tell him. Every piece of information she shares only leaves her more vulnerable. *But sometimes we need to take a chance on people.*

'I went to university with Will,' she says. 'He was my first serious boyfriend.' She looks away. 'Actually, he was my only boyfriend. I... I loved him. I think I did. No, I know I did.

Anyway, I didn't realise how much he was struggling with... life, I guess. I went to meet him after a lecture one day and... I had a key to his place.' She feels an unfamiliar twinge; she hasn't let herself think of Will for a long time now. 'He didn't answer so I let myself in. I thought I could just wait for him. He'd had a bad week so I just... I just wanted to cheer him up.' Her breath catches in her lungs, then comes in short bursts. *Is this a panic attack?* 'I found him. He'd... tied a rope around his neck and...'

Jack moves closer, pulls her towards him. 'You don't have to say any more.'

Rachel's grateful for this – she's not sure she has the capacity to relive that moment. 'I felt guilty for years,' she says. 'I still do. If I'd just realised how bad he was feeling... how desperate. But I didn't know.'

Jack lets her cry, her tears staining his T-shirt, and she's grateful for his silence.

'Everyone loses people,' Jack says, after a while. 'It's not your fault. Your husband is trying to make out that it is. He's taunting you. He wants you to suffer. It's disgusting.'

'Let's not talk about him,' Rachel says. 'Anything else but him.'

'Okay.' Jack reaches for the tub of sandwiches, holding it out to her.

She takes a ham and cheese one. 'Don't you want to be with someone?' Rachel asks. 'Someone to share your life with. You're spending so much time with me, how are you ever going to fit in having a love life?'

Jack takes a bite of his sandwich, chewing slowly. Perhaps she's offended him. They've never discussed their personal lives like this. Damien, yes, but only in the context of his abuse. 'I don't have the headspace for any relationship right now,' he says. 'Getting into something would mean explaining what I've done.'

'An awful accident,' she says, the words feeling like sharp knives in her throat.

'But still at my hands. Anyway, it's too messy. I'm not ready for that. I mean, when do I confess? Right at the beginning? Then she'd just run. Or a few months in? Then I'm being deceitful. There's no way to win, is there?'

'The right person will accept it. Full stop. And anyone who doesn't, you don't need in your life.'

'Is there such a thing as a right person?' Jack says. 'We grow up believing we all have a soulmate – just the one of course – but I don't believe that. I think there are many people all over the world we could click with and make a life with. We don't just have one friend, do we? Most of us have several, and we care about all of them.'

His words echo exactly what Rachel believes. Then she thinks about Holly. How, yes, she has other friends, but her friendship with Holly is far stronger than any other she's known. *And now it's destroyed by my senseless act.* 'I used to think that,' she says. 'Now I'm not sure any more. I'm not sure of anything. Maybe we just have to believe what works for us and gets us through life.'

'Good point,' Jack says, picking up another sandwich.

They eat in silence, as the sun bathes their skin in warmth, and birds trill in the trees above them. Rachel is calm here. Safe. A feeling she never has at home, even when Damien isn't there. 'I wish we could stay here forever,' she says. 'With Logan too, of course.'

Jack studies her. 'I know we can't, but you can still change your life. Walk away. You and Logan. You can be free of him.'

Rachel sighs, picking up an apple. 'This is the problem. People think it's all too easy to walk away from people who are... like Damien. *Just leave. He hurts you. Walk away.* And they assume we're not strong. That we let people walk all over us. We're passive. We let people control us.' She shakes her head. 'I'm none of those things. And I'm not the only woman in this situation who *is* strong.'

'I don't make those assumptions. Sorry if it sounded like I was. I just wish—'

'Have you stopped to think for just one second that I know what I'm doing? That there might be a reason I haven't left?'

'Tell me. Help me understand.'

'I can't. It's just something I have to deal with. But I know what I'm doing, don't ever think that I don't. And I'm putting my son first, above anything else.'

'So you're staying with Damien for Logan's sake? I understand that. So he has his mother and father around?'

She could tell Jack the truth now, lay it all bare. Maybe he'd even understand. But she can't. It needs to stay in her head for now. Until the time is right. 'Something like that,' she says.

Her phone pings, but she leaves it in her bag. She doesn't want a reminder that a world exists outside this park. Then she realises it might be Logan, so she digs her phone out of her bag.

'Everything okay?' Jack asks.

'It's my friend. The one with the little girl Evie's age.' Rachel stares at Holly's words. 'She's asking if I'll babysit Luna tonight. Her husband's away.'

'Oh,' Jack says. 'Isn't that a bit... I don't know. Insensitive?'

Rachel smiles. 'No, not at all. I've done it before.' And right now, it's just what she needs. Being with Luna, just the two of them.

Jack nods. 'Okay, well, I know you can handle it, then.'

Rachel laughs. 'Well, if I can handle this... you... whatever we're doing, then everything else is a walk in the park, right?'

Jack smiles. She likes it when he does, when his face brightens and just for a second his pain takes a back seat. Until the spark dies. It wasn't his fault. It could have been anyone.

They finish eating, and Jack suggests a walk.

She checks the time on her phone. Nearly half past two. 'I

need to get back,' Rachel says. 'Now that I'm babysitting this evening. I need to make sure Logan's sorted with dinner before I go.'

'I hope it helps,' Jack says. 'Even in some small way.'

'Oh, it will.' Rachel knows this for a fact. Being around Luna helps her more than anyone could know, or understand. If she told anyone else, they'd say it's not healthy, and that Rachel is fixating on her friend's daughter in an attempt to replace Evie. But they're wrong, so she keeps her mouth shut.

They pack away and head towards the car park. 'Can I give you a lift home?' she asks.

'Thanks, but I'm fine getting the train. I've got my laptop so I can do some work.'

'I know why I'm doing this, but what about you?' she asks, when they get to her car. 'Why do you keep wanting to meet up?'

'I've thought about this a lot,' he replies. 'And maybe to start with I wanted some kind of forgiveness. I needed to try and make it up to you in some way. Not that anything could ever make up for what happened, or replace Evie. I still want those things, but once we started meeting up... things changed. Or evolved. I don't know. I feel like we're... friends or something like that.'

Rachel nods. 'I get it. It does feel like that.' She gets into her car, shutting the door and winding down the window. 'But, Jack. You shouldn't prioritise me. You're still young, you should be out there, giving yourself the chance to meet someone. If you spend all this time with me, then... I just worry about you.'

'I'm glad you do, but you really don't have to. What was it you said earlier? You know what you're doing? Well, same here.'

She gets stuck in roadworks on the way back, and Logan's already home when she gets in, sitting at the table with his school books spread in front of him. She's proud of his work ethic, but it also saddens her to see him spending his Saturday afternoon this way, instead of with his friends. It worries her that he's cutting himself off from people.

She gives him a hug on her way to get a glass of water, pleased that it evokes a rare smile. 'How's it going?' she asks.

He shrugs. 'Okay.' He stops writing and looks up. 'Dad was looking for you.'

'Oh, is he home?' His car wasn't in the drive, so she's sure he can't be. It certainly doesn't *feel* like he's here.

'He went to work. But he said we could go to the cinema tonight. Will you come?'

She's sure Damien would have something to say about that. 'Um, actually I'm babysitting Luna tonight. Elijah's away and it's Holly's brother's fortieth birthday. It will go on too late for her to take Luna.'

Logan stares at her. 'Are you sure it's a good idea?'

He's been talking to Damien about her. But she doesn't want to put pressure on him by asking what his dad's been saying. 'I've done it before, remember? And I was fine.' Until she'd made that frightful mistake.

'But isn't it hard being around Luna?' Logan asks.

He has a mature head on his shoulders. Rachel takes her glass of water to the table and sits down next to him. She takes his arm, hoping it will reassure him. 'Did Dad tell you that I'm not okay?'

Logan looks away, running his hands over the page in his exercise book, over writing that's even neater than her own.

'Logan,' she urges. 'You can tell me anything. I hope you know that.'

'Can I?' he says quietly. 'I just don't want to upset you.'

Her breath catches in her throat. 'Listen to me – you never have to worry about my feelings. Okay? That's not your job. It's the other way around. Please remember that.'

Logan shrugs. 'Okay. I'll try.'

'I won't lie to you – I've found it really hard. Like I've been ripped to pieces. Shredded. It's hard to get a sense of who I am any more. Anyway, I just want to make sure *you're* okay.'

'I'm fine.'

'I've noticed you haven't been seeing your friends much. You used to always see them on Saturdays.'

'I don't play football any more. So...'

'But you could meet up after that? Please don't cut yourself off from people. It's important to—'

'I know, Mum. I haven't. I've got plenty of friends. I just feel like going to the cinema with Dad today. That's all. And I've got a load of homework to do before he gets home.'

Rachel senses he's getting anxious. She places a hand on his shoulder, then leaves him to get on with his homework.

At the door, she turns back, watching him. She wishes she could tell Logan that soon they'll both be okay.

'Are you sure you don't mind doing this?' Holly asks, as she puts in her earrings. They're beautiful. Small, eye-catching diamonds that glisten every time she moves her head. Probably a present from Elijah at some point along the journey of their marriage. Rachel's never seen them before.

'I wouldn't be here if it was any problem,' she tells Holly. 'Besides, I've done it before, haven't I? And I was fine.' She glances at Luna, who's sitting on the floor with her Duplo bricks, building towers then giggling as she knocks them down.

'I know you'll be okay,' Holly says, touching Rachel's arm. 'You amaze me. I don't know how I would have coped. But you... your strength.'

Rachel needs her to stop; she can't bear Holly's kind comments, not after what she's done to her friend. She feels like a fraud. 'Holly, there's something—'

Luna screams, and they turn to find her at the door, holding out her hand. 'Mama!' she cries. 'Hand catched.'

Rachel and Holly both rush to her. 'You get going,' Rachel says to Holly. 'I'll get this little one fixed up.' She checks Luna's hand. 'No blood. All good.'

'Want plaster,' Luna says.

Rachel's about to tell her she really doesn't need one, that they're only for stopping blood, but then she remembers Evie and how any time she got hurt she'd demand a plaster to make it feel better. 'No problem. One plaster coming up.'

Holly smiles. 'Cupboard above the dishwasher. That's if there are any left. Sorry to run, but I'll be late if I don't get going.'

'Enjoy yourself. No need to rush back. We'll be fine, won't we Luna?' She tickles Luna's cheek.

'Ray-Ray,' Luna says, smiling.

They watch Holly leave, waving to her from the door. As soon as her car disappears, Rachel feels that ever-present weight lift from her shoulders. She's got at least an hour before Luna needs to be in bed. Just the two of them. For the next sixty minutes, she can be the mother of a little girl again. She's not deluding herself – she knows Luna isn't Evie, isn't hers. But it's the next best thing.

Once Luna's in bed, Rachel makes herself a coffee and sits on the sofa, opening the poetry book she needs to teach her GCSE class next term.

She's on chapter two when she hears a key in the door. Disappointed that she won't get to spend more time in the house with Luna, she puts her books down and calls out to Holly. 'That was quick. Everything okay?'

But the figure who appears in the living room doorway isn't Holly. It's Elijah.

Rachel's face flushes. She hasn't set eyes on him since that night. Her head scrambles to work out what he's doing here.

Had she misheard? Did Holly say he was coming back later tonight? She's certain she wouldn't have misunderstood that. 'I thought you were away,' she says.

Elijah joins her on the sofa. 'Yep, I was. But when Holly said you were babysitting, I thought I'd leave early. All my meetings were finished anyway. No point hanging around until morning when I could easily catch a train tonight.' He smiles, as if this is a good thing, not a nightmare for Rachel.

She grabs her book and stands. 'Well, I'll get going, then.'

Elijah reaches for her arm. 'No, don't. Please stay. We need to talk.' He lets go of her. 'You haven't replied to any of my messages.'

'There's nothing to say.'

'We *slept* together, Rachel. There's plenty to say.'

An icy chill runs through her, similar to the one she gets when she's around Damien. By ignoring Elijah all these weeks, she'd been able to push aside what they did, even though she knows she has to address it.

Rachel goes to the door, listening out for Luna before she closes it. 'What we did makes me sick,' Rachel says. 'Every time I think about it. Holly's my friend. And you... it should never have happened. I despise myself for letting it.'

Elijah stares at her, and she tries to read his face. Shock? Hurt? Anger? Contempt? Perhaps it's a mixture of all of those things. 'That's harsh,' he says. 'You weren't complaining at the time.'

In that moment, Rachel sees even more clearly what she needs to do. 'We need to tell Holly. I can't keep lying to her. I won't.'

Elijah shakes his head. 'No. No way.' He pauses. 'She'll leave me. She'll take Luna.'

'Maybe it's what you deserve,' Rachel says. 'Me too. We have to face the consequences of what we've done.' Her heart sinks at the thought that this will give Damien another reason to ramp up the abuse, but she's willing to take the risk to put things right.

Elijah grabs her arm. 'You're not thinking straight. It's grief talking.'

'I've never seen things more clearly. We have to tell Holly. We both owe it to her.'

'This is crazy,' he says, shaking his head. 'I'm not destroying my family over this. And what about Damien?'

'It's wrong to keep lying to them. What you need to do, Elijah, is think about why you did it. Whatever problems you've got, they're not going to go away just because you pretend they don't exist.'

He stares at her. 'You're talking about Ross, aren't you? Has Holly said something?'

Rachel sighs. 'No, and it's not my business. It's for the two of you to sort out. All I know is that I won't keep lying to her. And please stop contacting me. It was a mistake. I don't know why you did it. I think we're both messed up. At least I can admit it.'

She opens the living room door, tempted to ask him if she can pop up to check on Luna before she goes. But it's best if she gets out of here.

'I'm not doing it,' Elijah calls. 'And I won't let you either. Do you hear me? I won't let you destroy my life. Not now, not ever.'

TWENTY-THREE

NOW

Holly

They've only been home a few minutes when the doorbell rings. Holly's not ready to face any visitors – she still feels deflated after Luna's therapy appointment this afternoon. As she'd half expected, they hadn't made any progress, and Luna had clung to Holly, refusing to leave her lap. Even the vast array of toys scattered around couldn't tempt her.

'We'll try again next week,' the psychologist had said. 'Try not to be too disheartened.'

Elijah looks out of the window. 'It's your mum! I didn't know she was coming.'

'Neither did I,' Holly says, rushing to the door. 'Mum. It's lovely to see you.'

Her mother throws her arms around Holly. 'Oh, my darling, you should have told me what was going on. I just can't believe it. I had to hear about it from friends as soon as I switched my phone on when I landed.' She comes inside, wheeling a large suitcase behind her. 'There's my little girl,' she says, as Elijah appears, carrying Luna.

'Hi, Liz,' he says, giving her a hug. 'This is a nice surprise.'

Liz holds out her arms and takes Luna, who Holly's pleased to see smiles at her grandmother. 'And you, my darling, are a brave little girl.' She turns back to Holly. 'I'm sorry you couldn't reach me. Just bad timing.'

'Yep. That's what happens when you go off-grid.' After retiring as a therapist, her mum runs meditation retreats all over the world, where technology is left behind and people have a chance to escape their anxieties and get in touch with nature. Spirituality. Whatever they're searching for. Holly gets it, but has never felt comfortable with the total loss of contact. Life might pause for the people who book onto a retreat with her mum, but emergencies still happen.

'I feel terrible,' Liz says. 'But I'm here now.' She hugs Luna more tightly.

'There's more,' Elijah says, and despite Holly shaking her head, he fills her mother in on every detail of Rachel's disappearance.

Liz lowers her voice. 'Do you think she took Luna, then? It would make sense if Luna was talking about her.'

Luna and Ray-Ray

Holly glances at Elijah, who averts his eyes. 'There's no evidence of that at all. It's just speculation. Rachel's a good person. What Luna said could have meant anything. They spend a lot of time together.' Although hadn't Holly been deliberately curtailing it? Allowing Elijah to persuade her that it wasn't healthy for Rachel to be so *clingy*.

Liz nods. 'People are always good people, until they do something to show they're not.' She beams at Luna, stroking her cheek. 'Anyway, I'll stay for a couple of days, just to help out.'

Holly's about to tell her there's no need, but the way Luna's responding to her mother convinces her to hold back. The smile that reaches further across Luna's face has been absent since her abduction. Maybe her mum can encourage Luna to talk about what happened to her. 'Okay,' Holly says. 'Thanks. Just a couple of days, then. I'm sure you've got somewhere you have to fly off to.'

'Morocco in four days. I do love it there. But if you need me, I'll cancel.'

'No,' Holly says. 'We'll be fine.'

Elijah stands. 'Might get some jobs done in the garden while Liz is here, then. Can't put them off forever.'

'Of course.' Liz smiles. 'I can entertain Luna.' She turns to Holly. 'And if there's anything you need to do, please go ahead. Make full use of me. That's what I'm here for. I know it doesn't make up for me not being here those days Luna was missing. I shudder to think how that must have felt.'

'Like absolute hell,' Holly says. 'Actually, there is something I need to do if you're sure you don't mind watching Luna?'

'It will be my pleasure.' Liz places Luna down, but Luna clings to her leg.

Holly waits for Elijah to leave the room before whispering to her mum. 'Please don't take her out anywhere. And don't answer the door. Don't take your eyes off her.'

'Okay. But—'

'Mum, please just humour me.'

'Of course,' she says. 'Whatever you want. I understand why you're feeling like this, Holly, but you can't keep Luna a prisoner. She needs fresh air. Normality. We could go to the park. I wouldn't let her out of my—'

'No. Definitely not the park. That's where she was found. We're not ready to take her back there.'

'Okay. The garden it is. We'll make the most of it, won't we, darling?'

'Thanks, Mum.' Holly knows her mum is right, and she doesn't want to deny her daughter the experiences she should be having at her age.

But she also knows a man was following them today.

. . .

Guilt clasps tightly around Holly's chest as she presses
Damien's doorbell, hoping to catch Logan at home. Rachel had
told her how much of a hermit he'd become since Luna died,
and how she'd hoped it was a phase with an end date, so there's
every chance he's here.

He opens the door, confirming her suspicion, and frowns.
'Dad's not back yet. Didn't you find him?'

'I did. But I was just wondering if I could ask you something? Can I come in for a second?'

Logan shrugs. 'I guess. Is this about Mum?'

'Yeah,' Holly says, stepping inside. 'That's exactly what it's
about.'

He glances past her. 'Where's Luna?'

'Oh, she's at home with my mum. Listen, Logan, I could
really do with your help. You know I'm doing everything I can
to find your mum?'

He nods. 'Yeah. But Dad thinks she doesn't want to be
found. He says she wanted to leave, and when people don't
want to be found they do everything to hide their tracks.'

She gestures to the kitchen. 'Let's sit for a minute.'

Logan's schoolwork is spread across the table and it hits her
that Rachel would be sad that he's spending his Saturday afternoon this way. 'You really care about your studies, don't you?'

He nods, briefly looking at his books. 'I want to do well. It's
important to me.'

'That's great. So many kids your age aren't interested. They
can't see what it will do for them in the future. It's hard to think
about all that when you're so young, I suppose.'

'That's all *I* think about. Mum's always saying how I need
to secure my future by doing the right things now.' He pauses. 'I
kind of don't know any other way to be.'

'Your mum's right. I hope Luna learns this too.'

'People are saying all kinds of stuff. Like we don't know what jobs there'll be in a few years, so how can we know what we're learning is relevant. But that's stupid. All knowledge is power, isn't it?'

He's a smart boy. And after everything he's been through, he still cares about his future. This only makes Holly more determined than ever to find her friend. To get Rachel back to her son, whatever it takes. And to get questions answered for herself. But to do that, she needs to be honest with him.

'Logan, I think your mum might have been in some trouble. I think she was trying to tell me something before she went missing. And if I can just piece together what was happening, it might help us find her.'

He stares at Holly. 'What... what can I do?'

'We need to find this other phone she was seen with. If she hasn't got it with her, then there's every chance it might have something on it. The police have already searched here, but I wonder if she had it at school. That's where she was seen with it. And you or your dad never saw her use it at home, so unless she had it with her, it could still be there.'

He nods.

'I know this is a big ask, and I don't know if it's possible, but I need to get into your school. Today. I know it's the weekend, but do you know if it's open? Is there any way I'd be able to get in? I imagine it's changed a lot since I went there.'

Logan frowns. 'They have tennis and basketball clubs on until six. So it's got to be open until at least then.'

Holly checks her phone. Two forty-six. 'I need to go now, then. Will you come with me? Just in case anyone wonders what I'm doing?' She knows she should check this with Damien first, but she can't trust him. There's no way that man cares about finding his wife – not when he's already made up his mind about what Rachel's done.

'Yeah, I'll come. I can show you Mum's classroom. Maybe

it's in there? And all the teachers have lockers in the staffroom. We could try that too.'

'Great. But your mum's keys weren't found so we won't be able to open anything. Do you think she locks her desk?'

Logan considers this for a moment. 'Yeah, most of the teachers do.' He pauses. 'Mum's so careful and organised – she has spare keys somewhere in the house. I've seen her check them before. They're on a keyring with suitcase keys and other ones.'

'But where could it be?'

He stands. 'Come on, I'll show you.'

Upstairs, Holly stays in the doorway of Rachel and Damien's bedroom while Logan goes inside. 'I'll wait here,' she says.

Logan gives a small nod, then goes straight to the wardrobe, rifling through the pockets of Rachel's clothes. 'Mum told me once that to keep things safe you have to put them in a place you'll always remember and keep them there.' He pulls something out of the pocket of a coral-coloured blazer Holly can't recall ever seeing Rachel wear. Come to think of it, since Evie died Rachel only ever dresses in dark clothing. Hardly surprising. 'Here,' he says, holding out a bunch of small keys.

'But how did you work out they'd be there just from Rachel saying that?'

He smiles. 'I didn't. She told me she kept them here. I just couldn't remember which pocket they were in.' Logan hands her the keys. 'I reckon if there's a spare one for her school locker and desk, they'll be on there.'

Holly stares at the keys. There must be at least fifteen. 'Worth a try. Let's go.'

Walking up the steps to the main entrance of Woodbridge School, Holly's glad Logan agreed to come with her, despite it being ethically questionable. *I'm doing what I must to find Rachel. That's all that matters.* There's no one at the reception desk so they turn right along a corridor and head through glass doors at the other end. 'The English block is out here,' Logan explains. Holly's conscious that she's walking the same corridors that Rachel takes every day, and it fills her with hope. How many times has her friend passed through here in the years she's taught here? Optimistic that there have to be some answers somewhere in this place, Holly urges Logan to walk faster.

They head out into a courtyard, walking across it to a separate new building. It definitely wasn't there when Holly was a student here.

'This is it,' Logan says. 'Not sure if it will be open, but I know some teachers come in at weekends to do marking and stuff. Mum does sometimes when she needs to get away.'

'Away from what?'

'Just the house, I guess. Maybe the memories of Evie.'

Or was there something else chasing Rachel from her own home?

Holly holds her breath as she tries the door. It opens. 'We're in,' she says. It's a small building with a narrow corridor and three rooms on each side 'Maybe the classroom doors will be locked.'

'They don't bother as they lock the outside one,' Logan says. 'I've never seen a teacher lock a door.'

This school doesn't seem tough on security, but that only serves Holly's purpose. She has no idea what they'll do if they can't get into Rachel's classroom. 'Right, which one is your mum's?'

'At the end on the left.'

Holding her breath, Holly turns the handle. To her relief, it opens and she steps inside Rachel's room, looking around. It feels like Rachel in here. It's bright, with displays adorning every wall. Everything neat and organised. 'I've never seen your mum at work,' she says. 'I bet she's an awesome teacher.'

Logan shrugs. 'She works hard. The other kids don't see that – but I do.' He looks away and stares out of the window at the huge sports field beyond the courtyard.

'Let's try these keys, then.'

It's a long process, and Holly begins to lose hope. But the second to last key slots in and turns, and Holly pulls open the drawer, sure her luck's about to run out. Logan hovers beside her as she rummages inside. It's crammed full of papers and stationery, not a state she can imagine Rachel keeping anything in.

She feels it before she sees it, and knows what it is before she pulls it out. Holly was so sure she wouldn't find anything that it takes her a moment to register what's in her hand. In a way, she'd been hoping Megan had been lying. Whatever's on here could change everything.

Beside her, Logan stares at the phone. 'Maybe it's just one she confiscated from a student?' he says.

'Do you know anyone who would have an old Nokia like this? I didn't even know they made these any more.'

'I don't think that's an old phone,' Logan says. 'They make them for kids so parents don't have to worry about them being online.'

'So it *could* belong to a student, then.' But Megan had seen Rachel using it. Talking to someone. Holly switches the phone on but it asks for a four-digit passcode. Her luck had to run out eventually. 'Any idea what your mum's passcode might be?' she asks.

Logan shrugs. 'Evie's birthday? Or mine?'

Holly's trying the first combination of digits when the door opens.

'What do you think you're doing in here?'

TWENTY-FOUR

BEFORE

Rachel

When he started at Woodbridge School, Rachel promised Logan that she'd never check up on him, and that she wouldn't single him out if she happened to see him. He could come to her, of course, if he needed anything, otherwise she'd assured him she'd keep her distance. Logan always smiles at her whenever they pass in the corridor, though.

And now, as she watches him head towards the PE block, he's like a spectre roaming the corridors. Pale. Almost as lifeless as his sister. She wishes she knew how to help him. Do other parents feel like this as their kids get older? As if they're standing by, helpless, watching their children drift further away.

'Miss?'

She spins around and sees Oscar Hobbs waving a sheet of paper in front of her.

'My homework,' he says. 'Sorry I forgot it this morning, but I ran home at lunchtime and got it. So it wasn't late. Technically, it's not the end of the day yet.'

'You're right. Thanks, Oscar,' she says, taking his sheet.

'I would have remembered it this morning for the lesson, but I've been a bit... There's been stuff going on.'

Rachel knows what he's referring to. There can't be a single person in the school who doesn't know what happened: that Oscar was accused of rape by another student. Megan Hart. And then just as suddenly, Megan withdrew her accusation.

'It's fine,' Rachel assures him. 'I've got it now, so nothing to worry about.'

He nods and turns to walk off. 'I didn't do it,' he says, changing his mind and walking back to her. 'People are saying I made her take it all back, but how could I? I don't have that kind of power.'

'Oscar, it really is none of my business, and you don't have to explain anything to me, or any of your teachers.'

He nods. 'Yep, I know. But I hate the way people look at me now. It's like—' Oscar pauses while a group of Year 7s shuffle past. A couple of them turn back to stare at him before scurrying off. This is what life must be like for him now. Rachel knows how that feels – all eyes are on her whenever she leaves her classroom. Pitying looks from adults she can just about cope with, but from children it's too much to bear.

'You'll get used to it,' Rachel says. 'I promise. Before long, something else will catch people's attention and it will all be forgotten. Believe me, I know.'

'I'm sorry about your little girl,' Oscar says. 'I saw you out with her once. And Logan. You all looked... happy. It's kind of weird seeing a teacher out of school.'

'Yes, I think half the time you all think we only exist in this building. How could we possibly be human, with lives outside these walls?'

'Is that from some book or something, Miss?'

Rachel taps her temple. 'It's from here. Anyway, you'd better get going – the second bell's about to go.'

Oscar smiles and heads off, but stops again and turns around. 'You might want to know that Logan's always on his own at break and lunch.' He shrugs. 'Don't know if that's important, but, well, no one should be on their own, should they?'

'Thanks for telling me, Oscar. I appreciate that.' She'd suspected this was the case, but hearing it from Oscar – who barely knows Logan – crushes her. Her breath quickens – the beginnings of a panic attack – and she doesn't know if she'll be able to dampen it down this time. She's learnt how to hide it from her students, how to soldier on, while inside she feels like she's suffocating, her silent anguish undetected. She'll reach breaking point because of this, surely. If she hasn't already.

She's grateful that she has a free period now, so she hurries to her classroom and shuts the door, leaning back against it while she tries to steady her breathing. She couldn't save Evie, but there's still a chance to save Logan, though she feels like she's running out of time. And it all starts with putting things right with Holly, then she can take care of everything else she needs to do.

Pulling out her phone, she messages Elijah.

Tell Holly what happened, or I will. Get your head together and do it.

Somehow, it helps to know there's a deadline. She's setting things in motion, starting with this. She needs to get things straight, because she won't live like this any more.

She'll lose her friend for sure – the closest one she's had in her adult life – but that's the price she has to pay. She did wrong, she's ready to face it. Even if it means Holly will no longer be in her life.

And no more Luna.

The thought of never seeing Luna again is unbearable.

.   .   .

Rachel's late home. Marking her Year 10 essays had taken longer than she'd anticipated so it's way past dinnertime. It will have to be something quick. No doubt Logan hasn't even noticed the time. It's Friday evening, just about the only time he lets himself relax and switch off from schoolwork. Rachel assumes he'll be on his Xbox.

She's surprised to see Damien's BMW in the drive. Even on a Friday, seven o'clock is early for him. Bracing herself, she parks her Peugeot next to him and prepares to face whatever mood he's in.

Damien's in the kitchen, dishing up what looks like a curry. She can't see any takeaway cartons, but she's sure he wouldn't have made it himself.

'You're home late,' he says, glancing at her before turning back to the food.

'Had marking to do. It was easier to just do it at school.' She's not sure why she's explaining herself to him – he's probably not even listening. She watches him, noticing he's only got out one plate. 'Where's Logan?'

'My parents wanted to surprise him and take him back to York with them for a visit. They've been in London.'

Rachel stiffens. He's done this on purpose. 'But he's got school on Monday.'

'They'll bring him back on Sunday. What are you stressing about?'

'It's a long way to drive just to have one whole day with him.' Rachel doesn't like being taken by surprise, especially by Damien. And especially when it concerns her son.

'You see, this is exactly why I didn't tell you. I knew you'd get like this. I was trying to save you the... whatever it is. Anxiety?' He smiles. 'Which reminds me – I found these in the bathroom bin.' Reaching into his pocket, he pulls out a neatly folded tissue and places it on the table. Then he opens it, and Rachel's staring at this week's pills she's thrown away.

'Care to explain?' Damien asks. Affable. Concerned. Wearing that mask again to try to confuse her.

'I don't need them,' she says. 'I feel fine.' It's a risk – Damien believing she's taking them has kept him off her back. He's stepped back a little, which has allowed her to breathe. And to stay under his radar with what she's doing. Now, though, he will be alert, watching her every move. And then how can she hope to gather the evidence she needs?

'I can't trust you, can I?' he says, still smiling. If anyone walked in now, all they'd see is a loving husband. 'What am I supposed to do? You're a teacher, Rachel. You really should be more responsible. More importantly, your Logan's mother. How can I believe—?'

'Stop!' she shouts. 'Just stop. I'm not listening to this... this—'

He grabs her neck, squeezing hard. 'Really? Not listening to me? How about now?' His grip tightens. Is this how she's going to die? Perhaps she's always known it. But then she thinks of Logan, and knows she has to fight for his sake, as well as her own. She kicks out with all her strength, kneeing him in the groin. Letting go, he falls backwards against the sink. 'You bitch!'

More venomous words fly from Damien's mouth, but she doesn't stay around long enough to take them in.

It would be Holly she would go to if things had been different, if Rachel hadn't messed up. Instead, she finds herself knocking on the door of the only other person she can trust.

'He's hurt you again, hasn't he?' Jack pulls her inside, quickly closing the door. 'Jesus, Rachel. Why can't you leave him? What hold has he got over you?'

She doesn't answer.

'Come on,' he says. 'I think you could do with a drink.'

'No,' she says. Never again will she touch alcohol. Not when it will only conjure up images of Elijah, and force her to relive that night all over again. Every sordid detail.

'At least have some water, then.'

It's funny how people think offering a drink will help in a crisis. 'I'm fine,' Rachel says. 'I just need to get my head straight.'

She's been to Jack's house a few times now and always feels comfortable here. It's minimal and uncluttered. Clean. Organised. And it's also too big for him to live in on his own.

'He tried to strangle you. I can see the bruise around your neck,' Jack says.

Instinctively she covers it with her hand. When she studied it in her car mirror, it was mulberry coloured, almost black.

'Okay, if you don't want to talk about it, that's fine,' Jack says. 'But if you do, then I'm listening.' He sighs. 'Come on, let's sit down.'

On the sofa, they sit in silence for a few minutes, lost in their own thoughts. Rachel wonders what she'd find if she could read his mind. She trusts him, as much as anyone can trust another person, and if she doesn't open up to him, then there's no way he'll ever understand. And she's got to share this, or it will eat away at her until... what? She has no idea, but knows it won't be good.

'You asked me what hold Damien has over me,' Rachel says, breaking the silence. 'Because why else would I stay with a man who emotionally and now physically abuses me. A man who was jealous of the attention his own baby gave me. A man who only knows how to control people.'

Jack nods. 'So what is it? Because whatever it is – you don't have to go through all this. Whatever you did, we can work it out. Find a way to get him off your back.'

Rachel lets Jack's words hover over her, and wrap themselves around her like a warm fleece blanket.

It takes her a moment to speak, because once she does there'll be no going back. Jack will be dragged into her life again, and it won't be good for him.

'It's not me who's done something,' she begins. 'It's Damien.' Her voice is quiet. Softer. Yet she knows her words hold power.

'What's he done?'

'He... he tried to kill someone.'

TWENTY-FIVE

NOW

Holly

Holly shoves Rachel's phone in her pocket and stares at the tall, wiry man standing in the doorway. He's dressed in a smart blue shirt and dark grey trousers, and she assumes he's a member of staff so she'll need to tread carefully.

'This is my aunt,' Logan says, before Holly can come up with an excuse. 'I left a book at school and I need it for homework. She drove me here to get it. I was just showing her my mum's classroom.'

'I see.' Stepping into the room, the man scrutinises Holly. 'I'm Mr Proctor, the head.'

'Nice to meet you,' Holly says, her words feeling excruciatingly out of context.

'I'm sorry about Rachel,' he says. 'We're all praying she comes home safely.' He offers a small nod. 'Is she your sister?'

'Sister-in-law.'

'Did you find your book?' Mr Proctor asks, glancing between them both.

'Afraid not,' Logan says. His cheeks have reddened and

Holly's sure the head teacher doesn't believe them. 'Maybe I left it somewhere else?'

'Only authorised people are allowed on school premises,' he says, gesturing to the door. 'I'm afraid you'll have to leave.'

'Not a problem,' Holly says, already making her way to the door with Logan following. She feels Mr Proctor's eyes on them and only hopes he doesn't email Damien about this.

They don't speak until they're in the car and Holly's pulling away. 'Well, that was...'

'Yeah, he's pretty scary,' Logan says.

'Still, we got what we needed.' Holly pats her pocket to make sure the phone is still there. 'I was just thinking... might be best if we don't mention this phone to anyone – even your dad – until I know what's on here. Is that okay?'

With some hesitation, Logan nods. 'But what if you can't work out the password?'

'I'll take it to a phone shop. Tell them I've locked myself out. That might work. Anyway, let me worry about all that. Let's get you home.'

'Will you let me know what you find on it?' Logan asks when they turn into his road.

'I promise.' As soon as she's said this, Holly realises that the contents of Rachel's phone might not be something Logan should know about. Still, she'll make that call when she knows what she's dealing with.

She waits until Logan is safely inside with the door closed, then pulls out Rachel's phone. She tries Evie's birthday, then Logan's. Neither of them work. Frustrated, she tries Rachel's birthday, but the screen remains locked.

Reaching for her own phone, she calls Ross. 'Hi. Are you at the office?'

'Nope. Believe it or not, I do go home occasionally.' He laughs. 'What's up?'

'Can I see you?'

'Yeah, course. I'm at home.'

'Alone?'

'No, the dog's here, but I'm sure he won't interfere in our conversation.' He chuckles. 'Is everything okay?'

'I'll be there in ten minutes.'

With everything that happened at the school, and knowing Luna is safe at home with her mum, Holly hasn't given much thought to the man who was watching them earlier. But now, as she glances in her rear-view mirror, she wonders if she's being followed. But the car behind her turns left, and there's no sign that anyone is tailing her.

Parking outside Ross's large townhouse, which overlooks a huge green on one side, Holly turns her attention back to the phone. There are answers on there, she knows it. Stuffing it in her pocket, she grabs her bag and locks the car.

Before she's even reached the door, Ross flings it open. 'You really know how to worry people,' he says. 'Are you okay?'

'Sorry. I'm fine.' Holly offers an apologetic shrug. 'I just wanted to ask you something.' She could have done this on the phone, but she didn't want to give him a chance to talk her out of it.

'Sounds intriguing,' Ross says. 'But why do I get the feeling I won't like this?' He stands aside and Holly steps inside.

She likes Ross's home – he bought it after his divorce and it's more than enough space for him and his son whenever Harry is staying. Set out on three floors, there's a huge open-plan kitchen-diner downstairs and it's tastefully decorated. Although the walls are a neutral mink shade, there are splashes of orange and yellow in the décor, making it feel bright and fresh.

In the living room, they sit on the large corner sofa and Holly pulls out the phone.

'Is that what I think it is?'

'Yep.'

'You actually found it. I only saw you a few hours ago. How did you—?'

'I'm very resourceful – you know that.'

Ross smiles. 'That you are.'

Holly tells him about going with Logan to Woodbridge School and finding the phone locked in Rachel's desk drawer, leaving out the part about the head teacher finding them.

'The only trouble is,' she says, 'I can't get into it. It's password protected.'

Ross frowns. 'Have you tried putting anything in? Her daughter or son's birthdays? Wedding anniversary?'

'Tried everything I can think of.' Holly had even entered Luna's birthday, just in case.

'You know what I'm about to say, don't you?'

'I'm not taking it to the police yet. I need to know what's on there first.'

Ross sighs. 'I do get that, but this isn't exactly legal, Holly. That phone is evidence in a missing person's case.'

'I know, but there are already enough rumours and lies about Rachel plastered all over the internet. I owe it to her to protect her privacy. There could be something on there she wouldn't want other people to see. Why else would she have a secret phone?'

Ross folds his hands together, resting his chin on them as he leans forward. 'Okay. But how are you going to get into it?'

'I'm taking it to a phone shop. I'll tell them I've forgotten my password.'

'You can't just go into a—'

'Yes, I can. Remember you told me about that time you couldn't get into yours? There was that place that didn't even verify it was yours?'

Ross frowns. 'That was years ago.'

'I need to know where it is.'

'It was in West Byfleet. Mobile Masters or something. I don't live there any more so I don't even know if it's—'

Holly throws her arms around him. 'Thank you.'

Ross's cheeks flush. 'I haven't even done anything. Look, I can see that nothing will change your mind, but just promise me one thing. If there's anything on that phone that might suggest... anything criminal – and I'm not saying there will be – then you take it straight to the police.'

'You have my word,' Holly says.

'And you need to prepare yourself. Because the only reason someone might have a hidden phone is if they're doing something they don't want anyone to know about.'

Holly's thought about this, and she doubts she'll ever be prepared for what she might find. She thought she knew her friend, but with every passing minute she's realising there was too much Rachel kept hidden. 'I've let her down,' Holly says, reminding herself why she's doing this. 'And I need to make it up to her.'

'I'm not trying to sugar-coat things – you know I hate all that – but of course you haven't. You were her friend.'

'She was trying to tell me something before she disappeared. And if I'd listened to her, then she might still be here now. She must have felt so desperate to leave Logan behind.'

Ross takes her hand. 'I hate to say this, but have you thought of the other possibility?'

Holly shakes her head. 'Of course I have, but I can't let myself go there. Not yet. Not until the police find...'

Ross hugs her, and for just a moment she lets herself get lost in him.

'Will you let me know as soon as you get into it?' he asks, pulling away. 'I want to support you – whatever happens.'

'Will do.'

'And also... just be careful.'

· · ·

At home, Holly finds her mum and Luna cuddled on the sofa reading *The Gruffalo*. Although she can't quite work out if Luna's actually listening, she seems happy enough, secure in the arms of her grandmother.

'I thought you'd be back ages ago,' Liz says when she reaches the end of the book.

'Sorry, I had to do some things in town.' She'd gone to the mobile phone shop after leaving Ross's and had somehow convinced the man behind the counter to unlock the phone for her. But he'd had a lot of phones to deal with before he could get to Rachel's. 'No point hanging around here,' he'd told her. 'May as well go home and I'll call when it's ready to collect.'

Holly had tried to get him to commit to at least a day, if not a time, and he'd shrugged and said it would be ready when it's ready.

'I meant to ask you,' Liz says. 'How did Luna's counselling session go? Elijah mentioned it but didn't have a chance to tell me any details.'

'Not well. Luna wouldn't leave my lap. But we'll try again next week. I told the therapist I'd bring Play-Doh next time, to see if Luna acts aggressively again. I'm sure Elijah's told you about that?'

'Yes, he did. And it's just not like her, is it?' Liz says, stroking Luna's cheek. 'Well, it's early days. Counselling will help eventually, you just have to be patient. Has she done anything else since?'

'No. Just that one time.'

'Then that's good. Maybe that wasn't a big thing, and we're reading too much into it.'

'Or she's just blocking it out.' Holly's tempted to remind her mum that she wasn't a child psychologist, and that adult brains must differ significantly. 'Anyway, we'll keep taking her and hoping it will help.'

'Counselling always helps,' Liz says. 'If you've got the right person.'

Holly needs to change the subject before her mum puts herself forward for the job. 'So, what did the two of you get up to while I was gone?'

'Ooh, lots. We read Peppa Pig books. Made sandcastles in the sandpit. I made Luna pasta for dinner.'

'That's great, Mum. Thanks. And you didn't notice anyone hanging around outside the house?'

Liz shakes her head. 'No. Look, you've got to stop. Luna is back and she's safe now. You've got to move on. But...' She hesitates. And that's not like her mum.

'What is it? Holly asks.

'Oh, I may as well say it, even though you won't like it. I've been talking to Elijah about your friend who's gone missing. He seems adamant that she had something to do with it. Do you think—?'

'No, Rachel didn't take Luna.'

'But you can't be sure, can you? You might think you know her, but how well do we ever know anyone?'

'I need to make dinner,' Holly says, grateful for something to take her mind off Rachel's phone.

Elijah gets home while Holly's preparing dinner, and he offers to take over so she can put Luna to bed.

By the time they've finished eating, there's been no call from the phone shop, and a knot of panic twists in her stomach. She'd told the man it was her son's phone, but what if he looked through it and found something that made him call the police?

On autopilot, she loads the dishwasher, making an excuse that she's too tired when her mum suggests they all watch a film together.

While Elijah and Liz settle in the living room, Holly sits in the kitchen, staring at her phone, even though no phone call will come this late. A bright flash of light catches her eye outside, and she heads to the back door, peering into the darkness. In the middle of the lawn, flickering flames sway in the breeze, casting an eerie glow across the garden. Holly grabs the first thing she can think of – the kettle, still full of water – and rushes outside. The fire is small, contained within a circle, and only when she gets closer does she realise there's something inside it, blackened and shapeless. Barely distinguishable. She steps closer and the realisation of what it is hits her like a sledgehammer. A child's baby doll.

Holly throws the water onto it and watches the fire slowly extinguish. She looks around, but there's no one in the garden now. Someone could have easily climbed over the fence at the back, escaping into the woods beyond the house.

Even though the night is muggy, chills shoot through her body.

As she makes her way back to the house, Holly notices the white envelope on the patio, a large stone sitting on top of it. She moves the stone away with her foot and picks up the envelope. There's no name on it, but she rips it open and reads the scrawled capital letters.

STOP ASKING QUESTIONS

TWENTY-SIX

BEFORE

Rachel

Jack stares at her, disbelief flooding his face. 'You need to tell me more,' he urges. 'What do you mean, Damien tried to kill someone?'

Now that Rachel is about to say it aloud, none of it seems real. So far, she's kept it all in her head, never speaking a word of it to anyone. 'Just before Evie's accident, a woman approached me outside school. Her name was Ren.' Rachel pictures her now: a thin woman with long light brown hair and large anxious eyes. 'She said she was Damien's ex and she needed to talk to me. I didn't believe her at first. Damien and I had been together for fifteen years – it seemed strange that she'd turn up to talk to me now.' Rachel pauses. 'I ignored her and started to walk off, but she followed me to my car. She begged me to hear her out. And then she showed me photos of her and Damien. Not on her phone. Printed ones. There were lots of them. Hugging. Kissing. Out and about in all kinds of places. He was much younger, of course, but it was him.' Rachel pauses. She hadn't realised how difficult this would be to talk about.

'Did you already know about her?' Jack asks.

Rachel shakes her head. 'When we first met, Damien would never talk about his past relationships, even though I'd told him about Will. He said it wasn't healthy. That the past didn't matter.' Rachel had always felt something was off, but she wanted to trust him. What was the point of a relationship without that?

Jack urges her to continue.

'Ren told me what their relationship had been like, and it mirrored my own. That's how I knew she was telling the truth. She told me how at first, Damien had been charming and atten-tive, but bit by bit he began to control her. In small ways at first, but then it escalated. He became physically abusive.' Rachel takes a deep breath. 'Ren said she tried to ghost him, cut him off, but one night he came over to her place and said he just wanted to talk about everything. She let him in, and told him their rela-tionship was over. Damien lost it and told her he would never let her go, and then he threatened to kill her.

'Even though he'd been abusive to her, she'd never consid-ered that he would actually want her dead.' There are tears in Rachel's eyes as she recounts what Ren told her. The parallels with her own story frighten her.

'She said Damien beat her to a pulp. Not just one blow, or two. She said she saw in his eyes that he didn't want to stop. He hadn't lost control – he knew what he was doing. He eventually stopped and calmly walked out, leaving her to die on her kitchen floor. Thankfully her sister was coming over that night and she found Ren and called an ambulance. Otherwise she'd be dead.'

'Jesus!' Jack shakes his head.

'She showed me pictures. Of her injuries.' Rachel can still picture them as clearly as if the photos were right in front of her. Barely a patch of her skin visible beneath the blood and bruising.

'But how did he get away with that?' Jack asks. 'Didn't she tell the police?'

'I asked her that, and she said she couldn't. Because the next day Damien visited her in hospital and offered her a lot of money to keep quiet, and he promised she'd never see or hear from him again. Ren told me she was torn – she didn't want him to get away with it, but she was scared she'd never be rid of him if she didn't take the money. And she admitted that she needed it. She was a student nurse at the time and could barely afford her rent. Damien knew this. He bought her silence.' *But he picked the wrong woman if he thinks he'll be able to do the same to me.*

'What did you say to her?'

'I told her what Damien was doing to me, gave her all the details of the psychological abuse he was inflicting on me. Then I tried to convince her to go to the police. I said I'd go with her to support her, but she was adamant that she couldn't. Then she said she was telling me this because she wanted me to leave him before it was too late. She said she knew I had children, and I should get them away from him before anything happened to them. Ren said it was terrifying to think what Damien was capable of.' Rachel pauses for a moment. 'I tried to get her number, so we could stay in touch, but she told me it was too dangerous. If Damien ever found out we'd been in contact, neither of us would be safe. When she walked off, I got in my car and tried to look her up online, but I only had her first name and couldn't find her.'

'And are you sure Damien doesn't know Ren tracked you down to warn you about him?'

'I don't think he knows. He's never said or done anything that suggests he might know. He's too smug and arrogant to believe his ex would ever dare to come back into his life in any way.' Rachel sighs. 'I tried so hard to find Ren, but then Evie...'

Jack hangs his head. 'I know.'

'It changed everything. I couldn't think about anything else. About Ren. Or myself. When Evie died, Damien actually backed off a bit. But that didn't last long.'

'He's a monster,' Jack says. 'And he must be clever if he could fool you and this other woman.'

'And he's a narcissist,' Rachel says. 'When I first met him, he was just so good at covering it up. I'm not easily fooled, that's what makes this so... awful. It happened so gradually. I suppose I was still grieving for Will, and I'd spent years putting up walls, not letting anyone else in. Then Damien somehow found a way to break my defences down. But I guess he could only keep up the charade for so long.' She pauses. 'I also think... I'm not sure, but his dad had some kind of accident and can't walk properly. They never talk about it, but I think maybe Damien had something to do with it. I've got no proof – just something about it doesn't feel right. The whole family shuts down whenever I mention it.'

'How can you trust him with Logan?' Jack asks.

Rachel's thought about this a lot over the years. Logan's the only person she's ever seen Damien show genuine love to. 'I don't think he'd ever hurt Logan,' she says. 'But that's now, when he's still young. He idolises Damien. I worry about the future, though, when Logan gets older. Their relationship will change – it has to.' She sighs. 'That's why I'm running out of time. If only Ren had agreed to go to the police. I've searched through all Damien's things but there's no trace of her in his old photos or anything. All I can do now is keep my son safe.'

Jack frowns. 'There must be a way you can get away from him.'

'He's made it clear that the only way I'll ever be free of him is if I'm dead.'

'Or we find Ren and try to convince her to go to the police.'

'I've already tried. And even if I could track her down, she won't do it. She made that clear.'

'But the next time you might not get away from him with just bruises. Please let me help you.'

'No,' Rachel says. 'You need to stay out of it. If he ever finds out I have anything to do with you, then...' She lets her unspoken thought sit between them. A warning to them both.

'Does he check your phone?' Jack asks.

'I don't know. He doesn't know my passcode.'

'Not sure that matters. I'm sure there'll be ways to check it remotely. I'll get you a spare phone. Not a smartphone. One where we can just message each other securely. Just in case.'

'I can get my own,' she says.

Jack shakes his head. 'Please will you let me just do this one thing for you?'

She gives a small nod, unsure whether she's fully agreeing or not. 'I've got to go. I need to get Logan from Damien's parents.'

'It's kind of late, isn't it? Where do they live?'

'York.'

'That's hours away. You can't go now. Why don't you wait until morning? You can stay here if you don't want to go home.'

Rachel stands. 'Thanks for the offer, but I can't leave it. I just need to be with my son.'

He calls after her as she leaves, but she doesn't turn back. Maybe because she knows he's probably right. There is no way Samantha will accept her turning up in the middle of the night. No way she'll let her take Logan home. But still Rachel gets in her car and pulls away from Jack's house. Away from the only place she feels safe.

. . .

It's nearly one a.m. by the time she reaches Samantha and Tobias's house. Surprisingly, there's a light on downstairs in Tobias's study; that should make things easier. Instead of ringing the doorbell, she raps on the window, trying to steady her breathing as she waits. Minutes tick by. Slowly. Painfully. And then finally Tobias peers through the shutters, frowning.

Moments later, he opens the front door, looking around, a mixture of confusion and pain on his face. 'Rachel. Hello. What's going on? Do you know what time it is?'

'Sorry, but I need to take Logan home.' Rachel doesn't have a plan. Even on the long drive here she couldn't work out what she'd say. Ultimately, though, she's Logan's mum and she doesn't need an excuse to take her son home.

The only plan in her head is that she can't go back to that house. Not after Damien tried to strangle her tonight. And not once he finds out she's come all the way here. She has to put her plan in motion now, and it starts with getting Logan away from these people.

'Rachel, this is insane,' Tobias says. 'Logan's asleep. Why on earth would you need to take him home?'

'It's an emergency. It's my uncle.' This is risky. Samantha and Tobias surely know she has no relationship with any of her parents' siblings, and that she didn't even as a child. 'He's in hospital in London and might not make it. It's important that Logan sees him as soon as possible. I need to take him back now.'

Tobias stares at her as if she's just spoken a language he doesn't understand. 'But you've never mentioned an uncle before. Neither has Damien.'

'We've been estranged. Which is exactly why now is the time to put everything right.'

Behind Tobias, Samantha appears, fastening the cord on her dressing gown. 'What on earth is going on? Rachel, what are you doing here?'

'Um, Rachel's come to take Logan home right now,' Tobias says, repeating the story Rachel's just told him.

'Absolutely not,' Samantha says. 'This is outrageous. I'm not letting you drive my grandson across the country in the middle of the night. Have you lost your mind?'

This isn't the first time Rachel's heard comments like this leave Samantha's mouth, and she lets it wash over her. 'Let's not talk about this on the doorstep,' Rachel says calmly. 'Can I come in?'

With a deep sigh, Tobias opens the door wider, while beside him Samantha tuts. 'This is unbelievable,' she mutters.

Inside, Rachel heads to the stairs.

'Just stop right there!' Samantha orders. 'I'm not letting you drag Logan out of bed. I'm calling Damien.'

Damien's phone is usually on silent during the night so it doesn't disturb him, yet her heart still pounds in her chest as Samantha makes the call.

'Damien, it's Mum. I need you to call me as soon as you get this message. No matter what time it is. Just call. Needless to say, it's urgent.'

'He's asleep,' Rachel says. 'He won't be up for hours.'

'Then you'll just have to wait here until morning,' Samantha says. 'Look, you're not thinking straight. Have you even slept?'

'I don't need to.' Rachel can't let them know that she and Logan will stay in a hotel somewhere nearby while she decides what to do tomorrow. 'I'm absolutely fine.'

'You've already lost one child, Rachel,' Samantha says. 'Come on, you must see that this isn't rational.'

She's playing her mind games, just like Damien does. Rachel won't let them break her. 'If you don't go upstairs and wake Logan, right now, I'll call the police. I'm his mum – keeping him here against my will is kidnapping.'

'Kidnapping!' Samantha exclaims. 'Listen to yourself. I

know you haven't been taking your pills – Damien's told us all about that. This is so hard for him. First, he loses his daughter, and now his wife's losing her mind.'

Don't rise to the bait. An outburst will only give them more ammunition.

'All I want is—'

Samantha's phone rings and she rushes to answer. 'Damien – thank goodness.' She disappears down the long hallway, shutting herself in the kitchen.

Rachel's about to go after her, but Tobias takes her arm. 'Why don't you have a seat in the lounge?'

'No. I'll stay right here.'

'Suit yourself. I'll wait here with you.'

She silently curses; if Tobias hadn't intervened, she could have rushed upstairs to Logan.

'How did your leg get hurt?' Rachel asks, when Tobias winces as he sits.

His eyes narrow. 'Why are you asking that now?'

Rachel sucks in her breath. There's something here, she knows it. 'I know it was an accident, but what exactly happened?'

Tobias glances at the door, his face stricken. 'I don't want to talk about it.'

Rachel lowers her voice. 'Does Damien know what happened? Can you just—?'

Samantha throws the door open and stares at them, shooting a glance at Tobias. She tucks her phone into her dressing gown pocket. 'Well, that was very interesting.' She walks over to Rachel and pulls the silk scarf from her neck.

Instinctively, Rachel covers her bruise, but it's too late. Samantha has already seen what she needed to.

'Damien's just told me what happened,' Samantha says, turning to Tobias. 'This evening he came home and found

Rachel with a rope around her neck, about to jump off a chair. Thankfully he got to her in time.'

Rachel freezes. A picture of Will forces its way into her head. How he looked as he hung there. Her chest feels tight, and she wonders if she'll stop breathing. Of all the things she'd expected Damien to say, this was never one of them. Using her pain against her. Never again will she underestimate the lengths he'll go to. She considers telling them the truth about how she got her bruised neck, but there's zero chance they'll believe her.

'Jesus!' Tobias says. 'Rachel, you need to get some help. You must see that.'

'Damien says we mustn't let her take Logan. He can't trust her.' She turns to Rachel. 'And he says you need to stay here until he can come and get you both in the morning. He's supposed to be working, but that's the sacrifice he makes for you. Honestly, Rachel. I can't believe you would do this to your son. He's already lost his sister, and now you want to leave him without his mother?'

'I need some water,' Rachel says, pulling her scarf back and heading to the kitchen.

She stops by the door, listening to Samantha and Tobias's hushed whispers.

'He told me to call the hospital and get her sectioned,' Samantha is saying. 'He said it's the only way to keep her and Logan safe.'

'Seems like we have no choice,' Tobias says.

The thought of leaving Logan here sickens her, but they've left her no choice. Turning on the tap so they can't hear what she's about to do, Rachel finds the key to the back door and unlocks it, slipping outside without bothering to close it.

And then she runs.

TWENTY-SEVEN

NOW

Holly

All night Holly has lain awake, drifting between consciousness and images of the fire flickering threateningly in the garden. The charred remains of the doll. When she'd told Elijah what had happened, he'd played it down, insisting it must just be teenagers messing around. She hadn't shown him the note. It would be all the ammunition he needs to fuel his campaign against Rachel. And until she knows something for sure, Holly will continue to defend her friend.

Luna sleeps soundly beside her, spread out like a starfish and taking up so much of the bed that Elijah had given up halfway through the night and gone to sleep downstairs. 'I love Luna, and I get why you want her right with us all night, but I need to get some sleep,' he'd said.

And in the spare room, her mum had settled for the night, oblivious to the terror that's kept Holly awake.

Before climbing out of bed, Holly switches off the house alarm from her mobile. She gets dressed while Luna continues sleeping, then checks the window before going downstairs.

Elijah's on the sofa, the blanket that's supposed to be covering him in a heap on the floor. She pulls the blanket back over him, then goes to the kitchen to make a strong coffee, hoping it will fully wake her.

A message comes through on her phone when she's checking her emails on her laptop.

Your phone is unlocked and ready for collection

Adrenalin pumps through her body as she pours the rest of her coffee in the sink. She messages Ross, her fingers flying across her phone as she types.

Meet me at the office at 10:30.

Elijah comes in, yawning. 'I'm guessing you didn't sleep well?' he says, pouring himself coffee.

'No.' And Holly won't until she knows Luna is safe and Rachel is home.

'I know it's hard, but we have to be rational,' Elijah says. No one's going to try and take Luna again. The Ring doorbell is coming today, and the CCTV's being installed next week.'

'Next week is too long to wait. I'm not taking any chances.'

He pulls out a chair and joins her at the table. 'Holly, we've got to start getting back to some kind of normality. For Luna's sake. She'll pick up on all this. And who knows how that'll affect her.'

'I'm being vigilant till I know she's safe.'

'She *is* safe.'

'How can you say that when someone got into our garden?'

'And they lit a controlled fire. It's not like they burnt anything down. I know it's weird, but they didn't come into the house, did they?' He pauses. 'Burning that doll *was* horrible, though. But I reckon it's just teenagers trying to freak us out.

We can't let them get to us. That's what they want. Look, I'm not saying we shouldn't be careful and pay attention when you're out, but I think it's easy to read too much into this. We all know who took Luna. And that's why she wasn't harmed. You don't want to believe it, but if you're honest with yourself, it's the only thing that makes sense.' He takes Holly's hand. 'Look, I understand how hard it is for you to wrap your head around it, but deep down you must know. Rachel's been obsessed with Luna. Harassing you to let her see her all the time.'

Holly shakes her head. 'She's a grieving mum, trying to get through it the best she can. Who are we to judge what works for her? Maybe I did think wanting to be around someone else's daughter wasn't the way I might handle things, but we're all different.'

She can tell that Elijah's not going to change his mind, no matter what she says. 'You don't like Rachel. I didn't notice it before, but I see it now. Why is that?'

He stands, picking up his mug. 'Let's not let this drive a wedge between us. We need to stick together.'

Holly checks her phone. 'I have to go to the office now. I need to finish this story I'm working on.' *And find out what's on Rachel's burner phone, as soon as the shop opens.*

'Will Ross be there?'

'Yeah. Why?' Holly knows why he's asking, she just doesn't want to admit it.

'It's Sunday,' Elijah says, avoiding her question. 'I thought we could all take Luna out. Get some fresh air. Maybe go for lunch. Your mum will be leaving tomorrow.'

'I can't. This is really important. I'll try not to be long. Anyway, I'm taking Luna with me.'

'Why? Your mum and I will keep an eye on her. Don't drag her to work again. And if you think someone was following you, wouldn't she be safer here with us?'

Holly considers this. Elijah's right. 'Don't go anywhere. Promise? When I get back we can all go out.'

Elijah sighs. 'Okay.'

After a quick shower, Holly checks on Luna then leaves before her mum wakes up and tries to persuade her not to go to the office. She starts the car engine and glances up at the house. Elijah's watching her from the living room window. He doesn't trust her – she can feel it. But there's something else. Something she can't put her finger on.

But she will work it out.

The office is eerily quiet when she arrives after collecting Rachel's phone, and Holly isn't prepared for the flutters of anxiety. She's never been a worrier, always faced things with optimism and the belief that she'll get through any challenge. But Luna being taken has changed her. She thinks of Rachel, and how Evie's death has left its scar on her. She must have changed beyond recognition. Silently, out of sight of Holly.

In her office, to distract herself while she waits for Ross, she goes through what she needs to do for the Oscar Hobbs story. Rachel's phone sits on her desk, but she's not going to look at it until Ross gets here, no matter how much she wants to. Whatever's on there, she might need Ross to help her put it into perspective. She's fully aware that she's biased when it comes to her friend. Ross might see something she can't. Or won't want to.

Once she's finished this story, she can focus only on finding Rachel. There's one more person she needs to speak to – Oscar's dad.

'Hey, sorry I'm a bit late,' Ross says, appearing in her doorway. He sits on the chair near Holly's desk.

'I'm nervous,' Holly admits. 'And that's not like me. Have

you ever seen me rattled before? Apart from when Luna was taken.'

Ross sits at her desk. 'Nope, can't say I have. But it just means you're human after all. Did you get the phone? Have you looked?'

'Not yet. I wanted to wait till you got here. I know that sounds weird, but—'

'I get it,' Ross says, with a faint smile.

Holly picks up the phone.

'Are you sure you're ready?' Ross asks. 'It could be nothing, but... I don't know. Maybe there's stuff on there you'll wish you hadn't seen.'

'I'm ready.' Holly stares at the phone. 'Okay, here goes.' She navigates through the phone, not surprised to find that there's no internet browser, no apps. Nothing other than calls and text messages. 'Why would she need this phone?' she asks. There's nothing in the call log, which could just mean Rachel deleted it, and when she clicks on messages, there's only one in there. 'There's a message,' she tells Ross. 'Just one. From a number with no contact name. It was sent weeks ago.' She holds her breath and opens it.

Have you done it yet?

Holly stares at it, willing the words to make sense. To mean something. To give her some answers. But that question could mean anything.

'What does it say?' Ross asks.

'It says *Have you done it yet?* Done what, though?'

Holly's mind is a frenzy of devastating thoughts. Is the person talking about Luna? Asking if Rachel has taken her yet? She turns to Ross. 'Oh, God. What the hell does it mean?' Without waiting for an answer, Holly stands and walks to the window and back again. 'What was Rachel doing?'

'Can I see it?' Ross asks.

She hands the phone to him, studying his face as he reads.

'I wish I could tell you,' he says. 'But don't jump to conclusions.' He must be thinking the same thing as her – *has Rachel taken Luna yet?* 'Do you recognise the number?'

'No.' She eases the phone from his hand. 'I'm calling it.'

'Wait. Let's think this through first. Don't do things in haste.'

But it's too late. Holly has already pressed call, holding the phone to her ear.

On the fourth ring, a man answers. 'Where are you? I've been s—'

'Who is this?' Holly asks.

There's silence, and then a click as the call is cut off.

'Shit! He hung up!' Holly calls again, but this time there's no answer. 'He must have thought I was Rachel.'

Ross mulls this over. 'Do you think she could have been having an affair?'

'If you'd asked me that weeks ago, I'd have said no chance. Rachel's the most strait-laced, moral person I know.' *But didn't she change? I saw it, I just didn't want to acknowledge it.* 'Now, though, I have no idea.' She pauses, unsure how much she wants to tell Ross. Rachel's still her friend. There's still not enough evidence that she's guilty of anything. 'I think there might have been problems in her marriage. I didn't realise it, but I've been piecing things together. Damien is... he seems a bit cold. Controlling. I don't know. She never spoke to me about it. I think it might be something to do with what she wanted to tell me before she went missing.'

Holly copies the phone number into her contacts – entering *Man* as the contact name.

'What's your next move?' Ross asks.

'I'll message him. If he was close to Rachel, hopefully he'll care about her enough to reply. But if he was threatening her, I don't know how I'll find out. Do you have any contacts who could trace the number?'

'No! There are limits to what I can do, Holly. I wish I could help. If he doesn't reply, then you should give the phone to the police and let them find him. He could be linked to her disappearance.'

'I know.'

'Holly, there's something I need to tell you.' Ross looks away. 'You're not going to like it. Um... Paul emailed me a draft of his story about Rachel. I had to tell him to tone it down. It read too much like an accusation. Focusing on how she was so disturbed she might have been capable of anything. I've edited it. Heavily. But I still don't think you'll like it. It paints her as a troubled woman, someone with mental health issues. Paul somehow managed to get an interview with her husband's parents. They've been quite open about the troubles she was having.'

'Can I see it?'

'Yes. But don't tell him I've let you have an early read.'

Even as she pores over the article, ingesting the damaging and hurtful words, Holly knows she's powerless to prevent it being published. She made a deal with Paul, and this story was the condition for him keeping quiet about the evidence he knows Damien handed her. Luna's cuddly lamb. At least he doesn't know exactly what it was. 'This isn't Rachel,' she says. 'These words are about a stranger.'

Ross nods. 'I know. That's why you're going to write your own piece. From the perspective of her close friend, not just a journalist.'

'Paul won't like it.'

'Let me deal with him. We have to be balanced here, don't we? That's what I've always said. He can't argue with that. Maybe we give it a few days, though.'

Holly considers this. There was nothing in her deal with

Paul about Holly not being able to write something of her own. And if Ross has given the go-ahead, there's nothing he can do about it. If they don't tell Paul before it goes to print, then he can't even attempt to stop it. Perhaps he'll threaten going to the police, but then he'd have to explain why he didn't come forward the second he knew. Paul has dug himself into a hole, and there's no clambering out.

'I'll do it,' Holly says. 'But first I need to message the man who answered the phone just now.' She picks up her mobile and begins typing.

I'm a close friend of Rachel's and I need to speak to you urgently. Please call me. I haven't told anyone about Rachel's other phone so there's nothing to worry about.

She shows it to Ross, and when he gives a small nod, she presses send, praying that she'll hear back from this man. Whoever he is.

'I'd better get home,' Ross says. 'I'm taking Harry out this morning.'

'Oh, you should have said. I wouldn't have asked you to come here if I'd known you're spending the day with him.'

'It was a last-minute thing. It's not my weekend with him, but I said I'd help out. His mum has to be somewhere. Didn't tell me where.'

'I almost forgot, you never told me how your date went,' she says.

'Oh, I um... I cancelled. Didn't really feel like meeting up with anyone.' He pauses. 'Anyway, you know I'm always here for you, right? Whatever you need.'

Holly thanks him and rushes off before he says anything else she doesn't want to acknowledge.

. . .

Outside Shania Hobbs's house, Holly sits in her car and waits. She would have headed straight to the door but instead she's been watching Oscar kick a ball around on the green outside. He's with two other boys, and they've stopped now, huddled together on the bench. Whatever they're talking about, the words are lost to Holly, but she's sure it's probably something to do with girls. Megan? Or is that all behind him now?

When they eventually wander off, disappearing around the corner in the direction of the parade of shops, Holly gets out of the car and walks up the short path to the front door.

Shania answers, dressed in loose jeans and a V-neck T-shirt. 'Hello,' she says. 'I was wondering if you'd come to the door. You've been sitting in your car for ages. I saw you when I was opening the blinds.'

'Yeah, sorry. I just had to send some emails and it took me a while.'

'Is this about the story? When's it coming out? I thought I'd have seen a copy by now.'

'Yeah, it won't be long. I'll have it to my editor in the next two days. I'm just putting together the final draft. But I was just wondering how you'd feel about me talking to Oscar's dad?'

Shania stares at her as if she's just insulted her. 'I see. You'd better come in.'

In the living room, Holly perches on the edge of the sofa, while Shania hovers by the window. Holly's keen to keep this visit brief, and senses Shania feels the same. Elijah and Luna will be waiting for her, and she still needs to talk to Oscar's dad, preferably before she goes home.

'Oscar doesn't even live with his dad,' Shania says. 'I don't think he ever even met Megan. What could he possibly tell you?'

'It's more to get a sense of how it affected him. As a father. This accusation will have affected the whole family.'

'False accusation,' Shania says.

'Yes. Anyway, speaking to him will add weight to the story. Help the readers get a real feel for how it impacted all of you, not just Oscar. I'm trying to show that false accusations like this have far-reaching consequences.'

Shania considers Holly's words. 'Yeah, I suppose. Not sure Ryan will want to talk about it, though. I'm guessing you want his phone number?'

'Yes, that would be a great help.'

'I'll send it to you now.' Shania gets out her phone and scrolls through it.

'Thanks. There's just one other thing. Would you mind telling me a bit about him first? I always like to familiarise myself with the people I'm interviewing. I've tried looking online, but couldn't find much.'

Shania frowns. 'What d'you want to know?'

'Anything to help build a picture of him. What's his relationship like with Oscar? What does he do? That kind of thing.'

When Shania's eyes narrow, Holly knows she might be pushing things too far. Shania doesn't trust anyone. 'We're not together any more. I barely know Ryan now.' She pauses. 'After all these years. That relationship couldn't be further behind me.'

'Do you mind me asking why you split up?'

'Lots of reasons. But mainly because he wasn't the kind of father I'd imagined for my child. Too busy out drinking with his friends to bother being there for Oscar. He just seemed to think we'd have a kid and nothing would change. That he could keep doing what he'd always done, as if he didn't have any responsibility. He just never grew up. Think he got the shock of his life when I told him I was leaving. He begged me to stay. It shocked me, actually. Think it was the first time I realised I might actually mean something to him.'

'But it wasn't enough to change your mind?'

'No. I didn't want Oscar growing up around him – thinking that was how men... fathers should behave. I wanted him to be a decent boy who'll make a good husband one day.' She studies Holly's face. 'Is that enough? There's not much more I can tell you other than he's a mechanic. Works for Toyota.'

'Thanks. That's really helpful.'

'I think you're wasting your time. He barely knows his son. Even now, he tries to convince me to give him another chance. Says we should all be a family together and that Oscar and I need him. He says he'll prove it. But we don't need him. And there's nothing he can do that will change my mind.'

At the door, she wishes Holly luck. 'I do appreciate you telling Oscar's story. He's been tainted with all of this, and just needs someone to speak his truth.'

As does Rachel.

Outside, Oscar and his friends are back, sitting on the grass eating whatever they've bought from the shop. And further back, sitting on a wall outside some houses is a girl Holly instantly recognises. Megan Hart. And she's watching Oscar.

Holly considers going over to her, but she doesn't want to cause a scene. What is she doing? Stalking the boy she accused of rape? It doesn't make sense. At least, not if Megan was telling the truth. But if she was lying about Oscar, then that might explain why she's there watching him with his friends. Holly doesn't know what to make of it. There was something about Megan she hadn't trusted – but then she had been telling the truth about Rachel having another phone. *Does that mean she was telling the truth about what Rachel said – about picking up her daughter from nursery, long after Evie had died?*

Holly gets in the car and fastens her seatbelt. She needs to think this all through. But first she needs to call Oscar's dad.

Before she has a chance, her phone pings. A text message. From Rachel's anonymous contact.

Meet me at 6 p.m. Woking Park by the bandstand. Come alone.

TWENTY-EIGHT

BEFORE

Rachel

'What the hell were you thinking?'

Rachel stares at their beige carpet, at the small red ball of fluff which must have come from her jumper, and tries to drown out Damien's thunderous voice. She'd expected his rage, violence even, she'd prepared herself for it on the long drive home from York. But now she's home, overwhelmed with exhaustion from a night without sleep. She just needs her bed. And Damien to leave her alone.

She had considered not coming home – of course she had – but she couldn't risk staying away, not without Logan. The time will come, but it's not yet.

'You lied to them,' Rachel says, her hands smoothing the bruised skin on her neck. The pain is still there, and she can still feel his hands squeezing. Would he have stopped if she hadn't lashed out?

Damien stares at her. 'I told them the truth, Rachel. I came home and found you trying to kill yourself. With that rope around your neck. God knows where you got it from.' He shakes his head – an actor playing his part. 'And then you go and try to get Logan in the middle of the night. *Steal* him.' He shakes the bottle of pills he's holding in his hand. 'This is why you need these.' He slams them down on the coffee table. 'You can't be trusted, Rachel. I just don't know what you're capable of. What if you'd really managed to hurt yourself? Or worse, what if you hurt Logan?'

Rachel shakes her head. To anyone else, Damien would sound so convincing. A concerned husband and father, trying to get his wife the help she needs. Rachel almost believes him herself. That's how he's got away with everything he's done. People just hang on his every word, as if everything he says is the sacred truth. That's where his power lies. 'You know what really happened,' she says.

'And now you've embarrassed me in front of my parents. Turning up at their house like that.'

'People do worse things than that,' she says, glaring at him. Silently defying him to challenge her about what she's inferring. It's dangerous ground to tread.

But Damien is too arrogant to consider for one second that Rachel might know what he did to his ex-girlfriend. It's a weapon she will use against him, once she's worked out how.

'Pull a stunt like that again and it will be the last time you cross me,' he says, walking across to her and pressing his hand down on her head so hard she thinks he'll crush her skull. He lets go after a moment, shoving her back onto the sofa.

Rachel's whole body screams to fight back again, and her hands clench. But if she got into a physical fight with him, one of them would end up dead, and whichever way it went, she can't do that to Logan. 'I'm leaving you,' she says. She hasn't planned to say it, even though she knew this time would come.

Damien turns back. 'What did you say?'

'You heard me. You must have known this would happen.'

Rachel tries to sound more assertive than she feels. She isn't ready for this. It wasn't supposed to be yet.

Calmly, Damien walks over to her. 'No, you're not. And do you know how I can be so sure of that? It's because you'll never give up Logan. And that's what would happen if you left me. See, you're right. I've fully expected you might do something like this. And I've prepared for that time. Got myself a little insurance policy. Can't be too careful, can you?'

'What are you talking about?' She hates asking, knowing it's exactly what he wants her to do, but she needs to know.

'Times, dates, places. Everything written down. It makes for some interesting reading.'

Jack. Somehow Damien has found out. He will accuse her of having an affair with the man who drove the car that killed Evie. He'll twist things to make it appear that Rachel didn't love her daughter.

'I've listed them all. Every – let's just call them *mental health episodes*. So there's no doubt, when the time comes, that any court in the country will know that Logan is better off with me. His stable dad. And you haven't helped yourself. Turning up like that to drag Logan home in the middle of the night is just more evidence for me.'

But Rachel's holding a trump card. Damien has attempted murder, she just needs to prove it.

'So, it's up to you, Rachel, my darling wife,' Damien continues. 'Are you going to risk losing your son? Or is it better for you to keep up appearances? Play the role of my wife like you've been doing all these years.' He smiles, stroking her cheek. 'What's it going to be?'

'I'm staying,' she says, each word lodging in her throat like a pill she can't swallow.

'And you're going to keep taking these?' He shoves her antidepressants into her hand.

Rachel nods.

'Good. That's what I thought. Now, why don't you go and
have a shower? My parents will be bringing Logan back soon,
and I want them to see that you're turning things around.
Taking your pills. Behaving like a decent mother. And make
sure you apologise to them.'

Rachel stares at him, imagining a trickle of blood oozing
from his throat. She nods. 'Yes, I think I'll do that.'

When she hears the front door slam, Rachel rushes to the
window to watch Damien leave. She waits until his car pulls
away and disappears from sight before she picks up her phone.

'I have to admit. I'm surprised you wanted to see me.'

They're in Dorking, in a coffee shop she's never been to
before. She doesn't know this area at all, but Elijah insisted on
meeting here, far away from Holly, Damien, everyone they
know. He looks smug, as if he's won a battle she was never interested in fighting. Still, him believing this will only serve her
purpose.

'I've been thinking about it all,' she says, forcing a smile.
'And what good would it do for it all to come out? I don't want
to hurt Holly. I realise I already have... but I don't want to make
it worse for her. What we did still doesn't sit right with me, but I
just think it would be awful if she were to find out. And
Damien too.'

Elijah barely knows her husband – they never gelled, like
she and Holly used to wish they would. Those family days out
with all of them together never happened, even before they lost
Evie.

He nods, lifting his Americano to his mouth, but putting it
back down before he drinks any. 'I want you to know something,' he says. 'What happened between us... it meant something to me. I didn't do it lightly. I'm not expecting you to
believe that, but it's the truth. I love Holly. Of course I do. She

and Luna are everything to me. But... she doesn't love me how she thinks she does. Oh, we're fine. We *work*. There's nothing dysfunctional about us. But... she's settling for me. I think I've always known it.' He takes a sip of coffee. 'And Ross is always hovering in the background, casting a shadow over our marriage.'

Rachel nods, trying some of her green tea. It's too strong, but it doesn't matter. She's nearly finished here. 'It meant something to me too,' she says, leaning into him and stroking his arm. 'In a different time and place, you and I might have worked.'

The smile on his face is exactly what she's hoped for. She inches closer so that her thigh rests against his. And when his mouth finds hers, she goes with it, cupping his face in her hands. Counting. One, two, three, four, five, and then she slowly pulls away, placing her hand on his chest. 'I'd better go.'

'Can I see you again? Tonight? Holly's working late again, and I can get my parents to babysit Luna.'

Rachel stiffens. This man doesn't deserve to be Holly's husband. And he doesn't deserve to be a dad. Poor Luna. 'How about I message you later?' she says, grabbing her bag.

'Okay.' He finishes his coffee then stands and pulls on his coat.

'I just need the bathroom,' Rachel says. 'I'll see you later.' She places her hand on his shoulder, gives it a squeeze.

As she makes her way to the toilets, she turns to watch Elijah leave, holding her breath until he's disappeared. Then she rushes to the young barista behind the counter. 'Did you get it?'

'Yep. Got the whole thing.' He hands Rachel her phone. She grabs it and finds the video the barista has just recorded, pleased to see that he's captured the passionate kiss between her and Elijah. Undisputable evidence of an affair.

'Thanks,' Rachel says, handing him the fifty pounds she promised him earlier. She's taken a huge risk doing this –

turning up early to convince the barista to film her. For the sake of her friend, she'd explained. She hadn't had to say too much – the offer of fifty pounds was enough to convince him. 'You don't know how helpful you've been.'

'Hope your friend gets rid of that sleaze,' he says. 'Good luck.'

Outside, Rachel takes in a deep lungful of air and places her phone in her pocket. There's no going back now. She doesn't want to. Holly deserves to know the truth, no matter what that means for their friendship.

She's heading towards her car when a heavy hand lands on her shoulder, spinning her around.

'What the fuck was that?' Elijah asks, his face crimson.

'I don't know what you're talking about. What's wrong?'

'Don't fucking play games. I saw you. That guy in there was filming us. Now what the fuck is going on?' He tries to grab her phone, but she's too quick and shoves it in the waist of her jeans.

'I'll fucking kill you!' Elijah shouts.

And for the second time this weekend, Rachel finds herself running, not stopping until it feels like there's no more breath in her body.

TWENTY-NINE

NOW

Holly

They spend the afternoon in a small playground near Luna's nursery, all of them watching her like hawks, never letting her stray beyond their reach.

Elijah seems distracted, and Holly asks him several times if he's okay. 'Just work stuff on my mind,' he says. 'Every day I take off means it's all mounting up.' He watches Liz pushing Luna on the toddler swing for a moment. 'I know she needs us around right now, but we still have to pay the bills, don't we?'

Holly sees beyond his words – that what he really wants to say is that she's still carrying on, while he's falling behind. 'I've got to meet someone this evening. An important contact. But Mum can stay with Luna. Why don't you go into work and catch up?'

He thinks about this for a moment. 'Yeah, I think I will. Might make me feel better.'

They sit on the small bench for a while, until Luna starts rubbing her eyes. It's four p.m., which means Holly's got two hours until she's due to meet Rachel's contact. She has no idea what the evening will bring, but she feels woefully unprepared. She needs to tell someone where she'll be – and give them this man's number in case anything happens to her. But when she turns to Elijah and notices the worry lines carved into his forehead, she knows it can't be him. He'd only try to stop her. Tell her she's crazy, and that she needs to go to the police. And her mum too would do everything to stop Holly going.

That leaves only one person she can tell.

While Elijah drives them home, she messages Ross, giving him all the details of her meeting this evening. He replies straight away – she can always depend on him to have his phone close by – warning her to be careful, insisting she call him the minute she's finished.

I need to know you're okay

At home, Holly makes chicken nuggets and mashed potato for Luna, wondering how much of it she'll actually eat. Before she was taken, she'd wolf down most things, but now it's a good day if she eats a couple of forkfuls.

'What's wrong?' her mum asks. 'You're distracted, I can tell.'

'I'm just worried about Luna.'

Liz puts her arm around Holly. 'She'll be fine. Our love will get her through this, you have to believe that.'

One thing Holly knows for sure is that finding out who took Luna is the only way she'll begin to heal. And that it's looking extremely likely that somehow it's tied to Rachel, even if she doesn't quite know how. 'You're right,' she says. 'Luna will be okay. I'll make sure of that.'

Holly serves Luna's dinner, watching as her daughter pushes the food around her plate. 'I just need to make a call,' she tells them. 'I'll be right back.'

Upstairs, she calls the number Shania gave her for Ryan Hobbs, Oscar's dad. Shania had warned her that he never answers his phone, so Holly has already planned the message she'll leave on his voicemail. She's so convinced he won't answer that when he does, it takes her a moment to get her thoughts in order. 'Ryan?'

'Yeah. Who's this?' He has a pleasant voice, deep and mesmerising.

'I hope it's okay to call you. Shania gave me your number.'

There's a brief pause. 'Did she now? And who are you?'

'My name's Holly Fisher and I'm a journalist from *Surrey Live*.'

Silence follows. Clearly this isn't going to be easy. 'Did Shania mention that I'm writing Oscar's story? Setting the record straight. I know as a family it was an awful thing for you to go through.'

'Yeah, it was. And Oscar told me about your story. I told him I'm not sure it's a good idea. What's the point of raking it all up? Keeping it in people's minds? It'll be forgotten about soon.'

'I understand,' Holly says. 'And I hope that's true. But I think Oscar feels it's important to get his side across. There are still people out there who believe Megan's allegation. And even though she dropped the charges, she hasn't come out and admitted she was lying. She's sticking to her story that it really happened.'

'That girl is a lying bitch.'

His language surprises Holly – it's so out of place coming from a man with such an enchanting voice. 'Could we have a chat about it? Get your perspective? I'll treat you to a coffee.'

'Never drink the stuff. But you want my perspective? Oscar needs to learn a hard lesson from this. Stay away from people who aren't good for him. I've told him a thousand times, but kids never listen, do they?'

'I'm sure you're right.' Holly's not going to get much out of this man. 'But—'

'Here's the thing about news,' he says. 'As soon as something else happens, stories that one day seem so scandalous are quickly forgotten. No one's talking about Oscar any more – not when there's something juicier for them to gossip about.'

Holly knows exactly what he's talking about, but she stays silent.

'That teacher stole a kid,' he continues. 'And now she's run off. That's got more meat in it, right? Why aren't you working on that?'

'Um, my colleague is,' Holly manages to say.

'Good. Is that it then? I'm on my way out.'

After dinner, Holly runs Luna a bath, pleased to see her daughter splashing around in the bubbles. 'Mummy's got to go out in a few minutes,' she says, handing Luna her blue bath whale.

Luna dunks the whale in the bath. 'Mummy go.'

Holly's heart lifts to hear Luna speaking, and she leans in and hugs her, soaking her clothes in the process. 'I'll be back soon. I'm trying to find Rachel. We miss her, don't we?' This approach might backfire, but Holly needs to try it.

Luna stops playing and stares at Holly. 'Ray-Ray.'

'Yes, Ray-Ray. I need to find her.'

Luna shrinks back against the side of the bath. 'Ray-Ray!' Then she grabs the whale, throws it against the bathroom mirror, and watches it fall to the floor.

'Luna, it's okay, come here.' Holly lifts Luna from the bath and wraps her in a towel, hugging her tightly. 'Mummy's here, everything's okay.'

'Ray-Ray bad, Ray-Ray bad,' Luna mumbles, rocking back and forth.

Holly strokes her hair, holding her until she calms down. 'Did Rachel hurt you?' she whispers.

'Bad. Bad.'

'Okay, okay. Shh. Mummy's here. You're safe.'

Her mother appears in the doorway. 'What's going on? I heard a crash. Did Luna hurt herself?'

Holly doesn't have the energy to explain what happened. 'Something like that.' She picks up the whale and puts it on the side of the bath. 'I'll put Luna to bed and stay with her for a while.'

'But don't you have to be somewhere at six?'

'This is more important. I can go when she's fallen asleep.'

'Okay,' Liz says. 'But I'm here, and I'm perfectly capable of putting Luna to bed.'

'I know, Mum. But please, I need to do this.'

Liz sighs. 'I'll make a stir-fry. Guess it's just me eating.' She walks off, tutting.

At five to six, Holly settles Luna into bed. She messages the man she's meeting, telling him she's with her daughter and is running late, promising to be there by seven-fifteen.

After five minutes, there's still no reply.

When Luna falls asleep – deeply enough for Holly to feel okay about leaving – it's twenty to seven, and she's still had no reply. Undeterred, she tells her mum she's leaving now, and that Luna is asleep. And then she gets in her car and makes her way to Woking Park.

Grateful that there's still at least an hour of sunlight ahead, Holly walks up to the bandstand, scanning the area for any sign of the man who was watching her and Luna. Not that she'd recognise him without that red hooded sweatshirt. Not with certainty. Is he the person who set the fire in their garden? It only occurred to her on the way here that he could be the man she's arranged to meet tonight. She takes a deep breath. Either way, if he turns up, then she'll soon have some answers.

If she makes it out of here unharmed.

There are a few people in the park this evening, people

soaking up the late-May evening sun, young couples mostly. A group of teenagers. No one who could be her caller.

At the bandstand, she sits on a step, waiting. It's only ten past seven, so if he got her message, he's not late. If he didn't, or if he's ignoring it, annoyed that she changed the time, she'll message him again.

When there's still no sign of him at twenty past seven, Holly calls him, ready to fight for answers. But he doesn't pick up. She walks around the bandstand, restless and frustrated, but not ready to give up. Luna's reaction to hearing Rachel's name this evening is more damning evidence, and she needs to know what of.

Her patience has a limit, though, and as it approaches eight, she decides to leave.

'I don't think you'll want to leave.'

She turns around, startled. Standing in front of her is a man around her age wearing jeans and a red T-shirt. His hair is dark and his brown eyes appraise her, questioning.

Holly lets out a deep breath. She doesn't think this stranger is the man who's been following her. 'Who are you?'

'That's a long story.'

He steps forward, and even though she feels anxious, there's nothing intimidating about him.

'Sorry I made you wait,' he says. 'I had to be sure about you.'

'So you were watching me?'

He nods, pointing to the trees in the distance. 'I had to. When you know everything, you'll understand. Shall we sit? Or would you prefer to walk?'

Holly looks around, comforted that there are plenty of other people in the park. 'Let's stay here.' She walks back to the step she's just been sitting on, and he follows. 'Who are you?' she asks, as soon as they're sitting.

'I think you'll recognise my name. Jack Parsons.'

Holly flinches. It's a name she'll never forget. This is the man who killed Evie. 'What the hell?'

'Please hear me out.'

Her mind is reeling, trying to comprehend why this man – of all people – is sitting here, next to her. She takes a deep breath. 'Go on, then – explain yourself.'

'I know this will be a lot to take in. It's huge. But after the accident, I contacted Rachel. A lot. I found her on Facebook. She'd never reply to my messages, though. But I never gave up. I had to tell her how sorry I was. Not that it would make any difference, or bring her little girl back. But it was something I needed to do.'

Holly stares at him. 'It sounds like you were stalking her.'

'No, not at all. It was just messages. I never tried to approach her in person. And it was never more than once in any day.' He sighs. 'I know that doesn't make it any better. Anyway, after months, one day she replied. And she said we could meet up.'

'No. I don't believe you. Why would she?'

'I wasn't really sure to start with why she'd agreed, but then I soon worked it out. From stuff she told me. I think she wanted to try and heal in some way. And maybe meeting me would help her find some peace. I don't know. I know this will sound weird, but I think she liked getting my messages. After my initial apologies, I'd just start telling her about my day. Things that were going on with me. I suppose she got to know me through my words. And believe me, there were a lot of them. I don't expect you to believe this, but somehow we formed a friendship.'

Holly still can't wrap her head around this. 'Why wouldn't she tell me? Something this major. We talked about everything.' *Until we didn't.*

'Maybe that was the case, but that changed after Evie died,

didn't it? Rachel told me. But I think she understood that it had to. Your daughter was a constant reminder of what she'd lost.'

'I know. But Rachel likes being around Luna. She's always asking to see her.'

'Yeah, I could never understand that. But if that's what helped her, then I had to support her.' He shakes his head. 'I know this is all going to be hard for you to get your head around. But Rachel and I became very close.'

'What exactly are you saying? You slept together?'

'No,' Jack says. 'Never. It wasn't like that. What we had was deep, though. Something that couldn't be defined. She told me things. Lots. About her marriage. The things Damien did to her.'

Every inch of Holly's body freezes. 'What... what things?'

'You didn't know, did you?' Jack says. 'I suppose she hid it well. And so did he. But that man was emotionally and physically abusive.' He pauses, giving Holly time to process this.

Holly's mind scans dormant information about Rachel and Damien, searching for any hint of truth in what Jack's telling her. Something that she might not have noticed at the time, but makes sense in this strange new context. But other than the fact that Rachel rarely spoke about Damien, there is nothing. And Holly had always just assumed she was protecting their privacy by not discussing her marriage. Of course, Damien comes across as cold and distant, but Holly's never considered it might go beyond that. Why didn't Rachel tell her? Unless this was what she was trying to tell Holly before she disappeared. 'How do I know you're telling the truth?'

Jack pulls out his phone, scrolling through his messages. 'Read these,' he says. 'Then you'll see.'

For over ten minutes, Holly reads through the long trail of messages between Rachel and this man, starting on Facebook then migrating to texts. The earlier ones from Rachel's normal phone, then more recently from the phone she'd kept hidden.

Rachel must have been deleting the messages as none of these were on that phone, other than the one Holly found.

And when she's finished, Holly knows with certainty that Rachel was trapped in an abusive marriage, and that Jack was trying to help her.

Before she hands back his phone, Holly checks the date of the last message. Two weeks before Rachel disappeared. Yet up until then, she and Jack had communicated several times a day. 'Why did she stop messaging you?'

Jack turns away. 'We... we had an argument. She told me she needed space, so I was giving it to her.'

'But what did you argue about?'

He watches a man walking his dog on the other side of the park, then buries his head in his hands. 'It was about Evie and the accident. I think it all became too much for her. She needed space from me.'

'So she could have disappeared because of you. You drove her away!'

'No! It wasn't like that,' Jack insists. 'I mean, yeah, it wasn't good that we argued. But... we'd been spending a lot of time together. And having met under the circumstances we did... I understood that she couldn't deal with it any more. But she cared about me. She wouldn't have gone because of me. And you must know she'd never have left her son.'

This has been what's bothered her since Rachel disappeared. It was so out of character. Being a mum to her kids meant everything to her. 'What did your text message mean? The one that said *Have you done it yet?*'

'I was asking her if she'd left Damien. She had this big plan to get him out of her life.'

'How?'

'I don't know. She said she couldn't tell me. That it would put me in danger.'

Holly stands, staring at Jack Parsons. 'I don't know what to think or believe. I just need Rachel to know that she can come home. I'll help her to get away from Damien. I'll be with her every step of the way. If you know where she is, just tell me! Even if she's told you not to.'

Before he can respond, Holly realises something she should have noticed immediately. That as a journalist she should have picked up right at the start. Throughout their entire conversation, Jack Parsons has been talking about Rachel in the past tense.

'I swear I don't know where she is,' Jack says, staring at the ground. 'All I know is that... Rachel is dead.'

THIRTY

BEFORE

Rachel

'You're being very quiet,' Jack says. 'Are you okay?'

They're in Bourne End, in Buckinghamshire – a place Rachel's never heard of until now. It's a pretty village set by the River Thames, and is where Jack's parents live. They're away for a week, and Jack is looking after Apollo, their dog. With Logan away on a school camping trip, Rachel jumped at the chance to get out of the house and away from Damien.

Walking along the river path, with the dog sniffing every bush he encounters, Rachel wants to tell Jack that she's okay. Or at least as well as she can be given her circumstances, but an overwhelming feeling she's had for a few days now is causing her anxiety. A sense that everything's leading up to something terrible. She's had anxiety before, but never this sense of impending menace.

'I'm all right,' she tells Jack, avoiding his gaze. Elijah's face when he realised she'd filmed him is ingrained in her mind, even though it was a few days ago. She's heard nothing from him since then, and the radio silence is worse, somehow, than being bombarded with his messages. But she knows he won't let it rest. He'll want to know what she was doing. It wasn't exactly how her plan was meant to go. Elijah will be threatening her for that video, and she could do without that.

At least Damien has left her alone for the last few days. That's not to say they've communicated as a husband and wife should. No, it will never be that way – but a sense of calm seems to have spread over the house. Over Damien. Which is exactly why she had to get out.

'I know I haven't known you that long,' Jack says, 'but I can tell something's different. And it's not just Damien. What's happened? I hope you can talk to me.' He stops walking to wait for Apollo to sniff some stones that have caught his attention.

'I'm running out of time,' she says. 'I've searched the house over and over and can't find any evidence of Damien's relationship with Ren. There's just no way for me to contact her, even if I could get her to go to the police about him. But even if she did, there'd be no evidence of what he did to her now, would there? Not all these years later.'

'I think you should go to the police anyway,' Jack says. 'They'll have ways of finding people. And what he's done to you is enough for them to start looking into his past.'

'And if they don't, or can't? Then Damien will be free to carry on. And it will only be worse for me if he finds out I went to the police.' They continue walking. Despite how close she's grown to Jack, there are still things she can't tell him. Elijah. Her plan.

'Why don't you come back to my parents' house?' he suggests. 'You've driven all this way. Logan's not home, so there's nothing you need to rush back for, is there?'

'No. But would that feel weird?'

'Everything about us is weird already. So no harm adding some more weirdness into the mix. Right?'

Rachel smiles. It's funny how Jack can lift her spirits, even in the depths of her despair. 'Okay. Maybe just for an hour.'

His parents live in a small cottage in the middle of the village, surrounded by charming shops and a church. A village green sits in the centre, with benches dotted around it, and Rachel can't help but smile again. It's like stepping back in time. 'Did you grow up here?' she asks, as he unlocks the door.

'No. Wish I had, though. My life might have turned out differently. Mum and Dad moved here from Surrey a few years ago. When they retired.'

They step inside, and Rachel's pleased that the cottage has the same homely feel on the inside. The narrow hallway is filled with low bookshelves, a multitude of trinkets and ornaments sitting on top of them, and paintings line the walls.

'They love art,' Jack says, noticing her taking it all in. 'Are you hungry? I can make some lunch. Might just be sandwiches. Not sure what else is in. Mum always uses up the food before they go away. She hates waste.'

Rachel's not sure she's hungry, but neither is she in a rush to go home. 'Sounds good,' she says. Looking around, it strikes her how easy it would be to start a new life. Perhaps a cosy cottage like this one. Somewhere for her and Logan that's completely different from the house they're living in. And Evie should be with them too. It should have always been just the three of them.

They eat ham sandwiches at the small kitchen table, and a sense of peace envelopes her. How strange that being around Jack does this, when it should have the opposite effect.

'Do you think you'll ever drive your car again?' Rachel asks. She hadn't planned to ask something so personal, to bring the accident to the forefront of his mind – but it's something that's always at the edge of her consciousness. She wants Jack to heal. And surely avoiding getting behind the wheel won't help him do that. She believes Jack's a good person, who something terrible happened to, and now that she's got to know him, his pain hurts her too.

'Not sure,' he says. 'London isn't far and I never drove to work anyway. I've got used to not driving. I prefer it.'

'Coming to see your parents on the train can't be straightforward,' Rachel says. 'And what if there was an emergency and they needed you to get here quickly? In the middle of the night? You have to think about things like this now they're getting older.'

'I hate putting people out. Asking for favours. But if it was that much of an emergency then I'd ask someone to help.' He smiles. 'Maybe you would?'

'I would if I was around. Course. But I won't be here for much longer.'

Again, Rachel speaks without considering her words, but it's too late to take them back.

'What do you mean?'

'Nothing. Just ignore me.'

Jack pushes his plate aside. 'Bit hard to ignore a statement like that, Rachel. What's going on?'

This moment has come too soon. She knew it would eventually, but she'd counted on having a little more time with Jack. 'We knew this couldn't last,' she begins. 'Didn't we? Because Logan would never accept it. He's too young to understand that relationships of any kind can be complicated.'

Jack's face visibly pales, and his eyes widen. 'Rachel, what are you saying?'

'It's time for me to go. Out of your life.'

'No. You don't have to do that. This works, doesn't it? Our friendship. We're there for each other.' He holds out his hand and takes hers. 'I've never had this with anyone. None of my other friendships feel like this. Even with guys I've known since school. I don't talk to them about stuff. *Can't* talk to them. You understand me.'

Rachel folds her hand over Jack's, liking how smooth his skin feels. It would be so easy to change her plan. Follow a different path. But she could never let Logan's and Jack's lives intertwine. And her son will always come first.

'I don't blame you for what happened,' Rachel says. 'You have my complete forgiveness, or whatever it is you need.'

'That's not what I need,' Jack says. 'Maybe to start with it was, but I've really grown fond of you. I don't want to lose you.'

'In a way, you won't,' Rachel explains. 'We'll always be connected. Through Evie. She's the tie that binds us, and in a funny way, being around you has kept her alive for me. But I have to move on.' She feels a tear in the corner of her eye, and wills it not to fall.

'Nothing has to change. Whatever you're planning to do – I can be part of it if you just let me in.'

Rachel almost caves at his heartfelt words. It would be the easier option. She could tell Jack everything she's planning, and let him knowingly be part of it. He would understand what she has to do. He'd support her, Rachel's sure of that.

But there are parts of her plan that he'd never agree to, and would try to talk her out of, and Rachel can't waver. This is what she must do. 'I have to do this alone,' she says. 'I'm dealing with Damien. I'm not going to let him have control over my life any more. And I need him out of Logan's life too.'

'You're scaring me, Rachel,' Jack says. 'What are you doing? Please don't do something you'll regret. Just talk to me.'

'I have to go,' she says, standing and taking her plate to the sink. The longer she stays here with Jack, the more she can feel herself faltering. 'Thanks for the lunch. It was lovely.'

'Wait, don't go like this. Let's just talk,' Jack says, reaching for her arm.

Flashbacks of Damien bombard her head, and she shoves Jack away. 'Don't touch me!' she screams.

He stares at her, and she sees something in his eyes she's

never witnessed before. Fear. Hate. Love. Maybe it's all of those things. All she knows is that she needs to get away. Because sooner or later, everyone becomes a danger to her.

THIRTY-ONE

NOW

Holly

Holly stares at Jack Parsons, hoping that her mind has conjured up the words he's just said.

Rachel is dead.

'Why are you saying that? What have you done?'

Jack's eyes widen. 'Me? No, no, you've got it all wrong. I haven't hurt Rachel. I would never. But I know her husband has. And every day I don't hear from her, I know this for sure. He's killed her.'

'You can't know that. Just because Damien isn't a good person doesn't mean he's a murderer. And he loves Logan. Anyone can see that.'

Jack studies her face so closely she almost looks away. 'He's done it before.'

'What?'

Jack leans back, exhaling as he stares up at the sky. 'Rachel found out about a year ago that Damien had tried to kill his ex-girlfriend.'

Once again Holly is stunned by the words coming out of

this man's mouth. 'That can't be... Why would Rachel stay with him if that's true?'

'She only found out just before Evie died, when this woman approached her and told her she was Damien's ex. He was physically abusive towards this woman, and one night he went too far and left her for dead. She survived, though, and would have gone to the police but Damien paid her to stay silent. A lot of money. That's why she never came forward. And she was terrified of him. But then she realised she had to warn Rachel. In case he did the same to her. I guess she didn't want that on her conscience.'

'If this is all true, and this woman was ready to tell Rachel, why wouldn't she go to the police now?'

'Two reasons,' Jack explains. 'One, she was ashamed that she'd taken the money. And two, she was scared of what Damien might do to her for talking. I suppose she's moved on with her life now and doesn't want to be dragged back to that time.'

Holly considers this. She can understand how difficult it must be to be in that situation. 'Then why didn't Rachel just go to the police herself?'

'Do you know how many times I tried to get her to? But Damien made it clear that if she ever left him, she'd never see Logan again. He'd been documenting things, trying to prove she was unstable and having mental health issues, but you know as well as I do that, other than grieving for her daughter, she was fine.'

But she wanted to be around Luna all the time. This thought smashes around Holly's head, and she tries to force it away but it lingers, taunting her. 'So... you think Damien's hurt her?'

Jack nods. 'Just like he did his ex. He's an evil man, Holly, and Rachel knew it. He must have found out she was trying to get him out of her life. She told me he would never let her go.' He stares up at the darkening sky and sighs.

Holly tells him about Luna going missing, and how everyone assumed it was Rachel.

'I read about that,' Jack says. 'But I had no idea it was your daughter who'd been taken. I'm sorry.'

'I know she wouldn't harm any child,' Holly says.

They both fall silent for a moment.

'What if Damien took her?' Jack says. 'Just to make Rachel look bad. So that if she ever left him, there'd be no chance she'd get full custody? Not if she was a kidnapper. He was always trying to manipulate her, and skew her sense of reality. But she was too clever for him – she knew exactly what he was doing. Every action he took was carefully planned to destabilise her. Rachel pretended she couldn't see what he was doing, but that was what she wanted him to think.'

Holly thinks of Luna's cuddly lamb. Damien claimed he'd found it, but she has no real proof of that; he could have been the one who took it. Until now, she'd never considered this. There'd been no reason to. Holly closes her eyes. She needs to process all of this new information. And it changes so much. Jack Parsons is a stranger to her – but clearly he and Rachel have come to care for each other, despite the shaky foundation their friendship is built on.

'What you're saying could make sense,' Holly says. 'But I can only work with proof. The police haven't found... Rachel. So we don't know that he's hurt her.'

'Then we need to find proof.'

'Let's just say I believe this is plausible. How exactly are we supposed to find proof of anything?' As she says this, her determination kicks in – to hunt for the truth no matter the risk. Or the cost. 'Actually, there might be something I can do. It might not come to anything, but it's worth a try.'

She tells Jack how she might be able to get into Rachel's house while Damien's out. 'Logan will let me in. I just have to find a good excuse to be there. He's already helped me and he'll do anything to help find his mum.' She'll need to be careful. She doesn't want Logan to be collateral damage in any way. 'I'll try tomorrow after school.' Holly has no idea what she'll be looking for, but it's worth a try. 'The police have already searched the house,' she says. 'And Damien's an intelligent man. He won't just leave evidence lying around.'

'No,' Jack agrees. 'But it's been a few days now, and everyone seems to think she's disappeared on purpose. Which is exactly what he wants us to think. He might be letting his guard down if he thinks nobody's pointing the finger at him.'

It's possible, and Holly wants to believe she'll find something that links Damien to Rachel's disappearance. Whatever it is. 'I'll call you when it's done.' She pulls herself up from the step, her body aching from sitting on the hard concrete. 'But just so you know – this doesn't mean I trust you.'

'I don't expect you to,' Jack says. 'And in a way, I'm glad you don't. It means you'll always be alert. Because if Damien finds out what we're doing, neither of us is safe.'

His words make her think of the man who was watching her. 'Have you been watching me? The other day when I was leaving my office?'

'What? No!' Jack frowns. 'Why d'you ask that?'

'Someone's been watching me and Luna. I didn't think it was you. I've only seen him from a distance but his build was different. He was stockier. And then someone lit a fire in our garden last night and left a child's doll burning in it.' She tells Jack about the note, even though she hasn't yet determined whether or not she can trust him. *Stop asking questions.*

She scrutinises Jack's face. She's usually good at detecting lies or inconsistencies, but she can't get the measure of him.

'You need to be careful. Maybe Damien sent someone to scare you so you stop digging around?'

'Maybe. Whoever it is, though, I'll find out.'

As she walks away from this man who's shattered so many

of her perceptions this evening, she turns back to find him still sitting, watching her.

Elijah opens the front door before Holly's even put her key in the lock. 'I've been worried about you,' he says. 'You didn't reply to my message.'

Her stomach tightens. 'What's happened? Is Luna okay?'

'Yeah, course. Sorry. I didn't mean to worry you. She's fast asleep and your mum's in her room with her. She said it's what you'd want.'

Holly smiles. Her mum knows her so well.

'I asked her if she'd mind if we went out for dinner. I know it's late but neither of us has eaten. You must be hungry.'

After the conversation she's just had with Jack Parsons, the last thing Holly wants is food. 'Would you mind if we don't? It's been a long day.'

'Which is exactly why we need to go for dinner. Sit and relax. Luna's safe with your mum, and you could do with switching off from work.'

'Maybe another time?'

'We need to talk, Holly. We've hardly spent any time together lately.'

She's about to refuse again but reconsiders. Elijah never asks for much, so this is the least she can do. 'Okay. But somewhere close.'

They pick a Thai restaurant, ten minutes' drive from their house. Holly, quiet on the drive there, lost in her thoughts, sits silently, still unable to force small talk.

'I know you're worried about Rachel,' Elijah says, once they've ordered. 'And I'm sorry I haven't been supportive. I just didn't like the way she was obsessing over Luna after Evie died.'

Holly doesn't want to talk about this – not to her husband, a man who will never have a kind word to say about her friend. 'Let's not talk about it,' she says. 'We'll never agree.'

'I just don't want you to think I'm not here for you.' He takes her hand. 'I love you. You and Luna mean everything to me. Let's not let anything get between us. Nothing. Not your work, or mine. We stick together, whatever we have to go through.'

Something about Elijah's words doesn't feel right. 'Where's all this coming from?' she asks. He's never been one for huge gestures or declarations. Their love has sat silently for the most part, comfortably private.

'I feel like you're slipping away,' he says, lowering his voice.

'There's been a lot going on.' Holly glances around the room. It's quiet in here tonight and there are only three other parties. No one is looking at them, yet she constantly feels as though there are eyes on her.

Elijah takes a sip of his red wine. 'I feel like you spend more time with Ross than you do with me.'

'*What?* Ross has got nothing to do with anything,' she says. 'Not sure why you're even mentioning him. I do spend a lot of time working, but that's the nature of the business. Ross is just my boss. Nothing more.' Holly wonders if she's protesting too much. Elijah's never spoken about this before, though she's sensed it's been simmering under the surface for a long time. She needs this conversation to stop; she doesn't want Elijah forcing her to confront things she doesn't want to think about, because once it's there in her mind, growing like a seed, how will anything be the same?

'I get the feeling he likes you,' Elijah says, determined to pursue this topic. 'I can tell by the way he looks at you. Don't tell me you haven't noticed.'

'He's my *boss*. And we've become good friends.' She's too tired for this conversation, too on edge.

'I have to be honest, Holl,' Elijah says, 'it makes me a bit uncomfortable that you spend so much time with him.' He holds up his hands. 'I'm not saying I have any problem with you working so much. But I just need to know' – he takes another sip of wine – 'that you don't feel the same about him. Because then it doesn't matter how he feels, does it? I can live with that. If I knew the feelings weren't mutual.'

'I would never have an affair,' Holly hisses. 'You must know that about me. I stand for the truth, whatever it is.' *Then tell him now. Tell Elijah you're afraid of your feelings. You might be able to control them, but you can't pretend they don't exist.* Holly can't bring herself to say any of this. He would never understand that she'd never act on it. That any feelings she has for Ross are safely constrained behind a wall that she'll never knock down.

'I know,' Elijah says. 'Sorry. Maybe all this stuff has just got to me. Luna. Rachel. It's taking its toll.'

Their food arrives, and thankfully Elijah changes the subject. 'We should get away for a bit,' he says. 'Before the summer holidays. Take Luna to Spain or Portugal. Maybe Greece.'

Holly loves the sound of this, but she can't go anywhere; not when Rachel is missing and Damien might be responsible. 'Maybe in a few weeks?' she says. 'I'll have a look as soon as I can and get something booked.' She doesn't want Elijah doing it too soon, she needs time.

Elijah smiles. 'It will do us the world of good,' he says. 'All of us.'

There's a change in him by the time they pull up at home. Elijah's spirits have lifted now that he's been reassured there's nothing going on between her and Ross.

He unfastens his seatbelt and leans across, gently kissing her. 'I love you, Holly,' he says.

Her phone rings as they're getting out of the car. 'It's Damien.' She answers quickly. 'Hi.'

'Holly... They've found her.'

'They've found Rachel! Where is she?'

There's a long pause. 'No... you don't understand. They've found a body. In the river about a mile away. I have to go and identify her now. Will you come and stay with Logan for me?'

Holly's head thumps, too loud for her to think straight. 'Yes, I'm coming. But it might not be Rachel. It can't be.'

'The woman they've found is wearing the same clothes. Dark blue jeans and a white shirt with a large bow. It *is* Rachel.'

THIRTY-TWO

NOW

Holly

Logan answers the door and collapses into her arms, sobbing, struggling to catch his breath.

'I'm so sorry,' Holly says, shutting the door behind them. 'Your dad's gone to the hospital now, to... to identify her. He asked me to come and stay with you.' She hopes this is okay. Maybe Logan won't want her here. Maybe it's too painful to have his mum's closest friend here, while Rachel is... She can't say the word. It doesn't seem real. Perhaps it never will. Now Holly's beginning to have an inkling about why Rachel was finding it hard to let go. Why she needed to be around Luna.

And I stopped her. What kind of friend am I? What kind of person?

'Maybe they've got it wrong?' Logan says, pulling back. 'It might not be Mum.'

When Holly doesn't say anything, his hopeful expression fades and Logan grabs her tighter, like a toddler needing his mum. She lets him take his time, and eventually he relaxes his grip, stepping back, his face pale and his cheeks red and tear-stained. 'Is it okay for me to be here?' Holly asks.

He nods. 'First Evie... and now Mum.' Logan's face crumples, and he erupts into tears again.

Holly hands him a tissue from her bag. 'I'm so sorry, Logan. This is all so devastating.' She takes his arm. 'Let's go and sit down. Your dad said they're sending the family liaison officer round soon. She's had some sort of emergency but shouldn't be too long.'

'I... I don't want the police here. I just want them to leave us alone. They can't bring Mum back, can they?'

'No, but they can find out what happened to her.' Holly leads him into the living room.

'She jumped into the river,' Logan says, flopping onto the sofa. 'That's what happened to her.' Again, he wails, leaning forward and clutching his stomach. 'It was all too much for her to deal with.'

Holly places her arm around his shoulders. 'Listen, whatever happened, we have to remember what a strong person your mum... was. How hard she fought each day without Evie, to be there for you. The pain she was feeling is unimaginable, but she kept going. She never gave up.'

He shakes his head. 'What are we supposed to do without her? She held this family together. I know Dad does what he can, but it was always Mum. Even when she could hardly get out of bed, she always made sure I had everything I needed. And then people just think she took Luna. She could never do anything like that.'

Holly sits beside him. 'I know that. And soon everyone else will too.'

Logan wipes his eyes, trying to stem the flow of tears. 'Will they? How? People will just say she killed herself because she took Luna and couldn't live with the guilt.'

But someone might have pushed her. Holly doesn't say this aloud – Logan's already in a bad enough state; she needs to minimise the impact if she can.

Instead, she tells him not to focus on that, and lets him cry on her shoulder while he rocks back and forth. 'People always die around me,' he says. 'Maybe it's all my fault? If I hadn't fallen off my bike—'

'No,' Holly says, pulling back so she can see his face. 'Look at me. Don't ever say that. None of this is your fault.' *But it might be your father's.*

Logan curls up and buries his head in a sofa cushion, muffling the sound of his tears. She sits beside him and waits. Eventually, when Logan calms down, she offers to make him some hot chocolate, grateful when he accepts. Of course a hot drink won't make anything better, but it will give her something to do while they wait for Damien, and will allow her time to work out what she's going to do.

In the kitchen, she spoons chocolate powder into a mug, and it hits her that perhaps she's in shock; no part of her brain is fully acknowledging that Rachel is gone. And all Holly feels is disbelief. Rachel can't be dead. Her friend will call her any second now and have an excuse for why she's been AWOL for the last few days. And as for the poor woman they've pulled from the river – well, that's awful too, but it isn't Rachel. Holly is numb. Confused. And she still needs answers, still wants to clear her friend's name.

She takes the hot chocolate into the living room and finds Logan asleep, still curled up, tears still damp on his cheeks. She decides against waking him; at least sleep will bring him some respite from his pain.

In case he wakes in the next few minutes, she places the mug on the coffee table, then, pulling the door closed, makes her way upstairs. Holly has no idea what she's looking for, and there's only a slim chance of finding anything that could provide answers, but there's nothing to lose by trying.

As she passes Rachel's room, she decides to have a quick look in there first. As Jack had said, Damien might have got confident, believing no one was looking in his direction, and that could have made him sloppy.

She begins in the wardrobe, sharp spasms shooting through her stomach as she rifles through her friend's clothes. Finding nothing except the keys that Logan must have put back in her coral blazer pocket, she moves on to Damien's, listening out for any sounds before she continues to search. There's nothing out of the ordinary, and not much in his pockets other than loose change and a couple of receipts: one for petrol and the other for an Italian restaurant. Nothing incriminating.

Next she checks their bedside tables, finding a laptop in Damien's. She pulls it out, switching it on. But of course it's password protected. In her pocket, her phone rings. It's Elijah. She quickly ends it before it can wake Logan, switching it to mute.

Turning back to the laptop, Holly contemplates what Damien might use as a password. She tries *PropertyDeveloper*, unsurprised when it bleeps and a red cross appears. She tries a couple more, wondering how many goes it will give her before it locks itself. And then she tries *Evie*, holding her breath when the screen comes to life and she's in. Surely there can't be anything on this laptop, otherwise he'd have selected a more secure password.

She goes to the top of the stairs, listening out again, relieved when all is silent. Then she peers through the blind to make sure Damien hasn't got home yet, or that the FLO isn't pulling up outside.

Sitting on the bed, she balances the laptop on her knees and starts poring through its contents. As expected, there's not much on there, and either he's never gone online on it or he's erased the internet search history.

Browsing through more files, Holly finds nothing of interest. Giving up hope, she clicks on the last folder, labelled *Work*, surprised to find only one thing in there. A video. Frowning, Holly clicks on it.

Her breath catches in her throat.

It's Rachel. Kissing a man who isn't Damien. Within seconds, Holly realises that the man is Elijah. Clasping her hand to her mouth, she wants to close it down, make it disappear, but she's frozen, unable to pull her eyes from the screen. Seconds pass before the video ends, and all Holly can do is stare at the now black screen.

She plays it again, no longer caring if Damien is outside. And watching it for the second time, she's no longer numb. Anger courses through her. Rachel. And Elijah. Holly should hate her friend for this, but she can't. Whatever Rachel did, something drove her to it. She wouldn't have done this recklessly.

Blinking away tears, Holly logs on to her Gmail. She needs to get a copy of this. It might be the only chance she has before someone destroys the evidence of this affair that's shocked her to her core. Sending the video to herself, she deletes the browser history a second before she hears a car pull up outside.

Switching off the laptop, she throws it back in the drawer and only just makes it to the bottom of the stairs before Damien opens the door.

He stares at the floor. 'It... it was her,' he says.

Holly feels as though her legs will buckle, and she can't form any words. How can these last few days have led to this?

'How am I supposed to help Logan through this?' Damien says. There's no sign of tears in his eyes. No sign of any emotion.

Holly can't be in this house with him. 'I have to go,' she says, brushing past him, half expecting him to stop her.

He knows about Rachel and Elijah; what she can't understand is why he hasn't said anything.

It hits her when she's in the car, driving away from the house with Damien watching her from the door. Damien is pretending he doesn't know. The affair gives him a motive for harming Rachel.

THIRTY-THREE

NOW

Holly

Elijah's watching her from the window as she pulls into the drive. He disappears, and seconds later the front door opens and he rushes outside in his socks. 'Was it Rachel?'

When Holly responds with a nod, he pulls open the car door and reaches in to hug her. 'I'm so sorry.'

Holly's body stiffens, and she can barely look at him as she gets out of the car. 'Is Luna okay?' she asks. 'And Mum?'

'They're both asleep. Holly, why didn't you answer my call? I was really worried about you.'

'You knew I was looking after Logan.' Elijah had been right there when Damien had called, so his behaviour is strange.

'I know, but when you didn't reply, I—'

'What? Worried about me?' She slams the car door and locks it. 'Or did you worry I'd found something out?'

He screws up his face. 'What are you talking about? You've been gone ages.'

Holly pushes past him and heads inside. She won't tell him that she's been driving around aimlessly, lost in a mass of confused thoughts, not knowing how to organise them into anything coherent. At first. But now she sees everything clearly, and she knows exactly what she has to do.

Inside, she peels off her jacket and hangs it on the coat hook, next to Elijah's. 'I have a question for you,' she says, staring straight at him. 'When were you going to tell me about you and Rachel?'

Elijah's face drains of colour, and his skin looks almost translucent. 'What?'

'My guess is probably never.' She prays that at the very least, Elijah won't try to deny it.

'It's not like you to be lost for words,' she says when he doesn't respond. 'Normally you have plenty to say.' Holly walks into the kitchen and sits at the table, burying her head in her hands.

It's not long before she hears him come in. 'You're upset,' he says. 'Rachel's just been found and it's bound to take its toll.'

She looks up. 'On you too. I'm guessing it must be hard to sleep with someone and not be affected by their death.' Maybe it was just a kiss. That video doesn't have to mean they slept together. Not that it makes any difference. It's the betrayal that matters more.

But when Elijah doesn't correct her, the truth hits Holly like a punch to her gut. 'When?' she asks. 'When were the two of you ever alone?' There are tears in his eyes now, and Holly wonders who he's crying for – her or Rachel.

He walks to the back door and stares into the darkness outside. It feels like a lifetime before he finally turns to her. 'It was that night she babysat for Luna. When you had your office party.'

Holly recalls that night. How ironic that she'd spent most of her evening avoiding Ross, because the excitement she'd felt when he'd touched her arm had terrified her. 'That was six months ago,' she says.

Elijah nods. 'It was the only time it happened – I swear to you.'

'No,' she says. 'It *wasn't* the only time.'

He frowns. 'We, um, we did meet up in a coffee shop. Just to talk about what a terrible mistake we'd made, but that's it. I'm telling you the truth, Holl. I messed up – I'm sorry.'

Holly wants to show him the video, so he'll know for sure it's game over for them. But she holds back, to let him dig himself deeper. 'So nothing else ever happened after that night?'

He joins her at the table. 'No, nothing. It was a one-off. A huge mistake. We both regretted it after.' He tries to take Holly's hand.

'Don't touch me,' she says, pulling away. 'How did it happen? You must have liked her before that night. You didn't just wake up one morning and suddenly realise you wanted to sleep with my friend.'

He doesn't answer immediately, staring past her out of the window, then back down at his hands, twisting his wedding ring around his finger. 'I wasn't in a good place. All this stuff with Ross—'

'Don't you fucking dare!' Holly shouts, slamming her fist on the table. 'I have *never* done anything with Ross. You know that. Don't put this on me!'

Elijah hangs his head. 'I'm not. I didn't... I know it's my issue. In here.' He taps his head. 'But I was stewing on it and... I made a terrible decision. To make myself feel better.'

'And Rachel just went along with it?' Somehow, this hurts more than Elijah's betrayal.

'She was drunk.'

'What?'

'When I got home, I persuaded her to have a drink with me. Then more. I think she was messed up, you know, because of Evie. And I... I took advantage of that.'

Holly struggles to get her head around this. Rachel wouldn't have let someone take advantage of her. Some part of her must have wanted Elijah. But she'd never paid him any attention before, had rarely even been around him. Then Holly thinks of Damien, and everything he was putting Rachel through. 'You knew she was struggling,' she says to Elijah. 'In a vulnerable place. You disgust me. You're despicable!'

'I know,' he says. 'Don't you think I know that? I've never tried to pretend I'm perfect,' he says. 'Not like Ross, who can do no wrong.'

Holly shakes her head. 'Ross isn't perfect. Ask his ex-wife. None of us are! We're all just trying to muddle along and do the best we can. But morality is a different matter. We can choose to be a decent person, Elijah. And you decided not to be.' *So did Rachel. I wish I could ask her why. So she could help me understand.* 'Everything I thought I knew about you isn't real.'

'One mistake,' Elijah says. 'Don't throw our marriage away because of this. Please, Holly, I'm begging you.'

'One time? That's all it was?'

He nods. 'I promise.'

Holly pulls out her phone, clicking on the email she'd sent herself from Damien's laptop. Without a word, she places the phone in front of him, watching his face as he registers what she's found.

Elijah doesn't wait to watch the whole thing. He stops it within a second, sliding her phone back to her. The last time Holly saw such anguish on his face was when Luna was taken. 'How did you get that?' he says.

'Does that really matter?' she asks.

'Rachel sent it to you.' He's mumbling now, and can't look at her. At least he has the decency to feel ashamed.

Holly stares at him – why would he think this? Her mind searches for explanations. 'Why would Rachel have sent it to me?'

He takes his time to answer. 'Because she wanted to tell you what we'd done. She felt awful. She was putting pressure on me to tell you, saying that if I didn't, then she'd tell you herself. And I suppose she wanted proof. She lured me to that coffee shop – she'd planned all along to get someone to film us. She didn't really want to do anything with me. I don't know why she wanted that video. Probably for evidence to show you.'

'How... how do you know Rachel planned to film it?'

'Because she made an excuse to go to the toilet and told me not to wait for her. Something just didn't feel right. I went back and saw her get her phone from the guy serving coffee.' He hangs his head. 'I tried to grab it off her but she ran.' He looks up at Holly. 'I'm not proud of any of this.'

'Damien knows.'

'What?'

'I found the video on his laptop just now. Hidden in his work folder. He knows, Elijah.' As much as Holly loathes her husband right now, she doesn't want any harm to come to him. No matter what he's done – he's still Luna's dad.

'But how did he get it?' Elijah asks.

This is what Holly has been puzzling over, and all she can think is that he found it on Rachel's phone. It doesn't surprise her that Damien might have been spying on Rachel. 'It doesn't matter how he got it,' she tells Elijah. 'The fact is he knows. Damien hasn't said anything, not to me anyway. And that's worrying. Why wouldn't he confront you? So I think you need to be careful.' Holly doesn't tell him about what Damien has already done to his ex-girlfriend. She can no longer trust Elijah. 'It's just weird that he wouldn't have said anything. But that doesn't mean he's not planning to.'

'I can handle him,' Elijah says.

He reaches for her hand, and once again she pulls away. 'I need you to get out,' she says. 'Just leave. Pack a few things and I'll make sure you get everything else you need.'

'No... please, Holly. Don't do this. We can work this all out. What about Luna? She needs both of us. She's been through—'

'She'll have us both. We don't have to live together to be her parents.' Holly stands. 'Go and pack. Now. I don't want you in this house any more.'

'Where am I supposed to go?'

Ignoring him, Holly walks out of the room, heading upstairs to check on Luna. After a few minutes, she hears Elijah in the bedroom, opening cupboard doors and drawers. And then his footsteps on the stairs. The front door opening and closing.

'We'll be just fine,' she whispers to her sleeping daughter. 'No more lies in this house. Ever.'

After watching Elijah drive away, Holly sits on her bed and calls Jack Parsons. It's late now – almost midnight – but she needs to be the one to tell him about the police finding Rachel's body. There's no answer so she leaves a message asking him to call her urgently. Then she goes to the window and peers outside. Elijah's car has gone. At least he left without too much fuss, although Holly doubts he will give up so easily.

She tries to call Jack again, but he still doesn't answer. Downstairs, she checks the front door is locked, and then all the windows, before putting the alarm on. She'll just have to hope her mum doesn't wake up for water in the middle of the night. Upstairs, she grabs her duvet and takes it to Luna's room.

Until she knows who left that doll burning in their garden and wrote the note, she's staying with her daughter all night.

All night, Holly has lain awake, with memories of Rachel running through her mind, and her cheeks damp with tears for her friend. She gets out of bed as dawn breaks, and creeps downstairs for coffee. She sits at the table, trying desperately to make sense of everything. Rachel is dead. Her mind won't let her accept this, trying to convince her this is a terrible misunderstanding.

And her marriage is over. Strangely, she feels at peace with that part.

The first thing Holly did this morning was check her phone, but there's no reply from Jack. The only message is from Damien – telling her he needs to talk to her.

Does he know she found the video on his laptop? Holly shivers, despite the warmth of the sun filtering through the kitchen doors.

She's finishing her coffee when her mum comes down, still in her nightdress, with a thin silk kimono dressing gown over it. 'I'm so sorry,' she says, throwing her arms around Holly. 'Devastating news.'

For a fleeting moment, Holly wonders if she's talking about Elijah, but her mum can't possibly know about that yet. 'How did you hear?'

'It's all over the local Facebook group. People are saying it was suicide.'

'I don't know,' Holly says. 'There's no way to know yet. I suppose we'll have to wait until the post-mortem.' Holly rests her head in her hands. 'I still can't believe it. *Rachel*.'

Liz pours herself coffee and joins Holly at the table. 'Has Elijah gone out already? I thought he had some more time off work?'

'Actually, Mum... it's complicated to explain – but Elijah and I are separating. He's moved out.'

Her mum's eyes widen, her mouth hanging open. 'But... why? You never said anything. You went out for dinner last night.'

It would be easy to tell her mum about the affair, but right now Holly doesn't have the energy to go over it all. 'We're just taking some time apart. I'll tell you all about it soon, but right now all I can think about is Rachel.'

Liz sighs and shakes her head as she blinks back tears. After a moment, she gathers herself. 'Of course. Whenever you're ready to talk.' Liz stirs her coffee. 'Can I do anything?'

'Actually, would you mind staying a bit longer? I know you have your trip to Morocco, but you said—'

'You don't even need to ask,' Liz says. 'Let me just make some calls, but consider it done.'

Even at seven fifteen, there are already several people at their desks, and Holly is hoping Ross will be one of them. She needs to tell him about Rachel, if he doesn't already know. But when she gets to his office, the blinds are down, bathing it in darkness. She carries on to her own office, closing the door behind her.

Rachel is at the forefront of her mind. She owes it to her to find answers. To get justice for what Damien did to her, and Ren.

Many people in Holly's position might resent Rachel for what she did with Elijah, but Holly knows that Rachel will have spent her last few months hating herself. And what would hate do but eat away at Holly? No, she needs to focus on compassion and understanding for her friend, because something drove Rachel to sleep with Elijah, something Holly's sure has nothing to do with immorality.

At her desk, she writes down everything she knows about Rachel's circumstances. Elijah, Damien, Jack and even Luna. Rachel is the common ground here, Holly just needs to look closer.

Someone knocks on her door, opening it before she's answered.

'Can I come in?' Paul asks, stepping inside.

'I think you already are.' Holly flips over her notepad. 'What do you want, Paul?'

He sits on the sofa by her window. 'I'm sorry about your friend. I wasn't expecting this to be the outcome.'

Holly doesn't reply; she has trouble believing that anything that comes out of Paul's mouth is genuine.

'I know I've been out of order,' he admits. 'You know, with the stuff I've said. The way I've acted towards you.' He pauses. Perhaps he's waiting for Holly to accept his apology, but she won't make this easy for him. 'I've had a word with myself, and... it won't happen again.' He sighs. 'Look, I respect Ross. He's a decent guy, and he'd never give someone a job just because... Anyway, I... respect you too.'

'I appreciate that,' Holly says. 'But you do realise your story on Rachel is extremely hurtful and damaging.'

'I know.' He holds up his hands. 'I've told Ross not to publish. In view of what's happened. Anyway, I think *you* should be the one to write it.'

Holly narrows her eyes, unsure whether this is part of some game Paul is playing. 'That's what I was saying from the beginning,' she says. 'But why have you changed your mind?'

'Because a woman is dead. And I'm not heartless.' Paul stands. Perhaps he isn't as bad as she's always thought. How is it that she's been so wrong about so many people in her life recently?

'Suicide is such a terrible thing for everyone who knows the person,' Paul continues. 'I hope you're not blaming yourself in any way.'

'What makes you so sure it was suicide?' Holly asks. 'We don't know that.'

'No, but it's the most likely thing,' Paul says, smiling briefly as he leaves the room.

Perhaps she wasn't wrong about him after all.

Her phone rings, not long after Paul's left. She considers ignoring it when she sees it's Damien, but she needs to make sure he trusts her.

'Hi.'

'Why did you rush off like that last night?'

'Sorry. How are you doing?'

'People think that because I'm not in floods of tears, or falling apart, I'm not upset. But we all grieve in different ways.'

Holly's tempted to tell him she knows about everything he did to her friend, until she remembers what he's capable of.

'Thank you for staying with Logan yesterday,' Damien continues. 'He said you really helped him.'

'He's very welcome. Look, I really need to—'

'I wanted to tell you that you've been wrong all along.'

'Wrong about what?' Holly taps her pen on the desk.

'Rachel did this to herself, and you need to get your head around that. She took Luna. Changed her mind and let her go. Then couldn't live with the guilt. The best thing you and Elijah can do is move on with your lives and put this all behind you.'

Holly can't find any words. What she wants to do is scream at this cold, heartless man. A man who tried to murder his ex-girlfriend. Someone he purported to love.

'Another thing,' Damien continues. 'I'm taking Logan away from here. As soon as we can. He needs a change of scenery. Another country. A fresh start.'

His words leave her cold. Holly knows she can never let that happen.

THIRTY-FOUR

NOW

Holly

She should go straight to the police. There's evidence of Damien's abuse in those messages Rachel sent to Jack. That might be enough to convince them to start digging into Damien. Holly's never been able to accept that Rachel could take her own life, even though everything she's learnt over the last twenty-four hours has shown her that she never completely knew her friend. But as she listens to the lies coming from Damien's mouth, she instinctively knows she can trust her gut, even without firmer evidence.

'Do you think it's a good idea to drag Logan away from his friends? School? Everything familiar to him?'

'It's exactly what he needs. He's in pieces. Absolute bits.'

Holly's unsure how to respond to the man who is very likely Rachel's murderer. Damien knows that Rachel had an affair with Elijah – this could have pushed him over an edge he was already dangerously close to. And the fact that he's staying silent about it could only mean that he's planning his own

revenge. The police will have to act if Holly shows them the
video – it gives Damien a motive.

But it also gives her one too...

'I need to ask a favour,' Damien continues, interrupting her
stream of muddled thoughts. 'If you'll help me out? I've got
some things to take care of today before I can make plans for me
and Logan to leave. There's some stuff I need to sort out with
the business and it can't wait. Especially as I won't be here.
Would you come and stay with Logan again? I don't want to
leave him and he won't come with me. You're the only person
he'll stay with. I promise, I won't forget your kindness.'

Holly should refuse. But Rachel would have wanted her to
be there for Logan. 'Okay. I can come in a couple of hours.'

He ends the call with a mumbled thank you, and immediately Holly feels a surge of regret. No part of her wants to be in
that house again, where Rachel suffered such terrible things at
Damien's hands. But she needs to be there for Logan. Perhaps
she can talk to him about Damien's plans to move to another
country. Plant a seed of doubt in Logan's mind, if there isn't one
already.

Holly immediately tries Jack again, tapping her fingers on
her desk as she wills him to pick up.

'Holly, sorry, I've only just—'

'Why haven't you been answering? I've tried calling you
loads.'

'I know. Sorry. Only just got your voicemail. My dad had a
stroke so I had to come to my parents' house. I haven't been
checking my phone.'

'Oh. I'm sorry. Is he okay?'

'Thankfully it was minor, so he should be all right. Anyway,
what's happened? Are you okay?'

'You haven't heard, have you?'

There's silence. Jack already senses what she's about to say.
'They've found her?'

'I'm sorry.'

Silence again. 'Where?' His voice sounds different now. Faint. Fearful.

Now Holly's faced with saying it again, the reality of Rachel's death consumes her. She explains what she knows to Jack, and his agonising gasp says more than any words. She wants to ask him if he's okay, but of course he isn't.

'She didn't jump in that river,' he says, after a moment.

'I know,' Holly agrees. 'We need to go to the police. We can show them your messages from Rachel. They paint a picture of Damien's abuse. It should be enough to get them investigating him. And when they do a post-mortem, it might show evidence of the abuse.'

'Maybe. But Damien's too clever. Too premeditated. And he's got money, and that means power. If he got away with it, he'd come for us. Look what happened to his ex. You've got Luna to think about. And your husband.'

'What if I've got something more?' An image of Rachel and Elijah kissing in that video forces its way into her mind. The last thing Holly wants to do is sully Rachel's name to a man who clearly cared about her, but she needs to persuade Jack to go to the police with her, and she has more chance of doing that in person. And that means causing him some pain.

'What is it?' Jack asks.

'Can you come here?' she asks. 'I can't explain it on the phone. There's something I need to show you.'

'I'm coming now,' he says, without hesitation. 'It might take me a while to get there from here. Where are you?'

Holly gives him her office address and ends the call, her mind whirring. She's sure there's something she's missing. Something that's right in front of her. But no matter how hard she searches her mind, it remains out of reach.

. . .

By the time Jack calls to say he's outside, Holly head is throbbing, her calf muscles aching from pacing the room. She stops by Ross's office again on the way to the foyer, surprised to find he's still not there. She doesn't recall him saying he was taking leave, or had any meetings away from the office today.

At the main door, she greets Jack and leads him to her office, grateful that Paul's not at his desk to see them as they pass.

'I drove here,' Jack says when Holly has closed her office door.

Holly frowns. 'Well, that's the quickest way to get here.'

He puts his car fob in his pocket. 'Ah, you couldn't have known, but until just now I haven't driven since the accident. I couldn't get behind the wheel. Rachel kept telling me I needed to try, but I just couldn't do it.' He sits on the sofa. 'Then when you called, I had no hesitation. Because it would be what Rachel wanted. I did it for her.'

'That's a huge deal,' Holly says.

Jack closes his eyes. 'I won't like this, will I? Whatever it is you need to show me. Otherwise you would have told me on the phone.'

He's an intelligent man; Holly can see why Rachel grew fond of him, despite him driving the car that killed Evie. 'I'm sorry,' she says, flicking through her phone. She finds the video and hands it to Jack. 'I found this on Damien's laptop. I don't know how it got on there – Rachel was the one who had it filmed on her phone. The man in this video is Elijah. My husband.'

She watches Jack's face as he presses play, and isn't surprised to see it crumple. 'I don't understand,' he says, handing it back to her before it's even finished.

Holly explains what she knows about the affair from Elijah's eventual confession. 'I know it must be hard for you to watch that. But we all make mistakes,' she says. 'Please don't let this change the way you think of Rachel. She was in so much pain. My husband took advantage of that.'

Jack takes a deep breath. 'Nothing could make me change my mind about Rachel. She... she let *me* into her life – the person responsible for her daughter's death. I owe her so much. She helped me to heal as much as I'll ever be able to.'

Holly smiles. 'That's why we need to fight for her. And going to the police is the only option. We need to trust in them. And this video, and your messages, will help.'

'Because it shows Damien could have been jealous of the affair. Motive for killing her.' Jack walks over to the window and stares out across the car park. 'I just hope when they do Rachel's post-mortem, they can actually prove that it wasn't suicide. Otherwise, Damien gets away with it. Because if he pushed her in, what's the difference between that and her jumping? Forensically, I mean.'

'I've thought about that,' Holly says. 'And Rachel was such a good swimmer. She always talked about how she wanted Logan to join his swimming club, because her parents never let her, even though she was the fastest swimmer in her school.'

'I never knew that,' Jack says. 'There were so many things we were yet to find out about each other, I guess. And I was really enjoying doing that.' He sighs. 'Okay, let's do it. But you do understand the risks?'

Holly nods. 'We could be suspects too.'

'Yep. You could have been jealous of the affair with your husband. And they could try to say that I was in love with Rachel. And couldn't handle her being with another man. They could twist everything.'

'We have the truth on our side,' Holly says. 'That has to be enough.'

'When do you want to do it, then?'

'There's something I need to do first,' Holly explains. 'Damien's asked me to stay with Logan this afternoon while he

sorts out some urgent things at work. At least that's what he said
he'll be doing. Who knows if he's telling the truth?'

'Going to his house doesn't sound like a good idea,' Jack
says.

Holly nods. 'I know. But I need to do this for Logan. It's
what Rachel would want me to do. That poor boy is a mess, and
last time I managed to help him a bit. Not sure how, but...' She
shrugs. 'And it makes me feel closer to Rachel.'

'Okay, I get it.' Jack studies her. 'I can see why you and
Rachel were so close. It must take a lot for you to forgive her.
And it took a lot for her to forgive me. I'm not trying to say what
I did can be compared in any way to—'

'I know.'

'I just mean – that's one hell of a deep friendship.'

A friendship that's lost now. Holly stifles her tears; now is
not the time to fall apart. She needs to get justice for her friend.
'I'll call you as soon as I leave Damien's. I've told him I can only
spare a couple of hours. Then you and I can go to the police.'

'Just be careful when you're there,' Jack says.

After he's left, with thoughts of Rachel sitting firmly in her
mind, Holly somehow manages to finish writing up the Oscar
Hobbs story. She's pleased with how it's turned out, and she's
sure Ross will be happy with it too. She messages her boss to see
where he is, but gets no reply.

On her way out, at just after two p.m., Holly asks Marley,
the office manager, if she knows where Ross is.

'Maybe he's treating himself to a lie-in?' Marley suggests.
'He works so hard – I wouldn't blame him.'

'Can you tell him to call me when he comes in?'

'Will do.'

Outside, Holly stares across the road, to the verge where
she saw that man watching her and Luna only days ago. In
light of what she now knows about Damien, Holly tells herself
she read too much into it. It was Damien who took Luna, to

make it look like Rachel was guilty, losing her mind somehow. That's the only thing that makes sense. But he wouldn't have risked doing it himself, because Luna could point him out any time. Intense confusion and anger churn inside her at the thought of what he put Luna through. There's every chance Damien has sent someone to try and warn Holly to stop looking into it.

Holly's heart feels as if it will tear as Logan opens the door and she takes in his appearance. He looks more dishevelled than yesterday, with unbrushed hair and blotchy red skin.

'Thanks for coming,' he says, and his politeness only crushes her even more. In a few

hours, his life will be thrown into further turmoil as he learns what his dad is capable of. Losing two parents at the same time will traumatise him, and Holly vows to always be there for him, for whatever he needs. She's sure Damien's parents will step in to look after him, but she needs him to know she'll be there too, helping to keep the memory of his mum alive.

'I know there's nothing I can say that will make anything better,' Holly says. 'But I loved your mum. She meant so much to me.'

Logan nods. 'Thanks for saying that. Everyone still thinks she took Luna. I just don't know how to change their minds.'

Holly steps inside and pulls off her jacket. 'People will know the truth soon. I promise you. I've... well, I can never let things go, and I've been digging around. I know it wasn't your mum, and I also think I know who took her.'

Logan stares at her. Perhaps he's as numb as she is. 'I hope you're right,' he says. 'For Mum's sake. Do you mind if I go to my room?'

'No, of course not. This is your house – do whatever you

need to. I'll just be around until your dad gets home. In case you need anything.'

'Thanks,' he says, making his way upstairs.

In the kitchen, Holly sits at the table and messages her mum to see how Luna is.

The reply is immediate: *She's fine. We're painting. See you soon x*

Next, she messages Ross again. She sent him the Oscar Hobbs story over two hours ago and he still hasn't replied. It's not like him to ignore a story, especially when it's overdue. And now that she thinks about it, he will surely have heard about Rachel, so why hasn't he contacted her, at least to see how she's doing?

Elijah calls again and she lets it ring out. She's not ready to communicate with him yet. He tries a second time and she turns her phone to silent, ignoring his voicemail.

She pictures Rachel sitting across this table from her, remembering the time they talked about Rachel going back to work. If Holly had understood what her friend was going through, things might have been so different.

She calls up to Logan to see if he wants anything to drink, and when he says no thanks, Holly gets herself a glass of water.

As she's filling the glass, the doorbell rings. Assuming it must be a delivery, Holly calls up to Logan. 'I'll get it.'

'Okay,' he calls back.

The doorbell rings again, just as she's putting down her glass. Then a third time. 'I'm coming!' Holly shouts. Rushing to the door, she pulls it open, gasping when she sees who is standing there. 'You!' she cries. She's made a huge mistake letting her guard down.

Before she can slam the door shut, a fist smashes into her face, sending her reeling backwards. Then come flashes of excruciating pain, like she's never felt before.

And everything fades to black.

THIRTY-FIVE

BEFORE

Rachel

It's been a couple of weeks since Rachel saw Jack at his parents' home in Bourne End, the charming cottage she could have stayed in forever. And she feels his absence like a gaping wound. She didn't think it would hurt this much to cut him out of her life, and hadn't expected to feel it so acutely, although she understands why it does. Jack has been a huge part of her life these last few months, someone she's come to trust, and whose company she enjoys, and the thought of never seeing him again, of such finality, feels like raw grief. But this is the way it has to be.

Upstairs in her bedroom, she stands by the window waiting for Damien to leave. Logan's still asleep, and she's got a few minutes before she needs to wake him for school. Damien is leaving later than she'd hoped he would this morning, and it's hard not to feel paranoid that he's doing it on purpose. All week he's been out of the house by six, yet today it's nearly eight and he's only just leaving. Does he somehow know what she's planning?

Once his BMW has disappeared from sight, she runs down-stairs to lock the front door. She can't risk him coming back and finding her. The thought of what he'd do to her makes her stomach cramp. Sweat coats her palms as she heads back upstairs, listening out for any sound from Logan's room. But all is silent.

Back in the bedroom, she takes Damien's laptop from his bedside drawer. It's not the one he uses for work – that one he would never leave lying around – but this one he calls his backup. And luckily for Rachel, occasionally he lets Logan use it for his homework. Otherwise, she'd never have been able to guess Damien's password. Guilt rushes through her as she recalls how she'd hovered behind Logan the other day, pretending to be busy tidying but watching as her son had typed it in. Lost in his own world, Logan hadn't noticed her, and would never have suspected what she was doing. She hopes her son will forgive her; soon he will realise that everything she's done is for him.

She types in *Conquertheworld83!* and crosses her fingers. She's in. There's still nothing much on there, no work files, and no evidence of what Damien's done. She's already checked several times. She takes out her USB stick, the one she uses at school – she can never trust the cloud – and opens it, scrolling through until she finds what she needs. She doesn't watch the video again – she doesn't need to; the thought of watching herself kissing Elijah sickens her. All Rachel has to do is find somewhere on this laptop to hide it. She creates a folder, naming it *Work*, and hides it in Damien's downloads folder. It doesn't matter too much how well hidden it is, Damien won't have a chance to find it. Not if this all goes to plan. Besides, she's been keeping track and he hasn't used this laptop for months now.

But for extra security, Rachel changes the password, just in case she needs more time. Damien's not particularly tech-savvy, so by the time he's got into it, it will be too late. And who would believe he can't remember his password?

She thinks of Luna, away from Holly and Elijah for two nights now. The poor little girl must be terrified. But Luna will be okay. This isn't like what happened to Evie. It can't be. She won't let it be. Rachel will join the search again after school. Just like everyone else. Elijah won't like it. He's still leaving her alone – probably afraid to harass her now that she's got this evidence, but Rachel's aware that he won't let it lie. Not when Rachel is a threat to his marriage.

That's another reason she has to get out of here, why she has to throw this bomb into her friend's life and watch it explode, because ultimately it will be for Holly's benefit. But she can't control when it will all come out. All she can do is pray that Holly will find a way to be okay. In the end. She'll have Ross, of course, although it might take Holly some time to realise that he's the man she's supposed to be with.

Rachel shuts down the laptop and places it back in Damien's bedside drawer, covering it with some papers, just as she'd found it. And then she goes to wake Logan.

She's distracted at school. Not only with thoughts of Luna, but setting her plan in motion has caused anxiety to ripple under her skin. She's on high alert, waiting. Hoping it will all work out as she's planned. She delivers her lessons as best she can, but wonders if her students can see through her. That everything is about to change. Not only for her, but for everyone she has any contact with.

Holly, most of all.

At lunchtime, she sees Logan in the playground. He's sitting on the low wall by the basketball courts, where he usually goes to have lunch by himself, tucking in to the ham sandwich she made for him this morning. Another boy walks up to him, and she strains to make out who it is. Oscar Hobbs. He sits down next to Logan and the two of them strike up a conversation.

Rachel smiles. Oscar's a good kid, really. He'd mentioned not long ago that Logan's always on his own, and now he's reaching out the hand of friendship. He might be four years older than her son, but age has nothing to do with friendship.

After the last lesson of the school day, she sits in her classroom marking a pile of exercise books. There can be no loose ends; she wants everything up to date. Nothing messy that will plague her.

With all the books marked, Rachel pulls out a piece of A4 lined paper and begins to write the note she's had planned in her head for days. As she writes, a tear splatters onto the page, smudging some of her words.

It's nearly six by the time she's ready to leave, and she places all the books in neat piles, in class order, on the table at the back of the room. It feels good to have done this. There are just a few more things she needs to do.

Outside, she walks through the courtyard towards the car park. It's deserted now, and she feels like she's the only person in this vast place. There are over a thousand students in this school, and Rachel has probably taught most of them at some point or other. Tomorrow they will all be talking about her. Rachel smiles at this thought.

As she reaches the car park, she hears voices coming from around the corner. A girl and a boy. Loud and heated. She stops and listens.

'Why are you doing this?' the boy asks. 'Just tell the fucking truth.'

'Because you deserve it,' the girl says. 'You so fucking deserve it.'

Rachel steps forward – whatever's going on, she needs to break it up and encourage them to go home. For the next few minutes at least, she's still a teacher.

But as she rounds the corner and sees that it's Oscar Hobbs and Megan Hart, she instinctively steps back. This is a conversation she needs to hear more of before she makes any move.

'I can't help it if I don't like you like that,' Oscar says. 'I'm not into you, Megan.'

'You liked me enough to sleep with me!' Megan hisses.

'And then I didn't want to any more. It's not a crime! You didn't have to accuse me of... of rape!'

Rachel flattens herself against the wall to remain out of sight.

'Just tell my mum at least. No one else has to know. Please, Megan. I just want my mum not to look at me with... that look.'

'I dropped the charges, didn't I? That's all I can do. And however your mum looks at you, you deserve it!'

'You're a dirty liar,' Oscar spits. 'You lied about Miss James too. She never said she was picking up her daughter from nursery. Why did you tell everyone that?'

'Just leave me alone!' Megan shouts.

Footsteps pound the concrete, and Rachel peers around the wall, watching as Megan flies around the corner, away from the school.

Oscar stands still, staring after her. Rachel needs to go to him, to tell him she heard everything and that she believes him. She always did. But as she opens her mouth to call his name, Oscar runs off too, in the opposite direction to Megan.

Rachel heads to her car. It must be awful to have the whole world think you've done something so terrible, when you're perfectly innocent. She has to let Oscar know she believes him. She can even tell his mum. That will take the strain off their relationship. He's got his GCSEs coming up – he doesn't need this distraction. If she's quick, she can fit in a visit to his house; she knows where he lives. It's on that newish estate with the green in the middle. She's seen him hanging around with his friends.

But first, there's something she needs to do, or her whole plan will fall apart.

Rachel parks her car in the drive but doesn't go in her house. Instead, she leaves her large bag of school things on the passenger seat. Taking only her handbag with her phone in it, she walks down her road, following the path to the nature reserve. She hasn't been there for years, and can't remember the exact layout, but she knows there will be people there. Dog walkers, joggers. Witnesses who will see her. Who will remember her when she's reported missing.

Inside the nature reserve, she wanders around, going over it, making sure there isn't anything she's missed. She's got to make sure this all goes according to her plan. There's no room for error. If any of this goes wrong, then Damien has won.

A woman walks towards her, holding two dogs on a lead. Rachel takes a deep breath and prepares herself, fixing a blank stare on the ground. As she gets closer, she recognises the woman approaching her, although she can't quite place her.

'Hi,' the woman says, stopping right in front of Rachel. 'Do you remember me? You used to teach my kids – Sam and Penny Ortiz.'

A light flicker inside Rachel's head. Of course she remembers them. They were sweet kids. Worked hard. 'Yeah,' Rachel says, turning to stare at the river. She remembers this woman's name is Gabriella. It's a name she would have picked if she hadn't chosen Evie instead.

'They're at college now,' Gabriella says. 'Doing really well.'

As much as she wants to, Rachel doesn't reply. She shifts her feet, staring down at the ground again.

'Well, I'll leave you to it,' Gabriella says.

If Rachel looked at this woman now, she'd surely see a frown on her face. Confusion. Perhaps worry. But Rachel can't let anything sway her. This has worked out perfectly. Not just a witness, but someone who knows her, and won't forget they've seen her. She lifts her hand in a half-hearted wave, then resumes staring at the muddy ground.

She doesn't dare to move until Gabriella's out of sight, then moving slowly in case she comes back, Rachel searches for somewhere to leave her phone and bag. Everything she's carrying with her, except for the note she checks is still safely in her pocket. This is it. There's no going back now. And even if she could, Rachel wouldn't want to.

Afterwards, she leaves the nature reserve, heading towards Oscar's house. She could do without this detour, but it's important she helps put things right for him. She's got time, everything will still work as it's meant to if she doesn't take too long.

When she gets to his house, she's pleased to see a light on upstairs. If no one was home, she'd have to write a note and post it through the letterbox. Again she thinks of the note she's got in her pocket. The most important part of the plan. The thing that will make sure there's little room for doubt about what's happened to her.

That note will point straight to the man who's responsible for taking Rachel's life.

She rings the doorbell and waits. Footsteps thud down the stairs and then Oscar answers the door. 'Miss,' he says. 'What are you doing here?'

'Sorry to turn up like this, but I heard you and Megan arguing at school just now,' Rachel explains. 'Can I come in, just for a second? I want to explain to your mum what I heard Megan saying. It's awful that she did that to you. I had to come and set things straight.'

Oscar's face reddens, and he glances behind him. 'Um, Mum's not in.'

'Well, maybe I can come in anyway? I'd like to leave a note

for her. To explain. I think it's really important that she knows the truth.'

'Can't you just call her or something? Tomorrow?'

'I actually won't be here tomorrow. When will she be back? If it's soon then maybe I can wait for her?'

'Um, she's gone away for a few days. With my aunt.'

Rachel frowns. 'So you're here on your own?' She knows Oscar's sixteen, but he's still a school child.

'No, I've been staying at my dad's. I just came back here to get some stuff for school. I'm going back in a minute.'

Upstairs, something crashes to the floor, followed by an ear-piercing shriek. Has Oscar got a girl upstairs? Is that why he's been hesitant to let her in?

And then Rachel realises the sound is nothing like a teenage girl screaming.

It's a toddler.

But Oscar doesn't have a sibling.

Rachel stares at Oscar. 'Who is that?' she asks, making her way towards the stairs.

But she doesn't need an answer from him. She already knows.

THIRTY-SIX

BEFORE

Rachel

Rachel flies up the stairs, ignoring Oscar's pleas for her to stop. She prays that she's got this wrong, and that it really was an older girl's scream, but instinctively she knows it was Luna's cry she heard; Rachel has paid enough attention to her friend's toddler to know exactly how she sounds. And that was an anguished scream.

Oscar's following her, and for a moment she expects him to grab her, to grip her neck so that this secret – whatever it turns out to be – dies with her. But he doesn't touch her, and instead races past her, throwing open the door before she can reach it.

Luna's inside, sitting on the floor in dirty pyjamas, her cheeks blotchy and tear-stained. Horror courses through Rachel's body, mixing with relief as she rushes to scoop Luna up. 'Come here my sweetheart. Everything will be okay now.' Intense rage burns her cheeks as she turns to Oscar. 'What the hell have you done?'

Oscar shrinks back. He's never heard her shout like this

before; Rachel never raises her voice in lessons. 'I haven't hurt her, I swear!' he says, his eyes pleading to be believed.

Rachel cuddles Luna tighter, smoothing her matted hair from her face. 'You took my friend's child! Why? Why would you do this?'

Oscar sinks back against the wall. 'I... I... I was giving her back. I...'

'How did you know where Luna lives?'

'I... I saw you once with her mum. I... I followed you to her house. And that night – I didn't know her window would be open like that. I didn't know for sure how I'd get in.'

'You'd better start explaining why you did this,' Rachel demands. 'I'm seconds away from calling the police.' As soon as she says this, she realises the vulnerable position she's in. She no longer has her phone, and nobody knows she's here. There's no way for her to call for help. But surely Oscar won't hurt her. He looks more terrified than she is. *He stole Holly's little girl, though. Who knows what he's capable of? When someone's desperate, they could do anything.*

'Talk!' she demands, holding Luna closer, wiping the tears rolling down the little girl's cheeks. 'It's okay, I'm going to get you home to Mummy,' she whispers into Luna's hair.

When Rachel turns back to Oscar, he's also crying, the tough act he puts on at school long forgotten. He sinks to his knees, burying his head in his hands. 'I haven't hurt her,' he says, repeating the words like a mantra. 'I wouldn't.'

'Then what have you done?' Rachel lowers her voice. 'What the hell's going on?' She checks Luna, relieved to see there are no visible bruises, nothing to suggest she's been physically harmed. Yet her pyjamas are soiled, and must be making her more distressed. 'She's filthy! You could have given her clean clothes.'

'I couldn't get any,' Oscar says. 'I would have. I've been feeding her and giving her water, though.'

Rachel shakes her head. This makes no difference. Even if Oscar hasn't harmed Luna, what he's done is unforgiveable. 'Tell me why you did this,' she says. 'Right now, Oscar.'

He stares at his trainers, taking his time to answer. 'I... needed money.' His voice is so quiet that Rachel can barely hear him.

'What?'

'I couldn't get a weekend job,' Oscar explains, staring at his hands. 'No one around here would give me a chance. I filled out loads of applications and went round places to ask in person. Everyone just said no. That's if they even bothered to get back to me.' He sniffs. 'And Mum doesn't have much money. It's Megan's fault. All of it. She messed everything up for me. All my mates have everything they want. Clothes. New trainers. Money to go out. I've got nothing.'

Rachel takes a deep breath. 'But what's this got to do with Luna?'

Oscar breaks down again, staring at the carpet. 'I started stealing a bit. Selling stuff. But it was too risky and I could never get enough money. I had an idea. I thought if I could... take a kid and... and ask the parents for a ransom, then I'd get a lot more. People would pay anything to have their kid back, wouldn't they? And I knew your friend had a kid cos I'd seen you all in the park together.'

Rachel stares at him, her whole body filled with horror. This is nowhere close to anything she could have imagined he would say. 'But... there was no ransom demand.'

'I was waiting. I got nervous. I had to make sure there was no way it could be traced back to me. I didn't want to do this—'

'But you *did!*' Rachel shouts. 'Luna could have been hurt. What if something had happened to her? What if she needed urgent medical attention? Would you have left her to die in case you got caught?'

'No!' Oscar insists. 'I... didn't think of that.'

Rachel tries to stem her anger. She has to remember that no matter what he's done – Oscar is still a child. 'She's not even three. She needs to be with her mum!' The thought of what Luna's been put through sickens Rachel.

He hangs his head. 'I know.'

'Where have you been keeping her?'

'Here.'

'But you said your mum's away and you've been staying at your dad's. So you left Luna here on her own?' Nausea churns in her stomach. 'Jesus, Oscar!'

'But I've been coming back here at night. Dad hasn't noticed. He always goes out at night.'

Rachel has no words, and becomes acutely aware of the lurching pain in her body. She glances around the room. It must be their spare room. There's a sofa bed, a desk and a grey beanbag chair. Some toys for Luna. 'Is that all she's had to play with?' she says, pointing to the fluffy rabbit and Lego bricks scattered on the beige carpet. 'That Lego is too small for her. She could have swallowed it and choked!'

'She's, um, she's not really been playing with anything.' Oscar shrugs. Is he even aware of the seriousness of what he's done?

'That's because she's traumatised!' Rachel is seconds away from throwing up at the thought of what this will have done to Luna.

Standing up, Oscar shoves his hands in his pockets. 'Please don't tell anyone! I'm begging you. I'll give her back. I won't ever do anything like this again – I swear!'

'I'm sorry, Oscar. You have to tell the truth. That's always the answer. You need to go to the police and tell them exactly what you've done. The fact that you're owning up will count for something.'

His nose begins to run and he swipes it with his sleeve. 'I've got my exams. I've been working really hard. Trying my best to do well. I'll go to prison.'

'I know you've been trying hard at school,' Rachel says. 'But you have to face the consequences of your actions, Oscar. We all do.' In her arms, Luna clings to her, burying her head in the crook of Rachel's arm. Just like Evie used to.

'Can I... I just need to get some water.'

Rachel nods. 'And then we call the police.'

She lets Oscar go downstairs by himself. The only thing he could do is run, and Rachel's not worried about that. He can't hide forever. And Luna is safe. That's the only thing that matters.

When he comes back, carrying a glass of water, Rachel is sitting on the bed with Luna on her lap, still clinging to her. She seems a little calmer now, but she hasn't said a word. Rachel turns to Oscar. 'Are you ready?' she asks.

He nods.

'I'll need to use your phone. I left mine at home.' Rachel needs this to be quick; she has to go – time is running out. But there's no way she's leaving Luna. It should be fine, even if she has to stay here until they come. She should still be able to finish what she was doing, and get Damien out of her life.

'I'll do it,' Oscar says, pulling his phone from his pocket.

Rachel nods. 'You're doing the right thing.'

Luna begins to cry, so Rachel picks up the bunny from the floor, only for Luna to bat it away. She wishes she had Luna's grey lamb, but she's locked it in the shed. Rachel had taken it from Holly's house, the last time she'd been there. After everything that happened with Elijah, she knew that would be the last time she'd set foot in there, and she wanted something to remember Luna. In a way, the lamb reminds her of Evie too.

'Hi, um, yeah,' Oscar says. 'I need to report something... I know what's happened to the little girl who was taken. Luna Fisher. I took her.' He hangs up, and turns to Rachel. 'I don't need to give them my address, it will only take them a second to get it from my number.'

'You've done the right thing,' Rachel says. 'You know that, don't you?'

'My life's over,' Oscar says. 'It's all over.'

Rachel considers offering Oscar some reassurance, but he doesn't deserve it. Not after what he's done to Luna. 'Let's go and wait downstairs,' she says, lifting Luna from her lap and carrying her out.

They wait in the living room, each of them silent as Luna clings to Rachel and Oscar paces the room. She wants to scream at him to stop, but she doesn't have the energy. Finally, the doorbell rings, and Oscar stops walking and sinks to the floor, wailing. Despite everything, Rachel does pity him. He chose the wrong path, and things could so easily have been different.

'I can't do this,' Oscar says. 'Please...'

Ignoring him, Rachel takes Luna with her to answer the door, praying that she won't have to spend too long talking to the police. She opens the door, ready to explain what she's found, but it's not the police standing there.

A man she's never seen before pushes her backwards, forcing his way in and slamming the door shut.

And that's when Rachel knows that this night is not going to end how she'd so carefully planned it.

THIRTY-SEVEN

BEFORE

Rachel

Luna screams, and Rachel shields her as much as she can. Before she can say anything, Oscar appears behind her, staring at them.

'You came,' he says to the man who's just forced his way in.

'Course I did. Someone's got to get you out of this mess. But this is the last time. You pull a stunt like this again and I'll wring your neck. First it's rape, then it's—'

'I didn't do that!' Oscar protests. 'She knows!' He points at Rachel. 'Tell my dad you know I didn't do it. You heard Megan say it.'

Rachel's so stunned that she can't speak. She stares at this man she's never seen before. Oscar's father. He's never been to a parents' meeting at school – that's always been Oscar's mum on her own. She sees the resemblance now. He has the same dark hair as Oscar, the same wide-set eyes.

Still shielding Luna with her free arm, and cradling her with the other, Rachel searches her mind for a way out of this mess. 'Please,' she says. 'All I care about is that Luna is safe. I can see she's okay and hasn't been hurt. Just let me take her back home to her mum. I don't have to say anything about Oscar taking her. I won't tell the police any of this.' When her plea elicits no response, she tries again. 'You're a dad, you must know how Luna's parents are feeling. They're distraught. Just let me get her back to them. All they'll care about is that she's home safe.'

Oscar's dad raises his thick eyebrows. 'Yeah, but then I'd have to spend the rest of my life wondering if you were ever going to spill our little secret. I'm not living like that. Constantly on edge, looking over my shoulder. No way in hell.'

'Please, Dad,' Oscar begs. 'Miss James won't say anything. I trust her. She's not like other teachers. She really cares. She didn't look at me like I was a piece of shit after Megan's lies.'

'I suggest you keep quiet,' Oscar's father says. 'This almighty mess is all your fault and I'm the one who has to sort it out. Best thing you can do is stop talking and take that girl upstairs. Now. I need to figure this out and you're making it worse.'

'No!' Rachel cries. 'Let me keep Luna with me. She needs me!'

But he ignores her, yanking Luna out of her arms and thrusting her into his son's. Oscar reels backwards, almost toppling over but managing to grab the banister in time to stop himself falling.

'Get upstairs!' Oscar's dad roars at him, grabbing Rachel's arm and dragging her into the kitchen.

'You shouldn't have come here,' he says, once Oscar's disappeared upstairs with Luna. 'Turning up at your student's house at night. What the hell is that all about?'

Rachel doesn't reply. She doesn't owe this man answers.

'Lost your voice all of a sudden?' He steps closer to her.

'It's not too late,' Rachel says, glancing at the knife block on the worktop. 'You haven't done anything – you can let me and

Luna go. I'd really owe you for that. And I wouldn't tell the police. But even if I did, Oscar's the one who did this – not you. You can wash your hands of it.'

With a sneer on his face, he edges towards Rachel. 'These hostage negotiator tactics won't work on me. He's my fucking son. Don't you get what that means? I have to protect him. Do what I can for him. His mum thinks I'm a useless dad, never there for him.' He smiles. 'If only she knew the lengths I have to go to for Oscar. Shame I can't ever speak about this to let her know what I'd do for our boy.'

Rachel's legs weaken. How much longer will they support her weight? 'What's your name?' she asks, trying to keep the fear from her voice. She'll try anything to get out of this.

'What the fuck does that matter?'

'Please tell me.'

'Ryan.'

'Please, let us go, Ryan. Me and Luna. You'll never see me again.'

He shakes his head, and sweat pools on his forehead. 'I can't. My hands are tied. I can't let this ruin Oscar's life. He's got potential. He can go places. Do whatever he wants in life. He's bloody *sixteen*. I'm sorry.'

Somehow, Rachel believes that Ryan just might mean he's sorry. But his desperation is terrifying. She knows the lengths people will go to when they feel they have no choice.

Again, her eyes briefly flick to the knife block. She didn't think anyone could scare her as much as Damien does, but Ryan Hobbs is a close match. This man's got just as much to lose by letting her go. He's right that Oscar's life will be over once the police know. But she can't let that sway her. *We have to take responsibility for our own actions.*

Rachel feels herself struggling for breath – she needs to act fast before it's too late. This night has already veered her off course, when she'd so meticulously worked everything out. She can't let this man ruin it.

She runs towards the knives, grabbing the largest one, knocking the block over as she drags it out. All she needs to do is injure him enough to give her time to get away with Luna.

But Ryan's reactions are too quick, and within a second he's lunging towards her, grabbing her around the waist and squeezing so hard she's sure her ribs will crack. The knife crashes to the floor, sliding away from her. Still grabbing hold of her, Ryan reaches for it, lifting it to Rachel's throat. She freezes.

'Were you really going to use this?' Ryan says. 'Do you even know how?' He pushes the knife closer, cold against her skin. 'Do you know the best spot to ram it in so that there's no doubt you'll end someone's life? Because you can't leave a job like that half done. Can't give someone the chance to come back for you. Someone like you wouldn't know any of that.' Pulling the knife away, he grabs a fistful of Rachel's hair and drags her into the living room. A scream escapes her mouth. She will fight this man, with every fibre of her being.

Holding the knife to her neck again, he roots around in her pockets. 'I'll need your phone,' he says. 'I can't trust you.'

'I don't have it. I left it at home.' How ironic that this is the truth.

'You're lying,' he says. 'Who leaves the house without their phone?'

'I don't normally. I forgot it,' Rachel says. Her voice sounds strange, as though it no longer belongs to her. She is not a victim. She refuses to be that.

Rachel's body stiffens when he pats the pockets of her jeans, but of course there's no phone in them. Nothing except for the note she's written, neatly folded up in the back pocket. If Ryan finds it, then it will offer him just what he needs. She holds her breath, praying he doesn't notice it, and only exhales when he gives up and pushes her back on the sofa.

Ryan stalks around the room, his face paler than when he first forced his way in. He doesn't want to hurt her. Perhaps Rachel can still appeal to him. 'You still haven't done anything,' she says. 'It's still not too late to let me and Luna go. Please, Ryan.'

'Shut up!' He waves the knife. 'Just shut up! I need to think.'

Upstairs, Luna's cries become more anguished. Rachel needs to get to her. That poor little girl has already suffered too much. 'Please, Ryan.'

He rushes towards her and grabs her neck. 'I said shut up!'

Oscar appears in the living room doorway, holding Luna, who is still sobbing. 'Dad, we need to let them go. Miss James won't say anything.'

Ryan loosens his grip, backing away from her. 'This is all on you,' he says, turning to Oscar. 'I should have made you sort it out yourself. But now I'm mixed up in it. And I'd go to prison. I'm an accessory now.'

Hearing these words, Rachel acknowledges that it's almost over. There is no way out of this. *But there's still a way to ensure some sort of justice is served.* While Ryan and Oscar argue by the door, she reaches into her back pocket and pulls out the note, slipping it in between the sofa cushions, making sure it can't be seen too easily.

'Take Luna out of here,' she says to Oscar, tears choking her words. 'Don't let her see this.'

But Oscar doesn't move, and Luna stares at her, wailing, reaching out her arms to Rachel.

It hurts too much to watch, and she knows Oscar's frozen. So Rachel closes her eyes and waits, thinking of Logan. Silently praying he will be okay.

'This is the only way,' Ryan is saying to Oscar. 'And we let that fucking kid go. I don't care where, just dump her somewhere. There'll be no tie to us, then.'

'Dad, no, please,' Oscar begs. 'We can just let her go too. She won't say anything.'

Footsteps stride across the carpet, towards Rachel, and then she feels Ryan climb on top of her, the weight of him pinning her down. There's movement, and she can't work out what he's doing, but she won't open her eyes. It's better not to know.

Silent tears fall from her eyes as she feels something cover her mouth. A cushion. It smells of fabric conditioner. And even though Rachel knows it's futile, she fights back, wriggling underneath him, trying to force him off her, trying to get her nose and mouth free from the fabric that's suffocating her.

The last thing she hears is Oscar's anguished scream. And her final thought is that she hopes he's turned Luna away so she can't see this.

THIRTY-EIGHT

NOW

Holly

Holly opens her eyes, and everything instantly floods back to her. It takes her a second to get her bearings and she realises her arms and legs are bound. The thick rope digs into her skin, piercing her flesh. She takes in her surroundings. Rachel's living room. A room that doesn't feel as if Rachel was ever in it.

And then she notices him sitting on the chair by the window, watching her. Holly stares back at him, and she's not sure whether it's fear or confusion she feels the most. Perhaps both in equal amounts. She knew as soon as she opened that door that she was in trouble. Recognition had struck her like a wrecking ball, pounding into her skull.

'Who are you?' she asks, her voice cracked and hoarse. 'What do you want?'

'I know it's your job to ask questions,' he says, in a voice Holly instantly recognises. One that's oddly pleasant, that doesn't fit with this situation. 'But I'll do the asking now.'

'We spoke on the phone,' Holly says, when she catches her breath. 'You're Oscar's dad. Ryan.'

'Genius,' he says, mocking her with his smile. 'I can see why you're such a good journalist. Digging around, always trying to uncover things that should be left alone.'

Holly ignores him. 'Where's Logan? What have you done? If you've hurt him—'

'I'm not here for that boy,' Ryan says.

Luna, then. Perhaps it wasn't Damien who took her after all. Never has Holly felt so out of her depth, unable to comprehend a single thing that's happened over the last few days. 'My daughter isn't here.' And Holly will never let him take Luna. Never.

'Didn't I just say that I'll be the one asking the questions? I'm not here for your daughter either. That girl's already caused enough problems for me.' He gazes at Holly, his mouth an amused half-smile.

'Damien sent you, didn't he? Doesn't want to get his hands dirty so he's paid you to do it for him. How much? What was the cost for my daughter?' It sickens her to even think of this.

Ryan raises his eyebrows. 'Perhaps you're not very good at this after all. I thought you were an investigative journalist. But you're way off.'

'I've seen you watching me. You're not so clever yourself. Isn't the idea of stalking someone to remain unseen? And you're the one who left that doll burning in my garden.'

The amused expression on his face changes. 'Yeah, maybe that was a mistake on my part, but I'd assumed you'd have the sense to stop digging around. But you haven't. I didn't want it to come to this. None of this had to happen. You've made life very difficult for me, Holly Fisher.'

Confusion still hangs over her like a thick grey cloud. No matter how hard she tries, Holly can't make any of the pieces fit. She's missing something but can't grasp what it is.

'You said this isn't about Luna. Then what—'

'I didn't say that. What I said was *I'm not here for your daughter.*'

Holly stares at him. 'I don't...' But then it becomes clear. The only thing that makes any kind of sense. 'But you *do* know who took her.'

Ryan Hobbs doesn't speak, but stares at her, shaking his head. 'It's a hazardous job, isn't it? Being a journalist? You have to put yourself in all sorts of dangerous situations.'

'I can handle whatever's thrown at me.'

'Brave talk,' Ryan says. 'Sadly, that's all it is.'

'Logan!' Holly shouts. 'Get out of the house! Run!'

'You're wasting your breath,' Ryan says.

Holly's seconds away from throwing up. 'What have you done to him?' she spits. 'His dad will kill you. If there's even a scratch on him – Damien will come for you.'

'Do you think I'm scared of anyone?' Ryan shouts. But his voice is quieter, less self-assured than it was moments ago. 'I'm just here to clear up messes that other people have made for me. I don't care about Damien. Don't even know him.'

'He's already killed his wife,' Holly warns. 'He won't hesitate to do the same to you.'

Ryan raises his eyebrows. 'And what makes you think that?'

'Why? Are you scared now? Just let me go. I need to make sure Logan's okay.'

'You know, you've done me a favour,' Ryan says, pulling a knife from his back pocket. 'If this Damien's already killed someone, then it's likely he'd kill you too. That makes things so much easier for me.'

Fear grips Holly, squeezing her breath from her. Up until now, she's believed there'll be a way out of this, that this man can't be as dangerous as Damien. Now it's becoming apparent that she's been wrong to assume this. 'What have you done that's so bad you have to do this? If you did take my daughter, I don't care now – she's safely back with us. I have nothing to go to the police with. Nothing that involves you.' Ryan must be lying about not knowing Damien. She's sure he's tied up in this somehow.

Ryan stares at her, shaking his head. 'Enough chit-chat,' he says.

Holly ignores him. 'At least tell me what the hell's going on. If you're about to use that knife on me, what does it matter if I know? I'm not getting out of this, am I?' She holds up her bound wrists, kicks her legs out. 'I can't run away, can I?'

Ryan stands. 'Yeah, yeah – this isn't some movie where the victim gets to find everything out. And everything gets neatly revealed. Real life doesn't work like that. It's messy. You don't need to know anything.'

He walks towards her, the knife in his hand, and Holly notices it's shaking. It's almost imperceptible, but it fills her with hope. If there's even a tiny flicker of doubt in his mind, then she can use that to get out of this.

'I hope Damien doesn't mind mess on his carpet,' Ryan says, lunging towards her.

Holly springs up, ploughing into him with as much force as she can muster. Ryan reaches out to grab her, plunging the knife into her side. Her body feels cold, but surprisingly it doesn't hurt. Unbalanced from the force of her knocking into him, Ryan falls backwards. Spasms of pain shoot through Holly's arm. She turns as Ryan falls to the floor, his head smashing against the sharp edge of the fireplace, a pool of blood oozing from his hairline.

'You fucking bitch!' he shouts, managing to haul himself up. He grabs Holly's neck; she tries to squirm, but his hold on her is too strong, and with the ropes around her wrists and ankles, Holly is trapped.

But she will never give up. Summoning every iota of strength in her body, she fights to escape his grasp. But it's futile. Her body begins to loosen, as if she's losing herself. She struggles for breath. Then comes an ear-piercing smash, and Holly wonders if this is the sound people hear when they're dying.

Then slowly, Ryan's grip loosens, his hands slipping away from her neck. She doubles over, taking in huge gulps of air as Ryan collapses to the floor, a pool of blood fanning around him.

It takes her a moment to realise that Logan is standing there, holding Rachel's marble fruit bowl. Holly had bought it for her birthday last year, when Rachel had seen it when they were out shopping. She'd loved that fruit bowl.

'Thank God you're okay. I thought—' Holly sinks to the floor, clutching her side.

Logan stares at Ryan, his eyes filled with fear. 'Is he... is he dead? What if I've... killed him?'

Moving closer to Ryan, Holly checks his pulse. 'He's still breathing. Can you check his pockets? I think he took my phone and car key.'

Logan hesitates, shaking his head. 'I... I don't want to touch him.'

'Please, Logan,' Holly begs. 'I can't do it with these.' She lifts her hands. 'And we need to get out of here.'

He hesitates for a moment, but eventually Logan kneels down, tentatively poking around in Ryan's pockets.

'Hurry!' Holly warns. 'We need to be quick!'

'Is this it?' Logan pulls out a phone.

'No, that must be his. Mine's an iPhone. Keep looking.'

Logan does as she asks, eventually finding her phone and key in the back pocket of Ryan's jeans.

'Do you think you could grab that knife and cut these ropes?' Holly asks, glancing at Ryan. 'I don't know how much time we'll have.'

Again, Logan hesitates. He looks like a child at least five years younger. Terrified. 'I don't think I—'

'Yes, you can. Just try. Be quick!'

Logan manages to slice through the rope, and once she's free, Holly grabs his arm and they race from the house, just as Ryan begins to stir.

They don't speak until they're driving away, heading towards the police station.

'You're bleeding,' Logan says. 'Your arm.'

Holly keeps her eyes on the road. 'It's okay. I'll be okay.' But the wound is beginning to throb, and Holly knows she needs to get it checked. It's probably only shock that's preventing her from feeling the full force of pain.

'But your jacket's soaked. And it's going all over the car!'

'Logan, please don't worry. We just need to get to the police station.' Where she'll begin when they get there, Holly has no idea. There's still so much that doesn't make sense.

'I think that man took Luna,' Holly says.

'What?'

'He's Ryan Hobbs. His son Oscar goes to your school.'

'I know Oscar,' Logan says.

Holly nods. 'He's been following me ever since Luna was returned. Maybe keeping an eye on me to see if I've been poking around.'

Logan stares out of the window, and tears glisten on his cheeks.

How will he handle it once the truth comes out about Damien? Somehow, Holly needs to prepare him for what's ahead.

'Logan, there's something I need to tell you.' She glances at him before turning back to the road. 'It's about your dad.'

Logan looks at her. 'What is it?'

Drizzle patters against the windscreen as Holly begins, and it's somehow calming. 'I know this will be a shock, but I think your dad had something to do with Luna's abduction. And that man tonight – he's involved too. I'm not sure how exactly, but

I'll need to tell the police all of this, and I wanted to talk to you about it first.'

'No,' Logan says. 'Dad wouldn't—'

'I know it's a lot to get your head around. And I know you love him. But it's the only thing that makes sense. When you know the whole story, about him and your mum, then you'll understand.'

'Him and Mum?' He stares at Holly. 'What do you mean?'

She stops at the traffic lights. They'll be at the police station soon. 'There were... a lot of problems in their marriage.'

'Yeah, because Evie died.'

She glances at Logan, then back at the lights as they turn green. 'It started before that. I think your mum was trying to leave him. I don't fully understand how Luna comes into this, but I think maybe your dad arranged her abduction to make it look like your mum did it.'

'No!' Logan shouts. 'No!'

His cacophonous outburst is so out of the blue it causes Holly to swerve the car. 'Logan, I'm so sorry. But you have to accept—'

'You're not listening to me! Stop saying it was my dad!' Logan's deafening shouts burn Holly's ears.

Holly should drop it – this is too much for Logan to deal with tonight. She turns right onto the road that leads to the police station.

'It wasn't my dad,' Logan says after a moment, his voice quieter now. 'Because... I know who did it.' He stares out of the passenger window. 'I've known all along.'

And it's at this exact moment Holly realises something she hadn't registered before: Logan was in the house the whole time just now, and Ryan knew this. Yet he left Logan alone.

THIRTY-NINE

NOW

Holly

The car veers to the left, mounting the kerb as Holly pulls over, both of them lurching forward as she slams on the brakes. 'What are you saying, Logan?'

Tortured sobs fill the car, drowning out the sound of the windscreen wipers.

'It wasn't my dad who took Luna,' Logan says. 'Or my mum. It was nothing to do with them.'

Holly's mobile rings: Elijah again. She rejects the call.

'It was Oscar.'

For a moment Holly thinks she's heard him wrong. But then it all becomes clear, like condensation fading on a window. Ryan Hobbs following her these last few days. Turning up at the house. Leaving Logan alone. 'Why would he do that?' she asks, when she can find her way to speak through the myriad voices exploding in her head. 'Why would Oscar take Luna? He didn't even know her. I didn't even know him until the day she disappeared. That's when I interviewed him. And I'd never even heard of him before I started working on his story.'

Logan rubs his eyes, so vigorously Holly can hear them squelch. 'He did it to get money,' he says. 'He was planning to demand a ransom to return Luna. You were meant to get a note, but he panicked and let her go instead.'

Holly stares at Logan, her best friend's son, a boy she no longer recognises. Every word he's uttered has flipped her world on its head. She's been so wrong about all of it. 'I don't understand. How did you know? Did you help him? Please tell me you didn't.'

'No! At least not really.'

'What does that mean?'

'I think maybe... I might have given him the idea. Without realising.'

Silently, Holly waits for Logan to continue. She can't make up her mind about all of this until she knows every detail.

'After Evie died, I had no friends,' he begins. 'People stayed away from me. I didn't notice at first, but then I was spending more and more time on my own. You know, at lunchtimes and stuff.'

Holly should tell him that she's sorry to hear this, that he has her every sympathy, but the words lodge in her throat. Everything has changed.

'Oscar started talking to me. And I thought he was... cool. He was much older than me and actually wanted to hang out with me. I felt so... lucky. I knew the trouble he'd been in with Megan. He'd lost a lot of friends over it. So we kind of got each other.'

'This doesn't explain why you'd conspire to take my daughter!' Holly says, unable to keep her voice calm.

Logan turns away to stare out of the window again. His knee is shaking. 'He was asking me about Evie one day, and I told him how hard it was for Mum. I said she'd give anything to have Evie back, no matter what it cost. I think that's what gave him the idea. You know, how far a mum would go for her child.

He asked me if Evie had any little friends, and I... I told him about Luna.' He turns to Holly. 'I'm so sorry. I didn't think it would happen how it did. And when he told me what he was planning, I thought he would give her back straight away. That's what he was supposed to do. He was meant to leave a note when he took her and I thought you'd definitely pay the money to get her back. I didn't think it would drag on past that night.'

Tears sting Holly's eyes and she tries blinking to force them back, but they're only replaced with more. 'People blamed your mum,' she says. 'And the whole time you knew.'

'I didn't think it would get as bad as it did,' Logan insists. 'I thought people would realise it wasn't her, because it wasn't! And I was scared. Because I was part of it with Oscar. I knew about it. I was scared what would happen to me.'

Holly takes a deep breath, leaning back against the head-rest. What would Rachel do if she was part of this conversation? *Anything she could to protect her son.* 'How did Oscar's dad find out? He must have known, otherwise he wouldn't have been following me.'

Logan shrugs. 'I don't know. Oscar must have told him.'

'Where did he keep my little girl?'

'His mum went away for a few days. He kept her there in the house.'

Holly's breath catches in her chest. 'On her own? What the—?'

'No, he said he was with her.'

The thought of Luna being in a stranger's house like that, not knowing when or if Holly would come for her, crushes her chest. And Holly was in that house talking to Shania, only hours before Luna was taken. She relives the pain of those days Luna was missing all over again, worse this time, because now she knows Logan could have prevented it from happening. 'You should have told me.' And then something occurs to her. 'Did your mum know? Is that why she—?'

'No! Mum would never have kept that from you. She would have dragged me and Oscar to the police station.'

Holly's lips form a flat smile; it's true. Rachel hated injustice. Even if Logan is her son, she would never have let Luna suffer. Or Holly.

'You do know we're still going to the police station?' Holly says, unable to look at him. *He's a child. Above all else, I have to remember that.*

'I know.'

She checks her mirror, reversing the car then pulling out. The rain falls harder now, like the tears meandering down her cheeks.

When they pull into the police station car park, Holly finds one free space flanked by two police cars. She pulls into it and turns off the engine. Her T-shirt is damp, and the ache in her arm gets more painful with every second. She turns to Logan, who hasn't removed his seatbelt. 'So you had nothing to do with Oscar taking Luna that night? Apart from knowing what he was doing?' *And that's bad enough.*

'I promise. I didn't even know when he was planning to do it. I don't think I even believed he really would. I thought it was all just talk. He didn't talk to me about it. I only knew for sure when she went missing.'

Holly lets this sink in, rearranging it in her mind until she believes she can find some peace with it. 'Then this is what we're going to do.'

Logan listens while Holly tells him what to say when they walk into the police station. That Oscar just came to see him and admitted what he and his father had done. That they'd conspired to abduct Luna for money, and had only given her back when they'd panicked and realised the enormity of what they'd done, and that they might not get away with it.

'What if they don't believe me?' Logan asks, wiping his nose on his sleeve. He still hasn't undone his seatbelt.

'That's a chance we'll have to take,' she says.

'We,' he repeats.

'Yes. I'm right here with you. I'm doing this for your mum.' And because Holly knows that once the truth comes out about Damien, that will be punishment enough for a boy who's just lost his mother too.

'Thanks.'

'Come on. Let's get this over with.'

Seconds tick by until finally Logan unfastens his seatbelt. Holly's phone rings again as they make their way towards the entrance of the police station. Elijah. This time she answers it, just to stop him calling her. 'I can't talk now.'

'It's important,' Elijah says.

She stops, and holds her hand up for Logan to wait. 'What is it?'

'Michelle called. The swab results have come back from Luna's clothes. I told her I'd call you, but you haven't been answering. Where are you?'

Holly ignores his question. He has no right to ask her anything. 'What did Michelle say?'

'There's been a DNA match. Someone who was in the database already. His name's Oscar Hobbs, and he's a student at Rachel's school.'

Holly hangs up. Elijah is too late. Everything is too late.

`

FORTY

SIX MONTHS LATER

Holly

Holly sits on the floor beside Luna, playing with the doll's house she's bought her for her third birthday. She holds her breath while she waits to see what Luna will do with the dolls, and is relieved when Luna puts the baby in its cot and sits the mother beside it. Luna looks up at Holly, and a faint smile appears on her face. 'Mummy and Luna,' she says.

'Yes,' Holly says, fighting back a tear. 'Mummy will always be with Luna. I love you.' Holly hugs her tightly, and feels a painful twinge in her side. She's still recovering from the operation she had after the knife wound. It had been far deeper than she'd thought, and it still surprises her that she didn't feel more pain, and that she was able to drive. In fact, it hurts more after the operation than it did before. Still, it's worth it to know that more time will be added to Ryan Hobbs's sentence. Child abduction and GBH. Yet there's no amount of time that will be justice enough for what happened to Luna.

Holly acknowledges that she has to learn to let this go, and leave it to the justice system, otherwise it will gnaw away at her until she no longer recognises who she is.

The doorbell rings and she jumps up to answer it, checking herself in the mirror by the door. The reflection staring back at her is that of a different woman. One who is more wary. Suspicious. The silent scars of what happened are visible only to her.

She takes a deep breath and opens the door. 'Hi, come in.'

He smiles. 'Are you sure this is okay?'

'Yes, definitely. Elijah doesn't live here any more.' Holly has used most of her savings to pay him his half of what he put in to the house, and the mortgage has been transferred to her name. She's free to do what she likes.

Jack smiles and steps inside, wiping his feet on the mat.

'Come and meet Luna,' Holly says, gesturing to the living room. 'It's about time, isn't it?'

'Are you sure she'll be okay meeting a stranger?' Jack asks, hesitating by the door.

'Her therapist thinks the sooner we start introducing her to new people, the better. So that Luna learns it's okay, and that no one's going to take her or hurt her.' As she says this, Holly wonders if this is right. She's anguished over it for weeks now, eventually deciding she has to try for some normality.

She opens the living room door. 'Luna, sweetheart, this is Mummy's good friend, Jack. He wants to say hello. Is that okay?'

Luna looks up, tilting her head as she appraises Jack.

'Hi, Luna,' Jack says, stepping inside the living room. 'What have you got there?' He crouches beside Luna.

'Doll's house,' Luna says, holding the dad out to him.

Holly stands back, watching them, marvelling at the strides Luna has taken over the last few months. Every day there are more glimpses of the little girl she was before Oscar Hobbs abducted her. Holly still hasn't taken her to the park, though. She doesn't think either of them are ready for that yet.

'We're taking you to a soft play today,' Jack says. 'How does that sound?'

Luna smiles and turns back to her doll's house, taking the baby from the cot and placing it in the bath.

Jack stands and walks over to Holly. 'Thanks for letting me meet her,' he says. 'It means more than you could know.'

'Are you okay? I know this must be hard for you. After Evie...'

Jack nods. 'It *is* hard. But it's also just what I needed. Rachel adored Luna. She used to talk about her all the time.'

'I know she loved her.' And every day Holly curses herself for even entertaining the notion that Rachel was becoming obsessive over Luna. All her friend wanted to do was spend a bit of time with her, just like she would have done if the accident had never happened.

'This makes me feel closer to Rachel,' Jack says.

'You really cared about her, didn't you?' Holly says. It's a question she needs no answer to.

Jack looks away, but not before Holly sees his eyes beginning to water. 'If we'd met under different circumstances, Rachel might have been a great love of my life. If she'd felt the same. Sometimes I think she did, then other times I second-guess myself and can't quite believe it. But no matter how I felt about her, I knew neither of us would ever be able to get past how we met. It would have always been there, hovering above us, threatening our relationship. Rachel was right to walk away from me. To try and go it alone.'

'I wish we knew exactly what happened to her,' Holly says. 'I go over and over it all the time, and we still don't know for sure who killed her.' She lets out a deep sigh. 'But at least the post-mortem showed that Rachel didn't take her own life. I knew she would never have left Logan.'

'Damien,' Jack says. 'There's no doubt in my mind.'

'Or Ryan Hobbs. Maybe Rachel found out Oscar had taken

Luna. And he was ready to kill me, so he could have easily done that to her. But Oscar swears Rachel didn't know anything, and I've spoken to him several times since he's been in that youth offending prison.'

Jack sighs. 'Maybe we have to make peace with there always being a question mark hanging over Rachel's death. I know it's hard, but...'

For a moment they watch Luna playing, then Holly checks the time. 'We'd better get going.'

In the car, her phone rings. Holly glances at the screen and sees Shania's name. 'I need to get this,' she tells Jack, pulling over.

'Shania. Hi.' Holly hasn't spoken to her since Oscar and Ryan were arrested, and she has no idea why the woman would call her now, after all this time. She'd half expected an email from Shania – something to say she was sorry for what her son did, but nothing came.

'I've found something,' she says. 'It's really important. Could you come over? I wouldn't ask if it wasn't urgent.'

Holly glances at Jack. 'Um, I'm just taking my daughter out, but maybe this eve—'

'No – it needs to be now. Please.'

Holly wants to say no – she's done with that whole family, but curiosity wins. 'Okay, I'll be there in a few minutes.'

They pull up outside Shania's house, and Holly hesitates before unclicking her seatbelt. 'I can't take Luna in that house,' she says. 'And I don't want to set foot inside either.'

'I'll stay in the car with Luna,' Jack offers.

'Thanks. I'll be quick.'

'It means a lot to me that you trust me,' Jack says.

'I have to get over what happened. I'll always be on my guard, though.' She looks across at the house. 'Here goes, then.'

Shania looks years older when she answers the door. There are greyish-purple circles under her eyes, deep lines carved into her pallid skin. She's wearing loose joggers and a T-shirt that swallows her. 'I didn't think you'd come,' she says.

'We can talk out here,' Holly says. 'I'm not coming in.'

Shania nods. 'I understand.' She looks past Holly towards the car.

'Is that your husband?'

'No. He's a friend of mine. My daughter's in the car. I wasn't going to bring her in your house.'

Shania's face crumples. 'I'm so sorry about what Oscar did. It's unforgiveable. I've tried to email you so many times but I end up deleting them. No words seem enough.'

Any would have done, but Holly doesn't say this. It's clear that Shania has suffered enough. 'Is that it, then?' She glances back at the car. 'I need to go. We're taking Luna out.'

'That's lovely,' Shania says, her words laced with sadness. Regret too. 'I have something for you. It was stuck under the sofa cushions and I only found it this morning when I was vacuuming under them.' She reaches into her pocket and pulls out a slip of neatly folded lined paper. The kind kids use at school. 'It's a note to you. From your friend.'

Holly stares at her, unable to move. 'What?'

'I didn't know what it was, so I read it. Sorry. It's from Oscar's teacher. Mrs James. Rachel.'

Confused, Holly takes the note and slowly unfolds it, holding her breath while she reads.

My lovely Holly,

This is the hardest thing I've ever had to write, but there are things I need you to know. But first, I have to tell you how much I've cherished our friendship – you are one of the most important people in my life. No, that's wrong – other than Logan, you are THE most important person in my life.

I made a mistake, Holly. One I'll regret till I die. There's no apology I can give you that will ever be enough. I did a terrible thing. I slept with Elijah. I can't explain why, and I won't try to make excuses. It was one time, and it's haunted me ever since. I'm telling you this because I know he never will, and you deserve to know the truth. I know this means the end of our friendship, but at least you will know.

I'm scared for my life. There are things I have never told you about Damien, things I've never told anyone. He's been emotionally abusive for years, forcing me to take anti-depressants, trying to make me feel worthless. At least he didn't succeed in this. I know my worth.

He knows about the affair. He has a video of me and Elijah on his laptop in our bedroom. And he'll never let this go. He'll never let ME go. I want you to know this, so if anything happens to me, you'll know it's Damien who's killed me.

He tried to murder someone before. His ex-girlfriend. I only know her name is Ren, and to this day she's terrified of him. Please tell the police this. There must be hospital records of the attack. The police need to find her and listen to her story. Now that Damien has killed me too.

And every day I pray Luna comes back to you, wherever she is.

All my love,

Rachel x

Tears blur Holly's vision. She stares at the writing – definitely Rachel's distinctive round letters with large loops on the letter Y. 'How did you get this? Why was it in your house?'

'I don't know!' Shania says. 'I just found it. I don't know how it got under my sofa cushion.'

Holly takes a moment to process Shania's words. And the contents of the letter. 'Oscar must have found it.'

'I went to visit him this morning. He swears he's never seen that note. He doesn't know how it got there.'

'And you believe him?'

'Oscar told the truth about Luna. He's never tried to deny anything. Why would he lie about that?' She points to the note in Holly's hand.

'I don't know anything any more.'

'I just had to give that to you. It's for you. And I'm guessing it answers some questions about what happened to your friend.'

It does, except for the fact that the note was found in Shania's house, where Luna had been kept. 'I have to go,' Holly says. 'Thanks for giving this to me.'

'I'm sorry,' Shania says. 'For everything that's happened.'

Holly turns and heads back to the car, relieved to be away from that house.

'Are you okay?' Jack asks as they're pulling away. 'What happened?'

Holly hands him the note. 'Shania found that under her sofa cushion. It's from Rachel. She doesn't know how it got there.'

While Jack reads, Holly tries to concentrate on the road. The last thing she feels like doing now is spending the afternoon at the soft play, but she won't break her promise to Luna.

Seconds tick by while Holly waits for Jack to finish reading. And in the back of the car, Luna protests that she's hungry. 'We're nearly there,' Holly says. 'Then we can have some lunch.'

Jack folds the letter up and puts it in the glove compartment.

'I don't know what to think,' Holly says, when Jack doesn't

speak. 'I know what it means, I just don't know why it was in Shania's house. She said Oscar has never seen it before and didn't know anything about it.'

'So much makes sense now,' Jack says.

Holly frowns. 'Well, care to enlighten me, then? Because it's just made me more confused.'

'Okay. Rachel told me once that there was only one way she'd be free of Damien – and that's if she was dead.'

'But why did she write a note? Why couldn't she just tell me?'

'Because it was part of her plan. I could be wrong, but what if Rachel was planning on disappearing? If everyone thought she was dead, then Damien would have no hold on her. She'd be free of him. He'd never be looking for her.'

Holly considers this. 'But what about Logan? Rachel wouldn't have left him.'

'I agree. Maybe she was planning to come back for him? I can't know for sure. She didn't tell me any of this, but now I look back, there were hints in some of the things she said. That last time I saw her, she was so full of determination and hope. It's like she knew she was going to get away from him.'

'I suppose it's plausible,' Holly says. 'It just doesn't explain why the note was found in Shania's house.'

Jack frowns. 'You're right. Unless...'

'What?'

'All this time we've thought it was Damien who killed Rachel. But what if it wasn't? I'm not saying he wouldn't have eventually, especially if he found out she knew what he did to his ex. But what if Rachel was at Oscar's house? Maybe she found out what had happened to Luna? I don't know how. But Ryan could have threatened her like he did you. It's a possibility, isn't it?'

This scenario smashes around Holly's head. She doesn't know what to think. And how will they ever know for sure?

And then she realises that it doesn't matter. 'Rachel wanted Damien to face the consequences of what he did to Ren. And to her. She wanted me to go the police.' With these words, it becomes clear to Holly what she has to do. 'That's why she wrote this letter. And if it was actually Ryan who ultimately took her life, he's paying anyway for his involvement in Luna's abduction.'

Jack is silent for a moment. 'Yeah,' he says. 'Damien got everything he wanted after Rachel died. His son to himself, with no threat of anyone ever taking him.'

Holly pictures him now – living a new life in Portugal with Logan. No Rachel. Just what he always wanted. 'We might never know what really happened to Rachel, but we can make sure everyone who hurt her is held accountable in some way.'

They pull up outside the leisure centre and park near the entrance to the soft play.

'So you're going to take that note to the police?' Jack asks.

Holly nods. 'Yes. I'm doing what Rachel wanted me to do.'

Jack squeezes her arm. 'If you need me to come, I'm happy to. I've still got Rachel's messages on my phone. And it's what we were about to do when Ryan Hobbs showed up.'

And then Holly told Jack they couldn't, that she needed to protect Logan. She nods. 'Yeah, come with me. Let's finally get this all out there.' She turns to Luna. 'Shall we get you inside and have some lunch, then?'

Facing Jack again, Holly asks him if he's sure he wants to come in with them. 'It will be bedlam,' she warns.

'Fine with me. It'll be good for me,' Jack says. 'After all, I might want to have kids one day so I could do with the practice.' He smiles at Holly as she gets Luna out of the car, and together the three of them head inside.

. . .

In the evening, once Luna's settled in bed, Holly curls up on the sofa with a cup of hot chocolate. Drinking it reminds her of Logan, and sadness envelopes her. She checks the time. Seven thirty-nine. The police have Rachel's letter now, and no doubt they'll have questions for Damien, and might already be organising for him to be brought back to the UK. She wonders what will happen to Logan. He's lucky that Oscar and his dad both kept quiet about his involvement. She assumes he'll end up with Damien's parents. According to Jack, they enabled Damien's treatment of Rachel, and his mum tried to control her almost as much as Damien did. Holly will always regret that Rachel never spoke to her about it.

At eight fifteen, the doorbell rings, and Holly jumps up to answer, checking on the doorbell camera, just to make sure. She doubts she'll ever stop doing that.

'Hey,' she says, pulling him inside. 'Luna's asleep and the lasagne is in the oven. I hope you're hungry. Think I've made enough for ten.'

Ross wraps his arms around her and kisses her. This is just what she's needed after today. She hasn't told him everything yet, but she will. There'll be no secrets between them. No lies. Everything laid out in plain sight. It's the only way this will ever work.

After a moment, she pulls back. 'How's Harry doing?'

'Yeah, he's great. Are you and Luna ready to meet him next weekend?'

'I'm looking forward to it,' Holly says, kissing his cheek. 'And it will be lovely for Luna too.'

In the kitchen, she hands Ross some wine, then checks the lasagne.

'Do you have any regrets?' Ross asks.

'About us? No. Do you?'

'Yes. I wish I'd told you how I felt before. Even if nothing could have ever happened. If something had happened to you and you'd never known how I felt...'

'It wasn't the right time.' Holly didn't know about Elijah then. And she never would have left her marriage otherwise. Not when she'd made a commitment. It was only when she didn't hear from Ross, that day he didn't turn up at the office, that she fully acknowledged to herself how she felt. The same day Ryan Hobbs tried to kill her. Holly had no idea that the reason Ross wasn't replying was that he'd spent the day looking after Harry, who'd caught a sickness bug and couldn't go to school. Ross had gone to his ex-wife's house to stay with him there while she went to an urgent meeting, and he'd left his phone at home.

'We just need to be thankful we've found our way to each other now,' Holly says.

Rachel never got the chance to see what her future held, and Holly's determined that she'll live her life as best she can, and cherish every moment. For the friend she'll never let herself forget.

A LETTER FROM KATHRYN

Thank you so much for choosing to read *Two Mothers*. I really hope you've enjoyed reading it as much as I loved writing it. This was a story I was itching to tell, and I hope I've done the characters justice in the way I've told their stories. I really felt as if I knew Rachel, and I could see her story unfolding like a film in my mind. I hope I managed to convey her strength and determination, despite the cards she was dealt. And Holly too, who fought tirelessly for her friend, even when she uncovered some shocking truths. As always, I hope the twists were unexpected and kept you turning those pages.

If you did enjoy the book, and would like to keep up to date with all my latest releases, please do sign up at the following link. Your email address will never be shared and you can unsubscribe at any time.

www.bookouture.com/kathryn-croft

Thank you for your love of books and reading. As a mother of two young children, every day I try to impress upon them the power of books to transform lives, to educate and to entertain, especially in a world which is becoming increasingly fragmented, driven by screens and social media. Books have got to be one of the only things it's safe and healthy to be addicted to!

While writing, I really escaped into the world of *Two Mothers* and I hope you did to. If you enjoyed the book, I would very much appreciate it if you could spare a couple of minutes to leave a review on Amazon, or wherever you bought it. I say this with every book, but reviews truly are invaluable to authors – your important feedback helps us to reach other readers who have yet to discover our books.

If you'd like to, please also feel free to connect with me via my website, Facebook, Instagram, or X. I'd love to hear from you!

Thank you again for all your support – it is very much appreciated.

And as Joyce Carol Oates said: 'Reading is the sole means by which we slip, involuntarily, often helplessly, into another's skin, another's voice, another's soul.'

Kathryn x

www.kathryncroft.com

facebook.com/authorkathryncroft

instagram.com/authorkathryncroft

x.com/katcroft

ACKNOWLEDGEMENTS

Every day I'm so grateful that I get to write books for a living, and tell stories that hopefully entertain and thrill readers. Thank you to everyone who buys, reads and reviews my books. You make this dream possible.

Lydia Vassar-Smith – it's always a thrill to work with you. Thank you for the brainstorming session that this book idea resulted from. And thank you for your sharp and insightful editorial skills which made this book far better.

Hannah Todd – always supportive and enthusiastic – thanks for the continued championing of your most annoying author!

The publishing team at Bookouture – I'm always grateful to be part of such a fabulous team – thank you for all your hard work.

Stuart Gibbon – thank you for all your police procedural advice – it's always a pleasure!

Michelle Langford and Jo Sidaway – of course I can't write a book without having police questions for you both, even if I try my best not to bother you. Which reminds me, I think we're overdue a long murder chat!

To all my family and friends – thank you for your unwavering support. It means everything!

PUBLISHING TEAM

Turning a manuscript into a book requires the efforts of many people. The publishing team at Bookouture would like to acknowledge everyone who contributed to this publication.

Audio
Alba Proko
Melissa Tran
Sinead O'Connor

Commercial
Lauren Morrissette
Hannah Richmond
Imogen Allport

Contracts
Peta Nightingale

Cover design
The Brewster Project

Data and analysis
Mark Alder
Mohamed Bussuri

Made in the USA
Middletown, DE
08 August 2024

58782093R00198